Praise for the bestselling novels of the "queen of romantic adventure"* MARSHA CANHAM

"Absolutely bloody marvelous!"
—Virginia Henley

"Exciting, sexy, and fun. . . . Canham leads readers on a sweeping tale that cements her place as a writer that knows no bounds."
—*Romantic Times*

"Canham's characters jump from the pages into the reader's heart. . . . Marsha Canham is setting the standard for historical romance today."—*The Literary Times*

"An exciting tale that will steal your breath away."—*Affaire de Coeur*

"A good read."—*Publishers Weekly*

"Poignant . . . heroic. . . . This gifted author has created an intriguing adventure that should not be missed."—*Booklist*

Romantic Times

The
Iron Rose

Marsha Canham

A SIGNET BOOK

SIGNET
Published by New American Library, a division of
Penguin Putnam Inc., 375 Hudson Street,
New York, New York 10014, U.S.A.
Penguin Books Ltd, 80 Strand,
London WC2R 0RL, England
Penguin Books Australia Ltd, 250 Camberwell Road,
Camberwell, Victoria 3124, Australia
Penguin Books Canada Ltd, 10 Alcorn Avenue,
Toronto, Ontario, Canada M4V 3B2
Penguin Books (N.Z.) Ltd, Cnr Rosedale and Airborne Roads,
Albany, Auckland 1310, New Zealand

Penguin Books Ltd, Registered Offices:
Harmondsworth, Middlesex, England

First published by Signet, an imprint of New American Library,
a division of Penguin Putnam Inc.

First Printing, March 2003
10 9 8 7 6 5 4 3 2 1

To the newest ray of sunshine in our lives,
Payton Taylor Glenna Canham.
Grammy and Grumpy have been waiting
a long time
to spoil a beautiful little girl.

Prologue

August 1614

*A*s she had often heard her father say in the moments before the first broadside was fired, it was a fine day to die. The sun was a searing white eye in a sky so blue and clear it pained the soul to stare upward too long. Staring anywhere for even the briefest split second was not an option, however, for in the blink of an eyelash there was another flash of cold steel, another shock of contact as the two blades clashed together, sliding their full length in a shower of blue sparks.

Juliet was beginning to feel the strain in her wrist. She withstood her opponent's enraged offense as long as she could, then broke away, spinning and crouching low in one fluid motion, letting instinct take over where strength was failing. A second shadow loomed behind her, the face bloodied but the eyes focused with lethal intent, and Juliet cursed. She sprang to the side but found herself cornered, the flames of a burning spar on one side, the fat barrel of a twenty-four-pounder demi-culverin on the other. The two Spaniards, desperate for their own lives moments before, saw her predicament and closed rank, crowding her against the rail. One of them muttered under his breath and grabbed his crotch. The other laughed and licked the filthy tips of his fingers in agreement.

Juliet's sword slashed out in a brilliant flare of sunlight. The laughing Spaniard saw those fingers fly off his hand and land with a skitter of red splashes on the deck. While he was busy finding the breath to scream, she swung on his cohort and cut a wider grin on his face, one that went from ear to ear and severed the jugular clean through. She used her boot to kick him aside when he started to fall forward, then leaped gracefully over the twitching body as another snarling attacker rushed to take his place.

Juliet raised her sword, her slender body braced to meet a mighty downward stroke intended to cleave her skull in half. The impact shuddered through her arms and jarred her shoulders, bending her back over the gunwall. The savagery of the blow drew a grunt, then a curse, but she was able to deflect the blade long enough to reach into her belt with her left hand and unsheathe her dagger. The blade was eight inches long, sharp as a needle, and it went through the Spaniard's leather doublet like a finger through lard.

Juliet barely had time to regain her balance when she caught the glint of a steel-pot helmet. The arquebusier stood just out of reach of a sword thrust, calmly balancing his weapon on a handy length of broken timber, the fuse smoking, the trumpet nose aimed squarely between her eyes.

Trapped against the gunwall, she could do little but watch as his finger squeezed the trigger to release the mainspring. She saw the serpentine lock trip forward and touch the fuse to the priming pan. The powder ignited in a small puff of smoke, lighting the main charge and sending the two-ounce iron ball exploding down the barrel.

Out of nowhere, a streak of violet and silver lace cut across Juliet's path. A slash of steel knocked aside the snout of the blunderbuss just as it discharged its round, and the shot went wild. The stranger's sword glittered again, finding a vulnerable gap between the arquebusier's iron cuirass and the exposed band of skin beneath his helmet, and the Spaniard heeled backward in a gout of bright red blood. Juliet saw the flash of a grin as her rescuer turned and extended a gloved hand to lift her away from the rail.

"Are you all right, boy?"

Juliet found herself staring into the deepest, darkest blue eyes she had ever seen. They were partly shadowed by the brim of an elegant cavalier's hat, the one side cocked up at a jaunty angle, topped by a plume dyed the same shade of violet as his doublet and breeches.

"Boy?"

Instead of answering, Juliet drew a pistol out of her crossbelt and fired it, her finger squeezing the trigger before the surprise could register on the stranger's face. The shot was propelled past a broad shoulder and thudded into the chest of a Spaniard who was about to slay one of her crewmen at the opposite side of the deck.

The midnight blue eyes followed the shot, then flicked back to Juliet. The grin reappeared, wide and very white through a neatly trimmed moustache and imperial.

"A fine shot. And yes, I can see you are very much all right."

He touched the brim of his hat in a salute, then was gone, leaping over what was left of the taffrail to rejoin the mêlée taking place on the main deck. He was not two heartbeats out of her startled sight when a massive, ear-shattering explosion rocked her off her feet and threw her hard against the barrel of the cannon.

Juliet averted her face as a blast of heat laden with particles of stinging debris swept across the deck. A huge pillar of red and orange flame rose to the sky, and the accompanying screams of those men caught in the open seemed to take the last of the Spaniard's resolve with them. By twos and threes the soldiers began dropping their weapons and spearing their hands upward in surrender. Some fell onto their knees; others raised their steepled hands to pray for mercy.

Juliet scrambled to her feet and ran to the rail. The waist of the galleon was a shambles, with bodies littering the deck from stem to stern. The explosion had not come from the Spaniard's powder stores, as she had initially feared, but from the deck of the much smaller English carrack that was bound to the galleon's hull by grappling lines.

It was this distraction, when the Spaniard had closed for the kill and boarded the English merchantman, that had allowed Juliet's ship, the *Iron Rose*, to emerge almost unseen from the banks of haze and drifting smoke. She had come in under full sail and poured a series of crippling broadsides into the exposed side of the galleon before snaring it within her own cobweb of thick cables. A cry of "up and over" had sent the crew of the privateer swarming eagerly over the side to join the fray. The crew of the beleaguered English vessel, perilously near the brink of defeat, had rallied as well and now, despite the fact that the two smaller vessels were shockingly outmanned and outgunned by the behemoth warship, the Spaniards were surrendering!

Chapter One

"We were lucky this time, lass. Dead lucky. There's a brace o' mortars in the stern that would've ripped our guts out sure as they ripped out the guts o' the Englishman, given half the chance. Sheer bloody luck o' the devil it was, an' I'd be damned to believe it if I hadn't seen it with me own eyes."

Nathan Crisp was quartermaster on board the *Iron Rose*. He stood all of five feet tall, which put his eyes on level with Juliet's chin, but he had the neck and shoulders of a bulldog, and could lift a man twice his size without straining a muscle. What he did not know about the sea, about guns, about sailing in fair weather or foul, did not bear knowing, and despite being crusty as a barnacle at times, Juliet trusted him as implicitly as she trusted her own instincts.

"How badly is the English ship damaged?"

Crisp shook his head. "I've yet to go on board and have a good look, but she's well down below the waterline an' the only thing holdin' her up are the cables attached to this bloody galleon. That last explosion took out her magazine an' half the upper deck."

Juliet scanned the hazy line of the horizon. "We have but a few hours of daylight left and a great deal to do before we can get underway. Where do you suppose the captain of this beast is hiding?"

"He scuttled below like a rat when this lot began to throw down their swords."

Juliet's eyes were pale, silvery blue, and at Crisp's words, they sparked with darker flecks of anger. "Hell and damnation! He'll be after throwing his manifests and logs overboard before we can see them."

The hatchway leading below to the captain's quarters was locked from the inside, but a few strokes of a battle-ax reduced the escutcheon to a decorative scrap of iron on the deck.

Juliet, holding two loaded pistols before her, led the way along the narrow passageway to the great cabin. As on most Spanish galleons, the captain's quarters assumed the entire breadth of the stern, and Juliet stood aside while Crisp smashed through the heavy oak door. In the instant it took for all the crimson velvet and gilded furniture to register on her senses, she saw two officers standing by the ruined mass of cherrywood that had once been a magnificently appointed escritoire. The *capitán de mar*, identified by the ornamented breastplate and wide, pleated neck ruff, was swabbing his forehead with a lace handkerchief while the officer beside him was stuffing papers and ledgers into a bulging canvas sack. The latter wore a cuirass dented from battle damage, and his face was streaked black with soot beneath the curved rim of his cone-shaped helmet.

Juliet raised both pistols, aiming them squarely at the captain's chest.

Crisp did likewise, grinning wide over a minimum of uneven front teeth. "Ah, but it's a clever lass who knows her enemies so well." In a louder voice, he addressed the two Spaniards. "Now then, what manner of foolery do we have here? Should we be thankin' ye kindly for actin' so quick to gather yer important papers together? Or should we be thinkin' ye're eager to hide something ye'd rather we didn't see?"

The captain was heavyset, with a girth as round as a barrel and legs the size of tree trunks squeezed into stockings so tight the seams were strained. His face was red, running with sweat that dripped onto the top of the desk as he started muttering under his breath to his first officer.

Crisp scowled, for he knew only enough coarse Spanish to tell an enemy to drop his weapon or the sharks would be feeding on his spleen.

It was Juliet who smiled and said in soft, perfectly accented Castilian, "And if he should indeed take one step toward the gallery door with the intent of throwing that sack overboard, Señor Capitán-General, I shall blow the top of his head off. His first," she added, shifting the aim of her guns to make her meaning clear. "Then yours, of course."

The captain looked over, startled by her fluency, and another droplet of sour sweat fell on the desk. He bore one small bruise on his forehead, the flesh an angry blue, and it was to this blow Juliet credited his blinking dullness for he did nothing but continue to stare. The officer by his side was a soldier, however, not merely a posturing figurehead. He stiffened with indignation, so much so the reflections of sunlight from the broken gallery windows cut briefly through the shadows beneath the rim of his helmet.

His eyes were small and close-set, black as empty sockets. Rage tightened his lips to a thin line as he responded to Juliet in equally excellent English, "You dare issue your paltry threats! Do you know to whom you speak with such crude impertinence?"

"I have no doubt you feel obliged to enlighten me."

His voice was a mere hiss of sound. "You have the effrontery to stand before Don Diego Flores Cinquanto de Aquayo."

"Aquayo," she murmured. Juliet searched her memory for the name—mentally giving thanks to the taskmaster who had drummed into her the importance of knowing every ship that patrolled the Caribbee—and came up with a match. "Then this must be the *Santo Domingo.*"

She tried to keep her voice level, her breathing even, but she could feel the sudden pounding of blood in her temples. She could also hear the involuntary catch in Nathan's throat and guessed that he had almost swallowed the glutinous wad of tobacco leaves he customarily chewed during an engagement. The *Santo Domingo* was one of the largest and finest warships in His Catholic Majesty's fleet in Nueva España. At eight hundred tons, mounting fifty-two heavy guns, she had been touted to be both invincible and unsinkable. Moreover, at last count, she had been credited with the capture or sinking of at least fourteen privateers from three nations who hunted along the Spanish shipping lanes.

"You are a long way from Vera Cruz," Juliet said calmly. "I would have thought, after you escorted the new viceroy from Hispaniola to San Juan de Ulloa, you would have remained to help celebrate his appointment."

"You are very well informed," said Aquayo, gasping for breath—or belief.

Juliet tipped her head to acknowledge the compliment. "We pay very high bribes to your port officials to ensure it is so. As for my threats, señor *maestre*"— Juliet switched her focus back to the military commander as she caught his hand inching toward the butt of a pistol that was partly hidden in the debris on the desk—"I can promise you they are not the least paltry, for at this close range, I expect the shot would remove the greater half of your skull even if my aim wavered by a twitch or two."

"An' that's never happened in all the years I've known her," Crisp warned dryly. "So unless ye want to insult yer capitán-general more by having yer brains splashed all over his fine gold braid, I suggest ye set the sack down slowly an' step carefully to one side."

The officer's coal black eyes narrowed and Juliet could see him weighing the odds of his reaching the gun and surviving long enough to fire it. He wore the thin moustache and pointed beard favored by the Spanish nobility, yet the fact that his rank had been earned through military service and not by royal appointment like his captain suggested there was some illegitimate taint in his bloodlines somewhere.

"You must be the one they call *la Rosa de Hierro*," he murmured. "The Iron Rose."

"My ship is the *Iron Rose*, señor. Those aboard her call me Captain."

"I will call you *puta*," he spat, "and it will give me great pleasure one day to spread your legs and encourage my soldiers to repay you for the trouble you have caused today."

Juliet pursed her lips to give the insult the consideration it merited. "I am sure their efforts would bore me, señor, as do yours."

"Spoken like a true whore-bitch. Just like your mother before you."

Juliet's expression did not change, but her eyes turned as cold as frost, a sight known to raise the hackles of those aware of their own mortality.

"You know my mother, señor?"

A smirk spread slowly across his face. "We are also well informed, *puta*, although the reputation of Isabeau Dante—a whore of such magnitude—comes without cost."

The Spaniard's grin was still full of insolence and arrogance as Juliet adjusted the aim of the pistols, gave the triggers a quick caress, and blinked through the delayed ignition of gunpowder. Both wheel-locks spun and fired simultaneously, the result of the twin explosions causing Aquayo to cross his arms over his head and drop to the floor with a scream.

"An insult to me is one thing, señor *maestre*," she said evenly, watching the army officer stagger back against the bulkhead in shock. "But an insult to my dear mother . . . well . . . that is quite another."

With the logs and manifests sent safely back to the *Iron Rose*, Juliet accompanied Crisp on board the English carrack to assess the damage. In truth, there was not much left to assess, for her masts were gone, her rails were little more than jagged spikes, and what timbers remained intact on the upper deck would not do so for long in light of the fires that raged from above and below. Dead and pieces of the dead were strewn everywhere, lying in rivulets of blood that flowed to and fro across the planking with the motion of the ship.

"How long before she goes down?" Juliet asked softly.

"She's drinkin' the sea faster than any ten pumps could spew it out. Nog's checkin' now, but he thinks she's been holed below the waterline. Looks to me like the Spaniards weren't in the mood to take her back to Havana. Or to leave any witnesses behind."

Juliet nodded grimly. "Target practice. For their gunners as well as their musketeers. How many survivors do you estimate?"

"I counted less than forty who can stand on their own," he said. "Only two of those appear to be officers. There's another score an' a half with minor wounds, but easily twice that number who'll be dead if we try to move them. I've not made a tally of the Spaniards yet, but I'd say we accounted ourselves well. We've less than a dozen injured an' only one death."

"Who?"

"Billy Crab. Caught a musket ball in the brain."

Red hair, a lot of freckles. Juliet knew every member of the crew well enough to take each loss personally.

"Who is in command here?" Crisp asked, raising his voice to be heard above the whoosh and crackle of burning fires.

"I must assume I am." One of the two officers Crisp had already identified limped forward through the smoke. He was young, perhaps five and twenty, but it was obvious he was no stranger to combat. His face, handsome enough on the one side, bore telling scars on the other. A melted plate of stretched, shiny flesh distorted the entire left side of his face from above the temple to below the starched line of his collar. His ear was a curled mass of pink skin, and his cheek, when he spoke, was stiffened by the scar tissue, setting his mouth at an odd cant.

Juliet, who had seen far more hideous disfigurements over the years, was not as concerned with the officer's appearance as she was with his character. The galleon was a huge and cumbersome ship, and would be difficult to sail without the help of the English seamen.

The officer instinctively addressed Nathan, and pulled himself together for the makings of a salute. "Lieutenant John Beck, His Majesty's Royal Navy."

"What ship?" Crisp asked.

"The *Argus*, under the former command of Captain Angus Macleod, God rest his soul."

"Might we ask what ye did to piss off the Spaniard?"

Beck's nostrils flared with indignation. "We did nothing, sir. We are a courier ship, bound for New Providence; we carry a minimum of cargo. We did absolutely nothing to invite their interest or provoke their attack. We came through the storm and she was there, riding the edge of the horizon. She saw us and gave chase, then the next thing we knew . . ." He tensed and wiped at a persistent trickle of blood that was flowing over his eye. When he blinked it clear, he studied Crisp's casual canvas trousers, the loose white shirt and double leather bandoliers that held an assortment of pistols and knives. "Might *we* venture to surmise you are not in the king's service, sir?"

"Ye might venture it, aye. But if ye're thinkin' our cap'n flies the *jolie rouge*, ye'd be mistaken again, for a pyrate would have let the Spaniard sink ye, then moved in to pick over the bones."

The words were hardly reassuring but Beck was gracious nonetheless. "I should like to take this opportunity to extend the heartfelt gratitude of myself and the crew, and indeed the crown, for coming forth against such odds and at such terrible risk to the safety of your own ship and crew. I stand humbled and in awe of your captain, whom I sincerely hope I shall have the honor of meeting forthwith."

Crisp shifted the wad of tobacco he was chewing from one cheek to the other. "Ye can have the honor now, if ye like. Lieutenant . . . Beck, was it?" He gave a half turn and held a hand out toward Juliet. "Cap'n Dante."

Beck's gaze seemed to take a moment to shift from Crisp to the tall slender figure standing beside him. Dark reddish hair was gathered back into a thick plait and covered by a blue bandana. The face beneath was streaked with grime, and a shirt that had once been white was stained with blood and black powder. Wide leather crossbelts slung over the shoulders housed an arsenal of pistols, daggers, pouches for powder and shot, and while the shirt was loose-fitting and could have hidden anything beneath, the breeches were moleskin and molded snugly to hips and legs that were suddenly all too obviously feminine.

"Good God, sir. You're a woman."

"The last time I looked, aye, I was," Juliet said, reserving her smile.

"A female captain? Of a privateer?"

Juliet crossed her arms over her chest and responded to the redundancies with a fine Dante glare.

Beck swallowed his astonishment and drew himself sharply to attention. "First Lieutenant Jonathan Grenville Beck, His Majesty's Royal Navy. At your service, Captain Dan . . . Dan . . ." His chin came trembling down as his jaw gaped again. ". . . Dante?" he whispered. "Surely not . . . the Black Swan?"

Juliet blew out a wry sigh and glanced at Crisp. "Really, this is too much. First I am mistaken for an iron rose, now a black swan. Are my features truly so vague and obscure?"

Nathan Crisp cocked an eyebrow. "Ye would benefit from a good scrub, aye."

"Please," Beck interjected. "I . . . I meant no offense. Isabeau Dante's name is well known throughout the fleet. Indeed, it is almost as legendary as that of—" He stopped again, but there was apparently not enough strength left in his body to absorb this most final and overwhelming shock. "You . . . would not happen to be any relation to the privateer, *Simon* Dante . . . would you?"

He almost looked as though he wished she would answer in the negative, but of course, that was not possible.

"He is my father."

"Your . . . ? Oh . . . my . . . good . . . God."

The lieutenant swayed through a rush of light-headedness as all the blood appeared to drain out of his face. Crisp clapped him stoutly on the shoulder. "Bah, she isn't half so frightening as all that, lad. Leastwise not unless ye prick her temper. Many a man on board the *Rose* can show ye the blisters to swear to that."

Over a frosty glare intended to curb Crisp's humor, Juliet indicated the deck with a tilt of her head. "You should see to your men, Mr. Beck. Your ship is sinking and they need to be removed from the *Argus* at once."

"Yes. Yes, of course. Wh-what are your intentions toward the crew of the galleon?"

"Do you care?"

The undamaged half of Beck's face tightened beneath the oily sheen of sweat and filth as he cast a slow glance around the broken ruin of the *Argus*. "They attacked without provocation and would have sunk us without qualm. Do I care what becomes of them? No. At this precise moment, God save me but no."

"Then get about your duties, Lieutenant, and leave the troublesome details to us."

He held Juliet's unwavering gaze for another moment, then offered a stiffly executed bow before leaving to supervise his crew.

Juliet watched him limp away, then pursed her lips and murmured thoughtfully, "A courier? What on earth would an English courier ship be doing in these waters?"

Crisp was already moving in the direction of the
stern cabins. "His Majesty's officers are almost as me-
ticulous as the Spanish in keeping good accounts of
where they have been an' where they are bound. I'll
see to any dispatches an' charts; you get yerself back
over to the *Rose.*"

He vanished into the wall of belching smoke and
Juliet was taking a last look around when an incongru-
ous splash of color caught her eye. Two bodies were
tangled together in the midst of the blackened ruins
near the base of the mainmast. The uppermost one
was wearing a violet doublet and lying beside him was
the cavalier's hat that had been so gallantly tipped by
way of a salute on board the Spaniard.

Juliet had almost forgotten about the champion who
had come to her aid in the heat of battle. He looked
dead and she guessed he had been caught in the blast
that had destroyed the ship's magazine, for everything
else around him was smoldering, scorched by the force
of the exploding gunpowder. Patches of charred velvet
smoked across his shoulders and buttocks. He had a
lump the size of a gull's egg at the back of his skull,
and a thin thread of blood was leaking from his ear
from the concussion. The splendid fan of plumes on
his hat had been reduced to burned and bristled shafts,
while the exquisitely jeweled dagger she had last seen
clutched in his hand lay several feet away, glittering
brightly against the rubble.

He was sprawled facedown, his arms spread wide
like a crucifix. Above his shoulders—which were impressively wide for a man who chose to wear purple
velvet—his features were obscured by the tumbled
waves of long chestnut hair. But his clothes were very
fine indeed. The peasecod doublet was trimmed in
gold braid, emphasizing the high waist in back and, if
memory served, the deep vee in front. The sleeves
were fitted, with a rolled band at the shoulder embroidered with gold stripes. Legs that were long and well
formed were clad in trunk hose padded to a bell

shape, worn over silk stockings that would have been the envy of a king.

Juliet's gaze returned to the dagger. It was as rich a trophy as any she had taken in a year's worth of plunder and she had to think it would be a shame not to have some memento of this stranger's courageous death.

She stepped over a broken spar and was reaching down to collect the dagger when a hand shot out and grabbed her around the wrist.

The Samaritan was not dead after all. He was very much alive and glaring up at her.

"Is it your habit, boy, to rob the men who save your life?"

She balled her fist and attempted to pull it free. "I thought you were dead."

He held fast to her wrist and gave his head a small shake to clear his wits. If the blood leaking from his ear was any indication, he was likely hearing a chorus of ringing bells, and the only thing he accomplished by shaking his head was to scatter a few droplets of red across the deck.

"Jesus God!" His fingers sprang open, releasing her. They rose to gingerly probe the lump at the back of his skull and he groaned again.

The sound was echoed by the body crushed beneath him.

"Beacom?" A violet-clad arm lifted to see what was beneath. "Good God, man, what are you doing under there?"

"Waiting for you to rouse, your grace," came the gasped reply. "Hoping that in your boundless compassion, you might even be willing to heave off me!"

"I would be more than happy to oblige," his grace said, "just as soon as I can coax my limbs to work again. You there, lad. Stop gawking at the bauble on my dagger—consider it lost to you now anyway—and lend us your assistance here."

Juliet arched an eyebrow and glanced to either side,

but there was no one else close by. Ignoring the hand
he extended, she straddled a leg on either side of his
narrow hips instead and, taking up fistfuls of charred
velvet, hoisted his upper body and held him while the
man pinned underneath him wriggled free.

When the deed was accomplished, Juliet dropped
him unceremoniously back to the deck while Beacom,
who had his back turned and was dusting the soot
and grime off his clothes, paused to flutter his hands
in gratitude.

"Oh, I thank you, good sir. I thank you so very
much indeed. My lord his grace the duke has been
most uncooperative in answering my many attempts
to waken him and I began to fear I might die for lack
of air before anyone came to our rescue."

Contrasting the colorful garments his master wore,
Beacom was dressed head to toe in somber, fastidious
black. He had a long, bony face to match the long
bony body, and his teeth, when he spoke, clicked together like castanets.

"I am roused now," said the duke, swaying to his
knees. "Give me a hand, damn you Beacom."

Juliet watched, somewhat bemused, as Beacom
paused in the act of straightening his shortcoat. A cry,
not unlike the squawk of a pinched chicken, saw him
whirl around and bend to assist his master, who appeared to be on the verge of careening nose down
onto the deck again.

"Your limbs, my lord. Are they sound?"

"Sound as a newborn babe's," the duke muttered.
"It is the deck that is spinning like a bloody dervish."

Beacom looked hardly strong enough for the task,
but he managed with a great deal of grunting, pulling,
and straining to haul his master to his feet. As soon
as he was able to stand unassisted, Beacom gingerly
probed the scorched layers of velvet and lace to search
for injuries.

Juliet was more intrigued by the duke himself, for
apart from her father, who had been awarded a
knighthood by Queen Elizabeth, he was the first mem-

ber of the English nobility she had encountered. His face, when he pushed the lanky strands of hair out of the way, was neither pointy nor vapid, as she expected it to be. The nose was long and regal, the eyes deep-set and shielded by lashes the same gleaming chestnut as his hair. His eyebrows were full and straight, meeting almost in the middle. A slender moustache marked a perfect line along his upper lip, while the neatly trimmed imperial elongated the squareness of his jaw. She remembered seeing a full rack of even white teeth—a rarity among seafaring men—and although his mouth was compressed now against the pain and dizziness, a smile that had been somewhat breathtaking.

Despite the lace at his throat and cuffs, the silk stockings and padded trunk hose, he had also wielded an extremely fine sword, one that did not hang about his hips solely for decoration or pomp. It was lying on the deck a few feet away and while Juliet went to retrieve it, Beacom continued to fuss and fret.

"There would appear to be no serious perforations, my lord. It is probably to your good account that you were not a step or two closer to the middle of the vessel."

The duke scowled his way through another stab of pain. "You will forgive me, Beacom, if I wait for these devils to stop dancing in my head before I celebrate?"

"I should not wait too long," Juliet said as she handed Beacom the sword as well as the jeweled dagger. "The pair of you would be wise to haul yourselves over the rail before the *Argus* takes on too much more water. Will you be able to manage him on your own?" she asked Beacom. "Or do you need help?"

The pinched nostrils flared. "I am quite capable of guiding his grace to safety. We will, however, require assistance with our belongings. If you can spare another moment, young man, there will be a coin in it for you."

"A coin?" Juliet rounded her eyes. "Gold or silver?"

"More than you'll earn by standing here and—"

Beacom's words were cut short on another squawk as the ship listed suddenly. The *Argus* settled deeper in the bows, sending the manservant and his burden staggering sideways against the base of the mast. From somewhere in the bowels of the ship came the sound of straining, popping timbers and a roar not unlike a monster rising up from the deep. Men bounded up the ladderways, including Nathan Crisp, who was soaked to the neck with seawater, enveloped in a huge cloud of steam that boiled out of the hatchway behind him. He carried charts and maps and a thick ledger bound in leather, tied with a red ribband.

"There's a hole as big as Lucifer's arse in the hull where the powder barrels blew out," he shouted. "Her back is broken. A minute or two, no more, an' she won't be able to keep her head up. We'd best cut loose or she'll drag the Spanish bitch down with her."

Juliet turned to Beacom. "You are certainly free to swim below and squander your life fetching milord's silver shaving cup if you like, but if I were you, I would hasten over the side *now*."

"Well, I . . ." The beginnings of what might have been an instinctive protest died on a startled gasp as the *Argus* rolled and wailed again. A flurry of chopping sounds could be heard as men began to take axes to the grappling lines to cut her free, each strained rope giving off a sharp *ping* as it snapped apart. "Yes. Yes, of course. To the side. At once. Come, milord. *Milord*—!"

The duke was still leaning up against the broken mast. His eyes were open and although they were fixed on Juliet with a kind of puzzled confusion, his jaw had gone slack and his body was starting to slide down the smooth wood.

Juliet cursed and slung his free arm around her shoulder. Hoisting the deadweight between them, she and Beacom dragged the barely conscious duke to the side of the ship where members of the *Iron Rose*'s crew stood on lengths of heavy cargo netting to help heave the survivors up and over the rail onto the *Santo Domingo*.

Swirling green water churned no more than ten feet below the level of the English carrack's deck but Juliet waited until the last possible moment before she gave the signal for the final tethering lines to be chopped. With one arm looped through the cables, she hung on as the galleon rolled free and righted herself. Cut adrift, the drowning frigate struggled to remain afloat through the surging backwash of waves but it was no use. In less than a minute, with the surface of the water bubbling and hissing, and with the weak cries of the men who could not be saved echoing across the distance, the *Argus* went down by the stern, leaving a wide circle of broken spars and burning canvas scraps to mark her demise.

Chapter Two

*J*uliet wasted little time or energy on niceties. The Spanish prisoners were bound together by wrist and ankle. There were well over three hundred captives crammed on two decks and even though they had surrendered their ship and waited in dazed clusters to hear their fate, they outnumbered the combined crew of the *Iron Rose* and survivors of the *Argus* by more than two to one.

Juliet's first priority was to ensure there were no hidden pockets of Spaniards burrowed below on any of the decks. Ten enterprising soldiers with muskets could undo the day's efforts and turn defeat into victory. She dispatched armed parties to scour each of the four decks, rooting out another score of men to add to the crush on deck.

Nathan Crisp led one such party to search the cargo bays and what he found there caused him to swallow his cud of tobacco whole. There were storerooms filled with crates of silver bars, all bearing the stamp of the mint in Vera Cruz. Four huge barrels contained pearls the size of a man's thumbnail. There were sacks of uncut emeralds from Cartagena, chests of gold from the mines in Peru, bales of spices and rubber in such quantities that the initial euphoria Juliet and Nathan felt upon opening door after door turned to consternation for it would take days to transfer all the treasure to the *Rose*. Even then, it was likely the privateer would sink under half the burden.

While it was not unusual for warships to carry treasure, it was definitely curious that a ship with the firepower and reputation of the *Santo Domingo* should be weighted so heavily with cargo. It implied she was going to be sent back to Spain with the September plate fleet. Twice yearly, in spring and fall, fleets of galleons loaded with treasure rendezvoused in Havana. They came from Vera Cruz in Mexico, from Nombre de Dios in Panama, from Maracaibo, Cartagena, and Barranquilla along the northern coast of Peru and Colombia. The trading vessels went from port to port along the Spanish Main, circling the vast gulf, touching on the islands of the Antilles and Caribbean until they arrived back in Havana, where they gathered into a single fleet to make the journey back to Spain.

In Havana, they were met by an armada of warships that did not winter over in the New World with the trading ships, but were there strictly to act as escorts to the treasure ships on their voyages back and forth across the Atlantic. In April and again in September, the *armada de la guardia* would deliver a new fleet to Havana and collect the ships that had spent the winter or summer filling their holds with treasure, then escort them back across the Atlantic to Spain.

Whatever stroke of luck or fate had put the *Santo Domingo* in Juliet's path, she was not about to lose either the ship or the immense treasure she carried. It was imperative, therefore, to off-load the Spanish crew as soon as possible and vacate these waters before any other curious ships happened by. Once the galleon's capture became known, word would spread through the islands like a fever, increasing patrols and raising the already staggering reward placed on the head of any privateer who bore the name Dante.

For over twenty-five years the Pirate Wolf, Simon Dante, had been the plague of Spanish shipping. He had fought alongside Sir Francis Drake and been one of Elizabeth's fearsome sea hawks who had helped defend England's shores against invasion by the Spanish Armada. Having won glory, accolades, titles, and estates, Simon had taken away nothing but letters of marque signed by the queen, official sanctions to harass, capture, and plunder ships of hostile nations, which, in the West Indies, was mainly Spain.

His wife, Isabeau Spence Dante, was the offspring of a red-haired giant of a pirate who had taught his daughter how to fire a cannon by the age of twelve and how to navigate a ship around the Horn before her twentieth birthday. Her maps and sea charts were prized by captains of every nationality who sailed on the ocean-sea, and to every cartographer in England, she was known as the Black Swan after the elegantly painted imprint that identified her work.

The *Black Swan* had also been the name of the ship Simon Dante had given to Isabeau as a wedding gift. She had returned the favor by presenting him with a son, Jonas, nine months later. Another son, Gabriel, had followed within three years, and Juliet ten months after that. None of the three had shown a desire to be anywhere else but on the deck of a ship, and with parents like Simon and Isabeau Dante, it was no surprise they would grow to be a trio of magnificent thorns in the Spaniard's side.

All three had fought for and earned the right to sail at the helm of their own ships. Armed with twelve heavy culverins that fired thirty-two-pound shots, and eight twenty-four-pound demi-culverins, the *Iron Rose* had been presented to Juliet on her twentieth birthday. The fact that her captain was a woman held no less terror for foreign crews who sighted her sails on the horizon. Most ships ran up as many sheets as they could carry and fled before the wind, for to see the *Iron Rose*'s pyramid of canvas turning into the chase usually meant her brothers' ships, the *Tribute* and the *Valour*, were not far off her beam. And woe betide the arrogant captain of any vessel who thought only to shake off the three pups pursuing him; chances were better than nine out of ten that the Pirate Wolf himself, Simon Dante, would have already circled his *Avenger* around to lie in wait off their bows.

On this occasion, Juliet had been alone, intending to take the *Iron Rose* to sea only to test the strength of a new rudder design. She had been startled herself to emerge from a tropical squall and stumble across the two battling ships. At first she had thought the rumble of guns to be lingering thunder, but when the rain had passed and the mist had thinned, the lookouts had spied the *Santo Domingo* blasting the *Argus* into kindling.

Now she had an enormous treasure, three hundred prisoners, and an eight-hundred-ton warship on her hands, none of which made her particularly happy at the moment.

"Loftus agrees with my estimate," she said, glancing at the *Iron Rose*'s helmsman, "that we are less than half a day's sail from Guanahana Island."

"We have no friends there," Crisp said, frowning.

"No, but look you, between there and here"—she stabbed a finger at a small dot of black ink on the map she had spread on top of the binnacle—"is an atoll. We could tow the galleon at least that far and set the Spaniards ashore. Once we are rid of them, we can think about what to do with the rest of the cargo, whether to risk making a run for Pigeon Cay, or to off-load it somewhere and return for it later with Jonas and Gabriel to guard our backs."

Nathan could see by the look on her face that the second option was not an option at all, for she had as much of a rivalry with her brothers as an abiding love and affection. Nonetheless, he sighed and shook his head. "We'd be trying to find this atoll in full dark. How the devil do ye expect to make a dead reckoning of a sandy pimple the size of my toenail at night?"

"I'll find it. Unless you fancy standing on guard for the next forty-eight hours straight until we find a larger toenail in daylight, we've little other choice."

"We could just heave them over the side," he grumbled. "It's more than they would have done for us."

"We could, but it would still leave us with one other small problem."

"Only one?" He snorted. "Ye have yer father's gift for understatement, lass."

"What do we do about the English crew? We can't set them adrift on the same island as the Spaniards or they'll end up either dead or chained to oars in the belly of some galleass. The closest port friendly to the British is at least a week away, which puts it a week beyond impossible. We're overdue as it is."

"The Frenchies would take 'em off our hands an' trade us a few barrels o' wine for our trouble."

"Yes, then they would turn around and sell them to the Spanish in exchange for trading privileges."

"Might I make so bold as to offer a suggestion, Captain?"

Juliet and Crisp both looked around as Lieutenant Beck stepped up behind them. They had been aware of him pacing the deck below for some time, working up the nerve to approach.

"Is there something you need, Lieutenant?" Juliet asked. "Something else we can do for your men?"

"You have been exceptionally generous already, Captain. In fact, I was rather hoping there was something we could do for you."

"I'm listening."

"Well." He clasped his hands behind his back and stood with his legs braced slightly apart. "It would appear to me that you have taken on somewhat more than you anticipated when you came to our rescue. This galleon, for instance. At a bare minimum, I estimate it will require a crew of seventy men to work the sails and keep her headed in the direction you wish to go—more if you should happen to cross the path of another enemy vessel. Your own ship carries a complement of how many? No. No, on second thought"—he held up a cautionary hand—"do not answer that; I should not want to be accused at any time of trying to prize information. My only intent is to establish that while your crew is more than adequate for sailing the one ship, it would be hard-pressed to manage two. You mention the possibility of towing the galleon, and I'm sure this would be feasible for a day or two, as long as the weather held steady and seas remained amenable. Of course, you also have the option of sinking the Spaniard, but she's a grand ship, an even grander prize, and while I can only speculate as to its value to your family's enterprise as a whole, I expect you would be loath to do such a thing if at all avoidable."

Crisp folded his arms over his chest and scowled. "Is it that ye like the sound of yer own voice, lad?"

"I beg your pardon?"

"Is there a point at the end of all this meandering?"

"A point? Why yes. Yes, of course. The point would be that I am offering the services of myself and my men in whatever capacity you might require. We are, each and every one, fully trained to the tasks of setting sails, rigging lines, manning the guns, even pumping the bilges if that is necessary to keep this monstrosity afloat. It is, if I might say, one of many advantages our navy has over, say, the French or the Spanish. A Spanish gunner is trained only to fire a gun; he would not know how to set a sail if his life depended upon it."

"Ye're offering to help us sail the *Santo Domingo* to a safe port?"

"I have under my command fifty-two able-bodied seamen who have no wish to be stranded in the middle of the ocean with the bloody Spaniards, sir." He looked at Juliet. "With respect, Captain."

She studied the unfortunately scarred face and decided she liked Lieutenant Jonathan Beck. He was earnest and outraged over the uncivilized behavior of the Spanish, grateful for his life and the lives of his men. But could she trust him? Having just boasted his knowledge of every aspect of a sailing ship, would he not be able to chart their course? Remember landmarks? Guess their position with reasonable accuracy from the sun and stars? Pigeon Cay was unique for a number of reasons, any one of which would identify it to someone familiar with the area. Moreover, she knew for a fact there was a reward of ten thousand gold doubloons on her father's head. A spectacular fortune for a man who made a shilling a month in the service of his king.

"Captain," he said, reading the hesitation in her eyes. "I am not unaware of the success your father has had in keeping his whereabouts in these islands a well-guarded secret. You have my word as an officer in His Majesty's Royal Navy that neither myself nor my men will jeopardize that secrecy in any way."

Juliet gave nothing away by her expression, but at length, she shared a long and searching look with Nathan Crisp. He, in turn, shrugged. "That's why ye're the captain. You make the decisions, I just do as I'm told."

"I could only wish," she said dryly. "Very well, Lieutenant Beck, I accept your offer and your word of honor. As for your men, I am not unappreciative of the strain it might put on their loyalties once they are back in London. In fact"—one auburn eyebrow made a casual hook upward—"for each man who agrees to join my crew of his own free will—however temporarily—and signs articles stating as much, I'm prepared to offer them a full crew's share when the prize is tallied."

Beck opened his mouth to protest, then clamped it shut again. Signing articles of privateering while still legally bound to the English navy was equivalent to desertion and the penalty for that was death. In effect, it would turn them into pirates, and for an officer to sanction such an agreement was tantamount to mutiny, treason, freebooting, and whatever other charge the navy council would throw at him if it ever came to light.

As a deterrent, however, going on account would certainly guarantee the silence of any man who signed. They had all heard the whispers concerning the cargo the *Santo Domingo* carried in her holds, and for sailors—half of whom had been pressed into service— even a tenth of a crewman's share would represent more than they could earn in a dozen lifetimes. A full share would likely be beyond any of their wildest dreamings.

"I would naturally have to put it to the men," he said, his eyes narrowing with new respect for the captain's cleverness. "But I can foresee no immediate impediment."

Juliet held out her hand. "In that case, welcome to my crew, Mr. Beck."

He was an inch away from extending his hand to seal the relationship when he blew out a puff of air and curled his fingers into a ball. "On second thought, there, ah, might be one slight impediment."

Juliet retracted her hand and rested it on the hilt of her sword. "And that would be . . . ?"

"That would be Varian St. Clare, his grace the Duke of Harrow. While I am not privileged to know his business in these waters, I do know he came aboard carrying documents that bore the king's seal. He is no common sailor, nor is he under my command. The bond I extend for my men would therefore have to exclude his grace and if his grace is excluded then I cannot guarantee the willingness of my men to sign your articles. In other words—"

"No need to hit us on the head with a truncheon, lad," Crisp said. "We see the way the boat is driftin'."

"Where is he now?" Juliet asked wearily, beginning to regret ever seeing a flash of purple velvet.

Crisp tilted his head. "We had him shifted over to the *Iron Rose*, like ye ordered."

"I did? Oh yes, I guess I did. And these documents he brought aboard?" Juliet inquired of the lieutenant. "You have no idea what they might be? Or where they might be?"

Beck glanced inadvertently over the rail as if he could see where the *Argus* rested on the bottom of the ocean. "I expect they are with the rest of the captain's papers, for I believe he entrusted them into Captain Macleod's care."

Juliet exchanged the smallest flicker of a glance with Crisp. "It would seem, then, the solution is obvious. You and your men, Mr. Beck, will remain on board the *Santo Domingo* under Mr. Loftus's command and his grace the duke will remain in ignorant bliss on board the *Iron Rose*. We need three days of fair wind and clear sailing, sir, and for that I promise a share of the prize as well as passage to the nearest British port after the *Santo Domingo* is in a safe anchorage."

Lieutenant Beck brought himself to attention. "In that case, Captain, I shall put the news to the men and we can begin to make ourselves useful at once."

She smiled. "See that you have that cut on your forehead tended first or you'll bleed to death and be no use to me at all."

Beck flashed a grin, the first she had seen since he had departed the *Argus*. It took ten years off the lieutenant's face and made his disfigurement all the more unfortunate.

When he was gone, she turned to Crisp and forestalled any objections that might be forming on his tongue.

"When we come within sight of the Cay, we will invite Mr. Beck and his crewmen to go belowdecks."

"A full crew's share?"

"They deserve it. They played as big a part in bringing the *Santo Domingo* to her knees as we did. And you saw the holds, Nathan. We can afford a little catholic charity."

He offered up a grunt. "I still say ye should just heave this lot overboard. It would save us all a deal of trouble."

Juliet followed his gaze to the huddled groups of Spaniards. Capitán Aquayo and his officers had been spared the indignity of being tethered together, but they were under heavy guard in the stern. Most of the light was fading from the sky, but Juliet had no trouble locating the one pair of piercing black eyes that had not stopped staring in her direction since she and Nathan had climbed to the tall forecastle deck.

Juliet's shots had blown away the bottom halves of the *maestre*'s ears, the lead balls cutting so close to his face they had left red scorch marks on his cheeks. The right lobe had been severed cleanly, the left had hung by a shred of flesh until his angry, groping fingers had found it and torn it off. His head was now swathed in strips of blood-stained linen that left little more than his eyes free to vow revenge.

"Might also have been for the best if ye'd just shot the bastard clean through instead o' toyin' with his affections," Crisp noted dryly.

"Ah, but this way he'll remember me each time he looks in the mirror."

"I've a feelin' he'll remember ye anyway, lass. With or without the ear bobbin'."

Chapter Three

$\mathcal{D}$arian St. Clare groaned the groan of a dying man and forced himself to roll his head toward the source of light that glowed red through his eyelids. His mouth was coated with a sour fur, his tongue was so swollen it felt like it might burst. His head was pounding, his ears were ringing incessantly, and whoever it was who had the nerve to be talking and laughing nearby would be shot the instant he could lay a hand to a pistol.

He groped in the vicinity of his waist, finding nothing but skin. He ran his fingers over the ridge of his hipbone and dragged them across the hard surface of his belly, skimming upward as he felt more flesh, hair, and a thumping heartbeat beneath his breastbone.

He was alive, though he was still not certain if that was cause for celebration.

He was also stark naked, covered by a thin, scratchy blanket. No sooner had he determined this, then more battered senses came into play, making him aware of a burning sensation on his left buttock. That, combined with the pungent smell of brimstone, made him brace himself before he dared open one dark blue eye.

Half expecting to find himself surrounded by sulfurous flames, attended by a hoard of leering, grinning demons, he peered through the merest slit of his lashes.

He was not in hell, nor was he on board the *Argus*. He had been in Captain Macleod's great cabin on many occasions and this, with its huge brass wheel suspended from the ceiling, was not the smallest part familiar.

He opened his eyes wider and his search for explanations ranged farther afield. Most of the cabin was in heavy shadow, for although there was a lantern suspended from every spoke of the brass wheel, only one was lit, casting its soot up to smudge a ceiling thick with lampblack. There was no way of telling if it was day or night; heavy sheets of canvas had been hung over the bank of windows that spanned the rear wall of the cabin.

A glint of metal drew his eye to the leaded crosspieces on a wire-fronted bookcase, then to another beside it lined with shelves that held an impressive array of pistols and powder flasks. The two cases appeared to be the only extravagance in a room fitted with an enormous desk, a chair, and a small washing stand nailed to the floorboards. The bed he was lying on was little more than a shelf set into the bulkhead. The mattress was barely wide enough to accommodate his shoulders and so thin he might as well have been stretched out flat on a board.

Moreover, he was not alone in this strange and spartan cabin.

Beacom was seated on a narrow bench at the end of the bed, his head drooping forward so far his chin touched his chest. Bowed over the desk were two men, one of whom was studying a map and scratching notations on the border while the other man watched, nodding occasionally to himself as if mentally comparing the jotted computations with those he had apparently made himself. He was short and burly with a face like a terrier chewing a mouthful of wasps. The one doing the jottings was taller, leaner, and wore a faded blue bandana over a single long auburn braid that hung halfway down his back.

A memory stabbed through the pain in his skull and took Varian back into the heat of battle where he recalled seeing the same lad with the blue bandana

cornered against the rail by three Spaniards. The boy
had been holding his own, wielding a sword like a
brilliant young master, and Varian had only felt the
need to intercede when an arquebusier thought to
take unfair advantage.

He remembered that much. He also remembered
leaping back on board the *Argus* in time to be blown
to hell and gone when the deck had exploded beneath
his feet. After that . . . nothing but flashes and
glimpses. Something about a dagger. The ship going
down. The boy again.

There had been something odd about the way he
spoke, too. Something about the way he looked . . .

Varian's experienced eye traveled along the lad's
slender form and hovered over the rounded curve of
the hip, the tightly molded moleskin breeches, the
crux of the thighs where there was neither a bulge nor
a codpiece allowing ready access to one.

His gaze shot back up to the face beneath the blue
bandana and confirmed a rather shocking suspicion: it
was a female. Her head was tipped forward in concentration and the light was directly above her, casting
most of her face in shadow, but there was no doubting
his instincts. The boy was female—the same female in
the same tight breeches and leather jerkin he had seen
fighting on the deck of the galleon!

If there was the smallest doubt that this was the
same person, it was dispelled at the sight of the elegant Toledo sword she still wore strapped about her
waist, the tip of which bumped against the heel of her
boot when she took a step around the desk. It was as
splendid a weapon as his own blade, which had been
made by a master craftsman and presented to him as
a token of appreciation by King James himself.

Varian willed himself to take another long, slow
look around the cabin. This time, when he turned his
head farther in an attempt to see what lay in the shadows behind him, such a violent stab of pain shot
through his skull he could not stop a sharp gasp from
breaking through his lips.

"Oh! Faith and happy day!" Beacom's shadow cut across the lantern light, blocking both it and the couple standing at the desk. "My lord his grace the duke is coming to himself again!"

Varian attempted to speak but his throat refused to emit more than a dry croak.

"Captain!" Beacom clasped his hands in an appeal directed across the room. "Might I trouble you for a dram of wine? I expect his grace is sorely in need."

"It's there on the sideboard." The burly man waved a hand. "Help yerself."

"I thank you, sir. You are too desperately kind."

A grunt acknowledged the compliment before he returned to his charts.

A moment later Varian felt a few drops of sweet red wine trickle through his lips. He let it fill his mouth and run down his throat, and what he did not sputter out on a ragged cough he swallowed with avid appreciation. When the cup was empty he lapped the air insistently for more, but Beacom was cautioned against it.

"Unless you want him puking it all up again," said a feminine voice. "Wait a few minutes. If he manages to keep that down, he can have another. He has taken a stout knock on the head and if the skull is cracked or the brain is swollen, you will only be wasting my good Malaga."

"My skull is fine," Varian rasped. "Where the devil am I? Where is Captain Macleod?"

"Captain Macleod is dead, your grace," Beacom explained quickly. "The *Argus*, I'm afraid, is lost. Gone. Sunk beneath the sea."

"Sunk, you say?" Varian frowned and struggled to squeeze out more memories.

"We were attacked by a vile Spanish warship," Beacom recounted. "You were injured when the powder magazine on board the *Argus* exploded. You knocked your head on a beam as you flew through the air and, ah"—he leaned closer and lowered his voice to a whisper—"your shoulder and left buttock were severely bruised. Right to the very bone, I dare say. The captain applied some dreadful concoction of oil and turpentine, claiming it would numb the flesh and help it heal faster."

"Nothing is numb, dammit," Varian hissed through his teeth. "And you have yet to tell me where we are and who the devil that woman is that she should dare tell me I can or cannot have more wine."

The auburn head came up under the lantern light, causing the bandana to glow a pale, luminous blue against the darker shadows. "You are presently on board my ship, sir, in my bed, and as captain, I can tell you any damned thing I wish to tell you."

"Captain?"

"Captain."

"*Your* ship?"

"My ship." She nodded. "The *Iron Rose.*"

Varian closed his eyes and tried to concentrate. The name meant nothing to him yet he thought it highly preposterous—and unlikely—for a woman to be captain of any ship, much less one that had defied the might of a Spanish galleon.

"If the accommodations fail to meet with your approval," she murmured dryly, bringing his eyes open again, "Mr. Crisp, here, can always sling a hammock in a sail locker for you and your servant."

Since the pounding in his head did not allow an appreciation for either humor or sarcasm at the moment, Varian decided to savor the lingering taste of the wine—which he recognized as being a damned fine vintage and nothing at all like the sour claret the captain of the *Argus* had enjoyed by the barrelful. "You say this is your cabin?"

"It is."

"Then I shall assume it is the best the ship has to offer and accept it graciously."

The girl lifted her head and her eyebrow at the same time. She set the stick of charcoal she had been writing with on the desk and stared at Beacom, who instantly wilted against the wall.

"Your man informs us you are a duke."

"The twelfth Duke of Harrow to be precise. Varian St. Clare at your service, mistress . . . ?"

"Captain," she said, correcting him. "Captain Dante . . . to be precise. The twelfth duke, you say?"

"We tend to live short lives," he snapped. "Dante?" Though he whispered the name, it set off such a violent hammering in his head that he had to set his teeth against a shiver. "Do you pretend to tell me the infamous rogue known as the Pirate Wolf is a mere woman?"

The question and his manner of asking it brought her out from behind the desk this time and Beacom's eyes rounded almost out of their sockets. His face engaged in a flurry of contortions, most of them intended to warn Varian, by means of elaborate movements of the mouth and eyebrows, not to test the patience of the woman who was now slowly crossing the room and approaching the side of the bed. When she threw a scowl in his direction, the frantic pantomime ceased and he looked up at the ceiling, but when she looked away again, he laced his fingers together in a desperate plea for his master to hold his tongue.

"I pretend nothing, my lord. My name is Juliet Dante and the rogue to whom you refer so capriciously is my father, Simon Dante."

"Your *father*?"

"So he told me," she said evenly, "and I have no reason to disbelieve him."

"Well of course that was not what I meant." Varian raised a hand to massage his temple. "It was merely a response to the astonishing notion of a woman such as yourself captaining a fighting ship."

"You English do appear to be having a difficult time grasping the notion," she agreed wryly. "But I am curious to know what you mean by 'a woman such as myself.' Just what kind of woman might that be?"

He stopped rubbing his brow and stared at her a moment. It was her eyes that warned him—eyes that sent the fine hairs across the back of his neck standing on end. Aside from the extraordinary silver blue color, they were bold and direct, inviting him to expand on the insulting platitude only if he had absolutely no desire to see another sunrise. They were situated above a nose that looked almost as if it had been broken at some time, for it tipped ever so slightly to one side. The face itself, although wanting a good scrub, was a surprising blend of characteristics, from the large, expressive eyes to the firm chin, neither of which suggested she was someone to be trifled with.

No helpless, blushing dove, this one.

"Young," he said carefully. "I was about to say you looked too young to bear such a burden of responsibility. I meant no disrespect, I assure you."

His bad attempt at a feint put the hint of a smile on her lips.

"In that case, to save you any further consternation, the gentleman standing over there trying to pretend he can make calculations in his head is my quartermaster, Nathan Crisp, and he is as old as Beelzebub."

"Not by half," Crisp objected.

Varian was still studying the girl's face. He had read every scrap of documentation with the Dante name on it before he departed England. He'd read the English, the French, the Dutch, even the Spanish reports dating back some thirty years and knew there were two sons who had followed in their father's footsteps. Nowhere had he found a reference to the Pirate Wolf having a daughter, much less one who commanded her own armed privateer.

He must have winced under the weight of his thoughts, for without warning, she reached out and laid a hand across his forehead. Her fingers were long and cool and although they were withdrawn after a moment or two, he continued to feel their imprint long after.

"You have no fever and we've not seen the wine again. I suspect, apart from the ringing in your left ear, nothing has been too badly damaged."

"How do you know my left ear is ringing?"

She reached out again and this time when she touched him, it was to scratch a small fleck of dried blood off his neck. "You were fairly close to the explosion. You're lucky you didn't lose your hearing entirely."

"Beacom said you tended my wounds. You are the ship's surgeon as well as the captain?"

"Necessity dictates that everyone learns to do a little of everything. Unfortunately, we don't have the luxury of a surgeon. The carpenter has some skill with a saw and auger; thus he usually handles the serious wounds. If you had a cut or a gash, the sailmaker would ply his trade, but a cracked head and a bruised rump hardly seemed critical enough to warrant special attention despite the"—she paused to glare at Beacom—"incessant and interminable wailings of your manservant."

Varian attempted a smile, one that showed a lot of straight white teeth and cost very little in effort. "You must forgive Beacom's enthusiasm. He served my father and my elder brother before me and has very rigid standards to which everyone—including myself— must aspire." And although she did not ask, he added, "I had two older brothers, actually, but neither had the foresight to produce an heir before they died, and so here I am, the twelfth Duke of Harrow by default. It is a tiresome and annoying responsibility, but it is mine and I must bear it as best I can." He paused, sweetening his smile with a small, seductive curve, one that rarely failed to soften a woman's heart and limbs. "May I say, Captain, since we are discussing merits, that I was impressed by your display of swordsmanship on board the galleon. I warrant not ten men of my acquaintance could have conducted themselves so admirably."

"I do not fight to impress anyone, my lord. I fight to survive a day longer than my enemy."

"Nonetheless, for a woman—" He stopped, feeling another warning thud inside his chest as she turned the full power of those remarkable eyes back on him.

"For a *young* woman such as yourself," he amended slowly, "I would perhaps have suggested a lighter blade. Your left shoulder tends to droop somewhat when you tire and a more diligent foe might be able to take advantage."

Her eyebrow arched. "You say that as if your expertise goes beyond knowing how to choose your plumage to match your founts of lace."

Beacom let out a gasp that sounded like it had remained strangled in his throat too long. "Good gracious heavens, madam! Milord his grace the Duke of Harrow is one of the most renowned swordsmen in all of England! His reputation is legion among the very masters of Europe. His sword, madam, was a gift from His Most Gracious Majesty King James, bestowed by his own hand. Moreover, for these past many years that selfsame sword has been at the king's right hand, there but to answer the crown's call at the merest hint of peril. His grace is a former captain of the Royal Guard, as well as a loyal and—"

Varian shot the spluttering Beacom a look that squeezed the valet's throat shut, reducing the last few accolades to soundless movements of his lips.

But the words that had already been spoken could not be unspoken and Varian saw Juliet Dante's head tilt slightly to one side as if she had caught a scent of something foul in the air.

"So." She crossed her arms over her chest and frowned. "We are in the company of a trusted confidant of King James. A former captain of His Majesty's garters."

"Th-that would be *guards*, madam." Beacom held up a spindly finger to protest. "C-captain of the king's *guards*."

Juliet did not take her eyes off St. Clare. "Mr. Crisp. If this wretched little man says one more word, take him out onto the gallery and drop him overboard."

"Aye. With pleasure," Crisp grinned. "Mayhap, if he swims fast enough, he can catch up with the Spaniards."

Varian looked shocked. "You threw the Spanish prisoners overboard?"

"In a manner of speaking," she said dryly. "We landed them a hundred yards off an atoll, in water shallow enough for them to walk the rest of the way. What business brings you to the Caribbee?"

"My own," Varian replied curtly. "And none of yours."

For the briefest fraction of a second her hand moved toward the hilt of her sword.

"Lieutenant Beck said the *Argus* was a courier ship, bound for New Providence. An odd choice of vessels for an English duke to go adventuring on . . . unless of course you have come to deliver copies of the king's new Bible in an attempt to cleanse our heathen souls and mend us of our larcenous ways?"

Crisp guffawed, Varian glared.

"Some might regard it as an adventure to sail half-way across the world in a leaking wooden bucket, madam, but I assure you, I considered it nothing shy of hell."

"Then why are you here? And spare me the further insult of denying that you are another of the king's lackeys sent to spout dictums of peace."

"I am no man's lackey, madam."

"And I am no man's dupe, sir. The king has been sending a plague of messengers here for the past five years and they all bring missives demanding the same thing. They want us to stop attacking Spanish ships; they want us to leave the Caribbean entirely. They—and I must presume it is not entirely the king's idea, for he holds his royal hand out readily enough when we send his percentage of the prize monies back to London—they presume to think that if we cease to harass the Spaniards, Philip III will happily open the ports to honest trade. The last buffoon who came brandishing his sealed and beribboned documents even threatened to rescind all letters of marque. A threat, I might add, which had us trembling in abject terror, as you can imagine."

Despite the contempt in her voice, Varian could not help but be intrigued. The pale blue of her eyes was sparked with azure flecks, changing their character entirely. Where there had been amused indifference and disdain a few brief moments ago, there was now a depth of anger and passion that almost took his breath away. The heat had moved into her face as well, burnishing the already lusty effects of the sun and sea, suffusing her skin with enough of a ruddy glow to make him wonder what she would look like if she removed the scruffy blue bandana and let her hair loose about her shoulders.

"Well?"

He blinked. "Well . . . what?"

"Do you honestly believe the Spanish would ever honor a treaty with England? Can you even *pretend* to believe it after your own ship was attacked without provocation? Hah! No, you cannot. There has been no peace beyond the line for a hundred years, and the fact that your king and his ministers now send a duke in fancy plumage to deliver more of their puling threats changes nothing . . . except, perhaps, the method of your removal from my ship."

Varian's temples throbbed anew. She had the distinct advantage in this duel of wits and words for he was wounded, naked, lying flat in a bed with no recourse but to let her flay him with her contempt. In spite of the way she fought and talked and looked beneath all the grime and dried blood that stained her clothing, she was still a woman, for heaven's sake, and he had never met a woman he could not seduce with a smile and a silky word. Yet this one appeared to be completely immune. She was not afraid of him, not impressed with his title or his position as the king's emissary, nor did she seem to be concerned in the least that she had just threatened to drown a peer of the realm.

Some of what he was thinking must have shown in the sudden tightness in his jaw, for she leaned forward and smiled. "Indeed, my lord, you are not in London now and there are no courtiers present. You have no friends on board this ship, no power, no authority, no influence over so much as the lowliest seaman. On board the *Iron Rose*, I am the only authority. I am the queen, the duchess, the countess, the high priestess, and the only one who decides whether you remain here as our guest, or become fodder for the first school of sharks we see swimming past. Had we not happened along when we did, the Spaniards would have sunk you and left no witness behind to the deed. Make no mistake, sir: it would not cause me a moment in lost sleep to do likewise."

Varian stared up into eyes as implacably cold as ice and had no reason to doubt her. He did not believe in coincidences, and while he might have been persuaded to believe at first that it was by the greatest stroke of good fortune he had wakened to find himself in the presence of the daughter of one of the men he had indeed sailed halfway around the world to find, nothing could convince him he had not simply wakened into another kind of hell.

He was not given to blushing like a shy dove either, but nothing in his experience had prepared him to do battle with this blue-eyed Amazon and he could feel the blood rising warmly beneath his skin.

Her point made and her position clear, Juliet Dante turned without another word and walked back to the desk. Crisp, whom Varian had already recognized as a man of few words, smirked at him with the belligerence accorded idiots and annoying children.

The duke drew a slow, calming breath. The wine he had enjoyed earlier now rolled over in his stomach with an audible gurgle and raised a sour bubble in his throat.

"Excuse me, *Captain*, but may I at least ask where we are and where we are bound?"

Juliet answered without glancing up from her charts. "You are about twenty leagues distance from where you were, and you are bound for wherever we take you."

"Are you by chance thinking to hold me for ransom? If so, you should know the king is exceptionally . . . penurious. I doubt he would pay much for my return."

"If I had the time to drop you off at a British port, believe me I would, sir, and not ask a farthing for the pleasure of doing so."

"In that case, Captain Dante, I would be verily obliged if you would take me to your father."

"I beg your pardon?"

"I said—"

"I heard what you said. I also heard you deny not five minutes ago that you were one of the king's lackeys."

"I denied being a *lackey*. I did not deny being dispatched to this forsaken place to meet with your father."

"Why?"

"I really am not at liberty to say at the moment. I will tell you this much, however, that if the *Argus* had made it safely to New Providence, and if I had met with . . . as an example . . . Captain David Smith, or Captain Frederick Mounts, or any of a dozen other privateers before ever hearing your father's name, I would have been able to discharge my commission for the king and be happily on my way back to London on the next ship. The fact that it was you who intervened today, and that your father happens to be Simon Dante," he added, "who also happens to be one of the men I have been empowered to meet with, bears no extra weight of importance other than it is an incredible coincidence that happens to be incredibly convenient."

"I do not believe in coincidences, sir."

"Nor do I. Nonetheless, it would seem that one has occurred, so we can either take advantage . . . or not. As you see fit, Captain."

She was standing under the lamp again, the bandana glowing, the fine wisps of coppery hairs catching the light and shining in a fiery tangle around her face. The air was as still and silent as the instant before a lightning strike. So silent, Varian could hear Beacom's knees knocking together.

"London," she mused at length. "I have heard it stinks worse than the bilge of a slaver. That the people are so *friendly* they throw their offal on the heads of neighbors passing on the streets below. I have even heard that the king himself"—she paused and a humorless smile played about the corners of her mouth—"prefers the companionship of pretty men in plumes and purple velvet."

Varian refused to take the bait. He did push himself up onto his elbows, however, a move that caused the folds of the blanket to slip down, baring his chest and upper arms. It earned what he thought was the first glimpse of a genuinely feminine reaction when her gaze coursed over the exposed breadth of muscle— very hard, well-formed male muscle that was not deserving of the insult. He also paid the price for his little show of vanity when his head thundered and the cabin took a wild spin. But at least he managed to remain upright and not careen facedown out of the bunk.

"Take me to your father," he said through clenched teeth. " If he throws me over the side, then so be it; I will at least have met my obligations."

Crisp snorted. "Sharks'll like that, aye. A man who has met his obligations. Makes for a tastier meal."

Juliet smiled thoughtfully. She snapped her compass closed and started rolling up the sheaf of charts. "Very well, my lord, you have won your audience. Not because you plead your case so well, but because we are pressed for time. If the wind holds, we can put another twenty leagues behind us before midnight and should make landfall no later than Friday, three days hence. Between now and then, however, perhaps Mr. Crisp will be able to find a spare shirt and petticoat to preserve your modesty."

"Or you could simply return my own clothes. Beacom?"

Beacom turned as pale as candle wax, his eyes bug-

ging out so far they threatened to squirt from the
sockets. "I'm afraid that is not possible, your grace.
Everything you were wearing was either scorched beyond repair or had to be cut away in order to treat
your wounds."

"Everything? *All* of my clothes?"

"E-even to your linens, sir."

"What of my personal belongings? My trunks? My
books . . . my *papers*?"

"Gone, your grace. Everything is gone down with
the *Argus*. A-all except your sword, which I have
here"—the valet stood hastily to one side to show that
it was hanging on a peg beside him—"and your
shoes."

"Aye, an' as fetchin' an outfit as that would make,"
Crisp said, chuckling, "I'd not wander about the decks
like that or ye'll be bent over with yer legs spread,
takin' it up the bottle before ye've done half a turn."

"He'll not be wandering about at all, Mr. Crisp,"
Juliet said flatly. "This is a working ship and we have
a great deal to do between now and when we drop
anchor in port. I'll not have passengers causing a distraction or getting in the way of the men going about
their duties."

Varian watched her slot the charts into pigeonholes
built into the side of the desk. The dark braid of her
hair slithered over her shoulder as she bent over and
his fingers ached to follow it, to curl around her throat
and squeeze until that insolent tongue was bitten off
between her teeth. But the urge passed, taking the
glowering expression with it, and when she glanced
his way before she and her henchman left, she saw
nothing but a politely strained smile of compliance.

When the door closed behind them, Beacom spun
on his heel and grabbed at fistfuls of the blanket, twisting the cloth with such passion he nearly snatched it
off the bed.

"Oh my good gracious God, sir! I thought sure we
were done for! We are in the clutches of dread pirates!
We are hostages! We are captives! We are prisoners

at their complete and utter mercy! We shall be forced to walk the plank. We shall be lashed and smote with hot irons, our toenails drawn from our feet with hot pincers, our tongues cut out, and our entrails fed piece by piece to the sharks! How could you ask to stay on board? How could you provoke her temper with such bald disregard for our well-being? How could you not plead for release at the first opportunity!"

Varian threw the blanket aside and swung his legs over the side of the bed. The movement caused his bruised body to scream in pain but he was too angry to pay heed. "Lashed, smote, *and* fed to the sharks? You predict a gloomy future for us, Beacom."

"With good reason, your grace. Have we not been regaled these past six weeks since departing London by stories of the half-man, half-wolf she claims as sire? Have we not had our hair sent rising straight off our heads at the tales of torture and brutality attached to the name Dante? You witnessed with your own eyes and ears how insensible she is to the proper respect due her betters."

"I doubt she could be rendered sensible by anything short of a blow to the head. Where the devil is the wine?"

Beacom pointed with a hand still clutched around a hillock of blanket. Varian strode naked to a side table and poured himself a goblet of wine from a heavy green flagon. He downed the first cup in three noisy swallows and poured himself another.

"Brace yourself, man," he said, glaring at Beacom. "For all that he may well arouse fear in his enemies, Simon Dante is still the king's man. One could pick at nits and say, rather, that he was the queen's man, but he still flies the flag of England on his masthead. As for the daughter—" He paused to throw back another measure of wine. "In spite of her apparent contempt, did she not come to the *Argus*'s rescue at considerable risk to her own vessel? You saw the size of that bloody Spaniard. Our shots bounced off its hull like noisome gnats. Now fetch another bottle of wine and for pity's sake, stop your trembling before you wear through the heels of your shoes."

There was iron in Varian's voice, iron in his body, too, gleaming across the broad expanse of his shoulders, down the hard flat plane of his belly, and in the long, sinewed legs.

Though Beacom's very bowels liquefied at the thought of being caught helping himself to the lady captain's store of spirits, he was more than passingly familiar with his master's temper and at the moment, he was not certain which boded worse for the state of his own well-being.

Drawing what comfort he could from the knowledge that he was at least not alone on this dread pirate ship, and that his master was an admirable adversary when it came to dealing with either sex, he released his hold on the blankets, and, after giving the covers a tremulous smoothing, ventured to the cabinet. There was only one bottle on the shelf, the contents amber when he poured them into Varian's outthrust cup.

"Oh dear. I should think it looks quite off, your grace."

Varian held the goblet to his nose. For the first time since he had wakened, the smile that spread across his face was genuine and the darkness of his eyes lit with a glint of pleasure. "It isn't off at all, Beacom. It is quite damnably on. Rumbustion," he explained with a hearty wink and took a long, satisfied swallow. "As lusty and restorative an elixir as God could provide."

"Nonetheless, your grace, you . . . you might want to exercise caution in restoring too much too soon. You have had nothing by way of food or drink for the past twelve hours."

Scorning his valet's advice, Varian tipped the goblet and drained it. For all of ten seconds he felt little more than the warming sensation of the tropical spirit gliding down his throat—he was, after all, no stranger to the sharp effects of spirits—but when the ten seconds passed, his body went numb from the waist down and his knees folded like sheets of paper. He would have gone down hard had Beacom not caught him under the arms.

"I have you, your grace," he said, scrambling to keep his own balance. "Shall I help you back to the bed?"

Varian could not speak, he could only nod. When he was safely back on the narrow berth he allowed himself a gulp of fresh air, but that caused the room to spin faster and the fire in his throat to blaze.

Beacom emptied the goblet into the washbowl and filled it with water from a pewter jug. Varian gulped his way through that and another before he was able to lie flat again, his brain giddy, his flesh prickling as if it had been charred from the inside out.

"She fights like a man," he rasped. "She smells like a fishmonger's trollop, and swills rum like a common jackanapes. A truly delicate creature, our Captain Dante—when she and her crew are not sacking Spanish galleons."

"Or slitting the throats of unwanted guests and feeding them to the sharks."

Varian's eyes rolled to the back of his head. "You will have to allow me the luxury of a day or two to decide which may prove to be the happier course."

Chapter Four

*J*uliet climbed the shrouds as nimbly as any crewman. She had been doing so almost from the moment she could keep her balance on the deck of a ship. The highest point on the mainmast was her sanctuary; from there she could imagine herself perched on the top of the world. If the ship was shrouded in fog, it felt like being suspended on a cloud; in full daylight, with the wind turning her hair into sleek, dark ribbons, it gave her the exhilarating sensation of flying. There were clouds tonight, fast-moving veils that glowed iridescent blue where they were flung across the path of the crescent moon. The wind was strong from the west, laced with the faint taste of spice, hinting that a storm was brewing somewhere, bringing the scent of the islands out to sea.

Part of her did not want to return home yet, was never anxious to exchange the powerful surge of the sea for the powdered white sand that meant she was land bound. Nor was she particularly eager to explain to her father how a simple sea trial had turned into a rescue of one vessel and the capture of another. Hopefully the sight of the *Santo Domingo* being led into the harbor behind the *Iron Rose* would mollify her father's temper somewhat.

Countering the beneficial effects of the captured galleon would be the presence of a ducal envoy on board the *Rose*. Perhaps Crisp was right. Perhaps they should have loaded his grace the Duke of Harrow and his valet into the longboats with the Spaniards. The duke, especially, had the look of trouble about him.

Unfortunately the *Iron Rose* was already long overdue and her father would be climbing the hills daily to watch for a glimpse of her sails. As it was, they would have to take a circuitous route back to Pigeon Cay, sailing well south of their destination to ensure there were no predators lying below the horizon. There was no excuse for failing to take such precautions regardless of the time or energy it took, and if a vessel did show an interest in following them, it could take several more days to lead it astray and circle back.

Pigeon Cay had been her father's stronghold for the past thirty years and although the Spaniards had been searching for it nigh on as long, none had been able to discover the Pirate Wolf's hidden base. On each galleon caught or captured, a careful inspection was made of her charts and maps, but none had ever been marked with the tiny island that held the Wolf's lair. Not even English ships knew the exact location of Dante's atoll—and from a distance, it looked like just that: a crown of barren volcanic rock thrusting up from the sea. Occasional news, messages, missives from England, were delivered to the port of New Providence in the Baja Más and retrieved at irregular intervals. Once a year, the Dantes sent a ship back to England laden with the crown's share of their privateering ventures, and while both Jonas and Gabriel had been to London on one of these voyages, Juliet had never been curious enough to trade warm sunshine and salty sea air for fog, coal dust, and rain.

Juliet's beloved grandfather, Jonas Spence, had overseen these voyages until his death four years earlier. He had been a villainous old sea lion but Juliet had loved him dearly. All bluster and brine as he was, she could only wonder what it must have been like sailing in the company of men like Jonas and her father, Sir Francis Drake, John Hawkins, and Martin Frobisher in the glory days of Elizabeth's sea hawks.

Were it not for the courage and daring of scores of
these privateers, England would not have had a navy
to defend her against Spain's invasion armada. She
would likely not have a presence in the New World
either, ensuring the need for the Spanish king to di-
vide his naval forces in order to keep a strong and
active fleet patrolling the Spanish Main.

Philip II had tried, two years after the Great Armada and again ten years later, to amass enough ships
to threaten England's shores again, but neither fleet
had left port. When Philip III had come to power,
there had been a marked increase in shipbuilding to
counter the fear that Britain's navy was growing too
strong. There had been noticeable changes in Spain's
Indies fleets as well, with galleons like the fifty-four-
gun *Santo Domingo* replacing the smaller forty-gun
zabras and thirty-gun India guards. And while the actual number of treasure ships in the plate fleets had
been decreasing steadily over the years, the number
of warships that sailed in the protective escort had
increased to ensure each cargo of treasure arrived
safely back in Spain.

Conversely, men like Simon Dante, Captain David
Smith, and Captain Frederick Mounts did their damned-
est to see that it did not.

Of the original band of Gloriana's sea hawks led by
el Draque, only Simon Dante remained active in the
Caribbean, and only he continued to elude the Spanish
hunters' best efforts to bring him to ground. The reward on the *Pirata Lobo*'s head—whether he was
taken dead or alive—had become a large enough sum
to tempt more than just Spanish carrion-eaters. It was
not that Juliet had any overt suspicions or doubt that
Varian St. Clare was here for any reason other than
to deliver another of the king's edicts for peace. She
thought it highly unlikely an assassin would travel with
a manservant who fluttered and fainted at the least
turn of a knife, yet his evasiveness annoyed her.

On balance it was simply the lesser of two potential
evils to take the Duke of Harrow to Pigeon Cay and

let her father deal with him. To discourage him from making too many forays outside the cabin, Juliet had deliberately sliced his clothes to ribbons, leaving him nothing but a blanket and a swollen temper. Between that and finding himself at the mercy of a "mere woman," he should be manageable for the three days it would take to sail to Pigeon Cay.

Juliet grimaced and flicked a piece of oakum out into the darkness.

Mere woman. She hadn't been accused of having many feminine shortcomings in a very long time. One did not live on an island in close proximity to Spanish shipping lanes without learning at a young age how to fight with sword and knife and musket. Her father— no poor swordsman himself—had taught her as soon as she could heft the weight of a blade that while God could be entrusted to take care of their souls in the hereafter, it was solely incumbent upon their own skills with steel and powder to ensure they did not join Him too soon.

It had been her mother who had taken Juliet's lessons one step further. Isabeau had taught her to go for the swift and sure kill. A split second hesitation debating the polite rules of engagement could not only cost her her life, but the lives of the men who depended on her to lead them. Regardless of her lineage, there was nary a crew on the ocean-sea who would follow a woman—or man—who demurred at the sight of blood, or who showed the smallest signs of weakness when strength and hard, unblinking courage were demanded.

Juliet's body bore the scars to prove it.

She had needed to earn the loyalty and trust of the men along with their respect, and while most of the crew on board the *Iron Rose* would gut any man for looking sideways at her, there had been a few over the years who thought her fair and easy pickings on a cold dark night. Too much rum had sent their eyes and hands wandering but they had quickly and painfully discovered she was neither fair nor easy. She was no swanning virgin either. It had been several years since she had lost her innocence as well as her maidenhead, but it had been by her choice, and on her terms.

Dominic du Lac had been her first lover. A tall, green-eyed Frenchman with a silver tongue and silky hands, he hadn't been particularly handsome, but he had made her laugh. He had picked wildflowers and braided them into her hair, and he had insisted upon showing her, one garment at a time, how to dress like a proper French demoiselle. Afterward, with equal deliberation and care, he had shown her how to remove each article and by the time he was finished, they had both been naked and eager to release the tension he had so deftly created.

Dominic had died of the yellow fever within the month, but in the short time they had had together, he had taught her wondrous things about her body. He had introduced her to pleasures and cravings that could not remain in mourning for long.

There had been three men after Dominic, each special in his own way, and although none had caused any poetic flutters of the heart, they had enjoyed her and she had enjoyed them without shame or reservation. The last had been over a year ago and the affair had ended, as they usually did when the sea was such a powerful mistress, with the abruptness of a musket shot. In truth, it had been many months since she had even seen a man who stoked her interest. Perhaps that was why she had felt a distinct stirring in her blood when she had sliced away the final layer of clothing and viewed the duke's naked body.

Crisp had initially balked at settling him into her cabin but in truth, it contained the only real bed on board and even that was not built for comfort. Most nights she slung her hammock on the narrow stern gallery, preferring to sleep to the sound of the wake curling off the hull.

She was also admittedly intrigued. She had heard that all English noblemen were as soft and slightly built as their women, yet this one was tall and strapping, his chest and shoulders were well defined, the flesh taut, the muscles solid to the touch. The dark hairs that covered his breast were thick and silky, narrowing to a finger's width over his belly before exploding again in a crisp nest at the junction of his thighs.

There, her gaze had lingered a few moments longer than necessary, for he was more than adequately endowed. Nudity was commonplace on board a ship and she had seen more than her fair share of men's privy parts in all shapes and sizes. The most outstanding appendage belonged to Lucifer, her father's gun captain, and while the duke's pride and glory did not come within a league of such prominence, it did raise a small tingle of speculation at the base of her spine.

A scandalized cough from the manservant had prompted her to draw the covers above the duke's waist, but not before she noted that the muscles in his thighs were as hard as oak, suggesting he was an avid horseman as well as an experienced swordsman—one who did not forgo practicing in favor of a game of cards or dice.

The bruises would heal in a day or two and he could be thankful his clothes had provided enough padding to keep the fire from scorching through to the skin. The lump on his head was more troublesome for there was no way of knowing if the bone was cracked beneath. The fact that he had regained his sensibilities was no proof his brains were not leaking, and she had seen men with similar wounds emerge from battle seemingly fit and hale only to slump over dead a few days later, bleeding from the nose and ears.

That he was a nobleman in and of itself did not awe her, nor would it win him any special favor on board. Simon Dante's bloodlines reached well back to a time when England was ruled by wild-eyed Saxons. Being the twelfth of this or the fifth of that would not impress her father any more than it had impressed her, and if Varian St. Clare wanted to keep all his skin intact, he would curb his arrogance and not enter into any meeting with his nose thrust too high in the air.

Juliet let the wind take the last scrap of twine from her hand, then walked catlike out across the yard, testing her balance against the pull and sway of the ship. With nothing to hold her, nothing below to break her fall, it was a dangerous game that would have brought snarls and shouts from Nathan Crisp if he had seen her. Most of the men who worked the yards ran their length several times a day as a matter of course, but they were not the daughters of Simon Dante; bringing them home smashed and broken would only earn a cluck of the tongue and a shake of the head over their foolishness.

She went to the end of the yard and did a graceful pirouette on the ball of her foot. Forty feet below, the deck was all shadows and very little substance for the *Iron Rose* ran dark, sailing without lights of any kind. Out in the open water, on a starless night, something as small as the glow from a pipe could be seen for miles, and Juliet had forbidden all lamps and candles above deck and only below under extreme caution. The gallery windows in her own cabin had been covered with thick tarps painted black.

Faint snatches of conversation drifted upward, but for the most part, the crew was taking full advantage of their respite after the day's events. It was a warm night and most had slung their hammocks on the open deck. At this height, they resembled so many maggots rolled into small white carapaces, pale worms against the darker boards.

Because of the *Iron Rose*'s superior speed, it had been necessary to drastically shorten sail in order to keep abreast of the much slower *Santo Domingo*. Juliet could just barely make out the ghostly tower of sails following in their wake. Otherwise, the ocean stretched out black and unbroken on all sides with only a faintly luminous froth of spindrift here and there to reflect the filtered light of the moon. If she closed her eyes, Juliet could isolate the sound of the wake breaking astern, the creak of cleats, the faint hum of the wind straining against the canvas. She could hear the ship breathing, feel the rhythmic throbbing of a heartbeat through the mast. She knew the *Iron Rose* as well as she knew her own body and could waken out of a deep sleep upon the instant if she sensed something was out of balance.

The ship rolled into a wave and Juliet compensated for the movement with a graceful, upward fanning of her arms. Her feet were swift and sure and she reluctantly climbed back down the shrouds, pausing midway to secure a loose corner of sail. She could feel eyes on her, marking her descent through the rigging lines, and when her feet landed on solid decking, she heard the growl behind her.

"You know, do you not, it'd mark the death of every last one of us if you were to slip and fall one of these nights. Your father would hang, draw, and quarter us all, and that would be *if* we survived the keelhauling your brothers would mete out and *if* your mother did not pluck our ballocks off with hot pincers and force us to roast them over a fire."

Juliet smiled into the scowling face of the ship's carpenter, Noggin Kelly. He had earned his name through the number of times he had been brained by beams and spars—blows that would have dented the skulls of most men but that merely scrambled his wits for a few moments before he recovered. Despite the fact that Nog reminded her of a perpetually aroused mastiff who thought himself too fierce and virile to ever be considered harmless, harmless he was. For even puffed up with manly indignation as he was now, he could be reduced to a flame-skinned schoolboy with a suitably inappropriate riposte or mention of the hot-tempered wife waiting for him in port.

"Roasted ballocks," she mused, "are considered a delicacy, I have been told, on some of these heathen islands, though I've yet to sample the fare. 'Twould make for a tasty meal, faith, would it not?"

"You might not take the threat too seriously, Captain, but there are a hundred men on board the *Rose* who do."

"Ahh, but think how much more freely you would be able to move about without all that cumbersome flesh getting in the way."

She left him pondering the thought and joined Nathan, whom she had spied leaning by the rail.

"Nog is right, ye know. Ye take more risks than ye ought. Ye've naught to prove to any of us, lass. We've all seen ye slit a throat an' climb a shroud in a gale"—he paused to aim a wry glance upward—"an' dance a yard in the dead of night."

"What if I am not trying to prove anything, Nate? What if I just enjoy being able to do these things?"

"Then you're as daft as yer mam an' it'll be up to the saints to save yer soul."

"Are you implying that Mother's soul needs saving?"

"Nay. She has yer father to keep her honest. Though, on a second thought, he's as daft as her so the pair are both doomed."

She laughed. "I hope you are not suggesting that a good man would save me?"

"No." Crisp snorted. "It'd take a *hellish* good man to do that. And like as not, he'd lose his own soul in the bargain. Like Addle-Brain there." He raised his unlit pipe to indicate the carpenter. "He's been lustin' after ye for years an' look at the state he's in. Can't even manage to piss on a downdraft after ye've said a kind word to 'im. I warrant he'll be walkin' around on three legs all night long now at the thought of ye roastin' an' eatin' his ballocks."

Unlike Kelly's, Nathan's tongue rarely tied in knots, regardless of the subject.

"Since we are speaking of ballocks," she said, "what do you think of the duke's?"

He scratched the stubble on his chin. "Well now, I didn't have as good a look as ye did, but I'll wager they're as big as the rest of him."

"That wasn't what I meant," she said on a sigh.

Crisp snickered. "No? Then I'm thinkin' he'll be trouble all the same. His tongue is too smooth an' his answers come too quick. Glib, he is. An' up to no good where ye're father is concerned, mark my words. Cap'n Simon won't be thankin' ye for bringin' him back to the cay." He leaned over the rail and spat. "I'm also thinkin' he'll lay a few stripes across yer rump for goin' up against a prime warship by yerself."

The silence stretched for a full count of ten before the sense of triumph they had managed to keep under tight rein for the past several hours finally exploded. Juliet burst out laughing only a second or two before Crisp snatched off his cap and beat it on the rail in keeping with his hoots and hee-haws.

"Can ye believe it, lass? The farkin' *Santo Domingo*! The supposed Terror of the High Seas an' we took her! By Christ's own cross, it won't just be the *almirante* of the fleet an' his fancy dons ye've aggravated. I warrant farkin' Philip of farkin' Spain will throw fits an' open up his Court of Inquisition again."

"Yes, but do you think Father will be pleased?"

"Pleased?" Crisp paused to reflect over the word. "He'll be tickled enough he might just let ye sail off his starboard beam the next time he goes on a hunt."

"Do you really think so?" Juliet's pleasure could not be contained and this time when she laughed, the entire composition of her face changed. The stern set to her jaw softened and her eyes sparkled with the moonlight. Her lips took on a gentle fullness that was not often conducive to barking orders and having them obeyed.

She would have liked to fling her arms around Crisp in a hug, but she knew their easy friendship had its boundaries. Instead, she looked forward to seeing the startled and much aggrieved expressions on her brothers' faces. The best they had managed on their own hunts was a brace of carracks off the coast of Colombia full of reeking boucan-eaters.

"Jonas and Gabriel will be green with envy. Positively green."

"Aye, they'll not take it kindly that their sister captured the biggest prize in the Caribbee. Ye'll have to watch yer back an' have a care not to walk out alone at night."

Juliet sobered a moment and frowned. "You don't think they would—?"

"*Praemonitus, praemunitus.* Forewarned is forearmed."

Juliet dismissed the admonishment with a wave of her hand. "With hunting season about to begin, they'll be too busy for childish pranks."

"They painted ye blue the last time ye vexed them. That pair is never too busy for pranks, an' well ye know it."

She studied Crisp's face through the eerie glow of moonlight. "You realize that with the *Santo Domingo*, we now have six ships. It would not just be the plate fleets that would sail in fear of the Pirate Wolf, for we now have the firepower to attack Cartagena, Maracaibo, even Panama itself."

"Ho, there lass. Ye've set yer sights a mite high, have ye not? Maracaibo? Cartagena? *Panama?*"

"The whole of the Spanish Main would be ours for the taking. Jonas and Gabriel would be the first to agree—"

Crisp interrupted with an expletive. "Aye, an' stab my liver with a spoon if I'm surprised that yer brothers would be game for such lunacy. As for the Spanish, d'ye think they've run out of ships to send after us?"

"Perhaps if they would just stop hunting Father like a dog—"

"Simon Dante would not return the favor an' well ye know it. It were a Spaniard what put the scars on his back, an' it were a bloody papist Spaniard what cost yer mother her arm. Nay, he has a long list of reasons to keep hatin' the dons, but there's a devil of a difference between attackin' ships on the open water an' formin' up a fleet to raid a well-protected port." He paused long enough to thrust his empty pipe into his mouth. "Such a thing hasn't been done since Drake attacked Maracaibo near forty years ago an' since then they've reinforced their land defenses, increased their garrisons by a few hundred thousand soldiers, an' built ships like the *Santo Domingo* to patrol the sea-lanes an' keep 'em clear of dogs like us.''

Juliet knew better than to argue with Crisp, especially when his teeth were clamping down on his pipe hard enough to snap the stem. In truth, there was little to argue. Simon Dante had spent five years chained to the oars of a Spanish galleass, and if the scars were not enough of a reminder of the hatred he bore the Spaniards, he needed only to see the empty sleeve that hung below his wife's left elbow.

It had happened almost five years ago. Simon Dante had taken his ships the *Avenger* and the *Black Swan* on a hunt off the Straits of Florida. With Isabeau assuming her usual command at the helm of the *Swan*, they had stalked the galleons of the plate fleet and set their sights on two smaller ships that moved slower than the rest of the pack. A third galleon sailed protectively in their shadow, one of the India guards, and at first glance, she seemed to be wallowing as if she was suffering steerage problems.

If the warship appeared to lumber, however, it was because of the weight of the sixty-four guns she carried on three decks, the lowest painted a dull black to disguise the row of closed gunports. If she seemed to have a foolish captain who steered her away from the main fleet, it was because she was eager to lure each of the privateers into a confrontation, beginning with the smallest of the raiders: the *Black Swan*.

Never one to balk from a fight, and knowing Dante's *Avenger* was circling around to attack the galleon's stern, Isabeau had sallied forth to answer the challenge. It was not until they were well within range of the Spaniard's guns that the ports on the lower deck opened and Isabeau saw the trap for what it was. Before she could break away the gunners unleashed a horrendous broadside that blew away most of the *Swan*'s mainsails and the tops of two masts, and raked her upper deck with terrible results. Standing helpless in the water, she could only watch as the great galleon bore down with the intent to ram her amidships.

Simon Dante had come beating in with moments to spare, the *Avenger*'s guns blasting the Spaniard with unrelenting broadsides as the Pirate Wolf placed himself as a shield between the galleon and the wounded *Swan*. Round after blistering round discouraged the Spanish captain from pursuing his advantage and allowed the *Black Swan* to limp out of range. Suffering heavy damage to his own vessel, Simon broke off and escorted Isabeau into safer waters, but it was not until several hours later that the two ships were able to come alongside one another and exchange hails.

That was when Simon learned his wife had been gravely injured. A round of Spanish shot—rendered inferior by the practice of cooling the iron too quickly—had disintegrated on impact. The pieces of exploding metal had swept the forecastle deck, killing three crewmen and nearly taking Isabeau's forearm off at the elbow. Despite the best efforts of both ships' surgeons, it had been necessary to remove the damaged bone and flesh before the threat of gangrene finished the Spaniard's bloody work. To add further insult, the *Black Swan*'s wounds proved fatal and she had to be abandoned before the day was out.

The loss of her ship had affected Isabeau almost more than the loss of her arm, and while she had never shown any outward reluctance to take to the sea again, she had not sought the command of another ship. Indeed, it was Isabeau Dante who had insisted the *Iron Rose* be given to Juliet, and not a day passed that Juliet did not do everything in her power to justify her mother's faith. Simon's had been harder to earn, for each time she took the *Iron Rose* out of port she could see, deep in his eyes, a little of the unutterable horror that had been on his face when he had brought his injured wife home.

Juliet's navigational skills, her fighting spirit, her seamanship, were the equal of any man. If her father

needed further proof that he had taught her well, it
was sailing behind her now, docile and subdued and
flying the British flag on her foremast.

"The Spaniard—Aquayo," she murmured through
a frown. "He praised us for being so well informed."

"Aye," Crisp said. "What of it."

"The *Santo Domingo* was brought to the Indies to
patrol the sea-lanes between Cartagena and Havana,
and to keep rogues like us at bay. Odd then," she
continued, thinking aloud, "that we found silver bars
stamped by the mint in Vera Cruz in the same cargo
bay as pearls from Margarita Island and emeralds
from Barranquilla. Even odder that so much treasure
should be packed on board a warship."

"Aye, well." Crisp blew out a long breath. "If ye
want to spend the next few hours porin' over the manifests, I'm sure ye'll find an answer to the puzzle. Me?
Since I can't read that fancy Spanish bilge, I'd be no
help, so I'm for a big plate of biscuits, a slab of cold
mutton, an' enough ale to set me on my arse till
mornin'."

"You deserve it. All the men deserve it, and if you
haven't done so already, break out an extra ration
of rum."

Crisp tugged a scruffy brown forelock. "I'll do that,
Cap'n. Right after I set the watches an' trim the sails.
Smells like a storm comin' up, an' if Loftus can't
squeeze more speed out o' that sow, we'll be waddlin'
right into it."

Chapter Five

An hour later, Juliet was still poring over the manifests taken from the *Santo Domingo*. She had not found the answer as to why a warship would be carrying cargo from three very distinct regions of the Spanish Main. She did, however, find the name of the officer whose ears she had made a little shorter, and the discovery made her own ears perk a little higher. Capitán Cristóbal Nufio Espinosa y Recalde. He was listed in the crew manifest as the *capitán del navío*, the military commander on board the ship, second only in importance to the *capitán de mar*, Diego Flores de Aquayo.

What triggered Juliet's intrigue was that up to a month ago—and she had no reason to doubt the accuracy of the reports her father's partner of thirty years, Geoffrey Pitt, gleaned from his legion of spies along the Main—Recalde had been the commander of the military garrison at Nombre de Dios. It was the main port for Panama and Peru, sited near a huge, festering swamp that was almost impossible to fortify by normal methods. Francis Drake had plundered it twice in his seafaring days, once in 1572 when he took over the governor's house for a week while his men sacked and burned the city. The second time, less than a year later, he ambushed the treasure train coming across the isthmus from Peru, but there was so much silver and gold on the mules, he had to leave half of it in the swamp.

Since then, the viceroy of Nueva España had insisted on having the best, most vicious and tyrannical officers posted at Nombre de Dios. They were placed in charge of the misfits and miscreants culled from garrisons elsewhere along the Main, the more brutal and bloodthirsty the better.

As the *capitán del navío*, Recalde would have been in charge of the attack on the *Argus*. Aquayo was little more than a figurehead, a nobleman who had been rewarded with a prestigious command as a show of favor by the Spanish king, but Recalde had chosen his profession and he obviously excelled in his work if he had been in command at Nombre de Dios.

Nathan might have been right. It might have been better had she been as cold-blooded as her brother Jonas, who would have placed the two shots right through Recalde's eyes without troubling to wait for any justification.

Sighing, rubbing her temple with a weary hand, Juliet removed her bandana and used it to swab the dampness on the back of her neck. The air in the cabin was stifling. She frowned at the blackened tarps, then at the shadowy outline in her berth. He hadn't moved, hadn't made a sound since she had returned to the cabin.

She filled her goblet with the last of the rumbustion in the bottle and glanced over at the second body. Beacom was stretched out on the floor like a corpse, his hands folded over his chest, the heels of his shoes touching together, the toes pointing straight up.

"Damned Englishmen," she muttered.

Taking the goblet with her, she pulled aside the section of tarp that covered the narrow door to the gallery, and opened it. Almost instantly, she could feel the heat being sucked out of the cabin and she opened it wider, listening to the sound of the wake curling out behind her ship. The clouds were thicker, completely blanketing the sky, and the wind had picked up considerably, tugging peevishly at the loose threads of her hair. The darkness made it more difficult to see the

Santo Domingo riding off their stern, but she was there, a dark shape against a smothered sky.

For the fleetest of moments, Juliet allowed her mind to reconstruct the picture of the Spanish warship closing on the crippled *Argus*, the monstrous cannon belching smoke and flame in such a continuous barrage the two ships had become engulfed in the sulfurous yellow clouds. Crisp had thought she was mad to take the *Iron Rose* in, but she had been flung back five years in her mind, imagining it to be similar to the predicament her mother had found herself in: a galleon bearing down, the valiant *Black Swan* in shambles, her decks on fire, her crew struggling to prevent the inevitable.

Fate, in the form of a hideous boil on the bottom of her foot, had kept Juliet at home on Pigeon Cay; otherwise she would have been on board the *Swan* during that doomed voyage. She knew . . . she *knew* there was little she could have done to affect the outcome one way or another, yet it still weighed heavily on her mind and conscience that she had not been at her normal place on the *Swan*'s quarterdeck. Instead, she had been lying on a beach studying astral charts while her father kept a terrible vigil by his wife's side.

Juliet closed her eyes and concentrated on steadying her hands.

Yes indeed, she had proved herself the equal of any man in the years that followed. Her crew deemed her fearless and looked to her to bring them victory and glory despite impossible odds, despite the clawing doubts that gripped her every time she gave the command that sent the gunners to their posts. They thought her iron-willed and ironclad, afraid of nothing, never hesitating to answer a challenge with her sword or her ship.

They never saw the aftermath, of course. The quiet hour when her hands shook and her bones shivered, when her chest felt so constricted she could scarcely catch a breath and hold it.

She raised the goblet to her lips and managed to hold it steady enough to drink the rest of the rum. It was not enough—it was never enough to erase the taste of blood and gunpowder—and she returned to her desk in search of more. The bottle, when she tipped it, was empty. Cursing, she went to the bookcase for another and her knee caught the edge of the chair as she passed. She kicked it savagely out of the way and when it did not instantly break apart, she lifted it by the two hind legs and smashed it against the wall, splitting the backrest from the seat and sending pieces of wood flying across the cabin. In a fit of added temper, she scraped the *Santo Domingo*'s manifests and logbooks off her desk, scattering papers into the air like snow.

Varian had managed to drift in and out of a fitful sleep through most of the evening. He had come instantly awake when Juliet had first returned to the cabin, but since she chose to work quietly at her desk, he elected to remain quietly turned on his side away from her and pretend he was still asleep.

It was impossible to ignore a breaking chair, however, or a woman who cursed like a London wharf rat.

"If you plan to hurl more furniture, could you at least give me fair warning?"

Juliet gasped and stared at the pale form on the bed. She stared for a full minute without speaking, which gave Varian time to roll onto his back without sending his head into another potentially fatal spin.

"I . . . I thought you were asleep," she stammered.

"That should give me comfort?"

"Your comfort," she said with narrowed eyes, "is not my prime concern. And I suppose I've disturbed *your* rest as well?" she asked, glaring at Beacom.

"Oh. Oh, no, madam. No, not at all."

"Good. Then you won't mind fetching me another bottle of rum, since my supply seems to be sadly depleted."

Beacom scrambled to his feet. "Indeed, Captain. Where might I find one?"

"In the galley. Ask for Johnny Boy, he'll show you where I keep my private stores."

"Th-the galley?"

"One deck down, in the stern."

Beacom looked to his master, who nodded imperceptibly and tipped his head toward the door. When it closed behind him, Varian glanced wryly at the shattered parts of chair that had flown all the way to the floor beside his berth.

"Bravo, Captain. Most women claim not to have the strength to lift a chair, much less the ability to reduce it to kindling."

"I warrant I can meet my Maker happily now, knowing I am so set apart from the more dainty creatures of your acquaintance."

"My dear Captain Dante, you may believe you were set apart the instant I first glimpsed you on board the *Santo Domingo*."

"Even with my shoulder drooping from fatigue?"

"Even so, madam." He almost smiled, relishing the knowledge that he had obviously pricked her vanity with his earlier criticism.

"Rest assured, you were set apart as well, sirrah."

He arched a dark brow. "Was I?"

"Indeed. I vow I have never seen such a delicate shade of violet on a man before."

"Ahh. I thought a kind word for my fighting prowess might be too much to expect."

"You got yourself blown up; that hardly merits praise for your prowess."

The light from the lantern cast a yellowish glow over her shoulders, drawing his gaze downward. She had removed her heavy leather doublet and wore only a voluminous white cambric shirt that was uncommonly vulnerable to light and shadow. The shape of her breasts was visible, as was the trimness of her waist.

For a rough-cut sea urchin, she appeared to be rather provocatively proportioned.

Thankfully she moved out of the circle of light. With a grimace that suggested she was human enough to have suffered some aches and pains after the day's activities, she lowered herself haltingly onto one knee and began gathering the papers she had scattered on the floor.

Ingrained manners sent Varian's hand to lift a corner of his blanket but a glimpse of hair and flesh stopped him. "Understand, Captain, that I would hasten to offer my assistance, but I still find myself at a slight disadvantage."

She waved his apology aside and put the first handful of papers on the table. For the second, she had to stretch farther afield and as she leaned forward, she tottered slightly and shot out a hand to keep from toppling over. In the end, she succumbed to the steadiness of the hard timbers and slumped down, propping her back against the desk. She noticed her goblet, which had been swept away with the rest of the detritus, and picked it up, tipping it with a sigh to show it was still empty.

"My compliments on your fortitude as well, Captain," Varian murmured with a small grin. "I had occasion to sample your rumbustion earlier and it took my knees out from beneath me."

She kept one leg bent but stretched the other out flat. "I am not sure I trust your compliments, my lord. You tend to speak them out the side of your mouth."

"Mockery was not my intent, I promise you. And if I seemed an ingrate earlier, I apologize again, for I am not accustomed to waking up in a strange bed, bereft of clothes, and bathed in camphor oil."

"Really? I would have thought it a common occurrence for a man of your ilk. That is to say, all save bathing in camphor oil."

"Oil has its merits—if the fragrance is sweet and

does not singe the hairs out of one's nostrils. And what, pray tell, qualifies as 'a man of my ilk'?"

"A pompous, overindulged nobleman with misplaced pretentions of greatness."

"And you say that you do not trust *my* compliments, madam?"

"You took that as a compliment?" Her laugh was soft and husky. "In that case, I need say no more."

She leaned her head against the desk and closed her eyes. It gave Varian a further opportunity to study her face in the lantern light. Without the distraction of the blue bandana, he could see she had a delicate, heart-shaped hairline that framed her features in fine auburn wisps. Her complexion, considering that most Englishwomen attacked the mere hint of a freckle with mercuric salts and rice powder, was dark enough to have scandalized every matron within a hundred-mile radius of the royal court. Tanned by the constant exposure to the sea and sun, the warm bronze coloring suited Juliet Dante's ferriferous nature well enough though, and once again he found himself wondering what she would look like with her hair spun in curls and her body clad in fine, clinging silk.

He frowned and set his thoughts on less dangerous ground, searching for some topic that might not be seen as a challenge of wits. "You mentioned earlier that you have two brothers?"

"You have a remarkable memory."

"No husband?"

She turned her head slightly to peer at him. "What the devil would I want with a husband?"

"Companionship? Comfort?"

"I have all the companionship and comfort I need. And when I want more than that, it is readily available."

"Ah."

"Ah." She mimicked the disapproving sound perfectly, then laughed again. "I have always found it puzzling that men believe it perfectly acceptable to take their pleasure where they may without guilt or recriminations, but when women do the same, they are branded whores and trulls."

Varian opened his mouth . . . then closed it with an audible snapping of his jaw.

She smiled and leaned back against the desk. "I see I have shocked you again. Shall we return to more politic ground? You mentioned earlier that you thought no one would pay your ransom. Have you no family pining for you at home? No wife? No mewling children to carry on the succession of Harrows? No more brothers to take your place if you blow yourself up again?"

"No wife as yet," he said easily. "I expect my mother would grieve a moment for my passing, but the moment would pass quickly enough and she would be more concerned with safeguarding her own stipend as dowager. As for brothers, there were only the two. One drowned after riding his horse into a flooded river, the other was killed last year."

Truth be told, she wasn't really interested in knowing the petty details of Varian St. Clare's life, but a note of obvious bitterness that had crept into his voice made her turn and look at him again.

"Most people would have said he died last year. You said he was killed?"

"He fought a stupid, senseless duel over a point of honor that could have been resolved if the two parties had just come together and talked through the misunderstanding."

"You condone talk over action, do you?"

"I advocate logic over madness. They argued over a woman."

Juliet's mouth curved at the corner. "Faith, and so you have become soured against all women for all time? You have departed England with a burr under your skin and have chosen exile over the possibility of ever again being tempted by some demonic young shrew in perfumed silk?"

His dark eyes narrowed slightly at the mockery, but his smile was easy enough. "Quite the opposite, in fact. I agreed to become betrothed shortly before I departed."

"How does one 'agree' to become betrothed? I would think you either were or were not committed to the deed."

Varian answered with a grim curl on his lip. "You think Beacom can be incessant and interminable? You should have to endure an evening with the Dowager Duchess of Harrow. Seven years worth of evenings, in fact, ever since I enjoyed my twenty-first birthday. It was one of the reasons why I remained in the military. It gave me an excuse to avoid her matchmaking efforts."

"But you have finally succumbed?"

"After my brother died last year, I was left with little choice. I was informed in no uncertain terms that I needed an heir and being in the same room with dear mater was like standing naked in front of a line of artillery cannon and holding up a painted target, only in this case, the ammunition consisted of young women of suitable age, fortune, and social standing."

"You let your mother choose your intended bride?"

"It is not an uncommon practice for marriages to be arranged to suit the needs of both parties."

"Ah, so your betrothed—rather, your about-to-be-betrothed—is rich?"

Varian frowned. "In a family as old as mine, there are certain social considerations and requirements that eliminate the luxury of deciding by sight and smell alone."

"I am sure there are. Do you love her?"

"I hardly think that is any of your business."

"Yet it is a simple question. Do you love the woman you are going to marry?"

"She comes of good stock with a fine lineage."

"And is in possession of all her teeth? Great good God, you sound as if you choose your wives like you choose your breeding stock."

"Pray, madam, bang the other side of my head with a mallet before you tell me you believe in love."

She stared into the shadows a moment, debating how to answer, for one did not grow up in the company of Simon and Isabeau Dante without believing in more than simple convenience. After all their years together, they could barely keep their hands to themselves and their lusty thoughts out of their eyes when they gazed upon each other.

Juliet smiled. "I want the man I marry to be uncomfortable every time I look at him. I want him unable to move when I come into the room, afraid to do so lest the air shatter and fall to pieces around him."

"An easy fear to understand," he said, glancing pointedly at the splinters from the broken chair.

"And if he is the right man, I will not care if he is a beggar or a king."

"But better a king, judging by the sparkle I see in your hand."

She looked down at the empty goblet she was holding. A tilt of her hand set the jewels that were crusted around the rim reflecting fractured points of colored light across the wall.

"The rewards of a hard day's work," she countered evenly. "In this case a small token from the private stores of Don Alonzo Perez, former captain of the *San Ambrosio*. We took her off the coast of Hispaniola last winter. She was wormy and not worth the effort to repair or refit, but we sold her cargo for twenty thousand escudos. I kept the goblet, just as I keep some small token from every ship we capture."

Another casual flick of her hand indicated the wire-fronted case behind the chart table that held an array of extremely fine looking weapons. They were long snouted wheel-locks for the most part, some of French design featuring inlays of mother-of-pearl, but most favored the Italian style with heavy gilt ornamentation. One pair in particular caught his eye, an unusual combination of match- and wheel-lock mechanisms with both ignitions controlled by a single trigger. The alliance of the two firing systems was reflected in the decoration on the walnut stock where a naked couple were depicted in the act of merging. He knew this detail, even though he could not see it at this distance, because the guns were his, and the last time he had seen them, they had been on his person on the deck of the *Argus*.

"Damnation! Those are my Brescians!"

Juliet followed his outthrust finger. "Hardly, sir. Those are *my* Brescians."

"Indeed they are not, madam. They were handmade for me by Lazzarino Cominazzo himself!"

"If memory serves, I took them off a boucan-eater named Jorges Fillarento, and if they resemble yours, then your gunmaker must have made two pair."

"I need only look at them to tell you upon the instant if they are mine or not."

"Look away," she challenged. "This instant or the next, it changes nothing."

Provoked beyond any concern for his nudity, Varian flung aside the blanket and swung his legs over the side of the bed. The bruises on his hip and shoulder made him suck air through his teeth as he stood, but the pain was superseded by the angry strides that carried him across the cabin. The case was not locked and he withdrew one of the elegant dueling pistols from the rack. When he held it to the light the glare bounced off the smooth surface of the gilt lockplate, where, instead of the intricately engraved Harrow crest, Varian was startled to see three unfamiliar initials etched into the metal with a flamboyant script.

"This is not possible," he murmured. He checked the inlay on the walnut barrel and there indeed was the entwined couple, the woman's neck and back arched as if in the throes of an intense orgasm. "You have my apologies, Captain, I was assured my guns were unique."

Juliet, still seated on the floor, found herself at eye level with the duke's groin. She had, of course, already seen all there was to see when she had examined his wounds, but there was something to be said for gravity and the way it altered the appearance of appendages that were impressive at the outset. There was also a good deal of muscled thigh to distract the eye; this close she could see the indent of taut sinews at his hip, the soft furring of light brown hairs that followed down his calves.

"Do all Englishmen take such extraordinary measures to ensure the sun does not creep beneath their collars? I vow I have never seen a body half so pale as yours nor one that was smothered under so many layers of clothing this close to the equator. The rash you bear would benefit greatly from a day or two with nothing more confining than air."

Varian was startled into looking down. The rash to which she referred was indelicately located in the vicinity of his privy parts and under his arms. Soap, as Beacom had discovered to his unmitigated horror, did not mix with seawater, and since seawater was all that had been permitted for laundering during the six-week voyage, the ducal linens had acquired an irritating salt residue. The aggravation had worsened when the *Argus* had sailed into tropical waters, for the infernal heat and sun offered no relief, nor did the sight of the ship's crew stripping down layer by layer as the heat increased. Most of them worked barefoot, dressed in airy canvas pinafores and loose trousers.

Bereft of such heathenish options himself, Varian had remained in his stockings and padded trunk hose, his fashionably quilted doublets, shortcoats, and capes, itching without mercy in the silent knowledge that he cut an imposing figure on the deck. The thought of walking anywhere naked was almost as absurd as the picture he presented now, standing bare as birth in front of a woman who was inspecting his privates with a shamelessly arousing curiosity that caused his flesh to jerk.

Since it was neither the experience nor the pleasure of Varian St. Clare to have any part of his body come under such close and uninvited scrutiny, he thrust the pistol back onto its rack and started back to the bed. Her smile broadened into a chuckle, then a laugh—a sound that pricked more than just his vanity and caused him to stop cold in his tracks. Without thinking ahead to any consequences, he turned around, bent over, and roughly pulled her up by her arms to stand before him.

What the devil he planned to do with her once they were eye to eye, he was not given the chance to decide, for despite the quantity of rum she had consumed, her reflexes were as fast and deadly as a cobra strike. She had a knife drawn and the point thrust under his chin before he had finished hauling her to her feet.

"You should be advised," she said, her voice as cold as the blade kissing his throat, "there are few men who would dare touch me without a very specific invitation to do so. Even fewer who have survived calling me a liar."

Varian tilted his chin higher in response to the dagger's steely inducement to do so. He released her arms and spread his hands slowly outward. "Forgive my impertinence. The guns are identical to mine; it was an instinctive reaction and I have already apologized for the infraction—something *I* rarely do, and hardly ever to someone who is too full of rum to respect it."

"Is that so?" she murmured, her eyes narrowing.

"Just so, madam. As for repercussions—" He clenched his jaw and lowered his chin, defying the pressure of the knife, feeling the sharp jab as the tip pierced his skin. "Considering the course our conversation has taken thus far, I find the greater concern lies in wondering if there would be consequences for *refusing* an invitation."

Juliet stared for a long moment. The sheer insolence of his presumptions—that she would invite him to touch her in any kind of intimate manner—nearly drove the blade deeper of its own volition. Instead, she traced the point of the dagger down his throat to his breastbone, down through the swirls of dark hair to the hard, flat plane of his belly. When the cool steel scrolled lower and rested across the base of his manhood, she angled it so that the weight of his flesh lay across the flat surface of the blade like a plated offering.

He did not even flinch.

"You show more courage than I would have credited you with, my lord," she said quietly.

"And you more bravado, Captain. Not surprising, however, with the advantage of a knife in your hand."

Juliet expelled a disbelieving breath. She rid herself of the weapon, tossing it with an expert flick of her wrist, sending it across the cabin and biting into the wood beside the door. At the same time she raised a booted foot and brought it smashing down on Varian's bare instep.

Before he could react to either action, she grabbed his arm and gave his wrist a savage twist, bending his thumb back so far the joint popped. The pain flared up his arm, doubling him over at the waist; a further twist and he was crumpling down onto his knees before her.

Juliet leaned over and pressed her lips into the waves of silky hair that covered his ear. "I have no knife now, my lord. Are my words still full of rum and bravado?"

He bared his teeth, girding himself against the agony as he reached around with his free hand and hooked his arm around the back of her right leg. He wrenched it forward, feeling the tension break and throwing her off balance. A second tug brought her crashing down onto the floor beneath him, hard enough that she was forced to release her grip on his wrist and thumb.

Barely had he gasped enough breath to form an oath when another whiplike twist brought her rearing up onto her elbows. Her legs snapped together like pincers and clamped tightly around his throat, squeezing off his windpipe, trapping whatever air he had managed to suck into his lungs. He tried clawing at her thighs to loosen them but it was like trying to pry two iron bars apart. He attempted to roll, to wrest

himself free that way, but she countered his efforts
with a savage wrench in the opposite direction, one
that locked him even tighter in her grip.

The blood started to swell behind his eyeballs.
Large black splotches began spreading across his vision, and his chest began to burn, his muscles to
scream for air. He uncurled his hands from around
her thighs but before he could slam his palms on the
planking to indicate his surrender, a brusque knock
rattled the cabin door.

At the sound of Juliet's snarled curse, it was flung
open by a skinny lad of no more than twelve or thirteen balancing a large wooden tray in one hand, a
thick crockery bottle in the other.

He hesitated a moment on the threshold, but if he
thought it odd to see his captain lying on the floor
with a naked man being choked between her thighs,
the expression on his face did not betray it.

"That funny little man came lookin' fer rum an' Mr.
Crisp thought ye might want summit to eat with it," he
said. "Should I just put the victuals 'ere on the table?"

"Aye. Thank you, Johnny Boy," she said on a panted
breath. "Take a bite of cheese for your trouble."

"Aye, Cap'n. Thankee, Cap'n. Mr. Crisp also said
to tell ye we've had to shorten the mains'l again, cuz
the . . . the 'great 'eaving sow' has dropped off another
point." As he said this, he cheerfully plucked a knife
from his belt and helped himself to a huge wedge of
yellow cheese from the wheel on the platter. He took
a bite and tucked the rest inside his shirt. " 'Ee also
says to tell ye the wind 'as shifted an' the sea 'as
picked up a chop. We'll likely be in a hard blow
afore mornin'."

Juliet swore. She unclamped her legs from Varian's
throat and sprang to her feet, leaving him splayed like
a starfish on the floor behind her, gasping for air.

"How far astern is the *Santo Domingo*?"

"We couldn't 'it her with a double-charged long gun
blowin' a light load."

The boy's standard of measurement indicated half

a mile, perhaps more. Too great a separation if a squall was blowing up.

"Tell Mr. Crisp I'm on my way."

With his cheek puffed out over the chunk of cheese, Johnny Boy asked if there was anything else the captain needed.

"A hammock for his lordship," Juliet said. "He'll be sleeping elsewhere from now on."

The lad paused in his chewing and cocked an eyebrow. "Where'll I put 'im?"

"Empty one of the sail lockers. It should be private enough."

The boy looked at Varian, looked at Juliet, then chuckled. "Aye, Cap'n. A locker it is."

The muted thump that marked the boy's departure brought Varian rolling over in his misery. From his position, lying prone on the floor, he was able to turn his head enough to see through the curtain of his hair. The lad was missing a leg. His right knee was bound to a padded cradle that sat atop a wooden peg. In itself, the sight was not uncommon, for seamen were often without any kind of medical treatment save the knife and saw. What caught Varian's eye was the carving on the stump and cradle. The former was whittled and polished to resemble the body of a serpent; the latter was an open mouth complete with glittering glass eyes and sharp teeth.

The duke groaned and closed his eyes again. His thumb was dislocated, his hand was burning like coals in a forge, his throat was only just beginning to respond to his efforts to swallow.

Juliet retrieved her dagger from the wall and crouched down on her haunches beside St. Clare. She could not see his face. Dark puffs of hair were being dragged in and blown out in the vicinity of his lips, and using the tip of the blade, she edged aside the curtain of gleaming locks and waited for one of the midnight blue eyes to roll up and look at her.

"Perhaps next time, sirrah, you will show more caution when you throw out your challenges." She glanced down at the hand he held cradled against his chest and clucked her tongue once in sympathy. "I'll wager that hurts a devil. Shall I pop the thumb back in for you, or can you manage it yourself?"

Through the white grate of his teeth, he released a hiss of air to coincide with the sharp twist and shove he gave his thumb. The bone clicked back into the socket with a dull *thwock* and though a shiver went up his arm, he did not take his eyes away from her face.

"Like you, madam," his voice rasped with fury, "I would prefer if you did not touch me again without a specific invitation to do so."

She let the hair drop back over his face and sent her gaze sweeping down his back to the tautness of his buttocks. "Depending on how one interpreted that, milord, it could be mistaken for another challenge."

He drew and expelled a breath before he answered. "Never believe for a moment that it is, for I would sooner invite the attentions of a toothless, three-bellied hag."

Juliet grinned. "Faith, if that is where your preferences for female companionship lie, I shall endeavor to keep any lusty thoughts I might be tempted to have to myself."

"Do so and I shall expire in a state of eternal gratitude."

"Not too soon, I hope. You have put the thought into my head that you might be worth a ransom after all. Your intended bride, for instance. What would she pay to have you back safe and sound and"—she glanced along the muscled length of his body a second time—"unsullied by the depravities of a rapine pirate wench?"

His hair had fallen over his face again but she could see the glitter of his eyes through the silky strands.

"Or perhaps," she said, leaning closer to whisper seductively in his ear, "I should endeavor to win you over with my charm?"

"Since the necessary tools are entirely lacking," he spat, "the risk is negligible."

Juliet braced her hands on her knees and pushed to her feet.

"Savor that feeling of righteous piety, milord, for you have yet to meet my father. You think me quick to take offense? Lift your nose too high in his company and he will slice it off without a thought."

Chapter Six

The weather held to occasional gusts through the night, but the dawn came up gunmetal gray with seas high enough to send gouts of green spume over the deck rails. A wide, growling swath of black thunderclouds was circling in the western sky, and while the *Iron Rose* could easily have piled on more sail and outrun the storm, the galleon could not. Compounding the stubbornness of Spanish shipwrights who refused to alter the design of vessels that were square-rigged and could only go where the wind took them, they insisted upon building huge castles fore and aft—towering wooden decks that severely hampered speed and made the already top-heavy ships unstable in bad weather.

Juliet would be damned, however, if she lost such a grand prize to the wind and the sea.

"Lash down everything that is not already nailed or tied, Mr. Crisp. We're in for a sweet one." She lowered her spyglass and squinted up at the roiling mass of cloud. "We did both say it had been too easy, did we not?"

Nathan blew out an oath and went aft, shouting orders at the men as he passed.

A jagged fork of lightning cracked open the clouds and Juliet counted the seconds before the sound reached them. Calculating one league for every three seconds, she guessed the blow was four leagues away and swirling in on them fast. The wind was cold and damp; it snatched off hats and rattled deadeyes. It changed direction sharply from one minute to the next, making the sails overhead boom like cannon.

Apart from the men assigned to stand by the lines, the crew remained below. Gun captains checked that the culverins were tied down, the ports sealed against water coming inboard, and wax plugs fitted into the noses and priming holes of the guns. The powder barrels were secured and the several hundred balls of shot were safely confined in the magazine. The pumps were oiled and manned. Lanterns that had not been lit during the night remained cold, for the greatest hazard on board a ship was fire; even the coals in the galley were smothered to guard against any accidental spillage.

Juliet tracked the approaching storm from the quarterdeck, her feet braced wide to counter the rolls and dips the *Iron Rose* took riding from one swell to the next. She had her bandana knotted snugly around her forehead to keep her hair from lashing into her eyes, but strands were constantly being torn loose, making her look and feel like Medusa.

One stony figure who undoubtedly shared her impression stood down in the belly of the main deck, his hands clutching the rail, his face turned out to the sea. Juliet had been surprised to see the Duke of Harrow venturing out in such heavy weather. She was frankly surprised to see him at all, dressed as he was in a rough-spun shirt and canvas galligaskins, neither very clean nor anywhere near a proper fit.

The shirt, which might have been loose on the wiry frame of an average-sized seaman, was tight across the shoulders and absent any laces, so that it gaped open across his chest. The breeches were similarly stretched at the seams and so threadbare she wondered how safe they would be if he had to bend over in haste. In combination with the fine leather shoes beribboned with rosettes that were the only personal items salvaged in the rescue, he made a somewhat comical figure and she suspected it was sheer stubbornness that had brought him topside at all.

She had not seen him since the incident in her cabin, had not troubled herself to inquire which locker Johnny Boy had elected to transform into his cabin. She only knew her berth was empty when she had fallen into it sometime after midnight.

A rare twinge of guilt prickled Juliet's conscience as she studied him. It was possible she had consumed a tad too much rum last night and her reaction to his touching her *might* have been slightly out of proportion to the actual crime. She had been startled, more than anything else, when he'd pulled her to her feet, for she had just been wondering, not half a moment before, what it would be like to have all that naked flesh pressed up against her body. The knife had been in her hand before she knew it, after which of course, there could be no backing down. Especially not after he accused her of having an unfair advantage.

From where she stood on the quarterdeck, she could not see his face. He did not seem the least interested in glancing her way either, which was rather like dragging a line baited with fresh red meat in front of a shark. She had one foot on the ladderway when the sky rumbled, the wind abruptly dropped off, and the underbellies of the clouds lit up with an ungodly green glow.

In the sudden, unearthly silence, Varian glanced upward and held his breath. Fiery, brushlike discharges of static were crackling and snapping from the mastheads and yards. Bright orange in color, they were like little bolts of lightning playing across the skeleton of the ship, leaping from spar to spar, traveling down the masts and setting the air hissing overhead.

"Most seamen have a superstitious fear of St. Elmo's Fire," Juliet said quietly. "They believe that anyone who dares to let the light fall on his face will be dead within a day."

Varian lowered his gaze grudgingly from the dancing lights. His hair had been blown about his face and clung to his cheek and throat where two days' worth of dark stubble snagged the strands.

"I have heard of the phenomenon, but never seen it."

Juliet tilted her head up, but the flickers of light were already beginning to fade.

"You are not superstitious?" he asked.

"About some things, yes. I would never begin a voyage on a Friday, for instance, nor would I bring a black cat on board. On the other hand, I do have the caul of a newborn babe hanging in my cabin and I never set sail without pouring a fine bottle of wine on the gun decks for luck. Mind, since the most dreaded curse on the high seas is supposedly having a woman on board, I tend to be more skeptical than your average cabin boy."

"And here I was advised on very good authority before departing London that gales and high winds would subside if a naked woman stood on deck."

"Which is why most ships' figureheads are of naked women. Nevertheless, you might want to take yourself below," she advised, blinking as a fat drop of rain splashed her cheek. "I have no intentions of stripping down, and the wind can toss you about like a child's toy if you haven't a good pair of sea legs beneath you."

"Thank you, Captain," Beacom said, peering around from behind his master's broad shoulder. "I was about to suggest that very thing to his grace: to retire below until this unpleasantness passes."

"Whereas I was thinking a bit of rain, a brisk bit of wind, might make for a stimulating change," Varian said tautly.

"Suit yourself," Juliet said. "But if you end up riding a wave *briskly* over the rail, we won't be turning about to fish you out."

Beacom made a sound in his throat, but Varian merely offered a small bow to acknowledge the advice, then turned to stare out across the boiling seas again.

"Stimulating?" Beacom waited until Juliet had returned to the quarterdeck before he questioned his master's sanity. "As stimulating as the storm we encountered off the Canaries on the voyage south?"

Varian's dark eyebrow twitched at the memory, for the gale that had battered them for four days and five nights had left the two men so weak from seasickness they would have welcomed a swift death at the end of a spiked bludgeon. Even so, the wench had thrown down a subtle gauntlet. Were he to retreat below now, with his thumb throbbing a reminder that she had lorded her superiority over him once already, it would suggest his legs were made of less stern stuff than her own.

"Go below if you wish," he said, squinting against the beads of rain. "I choose to remain here a few minutes longer."

The few turned into ten, and by then the blackest of the clouds were directly overhead, the wind was lashing across the deck, and rain was pelting down like needles. Varian was satisfied he had made his point.

With Beacom's teeth chattering too badly to express his gratitude, the two men began to make their way across the deck, but before they were safely through the hatchway, the planking shifted under their feet. The ship seemed to rise up beneath them, careening perilously to one side, tossing both Varian and Beacom hard against the base of the mast. Dazed, they could only brace themselves as a solid green wall of seawater crashed over the deck, beating down on them with enough force to carry them across the deck and flatten them against the bulkhead. The ship righted itself, then rolled in the opposite direction, sending Beacom skidding and sliding across the wet planking almost back to the rail.

Varian cursed and went after him, managing to grasp hold of a bony arm and drag him back to the safety of the hatchway. Above them on the quarterdeck, Juliet was shouting orders to the helmsman, who was doubled over the whipstaff, his hair streaming horizontally into the wind. One moment he was there, his full weight pressed into keeping the rudder on course, and the next he was gone, flung against the rail, saved from being swept overboard only by the length of cable bound around his waist.

"Your grace!" Beacom was screaming, hauling on his arm, but Varian could not move, could scarcely see more than a few feet in front of him. He tried to scrape the saltwater out of his eyes, but everything remained a blur. He could not see Juliet Dante. If she was still up on the quarterdeck, she was obscured by the sheets of driving rain.

If she was still there.

A thunderous crack startled Varian's gaze higher as a bolt of lightning struck the top of the foremast. The jagged white streak seemed to hang in the air a moment before dissolving into a fountain of brilliant red sparks, some of which showered the heads of the crewmen who were working the lines. Weakened in the battle with the *Santo Domingo*, the top of the mast fractured in two under the fiery strike, and a ten-foot section came crashing down toward the deck, the shroud lines popping and snapping as it fell. The broken length of oak cannonaded into the planking close enough to where Varian was standing to lash his face with spray.

"Your grace, I beg you: you must come below!"

Beacom's voice was frantic, but Varian's attention was dragged back to the quarterdeck. There was still no sign of Juliet. The helmsman was on all fours, his face bloodied where his forehead had hit the rail. Varian shook off Beacom's clutching hands and ran to the bottom of the ladderway. He vaulted up the steps two at a time and saw her. She was on the starboard side of the quarterdeck attempting to climb into the shrouds.

At first he could not see why she would be doing such an insane thing, but then he looked higher and saw the boy with the peg leg hanging upside down from the ratlines. A cable was looped around his good ankle, and Varian guessed that when the mast had come down, the line had been pulled taut and jerked the boy off his feet and up into the tangle of rigging. He hung there helpless, being swung to and fro with the movement of the ship, coming ominously closer to the base of the mast on each swing.

Doubled over against the force of the wind, Varian made his way across the open quarterdeck. He reached Juliet's side just as another mountainous green wave crashed over the bow, nearly flinging them both down on the deck. He circled an arm around her waist and another around the four-stranded lanyard lines, and held them both against the shrouds until the wave passed.

Unfettered lines snaked treacherously underfoot and the broken section of mast continued to pull on the rigging with each plunge and toss of the ship, snapping shearing poles, popping the chainplates out of the gunwall and freeing more cables to whip over their heads. Varian heard Juliet shout something in his ear, but his mouth and nose streamed saltwater, his hair was plastered flat to his skull, and he turned the wrong way just as the end of a rope whipped across his cheek like a cat-'o-nine-tails.

The painful sting added to his blindness and almost made him miss Johnny Boy as he swung toward the shrouds. Varian reached up to grasp a flailing hand but he misjudged the distance by half an arm's length and realized he had to climb higher to reach him. Pushing Juliet to one side, he put a foot to the rail and hoisted himself up into the shroud lines. He caught his balance in time to see the next wave before it struck, and turned his head to avoid the worst of it, but when he shook his head to clear the water out of his hair and eyes, the loose cable lashed him again. With a curse, he caught the end and looped it several times around his wrist, which was, he acknowledged too late, probably the most foolish thing he could have done.

The ship plunged into a trough, and the yard around which the rope was bound swung forward with the motion, carrying Varian with it. He was yanked off the shrouds and found himself in the same perilous situation as the boy he had come to save. The two made brief contact as they swung in opposite directions; then St. Clare was bounced out and around the far side of the shroud. Being considerably heavier, with much more rope at play, he was sent spinning out over the side like a whirligig and for a full ten seconds, there was nothing under his flailing feet but empty air and churning water.

As the ship reared to climb above the next trough, he swung back on board and this time was able to get a hand around the boy's arm before they parted again. The rope he was holding cut into his wrist, and his arm was nearly wrenched from the socket as he caught the boy and dragged his weight behind his own, but before the ship careened again, he was able to shove the lad in the direction of the shrouds where Juliet was now standing high enough to snag him.

Varian saw her reel Johnny Boy in. A second later, the duke was sailing outward over the side of the ship again, reaching the end of the arc with such a hard jolt, he felt the rope slide painfully through his hand. Fighting to claw his way fist over fist up the cable, he was caught by the next wave, his feet sucked forward by the force of the rushing sea. As the wave broke across the deck, his vision cleared long enough to see the solid shape of the mainmast coming up swift and deadly in front of him. A moment away from slamming into the oak, he felt hands reach up to grab at his legs. Someone shouted at him to release the "farkin'" rope and when he did so, he was plucked out of the air and thrown by his shoulders and thighs through an open hatchway.

He landed in the same wet heap as Johnny Boy, who had been tossed there only moments before. Nathan and Juliet stood glaring down at the pair a moment before closing the hatch behind them and returning to the haze of beating rain and sluicing water on deck.

Another shadowy figure loomed out of the corridor beside them.

"Mother, Mary, and Joseph," Beacom cried. "I thought you were gone, your grace. Gone! What possible madness could have inspired you to venture out of cover in this tempest?"

Varian's teeth were clenched too tightly to offer any explanations and the boy had already disappeared into the gloom. He accepted Beacom's help to rise first to his knees, then to his feet, but he shook off the older man's offer of a shoulder to lean on and staggered on his own through the gloom of the lurching gun deck in search of the tiny, airless locker he had been banished to last night.

After opening three narrow wooden doors and having sails, holystones, and spars fall on him, he swore and stumbled along another narrow companionway that led to the stern. The captain's cabin was empty and relatively clear of sloshing seawater, and he stood there dripping like a great shaggy dog, his hair hanging over his face, his borrowed clothing sopping wet and clinging to him like a soaked layer of parchment.

"Your grace . . . ?"

The agony of his previously bruised shoulder and hip did not bear dwelling upon but when he looked down, the front of his shirt was covered in a wide red smear of blood with more splattering down each second. He remembered the end of the rope lashing his cheek and searched his face with his fingertips, gasping at what he found.

"Your grace—?"

Varian whirled around with a roar and slammed the door. Over further protests and pounding fists, he threw the bolt to lock it, leaving Beacom outside in the companionway.

The storm battered the *Iron Rose* for another two hours before relenting and driving east. By late afternoon the rain had eased, though the wind remained at strength long after the thunder and lightning had been chased far out into the Atlantic. With the peculiar character of a tropical storm, the sky cleared enough by nightfall to offer a late glimpse of the setting sun where it sank like a coppery fireball beneath the choppy sea.

One man had died in a fall from the rigging; another had been washed overboard. There were tangled lines and torn sails, broken spars and debris on all the decks, but that was not what concerned those who stood on the quarterdeck searching the empty horizon behind them.

The *Santo Domingo* was nowhere in sight. With darkness rapidly descending, they did not even know in which direction to search; the sea appeared vacant for miles around. Juliet sent men with the sharpest eyes up into the crow's nest and refused to leave the quarterdeck or even hand off the spyglass until a twinkle of light was spotted well down on the horizon. She gave orders to bring the *Iron Rose* about, and as a precaution, cleared her guns for action in case the lights were not the ones they were expecting. Another anxious hour passed before they had closed the distance enough to be assured it was the *Santo Domingo*.

The galleon had been hammered, but the English crew had helped pull her through. When the *Rose* drew alongside, extra men were transferred aboard, including Nathan Crisp. With the seas rough, Juliet wanted to take no chances during the last stretch to Pigeon Cay.

Coming about again, they resumed their steady south by southeast course and it was only then that Juliet took time to go below and search out dry clothes. While it was still daylight, she had ordered the galley fires lit long enough for the cook to bring his cauldrons up to the boil, and she did not know which she was more eager for, a bowl of hot mutton stew or a stiff glass of rum.

The need to make a choice was delayed by the sight of Beacom standing miserably outside her cabin door.

"What the devil are you doing here? Where is your master?"

"He . . . he is inside, madam," Beacom said, wringing his hands. "I did my best to deter him. However—"

"He's inside? He is inside my cabin?"

"Yes, madam. I am afraid he is. And . . . and I am afraid he has locked the door behind him."

Juliet's eyes widened. She approached the door, put a hand to the latch, and rattled it. When nothing happened, she moved back a pace and kicked the bottom of the planks.

"Good my lord, you have two seconds to unlock this blasted door before I shoot off the damned hinges!"

When there was no immediate response, and knowing full well her pistols were locked inside with the duke, she cursed and kicked the door again, this time hard enough to send splinters flying off the timbers.

She was about to take a run at it with her shoulder when they heard the bolt slide across wood and the latch was turned from the inside. The door swung open half an inch before she hoofed it the rest of the way, slamming it with enough force it bounced off the wall.

Juliet strode into the cabin, her eyes sparking with hot blue flecks. "How dare you! How dare you come in here and—!"

She stopped cold and the breath left her lungs in a startled rush. Varian St. Clare was swaying on unsteady feet in front of her, his shirt scarlet to his waist, his breeches red to the knee. His eyes were so dark they looked like holes burned into his skull, part of which could be seen gleaming white where his cheek had been torn open to the bone.

An empty bottle rolled to and fro on the floor below the berth. The cup that dangled in his hand spilled a few drops as he took a few halting steps back.

"You seem to have acquired a fondness for my rum, sirrah," she said quietly.

He said nothing for a moment, then reached up and touched the flap of flesh that was hanging down his cheek. "I find myself requiring its effects more and more as the pleasantries of each new day in this tropical paradise unfold."

Juliet turned her head slightly and spoke softly to Beacom. "Go and fetch the ship's sailmaker. No, wait. He isn't on board, dammit!"

Varian started to pitch forward, forcing Juliet to scramble fast to catch him up under the arms before his weight bore them both down onto the floor. He made a peculiar sound in his throat, followed by a belch that reeked of too much rum.

"Puke on me, my lord," she warned with a grunt, "and you'll not live out the day."

"Is that a threat or a promise?"

"Both." She glared over her shoulder at Beacom. "Don't just stand there gawping. Help me get him into the berth."

The valet fluttered his hands once before hastening forward. Together they manhandled the duke over to the bed and forced him to lie down. Juliet splashed some water into an enamel bowl and fetched some relatively clean cloths. She set Beacom to bathing the blood off his master's face and throat while she rummaged through her sea chest and produced a small gold sewing case she had appropriated from some long forgotten ship.

When she returned to the bed, Varian's eyes were closed, an arm draped across his forehead.

"Is he passed out?" she asked Beacom.

"No, he is not," Varian answered thickly. "Despite his every good intention."

"In this case, it might be better if you had succeeded. Shall we wait, or are you braced enough to bear up under a bit of stitching?"

"That depends upon who is going to do the stitching."

"Unfortunately you are rather limited in your choices at the moment. The sailmaker is still on board the *Santo Domingo* tending the wounded from the *Argus*, and since you have expressly forbidden me to touch you without an invitation, that would appear to leave Beacom."

She held the needle out to the valet, who blanched the color of old ashes and quailed loudly enough to bring Varian's eyes open again.

"Oh for pity's sake," he sighed. "Touch me, kill me, sew my cheek to my foot, it is of no consequence."

"Come now," she said. "You were far too pretty anyway. A scar will give you character."

Juliet nodded at Beacom to bring a chair over beside the berth. She lit a lamp, then gave it to the valet to hold while she threaded a needle with silk. "Truth be told, I did sew two fingers together once—quite by accident, of course. The wounds were such that I could not tell where one digit ended and the other began."

Varian swallowed hard. "Perhaps I will have more rum."

"Faith, just try not to move. And if you feel the need to scream, warn me first so I do not stab you in the eye."

His chest rose and fell through a deep breath. The muscles in his throat constricted and his fingers curled slowly into a fist, remaining that way as Juliet eased the torn flap of skin gently back into place and began stitching the raw edges together with quick, efficient strokes.

" 'Tis a good thing it bled so much. The wound is clean and should heal without too much trouble. Furthermore, the stitching follows your hair and should only be visible within, oh, a hundred paces or so."

The midnight eyes opened and found hers only a couple of inches above his face.

"Truthfully," she said, drawing the thread slowly up through the puckered flesh, "it could have been much worse. You could have lost your eye, or your ear . . ." She worked for several more minutes, the tip of her tongue stuck at the corner of her mouth in concentration. When she was finished, she leaned back and frowned.

"What think you, Mr. Beacom? Will his lordship's sweet betrothed-to-be not find such a scar dangerously attractive? God's love, man, you can turn your head forward and look now."

One of Beacom's hazel eyes opened a slit, followed by the other. "Oh. Oh!" He leaned forward and almost smiled. "Verily, the captain speaks the truth, your grace. The cut is near the hair and the stitches are as fine as any I have seen on a silk gown."

After returning the needle and thread to the sewing box, Juliet replaced it in the sea chest. When she came back to the berth several minutes later, she carried a cloth soaked in some noxious tincture as well as a small jar wrapped in oilcloth.

"Do you think, Mr. Beacom, that you can find your way back to the galley? The cook should have put some hot stew on to warm the men's bellies, and mine is so empty it is rubbing on my backbone. There should be biscuits, too. And cheese. You might as well fetch a jug of ale while you are about it, and some cold beef if there is any to be sliced. Furthermore, just tell Cook his captain is ravenous; he'll know what to do."

Beacom glanced at Varian but did not wait for his assent this time before leaving the cabin. Juliet took her seat again.

"This might sting." She pressed the warm, wet cloth over his cheek, holding it there so long Varian thought his lungs would burst from the pressure of holding back a scream. By the time the incredible burning subsided, he was half sober and she had already shifted her attention to his hand. It was his left, the same one that had had the thumb wrenched out last night, and which now had angry red rope skids on the palm and wrist.

She dipped two fingers into the jar and scooped out

a brown, viscous paste. It smelled like the devil's offal but the instant it touched his burned palm, the pain cooled.

"It was a foolish thing you did," she said finally. "Especially in wood-heeled shoes with satin rosettes."

The dark eyes studied her face a moment before responding. "Is the boy all right?"

"He was shaken more than anything else. And you've impressed him enough that you'll likely not find yourself lacking a defender if someone raises their hand and sniggers behind your back."

"Including you?"

"I mock you to your face, sirrah, or hadn't you noticed?"

"I have indeed," the duke agreed dryly.

Studiously avoiding his gaze, she turned her attention to his thumb, applying more of the salve and massaging it gently around the swollen joint.

"You're lucky this did not pop out again."

"I would have been luckier had it never come out in the first place."

She curled her lower lip between her teeth and nibbled fitfully. "Yes, well . . . my reaction last night might have been a little overwrought. As it happened, you just chose the wrong time to test my patience."

"Good God," he murmured. "Is that an apology?"

She stared into the inky darkness of his eyes and felt a disquieting warmth at the base of her spine. "It is as good as you are likely to get."

"Then I shall accept it . . . on the condition you accept mine."

"Yours? For what?"

"For not knowing when to keep my mouth shut."

The self-deprecating bluntness brought a hint of a smile to Juliet's lips. It also brought a second rush of heat flowing through her body, stronger this time, centered between her thighs, and as he continued to stare at her, the pleasure intensified, spreading through her body in the most extraordinarily soft waves.

"Spare me the trial of a long answer, my lord, but what are you doing here? What could possibly have induced you to leave your cozy hearthside in London when, surely, as the twelfth duke of Harlow, you could have appointed someone more suited to the rigors of a sea voyage to take your place."

"Harrow. And I must suppose that the king considered me adequate to the task."

"Which is . . . ?"

He grinned faintly. "I've not had that much rum, Captain."

"Whatever your business here, it will likely be explained in my presence anyway."

"Then that must be by your father's choice, not mine."

Juliet expelled her breath on an impatient puff. "Faith, but I am losing interest anyway."

"I can see that. And if you rub my thumb any harder, you might just as well wrench it out again, for the pain could not be any worse."

She scowled and flung his hand aside. "I hope you know how to swim, sirrah. If Father finds your wit half as amusing as I do, you may have need of the skill."

Varian's smile hovered between amusement and curiosity. The only thing he had need of at the moment was more rum, for it had dulled most of the aches and pains in his body for the first time in two days. Moreover, he found himself increasingly intrigued with this sharp-tongued, clever-witted pirate urchin—and not just with her mind.

Several hours in the driving rain had accomplished what a neglect for soap and water had not, for the grime of battle was washed away, leaving her face clean and smooth. Her hair, half in, half out of the braid, was rid of its layers of dust and gleamed a rich dark auburn in the lamplight. The long strands that curled down her neck lured the eye into the deep, open vee of her shirt, and where the fabric was not completely dry it clung to curves that would have been better left to the imagination. Shapes and shadows that he had found unsettling the previous night set the blood flowing thick and insistent through his veins now, making him begin to entertain a notion that she was even beautiful in a raw, untamed sort of way.

Varian forced himself to look away, wary of the turn his thoughts were taking. If there had been one redeeming benefit to this hellish voyage, it was the refreshing absence of any women on board. Because of his family's wealth and prominence, he had been plagued for most of his eight and twenty years by grasping females who threw themselves in his path at every opportunity. In his youth, he had enjoyed their attentions well enough, had enjoyed his share of mistresses through the years. But after his brothers' deaths had made him the sole heir, the efforts to bring him to ground had risen to almost frenzied proportions. His own mother had been the worst of the lot, haranguing him unceasingly about the need to choose a bride and take the appropriate steps to produce a legitimate heir.

He supposed Juliet Dante's scorn had been justified when she said he had finally just succumbed. The dowager had culled the herd of potential broodmares down to the three richest virgins pure enough to carry the St. Clare seed, whereupon he had simply chosen one. All three had impeccable manners, the same faultless, flawless education that prepared them for nothing more strenuous than being the perfect wife, hostess, and chatelaine. In essence, they were all replicas of the dowager herself: cool, beautiful, sexless in a pale, elegant way.

Try as he might, he could not imagine his intended, Lady Margery Wrothwell, letting him see her with her hair disheveled, her shirt damp and clinging to breasts that were practically begging him to tear aside the damned fabric and bring them into his hands.

He shifted his legs, knowing the stirring he felt was mostly a product of his rum-soaked meanderings, but he was troubled by it anyway. The celibacy he had enjoyed for the past six weeks had its drawbacks and

he would be lying to himself if he thought he had
reached a state of premarital purity where the curve
of a lush breast had no effect on him.

Where the devil was Beacom?

As if reading his mind, Juliet glanced at the door
and muttered the same question.

"He has been known," Varian said lightly, "to take
a wrong turn at Harrowgate Hall even though he has
spent the past thirty years in service there. Mind you,
with sixty-five bedrooms and God only knows how
many main chambers, I have erred a time or two
myself."

She stared as if he had just claimed to have flown
to the moon and back. "Sixty-five bedrooms?"

"It . . . is a very old estate."

"And you live there by yourself?"

"Myself and a small army of about a hundred
servants."

Frowning, she pushed her chair back and carried
the pot of ointment back to the sea chest. She found
dry breeches and a clean shirt before she closed the
lid and propped one foot, then the other on top, using
it to keep her balance while she removed her boots.
Next, she unbuckled her belt and let it fall to the floor,
then pulled the tails of her shirt out of her breeches.

Varian watched, his eyes hooded and heavy, his
thoughts drifting, not really grasping what Juliet was
doing until she had drawn her shirt up and over her
head. When she set her fingers to the task of untying
the laces on her breeches, his eyes popped wide.

"I do beg your pardon, Captain, but . . . what are
you doing?"

"My clothes are damp, they want changing."

"Perfectly understandable, but—"

She paused and turned around, her hands resting
on her waist. This time there was nothing to fuel his
imagination but warm, naked flesh and had Varian
been standing, his jaw would likely have sagged to his
knees. Her breasts were full and round, tanned the
same olive shade as her face and arms. The nipples

were only slightly darker than the surrounding skin, with tips that peaked naturally like small, ripe berries. Her waist was trim, her hips taut beneath the formfitting black breeches.

Varian had seen all manner of women's forms, all shapes, all sizes, with or without corsets, silks, and buntings, offered seductively, modestly, and flirtatiously . . . but this . . . this unaffected, completely uninhibited presentation took his very breath away.

She stood unmoving for a full count of ten before she laughed that soft, unmanning laugh and tipped her head like a cat observing a mouse. "Have you never seen a naked woman before?"

"Yes. Yes, of course I have, but I . . . I hardly expected to see you."

"Well, unless you know of another way to change garments, you will simply have to bear up under the horror."

When he saw her hook her thumbs under the waist of her breeches to start peeling the moleskin down, he forced himself to turn his face to the wall. The rum as well as the temptation was raging through his blood, strong and pulsing, urging him to simply look and be done with it, but he dared not.

He heard each leg of the breeches being stripped away, heard water spilling into a bowl, a cloth being dipped and wrung, followed by the soft whisper of damp fabric moving over bare skin. He closed his eyes and ground his teeth together for he could feel himself growing thicker, fuller with each swipe of the cloth. And although he could not see it, he could easily imagine the shiny wetness left behind on her breasts, her thighs, the sleek vale between.

"If you take your shirt and breeches off," she said casually, "I can have Johnny Boy wash them. Or replace them with something more suitable. I warrant he will find something better than canvas breeks and a homespun pinafore, even if he has to swim over to the *Santo Domingo* and raid the Spanish stores of their velvet and lace."

Varian groaned inwardly and rolled all the way over onto his side, trusting the shadows to conceal his discomfort. Even so, the pain from the bulge in his breeches far outstripped the pain in his bruised hip, prompting his reply to come out in a strangled whisper. "Tell the boy not to go to any trouble on my account. Beacom can put me to rights when he returns. I thank you for the offer anyway."

Juliet shrugged and shook out the clean shirt. "Suit yourself. But if you keep straining those breeches without relief, your mother's concerns about a shortage of heirs will not be resolved by you."

Chapter Seven

*V*arian was wakened by the sound of Beacom's rattling snores. The cabin was dark, indicating it was still night, and when he rolled over to check the source of the light behind him, he saw that it was caused by the faint wash of moonlight coming through the gallery windows. The seas were not nearly as rough as they had been earlier, though the ship still leaped like a spirited filly from one wave to the next.

Juliet Dante had apparently gone topside again. Did she ever sleep? he wondered. She obviously ate, for the remnants of a huge platter of food littered her desk. All that was left of a small feast was a half-eaten biscuit turned nose down in a congealed pool of grease, a triangle of yellow cheese turning waxy at the edges, a few torn pieces of mutton that were marbled with globs of hard white fat. He knew this because he rose carefully out of the berth and went in search of a crumb or two to ease the rumbling in his stomach.

It occurred to him, as he munched on cheese, that he had eaten very little since coming on board the *Iron Rose*. Most of his sustenance had come from various bottles.

The line of stitches on his cheek, when he gently prodded it, was swollen and throbbing. His shoulder ached and the rope burns on his hand, while not uncomfortably painful, smelled of liniment. He had almost forgotten the lump at the back of his skull, but it did not forget him and he bowed his head between his shoulders, rolling it back and forth to ease the pressure. From that position, light or no light, he could hardly help but notice the dark stains on his shirt. The coarse homespun had been wet when he bled on it, and each drop had mushroomed two and three times its size, turning almost the entire front of the shirt red.

Mindful of his hand and shoulder, he lifted the shirt up over his head and crushed it into a ball. He debated, for a moment, throwing it at Beacom, resentful of the snores that continued with irritating regularity. Resisting the urge, he tossed it on the berth instead, then limped over to the washstand and sponged his chest clean in the same bowl Juliet had used earlier. The stand had a commode cabinet—he supposed the captain's share-all attitude did not extend to hanging her bottom over a hole in the beakhead—and while he was there, he relieved himself in the enamel pot. When he was finished, it was more than half full, and anticipating the look on Juliet Dante's face if she lifted the lid and found it well used, he turned instinctively to Beacom again.

This time the servant's name was a rumble halfway up his throat before it was rammed back down again. Emptying chamberpots was about as far below his station as he could possibly imagine, but when taken in perspective with all else he had endured recently, it seemed a trifling thing.

With fingertips only, he slid the pot out from beneath the wooden seat and carried it onto the stern gallery, a narrow balcony that ran the width of the cabin, good for little other than catching a fresh breath and emptying the contents of thunderpots.

And, it would seem, for slinging a hammock under the stars.

Evidently Juliet Dante did sleep, for she was stretched out on the canvas sling, one arm resting above her head, the other tucked alongside her hip. One leg was folded at the knee, the other hung freely over the side of the hammock, the bare toes gleaming like little pearls

under the moonlight. Varian had been provided with
one of the hellish devices the previous night and had
fallen out twice before managing to master it. But the
captain looked as comfortable as a kitten in a basket,
rocking gently with the motion of the ship, her hair
out of its braid and trailing over the side, the ends
drifting like a dark cloud as she swayed to and fro.

His hands tightened on the enamel pot and he knew
he should retreat with all haste before she wakened
and saw him standing there. His feet did not respond
to his command to take him back inside, however. His
eyes proved to be rebellious as well, choosing not to
look at the incredibly clear sky or the river of phos-
phorescent seawater that unfurled in a silvery path
behind the ship. They preferred to linger instead on
the pale arch of her throat, to follow the edge of her
shirt where it had become twisted to one side and lay
open over her breast.

As much as her offhanded stripping act had affected
him earlier, this moonlit display of casual nudity
nearly had him coming out of his skin again. For that
matter, he could not remember the last time he had
seen a woman's bare toes, or even a foot not hastily
tucked under covers or into a slipper. She had fine,
trim ankles, too. Supple calves. And thighs that had
already shocked him once with their sinewy strength.

"Have you never been told it is impolite to stare,
my lord?"

The whispered query sent his gaze snapping up to
her face. Her eyes were open beneath a dark brow
that was arched upward with curiosity.

"There is a difference," he said slowly, "between
staring and . . . admiring."

"Is that what you are doing? Admiring?"

"I am not a monk, madam."

"Faith, but it would be a waste if you were."

The observation was made with a husky honesty.
While the crescent moon had rendered Juliet's skin a
pale, creamy blur where it peeped through her shirt,

it gilded Varian's broad shoulders with bold strokes, emphasizing every curve of muscle on his chest, every hard band over the ribs, and the sight caused Juliet to experience something strangely like the sparks of St. Elmo's Fire they had witnessed earlier.

She had come awake the instant he had stepped out onto the gallery. Instinct had sent a hand into the sheath at her waist, but when she saw the vaunted twelfth Duke of Harrow emptying the contents of a thunderpot over the rail, she had relaxed and eased the dagger down by her hip. She had hoped he would simply creep back inside and return to bed, but when he continued to stand there, and then to fondle her with his eyes, she thought it best to end the charade before he noticed the effect all that visual intimacy was having on her own body.

"Whatever would your betrothed think," she mused aloud, "if she could see you standing there *admiring* another woman's breasts."

He did not answer at once. The wind funneling off the ship's hull snatched at his hair and cast it forward over his face so that all she could see was a faint glitter where his eyes should be.

"You do not make it easy for anyone to befriend you, do you?"

"Have I given you any reason to believe I need or even want more friends?"

"Not by a single word or deed, madam. In that you may be absolutely confident."

"You should tell your body that, my lord," she said, looking boldly at the obvious ridge in his breeches. "It would appear to need more convincing."

"I prefer to think my mind has a stronger will. Just as yours does, no doubt."

She smiled and folded her arm under her head as a pillow, further displacing the edge of her shirt. "Are you suggesting I am inwardly seething with the desire to bed you, sir?"

"I am suggesting nothing of the kind, although it

has been my experience that women do not usually strip down naked in front of a man unless they want to do more than simply change their clothing."

"Nor do men rise up like the mythical phoenix if their minds and thoughts are as pure as springwater."

"Forgive me if I repeat myself, but I am neither monkish nor insentient. Bare your breast and I will look. Bare it under moonlight and I will admire. Rest assured, however, there are more than enough deterrents to keep my lust duly restrained."

She laughed. "None quite as potent, I would argue, as a man clutching a pisspot in his hands."

Quicker than she thought him capable of moving, he tossed the enamel pot over the rail and moved to the side of the hammock. He caught her by the wrist and wrenched the concealed dagger out of her hand, then with a sniff of satisfaction, grasped the lip of canvas and jerked it with enough force to tumble her out the other side.

Juliet hit the deck in a tangle of arms and legs. When she sprang to her feet, he was ready for her. He caught both wrists and twisted them savagely around to the small of her back, locking them together in one iron fist while he used his big body to pin her against the rail. Conscious of the scab under his chin where she had pricked him last night, he was pleased now to press the sharp edge of her own dagger against her throat and let the cool steel caress the strained white arch.

"Be advised, *Captain*," he said evenly. "I learn from my mistakes and rarely make the same one twice."

"Brave words," she spat, mocking his accusation from the night before, "with a knife in your hand."

The knife went spinning away over the rail. He crowded closer and wrapped his hand firmly around her throat so that her chin was in a cradle and his fingers were able to locate and pinch a sensitive cluster of nerves below her ear. There was enough ruthlessness in his fingertips that her body sagged and her lips gasped apart with the pain.

"I am without a pisspot now, madam," he hissed against her cheek. "Shall I warm myself elsewhere?"

Her curse came out a strangled gasp. Taking crude advantage, he turned his head and kissed her hard on the mouth. When she tried to clamp her lips shut, he gouged his fingers deeper into her neck, winning another cry, another shuddered gasp of pain. His tongue plunged between her open lips and he took what she refused to give, using his mouth, even his teeth to stifle her efforts to dislodge him.

When she managed to wrench her mouth free, he captured it again. When she tried to kick and wriggle out of his grasp, he wedged a thigh between her legs, lifting her until her feet were raised off the deck and she was perilously close to tipping over the rail.

His tongue plundered her mouth without mercy, without allowing a scrap of air or sound to escape. Her hands escaped and in one pounding heartbeat, she transformed all the rage and anger she was feeling into defiance. Fisting her way through his attempts to recapture her hands, she clawed them up into his hair and, instead of pushing him away, held him fast and began to return each thrust of his tongue, to match each slant and turn of his lips as he ate at her mouth.

Shocked by the sudden and completely unexpected reversal, it was Varian's turn to try to break free but Juliet twisted her fingers around clumps of hair, threatening enough force to tear chunks out of his scalp if he pulled away. She used her body too, pushing her breasts against his, riding the wedge of his thigh until she found something more vulnerable and volatile to abuse. He was already half aroused from his imagined triumph, but now the friction and her eagerness in applying it brought them both straining together, feeding one off the other, neither sure who was the aggressor and who the victim now.

It was that uncertainty that caused Juliet to push his mouth away. She knew it had been too long since she had felt the heat of a man's body between her thighs, but she also knew this was the wrong man to want there. Any man, at the moment, would be wrong, but this one in particular was too potent, too unsettling, and for someone who decried the very notion of trying to seduce her, he was doing a damnèd fine job. Her mouth was hot and wet with the taste of him and now her flesh was betraying her. There were tremors in her arms, in her legs, and if the hand that had been sliding boldly down her hip had been allowed to curve a few inches lower, there would have been tremors elsewhere she would not have been able to control.

On the other hand, despite his own obvious arousal and the hard glitter of fury in his eyes, he was making no attempt to overcome her rejection and pull her back into his arms.

"You disappoint me, my lord," she said harshly. "You call yourself a master swordsman, but even a novice knows better than to attempt a finesse when he has not the strength or wit to see it through."

His eyes continued to glitter, his hands to flex and unflex by his sides. "It was . . . an unconscionable reaction to an unconscionable situation and I can only offer profound apologies for my conduct. If I have misrepresented myself in any way—"

"You haven't," she assured him bluntly. "I thought you were an arrogant, self-indulgent bastard when we first spoke, and nothing has happened to change that now."

She dragged the back of her hand across her mouth to wipe it clean and pushed away from the rail, striding past him without another word or glance. She was too furious with herself, too furious with him to trust herself to remain in his company a moment longer. Her mouth was tender, her breasts ached. Her knees were weak and her limbs felt like jelly. Her body was throbbing with a violence that made her want to walk up on deck and ravage the first man she found—to strip him, ride him until they both screamed for mercy, then toss him over the side with the galley scraps.

As a poor alternative, she snatched her doublet off the hook, grabbed her boots, and left the cabin, spending the rest of the long and sleepless night alone on her perch in the mainmast.

Chapter Eight

The sun was well past noon when the shout of "land ho" brought Juliet to the quarterdeck at a run. The faint purplish smear off the larboard bow was no more than a jagged bump on an otherwise smooth horizon, but when they drew closer and that one single bump proved to be five distinct islands, the crew of the *Iron Rose* was all smiles. Within the hour, the order was given to shorten sail, to reduce the sheets to steerage only. Riding in her wake, the *Santo Domingo* did likewise.

The reason for this became clear when they passed through a band of pale blue water. A reading off the cable put the depth beneath the keel at six fathoms—roughly six times the span of a man's outstretched arms—up drastically from the hundred fathoms of inky blue that had been beneath them for most of the morning. Less than a league later, the water became a bright turquoise that changed after another two hundred yards into pale cobalt. In all there were seven distinct bands of blue that formed a shimmering aura around the cluster of atolls. The palest bar measured a mere three fathoms of clearance, the bottom so close and the water so clear, the crew could see schools of yellow tiger fish feeding on the crowning heads of coral.

The broken ribs of shipwrecks were also visible, lying in their watery graves. An untold number of captains had allowed their curiosity to bring them too close onto the reef and for their trouble, they'd had their keels ripped open stem to stern. One ship in particular, whose identity and origin was unknown, lay almost intact on the bottom, her single mast pointed in a southwesterly direction. It was this marker that the lookout in the crow's nest searched for and located with an excited shout.

Juliet quietly relayed an order to bring the *Iron Rose* about on a course that followed the outstretched finger of the sunken mast. After calculating wind speed and direction, she turned a specially marked sandglass on its end. There were two men on cables now, one of whom continuously called out depth readings from the bow, while the other dropped the logline off the stern and counted the number of knots that played out over the course of a minute to measure their speed. The rest of the crew stood silent, half of them poised in the yards, ready to act upon any orders the instant they were given. The other half stared forward to where Juliet now stood perched at the very tip of the bowsprit, communicating instructions to the helmsman by way of prearranged hand signals. Although she knew these waters as well as she knew the rifts and valleys of her own body, there was only one way through the reef, only one narrow channel of deeper water that took several twists and turns and did not forgive the arrogance of any pilot who failed to show the proper respect.

Almost to the mark, as the helmsman signaled that the last grain of sand had fallen through to the bottom globe of the hourglass, Juliet waved that the bow was over deep water again. Balancing between the taut stay lines, she returned along the bowsprit and jumped lightly down onto the forecastle deck, where Johnny Boy was waiting with her spyglass. She took it, snapped open the brass and leather tube, and trained it anxiously on the much larger *Santo Domingo*, which was just beginning her run through the reef.

"She turns like a pig," Juliet muttered. "I warrant Nathan has chewed his cud to mush."

"I'll wager Cap'n Simon is chewing a thing or two as well," Johnny said, grinning.

Juliet swung the glass around and brought the islands into sharper focus. Four of the atolls were just that: caps of ancient volcanic rock that had pushed up through the surface of the sea. They were covered with tangles of brush crowned by a few scattered palms but were inhabited mainly by turtles and lizards. They offered no anchorage and promised nothing to passing ships except a splendid view of massive white waves crashing with spectacular violence against the barren rocks.

It was the fifth island, nestled in the middle and rising higher than the others, that housed the most sought-after secret in the Caribbee. Formed roughly in the shape of a C with overlapping arms, it had once been the uppermost rim of a volcano. An ancient upheaval on the seafloor had cracked the rim and created a natural deep-water harbor in the bowl of the crater, a harbor completely shielded by walls of seemingly impenetrable rock. Simon Dante had discovered the island sanctuary purely by accident some thirty years before when a storm of horrendous proportions had produced fifty-foot waves and swept his ship over the razored teeth of coral reef. It had taken him nearly six months to repair the damage to the keel of his beloved *Virago* and find a way out again—time enough to explore all five islands. He named the largest Pigeon Cay, after the small clutch of gray birds his quartermaster had brought on board. They had been the first, when released from their cages, to fly straight at the base of the most improbable wall of sheer rock and show them the way through the entrance to the crater.

As keen as Juliet's eyes were, even aided by familiarity, she would not be able to see the entrance until they were past the two outer islands. In her mind's eye, however, she could clearly picture the lookouts on the summit clanging the alarm bells that would bring men running to the heavy battery of guns that guarded the approach. Never in all her twenty-one years had Juliet known a single cannon to be fired in defense of Pigeon Cay yet she could not help but smile at the confusion that must be on some of the faces as they watched the massive Spanish warship maneuvering its way through the coral passage.

"If this were the *Tribute*," she murmured, "and I was my brother Jonas, I would be tempted to loose off a broadside just to get their blood flowing a little faster."

"Ye'd best be showing a friendly flag instead," Nog Kelly suggested over his shoulder. "Unless my good eye deceives me, there be men bristling on them gun emplacements getting ready to offer us a warm welcome."

Juliet trained the spyglass on the ledges she knew were halfway up the face of the cliffs. Sure enough, she could see the dull gleam of sunlight on metal and knew the snouts of twoscore heavy cannon had been cleared of the vines and brush that concealed them. The sentries would have seen the two ships from several leagues out and while the *Iron Rose* was as familiar to them as the backs of their hands, the fact that she was accompanied by a Spanish warship of the *Santo Domingo*'s size and firepower would have set hackles rising.

"D'ye think Cap'n Simon will be pleased with the prize you've brung home?"

Juliet lowered the glass a moment to smile at Johnny Boy. "Captain Simon will indeed be pleased with the *Santo Domingo*. It's the rest of what we're bringing him that might cause a vein or two to bulge in his forehead."

She glanced pointedly down to where Varian St. Clare was standing by the rail and her smile turned into a scowl.

"Why is he on deck? I gave specific orders he was to remain below."

Johnny Boy snorted. "As much as he knows about the sea, Cap'n, I doubt he could find his way back here in a thousand years."

Juliet glared at the lad. "And just how would you know how much he knows about the sea?"

"When I fetched him his biscuits an' ale this morning, 'ee asked me where we were. I showed 'im a chart of the Tortugas an' Cabecas de los Martyres an' 'ee nodded like 'ee knew what 'ee was lookin' at. I also told 'im we were ten degrees off the equator, an' he just nodded again."

"Telling him we are two hundred leagues north of where we are is hardly proof of his ignorance, and if you're wrong, you'll be accounting to Captain Simon for the lapse. I suppose you were also the one who fetched him those clothes?"

"Weren't no trouble, Cap'n. I found 'em in some o' the chests we brung over from the Spaniard an' I didn't think 'ee should meet Cap'n Simon in torn breeks an' a bloody apron. Looks a proper duke now, don't 'ee?"

Something—probably the heat of silvery blue eyes drilling into the back of his neck—prompted Varian St. Clare to turn and look up at the forecastle. His jaw was cleanly shaven, the moustache and imperial had been restored to precisely trimmed neatness. The bloodstained shirt had been replaced with one of fine Spanish linen, the cuffs and collar edged with lace. In place of the threadbare galligaskins, he now wore dark green Venetian breeches buckled just above the knee with gold silk bands. Dark hose, a pillow hat set on a rakish angle, and a surprisingly well-fitted emerald velvet doublet completed the restoration from shipwreck survivor to royal envoy. If not for the bruising and the line of stitching down the left side of his face, she would have thought he had just come from the king's court.

The midnight eyes held hers for a long moment before he bowed low to acknowledge her interest. She had not seen or spoken to him all morning and had no wish to do so now. It was enough to feel the residual heat smoldering under her skin and to know that if she did go near him, she might be tempted to throw him overboard and make him swim ashore.

"Arrogant bastard," she muttered under her breath. "We shall see who mocks whom before the day ends."

With an effort, she dragged her attention back to the *Santo Domingo*. It seemed to take forever for the heavy galleon to clear the reef but once through, with the *Iron Rose* taking the lead again, the two ships made straight for Pigeon Cay. When she was close enough, Juliet raised the glass again and was able to identify some of the tiny specks that stood in clusters along the gun emplacements.

Her father was at the main battery, a tall, imposing figure who was equally at ease standing on the deck of a ship heading into battle as he was manning the defenses of an island fortress. Standing by Simon Dante's side, as ever, was Geoffrey Pitt, a man of inestimable knowledge who presented a scholarly appearance and gentle demeanor to the world but whose skill and ruthlessness at the helm of a fighting ship was second only to Dante's.

Towering over the pair, his bald head shining in the sunlight, was the huge, black-skinned Cimaroon who had once been shackled beside Simon Dante in the belly of a Spanish galleass. His hatred for his former captors was near as legendary as that of the man who had commanded his loyalty for the past three decades. Lucifer was Dante's master gunner and there was not a cannon forged or a pistol made that he could not fire with frighteningly precise accuracy.

There was a fourth figure standing beside the lethal trio, smaller, slighter of build, with an empty sleeve knotted below the left elbow. Isabeau Dante had taken the loss of her arm in stride. She had spent all of her life at sea and just as Johnny Boy had learned to adapt to a missing limb, so had Beau adjusted and invented new ways to keep her husband and family on their toes. She did not seek any man's sympathy, nor did she respect it when it was offered. In fact, when Juliet had left on this last sea trial, Isabeau and her aged first mate, Spit McCutcheon, had been working on a contraption that would fit the stump and allow her to hold a sword or a pistol.

"The flags, Cap'n?" Kelly shouted a reminder.

Juliet nodded and one of the crewmen ran out the pennons, the first a crimson wolfhound and a blue fleur-de-lis on a black field: the arms of Simon Dante, Comte de Tourville. Directly beneath it flew a second black and crimson burgee with a swallowtail, this one depicting the wolfhound with a gilded rose clamped between its teeth. A third plain green square of silk went up the mast, a prearranged signal that would relieve any concerns up on the ramparts that a Spaniard had somehow overtaken and coerced the *Iron Rose* into leading them to Pigeon Cay.

Within minutes of the flags snapping open in the breeze, the massive siege guns were hauled back under cover and their crews stepped forward, waving and hooting even though they were still too far away for the sound to carry. Geoffrey Pitt even removed his hat and raised it in a salute, which Juliet interpreted as a good sign despite the fact that her father had not budged. He stood with his long legs braced wide apart, his hands clasped behind his back while he watched their approach.

Well into his fifth decade Simon Dante was still a handsome man. His body was iron hard with muscle and aside from a few deep creases earned by raising three children and keeping a hot-spirited wife by his side, his face had not changed much over the years. Clear, silvery blue eyes could still strike terror into the hearts of his enemies. The stern, authoritative voice could command the bloodless silence of a thousand men or, conversely, deliver a quip that could send the company around him into gales of irrepressible laughter. His expression gave nothing away that did not want giving and even though Juliet knew that enormous heart loved her beyond any mortal measure, she still felt butterflies beating madly in her belly. An angry word from those lips had the power to crush all her courage and bravado into dust. The smallest hint of disappointment in his eyes could gut her quicker than a knife.

Isabeau Dante was only slightly less terrifying.

"Bring us in, Mr. Anthony," Juliet said quietly, glancing at the helmsman.

"Aye, Cap'n. The lads are that anxious to be home an' braggin', they'll likely have the boats lowered before the anchor splashes down."

Juliet did not return his eager smile. "There will be time enough for bragging and boasting when everyone's job is done. I'll not want to see a scrap of rope left on deck or a single hatch unbattened. Moreover, I want the powder kegs rotated and the deck guns oiled and bunged before a drop of rum passes anyone's lips. Mr. Kelly"—she turned to the carpenter—"by noon tomorrow I will expect to see a new foremast mounted on the *Rose* as well as a detailed list of the repairs that are needed on board the *Santo Domingo*. I'm sure there will be no lack of help from shore to off-load whatever cargo may be in her holds, but I want her searched thoroughly and any unnecessary weight removed. Strip her to the beams if you must, but I want to be able to call up another five knots in speed."

"I could cut off what's left of those bloody castles fore an' aft; you'd gain two points off the wind and an extra rung above the waterline."

Juliet shook her head. "Let us see how she handles with those new fittings and balloon sails we discussed before we go changing her silhouette too much. You never know when a Trojan horse might come in useful."

"Eh? Ye're gonny use her to carry horses? Great Gomorrah's entrails, what do we need with horses?"

Juliet sighed and waved away any attempt at an explanation. "Just trust me when I say she may be useful."

"Cap'n Simon might just have something to say about that. Horses is nasty creatures. Got bit on the arse once when I were young. Still have the mark."

Juliet peered through the spyglass. "Yes, well, unless the vaunted *Pirata Lobo* has taken it upon himself to rewrite the articles of privateering we signed, the *Domingo* is mine. I won her. I brought her home. She's mine to do with as I please."

Kelly threw his hands up by way of expressing his final opinion on the matter. "I'd be the last to argue with ye, Cap'n. I'm just sayin' ye could sell her to the Portugee and make yourself a tidy sum."

"I already have a tidy sum, enough to suffice into my old age."

Juliet took a final sweep of the waves crashing against the base of the cliffs, noting the lines of foam and spindrift that marked the flow of currents around the jagged breakwater. This time of day, the tides would be more favorable to ships leaving the hidden harbor than to those arriving, and a careful eye had to be kept on the swirling eddies and whirlpools at the base of the cliffs. Once inside the curved spit that guarded the entrance, attention had to be paid to holding speed and not succumbing to the drag that wanted to pull them back out the mouth. There were men with ropes and grappling lines on either side of the channel to assist in hauling a ship through to the harbor if necessary, but Juliet had only been towed once, when her rudder had been jury-rigged and she had not trusted the temporary repair to hold against the current. Her brothers, on the other hand, had been towed in more often than not and it was a matter of pride for her to maintain the *Rose*'s speed until the very last possible instant.

Most of the crew knew of the unspoken rivalry and held their breath in those final moments of the approach. The slightest miscalculation could send the ship careening into the rocks and as Juliet made her way onto the quarterdeck, all eyes turned to the towering ramparts of the cliff and the huge fountains of white spume that exploded at its base.

Varian St. Clare had spent nine years in the army. As one of the youngest officers to earn a promotion to captain, he had won accolades for his bravery and courage under fire. He had served three of those years as Captain of the King's Royal Guard—no mean feat considering the number of papists who cursed the day Scotland and England united under one ruler. He had faced down the zealot Guy Fawkes, who had tried to kill the king and all his ministers by blowing up the Parliament buildings. He had calmly, if stupidly, walked into a cellar packed with thirty barrels of black powder and cut the burning fuse without flinching an eye . . . yet he found himself backing cautiously away from the rail now, with clammy beads of sweat rolling between his shoulder blades, as the *Iron Rose* rushed headlong toward what appeared to be an inevitable collision with six-hundred-foot cliffs.

Search as he might, he could see no cracks, no breaks in the rocks, no caverns, that might allow forty feet of masts to sail beneath. Although he glanced frequently at the madwoman standing on the quarter-deck, she seemed more intent upon watching the flight of a gull circling overhead than marking the thunderous fury of the breakers ahead. She did not even acknowledge the helmsman when he started shifting from one foot to the other and removing his hands from the whipstaff every few seconds to dry them on his breeches.

"Now, Mr. Anthony," she said clearly. "Haul in sail if you please and bring her hard to starboard. Leave me the mizzen for steerage and have men ready on the bills."

Varian looked up as a hail of shouts relayed the orders and the men in the yards came alive. They reeled in the sheets of canvas as fast as their hands could pull the cables, tying them off in thick bundles that lined the spars like rolls of sausage. On deck, men took positions along both sides of the ship holding thick oak staffs whose purpose Varian could only guess.

Their speed did not noticeably decrease. If anything, the ship seemed to gather momentum as she began to turn and was carried sideways by a wave. The surf took them sliding gracefully around a spit of rock and it was then that Varian saw the opening. For a moment he thought they might yet sweep right past it and he looked hard at the waves crashing not two hundred yards off the larboard beam, close enough he could feel the mist dampening his face.

But he could also see the faces of the men in the tops and lining the rails. Some were laughing outright, enjoying the exhilaration of the ride.

"Oh my good sweet God!" Beacom wailed into his hands. "We are doomed! We shall be wrecked! Dashed upon the rocks! Drowned after all that we have endured!"

"For pity's sake, Beacom, we are not going to drown. Open your eyes, man," Varian added with dawning comprehension, "and behold a feat of unparalleled brilliance."

He moved to the rail again. The timing had been precise, the turn had been exact, and the ship was gliding smoothly forward between two sheer walls of rock, leaving the roaring tumult of the waves behind. The need for the stout poles came clear at once as the stern threatened to swing too far and grind against the rocks, but the *Iron Rose* answered her rudder and righted herself, holding regally to the middle of the channel.

Steep walls covered with lush green vegetation rose on either side of them, narrowing overhead, so that the tangled vines filtered most of the light and turned it green. There were paths hidden behind the drooping palms, and the greetings exchanged between the men on board and the men who ran along the concealed ledges echoed back and forth across the water. Despite the steady decrease in their speed, the ship continued forward, and Varian was amazed yet again to see a bright opening at the end of the overgrown tunnel. Another hundred feet and they broke through to clear water and bright sunlight, and this time, the sight that unfolded before him was nothing short of astounding.

They appeared to have sailed into a huge enclosed harbor that stretched two miles or more at its widest point. Far from being the gnarled and uninviting crown of sparsely vegetated rock the island presented to the outside world, the interior boasted lush green slopes and masses of thick palm groves. Peppered in among the trees were clusters of thatched huts and stone cottages while pastures higher on the rim held flocks of sheep and cattle. Lime and lemon trees grew in profusion and on the far side of the bay, a large pan of rock used for extracting salt crystals from the seawater gleamed white against the distant green shore. The sun had already dipped below the westerly rim of the crater, casting most of the slope in thickening shadows and at the base, there were already lights twinkling to life in some of the huts, suggesting there were taverns and shanties down by the main jetty.

The latter would have rivaled any busy wharf on the Thames. There were warehouses and long flat buildings built of timber, loading docks and enormous winches hung with cargo nets. There was even a road following the shoreline, crowded with carts and wagons. At the far end was a church, its steeple rising white above the shadows.

There was also a trio of tall ships sitting at anchor. Two of them were similar in size and tonnage to the *Iron Rose*; the third was larger, showing twice the number of gunports on her decks.

"That be Cap'n Simon's ship," Johnny Boy said, coming up beside him. "The *Avenger*."

Varian was too overwhelmed to do more than nod. He was also duly impressed, knowing he was likely

among the privileged few who had seen the vaunted
privateer this close without her guns blazing. As the
Iron Rose glided past, he studied the sleek lines of the
ship that had been throwing terror into the hearts of
Spanish captains for over two decades, his gaze stalling
when it came to the unusual figurehead on her bow.

The face bore an astonishing resemblance to Juliet.
The exaggerated abundance of carved hair was spread
back on either side of the bowsprit, making it seem
as if the wind were sending the wavelike curls flowing
out behind her. The thin slip of a garment she was
wearing had fallen down, baring an oak breast that
was as perfectly shaped as the one Varian had beheld
last night. Below that, however, the similarity ended,
for the body was that of a swan, the feathers looking
as real as if they had been plucked out of a bird and
glued there, the enormous black wings spread back
against the wind.

"That be the Cap'n's wife, Miz Isabeau," Johnny
Boy said almost reverently. "It were the only thing he
saved from her ship, the *Black Swan*, before they had
to scuttle 'er. Not Cap'n Beau, of course. Just the ship.
An' that lady over there"—he pointed to a sleek two-
masted vessel that had been partially hidden by the
larger privateer—"is the *Christiana*, Mr. Pitt's ship. He
designed her himself an' she's the fastest thing ye'll
ever see on the water. Leastwise she will be when he
finishes her. The other two, over yon, are the *Tribute*
an' the *Valour*. They belong to Cap'n Jonas an'
Cap'n Gabriel."

There were a dozen lighter pinnaces anchored
closer to shore, single-masted vessels that were used
mainly as transports for ferrying supplies. They had
no specific captains, Johnny Boy explained, since they
were made to be broken down and stowed in the bal-
last of a bigger ship. They had also passed a considerable flock of longboats filled with men, oars, and
cables waiting at the mouth of the channel to row out
and fetch the *Santo Domingo*. The *Rose* had traversed

the currents and whirlpools safely, but the Spaniard would need a tow.

Varian nodded mutely throughout the boy's chatter, but his attention had strayed elsewhere. Higher up on the eastern slope of the crater, where the last of the sun's rays still washed the hill with light, a sprawling two-story manor house had been built on a natural green terrace of land. It was as large and fine as anything that could be found in the English countryside, built of white stone with red clay tiles on the roof and latticed verandas wrapping around the outside of the upper and lower floors. The road that led from the manor to the harbor looked like a ribbon where it trailed down through the greenery, and as the *Rose* sidled to a halt and the anchor chain began rattling through the hawser, small puffs of chalky dust could be seen in the wake of two riders charging toward the docks.

"That'll be Cap'n Jonas an' Cap'n Gabriel," Johnny Boy guessed. "Folk call 'em the Hell Twins for good reason, so ye might want to have a care. They don't take kindly to lubbers. Specially Cap'n Jonas. He has the red hair o' a demon and the temper to match."

"I plan to be on my best behavior."

The boy smirked. "If that was yer plan, it didn't work with Cap'n Juliet, did it?"

Varian glanced sidelong and bristled under the lad's grin. "How old are you, boy?"

"Twelve come Michaelmas," he answered promptly. "My ma says I were born under the sign of the holy star. Mr. Crisp says it were just a lamp shining up on the hill."

"Mr. Crisp sounds like a practical man."

The boy shrugged his narrow shoulders. "He's my da so I'm bounden to listen to him but I like the story of the holy star better."

"Mr. Crisp is your father?"

"Said so didn't I?"

"I meant no offense, I just . . ." Varian glanced

down at the ornately carved stump that served as the boy's leg. "Well, I find it odd a man would allow his son in harm's way when so much harm has been done already."

"Ye mean my leg? Aye, I paid the butcher's bill wi' that one. Were my own fault, though. I were carrying a charge of powder and set it too close to a burning fuse. I looked away for just a blink and *blam*! Off it went. Mr. Kelly made this for me," he added proudly, rapping his knuckles on the carved snake's head. "Cap'n Juliet give me the emerald for his eye. Miz Beau gave me the pearls for the scales, an' Cap'n Simon, well, he gave me bloody hellfire for not havin' better sense. But I was only six then an' didn't know much better. Now I'm twelve an' Cap'n Juliet is teaching me how to read charts an' plot a course."

"I am sure you will make a fine navigator some day."

"Terror o' the Seas. That's what I want to be. Just like Cap'n Dante." The boy beamed and tugged a forelock. At a shout from the helm, he moved farther along the rail and unlatched the section that swung open at the gangway. Several jolly-boats had pushed off from various points along the shoreline and were converging on the *Iron Rose* like iron shavings to a magnet. The one carrying the Dante brothers was the first to arrive and Varian moved discreetly back from the gangway as it bumped against the hull.

The brothers climbed up the steps set into the ship's hull and vaulted through the gangway, shouting for the captain before their boots were planted solidly on the timbers. They were similar in height and build, but that was where the resemblance ended. Thanks to Johnny Boy's description, Varian could identify Jonas Spence Dante by the violent shock of flame red hair that curled over his burly shoulders. His jaw was square, stubbled with the same titian hairs that bristled across his brows and lashes. A visible scar dented the left side of his chin, another crossed his neck above the collar of his battered leather doublet.

By contrast, the younger of the Hell Twins, Gabriel, had a face like a deposed archangel. Dark mahogany hair surrounded a handsome face dominated by large, expressive eyes and a sinfully shaped mouth that would have set women swooning in droves were he to walk into a crowded London ballroom. Where his brother looked at home in leather and coarse cotton, Gabriel's shirt was made of the finest white cambric, his jerkin was embroidered brocade, and his long legs were encased in supple chamois.

"Well, where is she?" Jonas's voice boomed out like thunder. Eyes the color of tarnished gold scanned the grinning crew from beneath the wide brim of his hat. "Where is the captain of this sorry excuse for a sailing ship?"

The forward hatchway opened and Juliet Dante stepped through.

Varian followed the sound of men cheering and had to blink to double-check his vision, for the chameleon had changed her skin again. She was dressed in tight black doeskin breeches and a snow-white silk shirt that had fonts of lace circling the collar and cuffs. The trim shape of her waist was now accentuated by a formfitting black leather doublet that glittered with bands of seed pearls. A short satin cape was draped artfully over one shoulder, the lining scarlet, the wings turned back to leave her swordarm free. Her hair fell in a mass of auburn curls down her back, covered by a flamboyant hat with a sweeping scarlet brim. Tall black boots had wide cuffs folded down over the knee, and at her waist, the exquisitely wrought Toledo sword.

Varian almost forgot whom he was staring at as he watched her stride across the deck, the image of a proud, triumphant privateer.

"Who let these two whoremongers on board my ship?" she demanded. "A pair of gold doubloons to any man brave enough to throw them overboard!"

Despite the excited murmur that went through the crew, none were imprudent enough to step forward and it was with an exaggerated sigh that Juliet withdrew her rapier slowly from its sheath.

"I see I shall have to do the honors myself, then," Juliet announced. "Who first? The mongrel or the pup?"

Jonas Dante grinned hugely and drew his sword. "If she's still dry when I'm finished with her, Gabe m'boy, you have my permission to lay a stripe or two across that saucy arse of hers."

"And you have mine, Gabriel dearest," Juliet said, flexing the thin blade of her rapier in a shiny arc, "to carve that rather overboastful codpiece he wears down to its proper size. Unless, of course, I attend to it first."

A raucous cheer went up from the crew of the *Rose*, who were hanging over the rails on the foredeck, draped over yardarms, gathered three-deep on the quarterdeck. Wagers were shouted and shoulders slapped to make room as brother and sister slowly began to circle one another, their blades hissing to and fro, slicing the air as they warmed their arms and readied themselves to engage.

"Gracious good heavens, my lord," Beacom whispered over Varian's shoulder. "Do you suppose they intend real harm to one another?"

But Varian only held up a hand to command silence, intrigued by the spectacle unfolding before him. He and his brothers had often practiced their swordsmanship, but never with unblunted blades, never with such fearsome intensity in their eyes.

Jonas broke first, taking advantage of a clever feint to open the attack. Juliet deflected the initial series of parries with ease, countering each with a lethal deftness that forced the much larger Dante to scramble into a hasty retreat.

A second prolonged engagement saw the two leaping catlike between the anchor capstans, lunging over and around barrels and crates, pushing the wall of roaring crewmen back to the rail. The sound of steel

ringing off steel was accompanied by flashes of blue
sparks and grunts as both combatants were forced to
think quick on their feet as the strikes came faster,
closer to their marks.

Sheer size should have given Jonas the advantage
of strength, but it became shockingly evident that Juliet was far superior in skill. Her ripostes were delivered in a blur, her attacks measured out in precise
quadrants. Her balancing arm rarely left the narrow
indent of her waist long enough to flutter the wing of
her cape nor was her hat ever in jeopardy of being
dislodged. Every attempt her brother made to break
into a charge or overpower a thrust by brute strength
was met with an adroit twist or an acrobatic leap that
put her somehow behind him, above him, beside him,
prodding his rump with the tip of her blade. When
he whirled around, she laughed, offering deliberate
openings and slashing them shut again with a swiftness
that left her opponent lunging ineffectually at vacant
space.

Varian's instincts rose to the surface, stinging with
manly indignation each time he saw Jonas miss a
failed opportunity, or stagger back in a clumsy retreat.

The torment ended soon enough as Jonas was
herded toward the open gangway. With the offending
codpiece hanging by a strip of cloth at the crux of his
thighs, the coup de grâce was delivered and he was
propelled, howling and cursing, through the rail and
out over open water.

A great roar went around the deck, and Juliet—
barely winded—spun on the balls of her feet and
brought the tip of her blade to a glittering rest beneath
the chin of Gabriel Dante. He responded with a casual
shrug, raising his hands to show he held no weapon.

"In no mood for a swim tonight?"

"The water is a little chilly for my taste," he said,
sighing. "And this is a new feather in my cap, dammit.
I'll not squander it on a brother's conceit."

"I'd not squander it either," she said, examining the

plume with interest. "Though I may pluck it for my own if I am not accorded a properly respectful greeting."

Gabriel lowered his hands, presented an elegant leg, and swept forward in a bow that bent him gracefully in half. It also put him in the perfect position to reach out and circle his arms around his sister's upper thighs as he was rising. With a maniacal shout of glee, he flung her over his shoulder and used his forward momentum to carry them both toward the side of the ship. A step away from tumbling her over the rail and into the drink, he was halted by the sight of two new arrivals standing in the gangway.

The more formidable of the scowling faces belonged to Simon Dante de Tourville, who stood with his arms crossed over his chest and his eyebrow raised in askance. Less threatening but no less daunting was the frowning visage of Isabeau Dante, whose head was shaking over the antics of their three adult siblings.

"Put me down, you sodding son of Beelzebub," Juliet cried. "Put me down or so help me I'll skin your ballocks with my teeth and—"

Gabriel grinned and swung around so that Juliet could see what had caused his momentary burst of brotherly mercy.

Raising her head, she shoved aside the curtain of hair that had tumbled over her face. "Oh. Good evening, Father. Mother. Welcome aboard."

Chapter Nine

"**Y**ou sail in here a week overdue dragging a bloody great galleon on your heels and that is all you have to say: 'Welcome aboard'?"

Juliet squirmed just enough to loosen Gabriel's grip and slip off his shoulder. She snatched her hat off the deck and resheathed her sword, then offered up a wide smile. "Welcome aboard, Father, Mother; I am very happy to see you both."

"We have been worried, young miss," Isabeau said, "and a sharp tongue will earn you no favors here. Where have you been? How in God's name did you come to be in possession of a damned warship?"

"It's a very long story, Mother, and—"

"We have time," Simon said, interrupting her in a voice that was as smooth as silk yet sharp as a razor. It was a voice she knew better than to defy but it brought a smile to her lips anyway.

Folding her arms across her chest in a fair imitation of the man glowering down at her, Juliet relayed with brusque efficiency the details of incident involving the demise of the *Argus* and the attack on the *Santo Domingo*.

"We took advantage of the Spaniard's distraction long enough to come up on her blind side, board her, and take command," she said, finishing the tale in a silence so complete one would have thought the crew was hearing it for the first time.

"You boarded her?" Isabeau Dante's amber eyes

narrowed. "An armed Spanish galleon three times the size of the *Iron Rose* and you simply sallied forth and boarded her?"

"Hell no, Cap'n Beau," came an anonymous voice from somewhere in the crowd. "We peppered her good, first. Swept the decks clear o' all them tin-breasted wogs an' grappled to her tighter 'n a whore's fist. Then the cap'n tells us 'up an' over' and up we goes an' over to the last man. We'd do it again, too, if'n she asked us."

A murmur of general assent rippled across the deck, but it only whitened the lines around Isabeau's mouth. She was certainly no stranger to the risks of engaging any ship in battle—the empty sleeve that hung at her side was proof of that. She also knew her daughter all too well and could be fairly certain that whatever account Juliet or any of her loyal crew gave of the action, it would not be one-tenth as terrifying and perilous as the reality had been.

Simon Dante was also searching the faces of the crew, stalling here and there when one of them was too slow to erase a cocky grin. He tipped his head and peered up at the masts, noting the fresh timbers that braced the broken foremast, the newly spliced lines of rigging, the repaired sheets of sail.

"We were also caught in a storm yesterday," Juliet added. "We took some small damage there, too."

The crystalline blue eyes settled upon his daughter.

"You were aware, were you not," he said slowly, "of the identity of the *Santo Domingo* before you decided to interfere? You knew her complements and firepower? You knew that no one in full possession of their wits would consider challenging her on their own, regardless of how distracted the galleon was with a kill."

Juliet's reply was as calm as the steadiness of her gaze. "I took offense that the *Argus* had surrendered yet the Spaniard did not withdraw her guns. She was, in fact, preparing to hull the Englishman, to sink her and leave no witnesses behind."

"And because of this indignation, you threw yourself, your crew, and your ship in the path of completely unwarranted peril?"

"No. I tried to imagine what you would have done in a similar situation."

Simon Dante narrowed his eyes. A full count of ten passed before he responded, "Yes, but I am generally thought to be a madman and I had higher hopes for my children."

"If that was the case, my love," Isabeau muttered under her breath, "you need only look at Jonas and Gabriel to know how miserably you failed before Juliet ever set foot on a deck."

The black brows crushed together and the great pirate lord glared down at his wife. The silence stretched for another fistful of heartbeats before the sound of a chuckle began to rumble up his throat. It turned into full-bore laughter as he threw his head back and half cursed, half praised his fortune in finding himself with such a family as this.

His broad shoulders were still shaking as he plucked Juliet's newly reseated hat off her head again and tossed it in the air, a signal for the pent-up cheering in a hundred throats to erupt and erupt again until the ship was engulfed in a clamorous roar. Meanwhile Juliet was swept into the circle of her father's arms, lifted, and spun until she was dizzy and laughing too hard herself to even beg to be set down. It was the cue for two hefty seamen to roll a big barrel of rum onto the deck, to knock out the bung and fill the eager cups and pannikins that were shoved under the golden stream.

Elbowed to the side and all but forgotten in the celebrations, Varian St. Clare stood with Beacom by the rail.

"What do you think of this then, Beacom? I expect the word *unique* will find its definition strained to the bounds by all the members of the Dante family."

"I think they are *all* quite mad, your grace. Quite unequivocally mad and the sooner we are free of these

wretched corsairs, the safer our throats will be at
night."

"If you intend to insult us, sir, you might at least
use the correct term."

Every last drop of blood drained from Beacom's
face as he slowly swiveled his head and saw Simon
Dante standing beside him.

"Corsairs are Saracens and ply their trade in the
Mediterranean," explained the Pirate Wolf casually.
"Here in the Caribbee, you might find boucan-eaters
and pirates, filibusters and freebooters, but never the
other. We brethren are very territorial, you know."

Beacom's mouth trembled, then began to flap like
a beached fish. No sounds came from his throat and
after a moment, his eyes rolled to the back of his head
and he slowly crumpled into a heap on the deck.

Dante looked down, then pursed his lips. "Does he
do that often?"

"Fairly regularly," Varian sighed.

"And he belongs to you?"

"He is my manservant, yes."

Up to that moment, Varian had been content to
merely observe and study his quarry. To be sure, the
man known as the *Pirata Lobo* was awe-inspiring in
a ruthless, wolflike way, boasting the powerfully muscled arms and shoulders of a man half his age. It was
also plain to see where Juliet Dante had inherited her
ability to cut a man to the bone with a single glance,
for Simon Dante's eyes were so penetrating they felt
like needles stabbing all the way to the back of the
skull.

Hair as black as ink showed but a few silvery
threads. It hung well below his shoulders in gleaming
waves, with a dozen tiny braids woven at the temples
to hold it back from his forehead. The wink of a thick
gold loop in his ear did nothing to lessen the impression that he was a man poised on the very fine line
that stretched between privateer and pirate. His wife
presented no less a striking figure with her dark au-

burn hair and tigress eyes. The fact that she was missing an arm had come as somewhat of a surprise to Varian, but it was plain to see she had not allowed the loss to cripple her. Such an injury suffered by a member of the English nobility—and by virtue of her marriage to Simon Dante, Isabeau was a comtesse—would have meant permanent exile behind closed doors.

One of Simon Dante's black eyebrows assumed a decided upward slant. "My daughter tells me you are an envoy from the king. How is the sanctimonious Scottish bastard? Juliet mentioned he sent a crate of Bibles in the hopes of saving our souls, but they were lost with your ship."

Varian shot a glance in Juliet's direction. She was standing a few feet away, her mouth trembling with amusement. Seeing the two of them together, father and daughter, Varian could see that she had inherited more than just the unusual silvery blue color of his eyes.

"His Majesty sends his compliments."

"I am sure he does."

The duke waited, but since it appeared no one else was going to step forth and make introductions, he did so himself. "Varian St. Clare, your servant, sir."

He was midway through a courteous bow when Juliet hooked her arm around her father's elbow.

"He is being modest, Father," she said. "He is a duke. A genuine member of the House of Lords—unless my education was lacking—sent by the king to stamp his noble foot and demand you cease molesting the Spanish trade routes."

Simon offered up a crooked grin. "I suppose we should not be too surprised. It has been what, four? five? months since the last envoy sought to convert us from our corrupt ways?" He paused and took note of the bruises on Varian's face, the row of knotted threads that followed his hairline. "I trust you've not been overly harsh on the poor fellow."

"Faith, no, Father. I have been the soul of hospitality. I have fed him and clothed him, even invited him to share my bed."

Dante's gaze flicked between the two of them and Varian gasped with shock. "I assure you, Comte, nothing improper occurred at any time! It was simply—"

The Pirate Wolf held up his hand. "Please. I have not been addressed as the Comte de Tourville for a good many years. And if you had attempted something improper, I expect it would be more than your head she would have cracked open. Ahh, here is young Johnny Boy with refills. You will join me in a cup of rum to toast the safe return of our *Iron Rose*?"

Without waiting for an answer, Simon Dante extended his cup. Johnny Boy scooped a wooden ladle into the bucket he was carrying and filled it, then splashed some in an extra cup which he offered to Varian. Simon touched his cup to his daughter's, then waited expectantly for the Englishman to do likewise.

Varian obliged with a solemn "To the unquestionable valor of the *Iron Rose*, to the courage of her captain and crew."

"Well said." Dante nodded with approval and emptied his cup.

"As for what brings me here, Captain Dante—"

The Pirate Wolf held up his hand a second time. "Any business you have that may or may not interest me can be discussed at a more appropriate time."

"Captain, it is both pressing and urgent. Any further delays could result in serious consequences to you and your brethren here in the Caribbean."

Dante glanced at Juliet, who only shrugged. "He has not deigned to tell me."

"Then the matter cannot be as urgent and pressing as you imply."

"His Majesty and the first minister were quite insistent that I convey his edict at the first opportunity."

"An edict, is it?" He glanced down as if to see if Varian was, indeed, stamping his foot. "You have kept the faith this long, St. Clare, another day or two will hardly affect the way the sun rises and sets. Further-more, you are in another hemisphere, sir, where things move a good deal slower than they do between chambers at Whitehall. Take your ease. Enjoy our beautiful tropical air. As my daughter's guest, you are welcome to come ashore under her protection, but do not bandy the king's name around and expect the walls to quiver in awe. We are a long way from court, and the whims of a lisping peace-monger carry little weight here." He set his cup aside and draped an arm around Juliet's waist. "Now then, daughter, you doubtless have stories to tell and a fair amount of bragging to set the ears of your brothers ringing. Shall we save them until we are ashore where we can toast each one without fear of drowning on the way to our beds? Oh, and before I forget . . . Mr. Kelly!"

The carpenter turned too quickly to answer the summons and banged his head on the lower edge of a spar. His eyes crossed a moment before he was able to shake them clear. "Aye, Cap'n?"

"You're not forgetting the reason the *Iron Rose* was sent out on sea trials in the first place?"

Nog scratched the stubble on his chin a moment before the recollection sparked in his eyes. "No, sar! Worked a charm, it did. We tried her at six, eight, and twelve knots and she turned without spillin' the soup out o' the pot. Rode the storm like a damned princess, too."

Dante nodded and elaborated for Varian's sake. "Now *that* is urgent and pressing business. A new rudder design that increases speed, improves steerage in bad weather, and provides greater stability in a turn. How soon can you rig the other ships, Nog?"

The carpenter tugged his forelock. "Cap'n Juliet has me strippin' down the Spaniard, but once she's done . . . it'll take a fortnight at least to do all three ships . . . unless ye want 'em belly up at the same time. Then it could be done in a week or less."

"I'll give it some thought. In the meantime"—he gave Juliet's shoulder a squeeze—"it looks like we'll have something else to celebrate tonight. You've done well. Next thing we know, you will be designing entire ships and giving Mr. Pitt a reason to look over his shoulder."

"Mr. Pitt did not come aboard?" she asked, suddenly noting the lack.

"He was detained elsewhere, I'm afraid. Another boy, delivered yesterday."

Juliet's face lit up with a wide smile. "Faith, but is that eight or nine?"

"Nine boys, four girls. I will have to start sending him out to sea more often. He obviously has too much time on his hands. But enough of this. Tonight, we celebrate the capture of the biggest prize"—he raised his voice so that it boomed from stem to stern— "taken by the boldest crew in the Caribbee!"

The ship's company broke out in another raucous chorus of cheers and stomping feet. It was high praise indeed coming from the Pirate Wolf, and many shed unabashed tears of pride. The cheering followed Simon Dante to the gangway, where he was met by Isabeau, Gabriel, and the sopping wet Jonas. After cautioning Juliet good-naturedly not to linger on board too long, the four descended to a waiting long-boat and were rowed back to shore to prepare the house for a great feast.

As the oars dipped into the water and carried them farther from the *Iron Rose*, Isabeau leaned into her husband's shoulder and released a tremulous sigh.

"Dear God, Simon. What have we done, you and I?"

He could barely hear her whisper above the rush of the water moving beneath the keel.

"What do you mean, love?"

"We both encouraged her to take this path, though I admit the fault lies more with me than you. You wanted to send her to France for her schooling, for a chance to become a proper lady. I was the one who urged you to let her choose for herself."

Dante pressed his lips into the crush of his wife's hair. "Next to you, my lovely *cygne noir*, Juliet is the most proper lady I know. She has heart, she has courage, she has honor . . . and she has fear. More fear than these two rapscallions, I warrant," he added, tilting his head in the direction of their two sons sitting in the bow of the longboat. "And that is what will keep her safe."

"A good man wouldn't hurt either," Gabriel said over his shoulder. "If one could be found addled enough to take her."

"Eh?" Jonas swiveled around. "What are you talking about?"

"The size of your brother's ears," Isabeau snapped. "And unless he wants them soundly boxed, he'll keep them pointed straight ahead."

Chapter Ten

Once again, Varian found himself at odds. Beacom recovered enough to dust himself off and retire below to fetch the small chest Johnny Boy had appropriated for their use. There was not much in it: a spare shirt and stockings, some linens, and a horsehair brush, but it gave the valet something familiar to do to keep his mind off slashed throats and boiled entrails.

As for Varian, he was not accustomed to being dismissed out of hand nor being set aside like an afterthought, and it angered him enough that he followed Juliet to her cabin after the revelry had come to a happy end on deck.

He paused only fractionally, his hand on the latch, before his fingers curled into a grudging fist and he knocked on the door.

"Come."

She was at her desk gathering up the ledgers, maps, manifests and other assorted documents they had collected from the *Santo Domingo* and the *Argus*. She had removed her hat, and the lantern light was pouring over her shoulders, gilding the dark waves of her hair with streaks of red and gold fire.

When Varian entered, she glanced up and sighed.

"You have the look of a grievance about you, my lord. Be warned, my patience is strained and I have my pistols close at hand."

He clasped his hands behind his back. "The correct

form of address, which you have thus far chosen to ignore, is in fact 'your grace.' "

She finished shuffling a handful of papers and straightened. "I am sure you have not come here, all puffed up like a quail, to instruct me in proper manners."

"I fear you are already well beyond salvation in that respect, Captain. I have come to inquire after the meaning of your father's words: that I am welcome to come ashore *under your protection*."

"It seems clear enough to me, *my lord*," she said, deliberately misusing the address again. "In essence, you were captured along with the galleon, which makes you part of the spoils, if you will. It follows then, by the purest definition of the articles of privateering, that you have become my property and therefore my responsibility. Trust me when I say I am no more pleased than you with the designation, but there you have it. Even pirates have rules of order." After holding his gaze a moment longer, she bowed to her task again. "On the other hand, you should be thankful Father did place you under my protection; otherwise my brother Jonas might have shot you out of hand."

Varian's mind was still stumbling over the word *property*. "Your brother? What has he to do with any of this?"

"He hates the Spaniards even more than my father, though one would be hard-pressed to find the grain of sand that weighs the balance in his favor. And if you have come here to deliver more of the king's petulant demands that we uphold the peace . . . well . . ."

She glanced up as Johnny Boy came stumping through the open doorway to tell her the *Santo Domingo* had been towed into the harbor.

"Yes, all right. Thank you. Here, you can take these topside for me—" She stuffed the last wad of documents into a bulging canvas sack and handed them to the boy. "Have a longboat made ready. We will be going ashore as soon as Mr. Crisp gives a signal."

"Aye, Cap'n."

"Hold up there a moment," she called, stopping him at the door. "What did you do to your leg?"

Johnny Boy craned his head around to look at the dark circle of blood that stained his breeches above the cup of the carved peg. " 'T'ain't nothin', Cap'n. I backed into a gun carriage and scraped it on a bit of wood."

"Make sure you clean it well before you go ashore. I'll not be pleased if we have to trim another inch off the stump because you were careless."

"Aye, Cap'n." The boy grinned. "I'll scrub it till it squeaks an' piss on it twice a day."

When he was gone, Juliet noted the look on Varian's face.

" 'Tis the best way to clean a wound, sir, and prevent corruption." Her gaze danced across his cheek a moment, but instead of compounding his shock by confirming the nature of the stinging tincture she had dabbed over his wound, she settled her cavalier's hat on her head and snatched her gloves off the desk. "Shall we go topside, my lord? I've a few more details to attend before we disembark."

Frustrated by the fact that he had come in search of answers only to be left with more questions, he reached out and caught her arm as she started to walk past. Exactly what he meant or wanted to say was cut short when she glared at his hand, then glared up at his face. He released his grip at once, but the daggers were already in her eyes, the steel in her voice. "I thought you said you learned from your mistakes?"

"I am trying desperately to do so, believe me. Unfortunately the rules seem to change every time I turn around."

"You will just have to turn a little faster then, will you not?"

"Believe me, I am spinning now, madam," he mut-

tered, but she was out the door and halfway up the
steps to the quarterdeck.

An hour later, Juliet was finally ready to go ashore.
The *Santo Domingo* was securely anchored fifty yards
astern and had become a magnet for swarms of jolly-
boats. It was long past full dark and lanterns had been
hung from her lines and rigging, flooding the decks
bright as day. Men were already banging together
winches that would be used in the morning to off-load
her cargo of treasure.

Juliet was heading toward the gangway when she
noticed how closely the Duke of Harrow was watching
the proceedings on board the *Santo Domingo*. He was
squinting to see through the glare, and when Juliet
searched the far deck to see what had piqued his interest, she saw the English lieutenant, Beck, moving
freely among the crewmen on board, even supervising
the men as they lowered huge nets into the belly of
the galleon.

"If you want to come ashore, my lord," Juliet said,
drawing Varian's attention away from the *Santo Domingo*, "we are leaving now. But take fair notice that
if you make a nuisance of yourself, you will be carried
back here like a sack of grain."

Apart from a small muscle that quickened in Varian's cheek, he remained silent.

By contrast, Beacom took one look over the open
rail at the gangway and blanched. It was a steep descent down the outer skin of the hull with nothing to
cling to but the narrow rungs that were set into the
timbers. The sky was black overhead, the water an
eerie confusion of shadows and shapes below. The
lights had attracted schools of fish, some who swam
near the surface and darted about like iridescent
streaks. Some of the darker shadows on the bottom
moved independent of the longboats above, huge
round, flat creatures with long whiplike tails snaking
out behind.

"Dear me, your grace." Beacom melted back from the rail. "I think I should prefer to wait for a chair."

Varian watched Juliet flick the wing of her cape over her shoulder and disappear below the level of the deck. "I doubt there are more than two ways of disembarking, Beacom," he said dryly. "Her brother took the one earlier today, and you see before you the other."

"Ho there!" Juliet shouted from below. "We haven't all night. If you fall, just give the barracuda a few sharp kicks and they get out of your way."

Beacom whimpered and Varian sighed. "Perhaps you would prefer to remain on board? I'm sure the ship's company will find ways to amuse you."

The valet's pale hand fluttered up to clutch his throat. "I'll not abandon you now, your grace. Lead on."

"Follow close behind me. I'll guide your feet and catch you up if you put one wrong."

Beacom gave a jerky nod and waited until Varian was three steps down before he stretched a foot gingerly over the side. Terror more than aptitude kept him moving down the ladder, and he did not stop or open his eyes until he felt a hand clamp around his ankle and guide it onto the rocking longboat.

As soon as Beacom and Varian were settled, one of the oarsmen used his paddle to push away from the side of the *Iron Rose*. It presented an odd perspective, gazing up from the water, and Varian felt dwarfed by the enormous bulk of timber, the towering masts that rose high into the night sky. He could see gouges in the wood, scars from past conflicts. He also counted the gunports and realized what a truly powerful, deadly vessel he had been aboard.

When they pulled around the bow, his attention was caught by the carved figurehead. It was a woman, naked but for a ripple of linen lying on a diagonal across her groin. Her hands were reaching forward as if to support the thick arm of the bowsprit; her legs were straight and shapely, the feet pointed down like those of a dancer.

They reached the towering hull of the *Santo Domingo* and waited but a moment for Nathan Crisp and Lieutenant Jonathan Beck to clamber down the side. The two men were sharing a laugh over something the crusty old sea dog had said, but when Beck saw Varian sitting in the longboat, he sobered at once and extended a polite bow.

"Your grace. I had heard you were recovered from your wounds and was pleased to learn they were not fatal."

"No more so than I, Lieutenant. We have not had an opportunity to speak since the incident, but please accept my condolences over the loss of your ship and the brave men in your crew."

"Thank you, sir. Captain Macleod was a good man, a fine sailor, and will be sorely missed."

"He trained his men well, at any rate," Crisp announced for Juliet's benefit. "Loftus tells me if it weren't for the crew of the *Argus* manning the lines, she would have floundered in the storm and been driven out into the Atlantic. As for the lieutenant here, it's a shame he hasn't a larcenous nature. I'd put him at the helm any day. He maneuvered that bitch through the reef like he'd done it a hundred times."

"I was raised in Cornwall, sir, where the currents and breakers have cracked the spines of many a fine ship."

"Take the compliment in the spirit it was given, Mr. Beck," said Juliet. "Mr. Crisp hoards them like a spinster does her kisses."

The oarsmen took up the stroke again and within minutes they had cut across the bay and were approaching the lights along shore. Higher up on the slope, the huge white house glittered like a cluster of jewels. When the longboat bumped into the dock, Juliet and Crisp leaped out first and while the others disembarked, they stood together talking in low voices.

Varian, after the first few steps on solid ground, was surprised to discover he was as queasy and unsteady

in the knees as he had been during his first days at
sea. To his quiet disgust, he recalled he had spent
some of that time with his head bowed over a slops
pail and it was no comfort to know he was susceptible
to the same weakness going from the sea to land.

A carriage was waiting to take them up to the big
house. It rattled like the bones of a skeleton over the
rough road, and Varian's teeth nearly snapped off at
the gums with the effort it took to bear the renewed
hammering in his head as well as his hip and shoulder.
By the time they rolled to a halt, he was ready to
throw his body out the door and hug the closest tree.

"I would like a moment alone to speak to the duke,"
Juliet said, waving for the others to step down. "Take
these inside for me," she said and handed Crisp the sack
of charts and manifests that had ridden beside her on
the seat. "Have someone show the lieutenant and Mr.
Beacom to rooms with clean sheets and hot baths."

The carriage had stopped in front of the big house.
Lamps hung from every pillar and post along the
hundred-foot length of the wide veranda; every window on both stories blazed. There was only one corner
of the coach where the shadows had not been chased
away and while Juliet Dante had the advantage of
being able to see every crease on Varian's face, every
hair on his head, she remained for the most part in
darkness save for the ruff of white lace at her throat.

The irony of her wearing lace and velvet was not
lost on him. At the same time, he had to admit the
black and crimson suited her nature, worn not out of
any need to comply with fashion, but simply because
it reflected her power, her confidence, her lethal grace.

She sat with her hands tapping lightly together on
her lap for a few moments, then, seeking some way
to occupy them, began stripping off her leather gloves,
one finger at a time.

"I was burned once," she said as a casual matter of
fact. "My shirt caught fire and I lost a few layers of
skin before the men could douse me. Since then, I've
had cuts and musket holes that have not hurt half so

much. I admire the lieutenant's fortitude; he must have suffered immeasurably. Do you know how it happened?"

"I am afraid I was not made privy to the information."

"You were at sea with him for six weeks and never thought to ask?"

"One simply does not ask a man outright how he burned his face."

"One doesn't? Plague take my manners then, because I did. It seems he was betrothed and—much like yourself—eagerly returning home to marry his sweetheart when his ship encountered a Dutchman off the Canaries. Shots were exchanged and one of the sails came down in flames. He had powder on his cheek from having discharged his musket several times and the fire caught his shirt, his hair, his face. When he arrived back in England, his sweetheart took one look at him and screamed in horror. He returned immediately to the navy, where he knew life was more tolerant away from the vulgar niceties of a well-bred society."

"I will own that there are those who judge their fellow man more harshly than others, but to say that all of English society as a whole is vulgar—"

"Am I so wrong? Do you really believe my mother would be well received at court? Would she be invited to dance a galliard, to play a game of bowls on the green? Would she find no lack of partners willing to sit next to her at a dinner party when she uses her stump to hold the meat for cutting?"

He searched the shadows. "Are you deliberately trying to shock me, Captain, or are you simply trying to get me to admit that we are all conceited boors? If so, then yes, I will admit it . . . if you will admit that you hold a similar degree of conceit—it is merely seen from the opposite side of the mirror. You wear your scars and ferocious nature proudly, and you scorn any man with uncalloused hands and rosettes in his shoes. As you say, it is not likely that the one-armed wife of

a pirate lord would be made lady-in-waiting to the
queen, yet how likely would it be for men like Beacom
and myself to be treated as equals at your dining
table? The very first time we spoke, you insisted I
address you as 'captain,' yet you mock my own rank
at every turn. You cannot have it both ways, Juliet.
You cannot cry foul when you are guilty of the
same crimes."

She was so still and so quiet he could almost hear
her lashes blinking together. It was the first time he
had used her proper name and he suspected it did not
sit well.

"I did not hold you back to receive a lecture on
social conceits, *your grace*. I thought only to save you
from further embarrassment by advising you, in all
good faith, against going inside the house and spouting
your directives and demands from the king. They will
not be happily met."

"You have yet to tell me why."

She responded with a shallow puff of disdain and
he spread his hands to show he had won his point.
"You chastise me for not asking the lieutenant a simple question, yet when I attempt to do the same with
you, you stab me with a blade."

"I have stabbed you with nothing, sir."

"You think not? If your eyes were weapons, madam,
I would have been bloodied from head to toe a dozen
times over."

She drummed her fingers again. She turned her
head when she heard footsteps outside on the crushed
stones, but her glare sent whoever it was into a
hasty retreat.

Her fingers stopped. Her hands curled around her
gloves, and she turned to look at him again.

"Our grandfather, Jonas Spence, was killed on
board the *Black Swan*, in the same battle that cost my
mother her arm. After fifty years at sea, he had few
of the original appendages he was born with. He had
but one leg, one arm, his body was a map of scars
and deformations that would have made Lieutenant

Beck seem positively handsome by comparison, yet he never once chose to remain behind when there were adventures to be had. He never balked from a fight, never ran from an enemy, never took a half measure when the whole was required. My brother Jonas was always by his side, mimicking his great lusty laugh, catching him when he tipped over from too much rum." She stopped, thinking perhaps she had said too much already, and finished with an edge of impatience in her voice. "Had you seen the look on my brother's face when he carried Grandfather's body off the ship, you would not have to ask why he would never abide by any edict for peace with the Spanish. Neither would my father, or my mother. Or me, for that matter."

He shook his head. "Would that not make you hunger for peace even more?"

"Peace, aye. Capitulation . . . never."

"No one is asking you to capitulate."

"Are they not? The Spaniards will never honor a peace treaty that allows foreign ships to sail these waters. They have too much at stake. They have an entire New World at their command, for heaven's sake, and as long as they hold it, they maintain their supremacy on the sea. While the Virgin was on the throne, Father used to receive official missives demanding he return to England for an audience with his sovereign, insisting he cease his attacks on Spanish shipping, scolding him, threatening him with all manner of repercussions if he disobeyed. Yet there were other communications, delivered secretly and often encoded so that they made sense to Father's eyes only. They praised him for his successes, even encouraged him to increase his attacks, to do everything in his power to disrupt the trade routes and strike the Spaniards where it hurt most: in their treasury. The old queen understood that if you stopped the flow of gold and silver from the Main, the Spanish king would have no money to build ships, to pay his armies, to garrison ports a thousand miles away from Seville. There were dozens of privateers in these waters, most of whom received the same veiled winks from Elizabeth as my father, and their efforts had results. While Spain's coffers emptied, England's filled with the one-tenth share of the treasure taken from every captured ship. A good part of England's navy was built with the ill-gotten gains of Elizabeth's sea hawks.

"But then she died and James Stuart took the throne. He had no knowledge of the queen's private dealings with men half a world away, or if he did he chose to ignore it. He had his navy, his treasure chest was full, and it was time to woo the Spanish monarch with his good intentions and order men like Father to haul in their guns. He had no control over the Dutch or the Portuguese, of course, but most of the English privateers drew back rather than risk being branded as pirates. They were wealthy, they had lived their adventures. A good many of them returned to England as ordered and retired to their country estates to grow fat and raise sheep."

"But your father refused."

She sighed. "He refused to walk away from everything he had fought so hard to win. This is our home now. Are we not supposed to defend it?"

"Defend it, yes, but—"

"Have you heard the phrase 'no peace beyond the line'?"

"You refer to the imaginary line drawn by Pope Alexander VI that runs down the middle of the Atlantic and divides the world's territories between Spain and Portugal?"

Juliet nodded. "It was drawn the year after Columbus discovered the New World, at a time when England barely knew how to navigate across the Channel, yet these are the boundaries Spain insists we must all uphold. It is the treaty Spain uses to defend their actions each time they attack and destroy one of our ships, regardless if that ship is engaged in lawful trade or simple exploration."

"The kings of England, France, and the Netherlands are trying to change that, as is Philip III of Spain,"

Varian said. "But the negotiations for peace and open trade will not, cannot be successful unless the guns on both sides are silent."

"I am surprised you can even say those words with any measure of conviction after what happened to the *Argus*. To be sure, Father will never acknowledge them or the notion of peace with Spain."

He leaned forward, the leather on the seat creaking softly as he did so. "I am more than just a little aware that I am well out of my depths here, Juliet. I admit freely that I do not understand your way of life, that I would likely be dead within a week if you were to set me adrift on an island where you, under similar conditions, could probably survive for a year. By the same token, I am a soldier—a damned good one—and I resent the implication that I would rather fight with words than deeds. Put me on a battlefield with artillery and cavalry, and I'll fight your battles and I'll win your wars. But set those battles at sea and frankly . . . it changes all the rules I know, all the certainties I have come to expect. There is no room for error. You attempt to surrender honorably and your enemy sinks you anyway. You lose a battle and you do not live to fight another day—you drown. In that respect alone, I cannot even begin to comprehend the strength and courage it takes to sail out of this harbor and know that there are bigger ships with bigger guns waiting just over the horizon to smash you to bits. Nor can I conceive of any reason why you would not support the king's efforts to negotiate a peace." He paused and sat back again. "As I said, I am trying to understand, but you make it difficult, to say the least."

A lamp outside the window cast a ring of distilled light on the side of the carriage, swaying as the branch it hung on was moved by the breeze. The light touched her eyes, then receded, touched again and held until she turned her face away.

"In truth, there are times I don't understand it myself," she admitted finally. "But then I look at my mother's empty sleeve and the empty seat at the dinner table where my grandfather used to sit, and I don't have to think about it. That is all the justification I need."

Varian studied her in silence, his hands clasped together, his forefingers steepled under his chin.

"So now you have your explanation," she said. "You can see why you have been sent on a fool's errand."

"Would it make a difference if I said the king and his ministers intend to rescind all letters of marque, and that to refuse to obey the king's orders will result in charges of piracy and treason being levied against your entire family and all those who sail on account with you? It would mean that your father would be hung like a common thief if he was caught."

Juliet smiled. "They would have to catch him first, would they not?"

"Might I remind you," he said softly, "that everyone is fallible?"

"And might I remind *you* that you are in no position to issue threats or point out fallibilities. We could as easily have marooned you with the Spaniards."

"Yet you took me on board, you kept me"—his chin came slowly off his fingers—"as a prisoner? Or as a hostage?"

She shrugged. "Either way, *your grace*, you may consider whatever business you have brought from the king to have been lost at the bottom of the sea with the *Argus*."

She raised a hand and passed a signal out the carriage window. Varian heard footsteps on the stone again, and a moment later, two burly men were standing at the door.

"I would not advise you to do anything foolish. You are here under my protection and as such you will be treated with any respect you are due. But you are on an island, there is absolutely no escape, and make no mistake, these men will kill you at the snap of a finger."

The door opened.

Juliet disembarked first and, after murmuring orders to the two men, strode into the house without a backward glance.

Chapter Eleven

*J*uliet walked unaccompanied into the house, her sword slapping the heel of her boot with each angry step. The family was gathered in the great room; she could hear them before she could see them, and she forced herself to slow down, to relax her face into a more pleasant expression. This was, after all, a night for celebrations. She had almost forgotten all about the damned rudder design, something she and Nog had been tinkering with for some months, but its success was indisputable. The increased speed and maneuverability had allowed her to cut in much closer and faster to the *Santo Domingo*, bringing the *Iron Rose* under the arc of the Spaniard's heavy guns before they could be put to good use.

Juliet arrived at the great room and stood on the threshold a moment while the warm familiarity of one world replaced the salty exhilaration of another. The musky scent of leather books and a crackling fire reminded her of the hours spent poring over lessons, learning how to chart the sea and stars, how to calculate wind speed and currents, how to mix and measure a prime charge of gunpowder.

At ten years of age, her classroom learning had been supplemented with time served on board the *Avenger*, where she had learned how to translate the practical knowledge found in textbooks into common good sense. When she turned sixteen, she could plot a course and navigate a ship from point to point within

a few leagues of error. When she was eighteen, she
had proved her mettle during battle by stepping over
a crush of dead bodies to take command of one of
the heavy thirty-two-pounders.

Two years later, she stood at the helm of her own
ship, the *Iron Rose*.

Jonas had served his apprenticeship on the *Black
Swan*. While he had mostly learned to control his violent urges under their mother's watchful eye, he was
too much like his grandfather and given to magnificent
rages passed down through the Spence bloodline. Gabriel, on the other hand, had benefited from the tute-
lage of Geoffrey Pitt and therefore had come to
appreciate the lethal difference a rational, clear-
thinking head could make.

Her father stood with Pitt by the unlit fire in the
hearth, the two men speculating, no doubt, on the stir
it would cause up and down the Spanish Main when
it became known a Dante had captured one of Spain's
most celebrated warships.

Isabeau, Gabriel, and Pitt's wife, Christiana, sat together by the open french doors that led to the veranda. In all her life, Juliet could have counted on the
fingers of one hand the number of times her mother
had voluntarily shed her breeches and doublet for the
more feminine trappings of a skirt and bodice. The
surprise of seeing her dressed tonight in a gown of
pale blue silk was surpassed only by the pleasure of
seeing her father in full court regalia, complete with
the decorative, gold-embossed baldric and the sword
Gloriana had presented him following the demise of
the Spanish Armada.

Gabriel was his usual cool and fashionable self, his
hair curling in glossy waves over his collar, his long
legs stretched out and crossed at the ankles. Jonas had
changed into dry clothes, but since his wardrobe rarely
varied from brown breeches, leather doublet, and bil-
lowing white camlet shirt, there was little difference
in his appearance.

The last familiar face able to put a faint smile on

Juliet's face was Lucifer, who after all these years, had still not acquired a liking for more clothes than he could remove with a flick of the wrist. He stood behind Simon Dante like a glowering watchdog, black as sin, dressed in half breeches and a striped doublet. He had been guarding the Pirate Wolf's back for three decades and it was his bald head that turned now, his gaze drawn to where Juliet stood unobserved in the doorway.

Though his face seemed not to have aged in all the years she had known him, the patterns and whorls of dotted tattoos had grown and spread. From the earliest markings that had spiralled across his cheeks, the inkings had spread down his throat and across the gleaming black marble of his chest and shoulders. There were even characters etched on the pendulous bulk of his sex—a testament to his threshold for pain— a cobra's head whose body swelled and stretched into layers of gleaming scales when roused.

Lucifer's lips parted around a murmured word to his captain before widening into an enormous grin. It was a sight that normally sent grown men cringing, for his huge white teeth had been filed into wickedly sharp points. When she was a child, Jonas had told her he had sharpened them for tearing his enemies apart and eating their entrails. The truth was somewhat less dramatic, for the filings were the mark of a great warrior in the village where he had been born.

Some of that warrior-like bloodlust came through in the snarl that brought him striding to the doorway. There, he did something she had only seen him do on very rare occasions: he offered a deep and formal bow to salute the great victory of the *Iron Rose* and acknowledge the courage of her captain.

"You have done us proud, Little Jolly," he said, addressing her by the nickname he had used since she was a child. "You have learned well on the heels of your brothers. So well they sulk and scowl now like mewling chicks."

"We are not scowling," Gabriel protested. "In fact,

I stand in awe of our little sister," he added, rising to his feet, "and have no doubt that in time, she will bring us back the entire Spanish fleet. By hell's burning flames, we could probably send her to Spain and she would bring back Felipe himself, still seated on his throne."

Geoffrey Pitt came forward and took up her hand, bestowing a gallant kiss. "Ignore the great buffoon. He is as jealous . . . and as proud . . . as the rest of us. Fifty-two guns, by God, and you took her with barely a scratch. The cannon alone are worth twice their weight in silver bars, for the Spanish are particular about the quality of brass they use in the castings."

"I understand you deserve congratulations as well. Another boy, is it? You'll have enough soon to fill the crew of your new ship."

Over his blushes, she gave him an enormous hug and kiss, then walked over to Christiana. She was petite and dark haired, possessing the face of a cherub and the body of a waif despite giving birth to thirteen babes.

Juliet reached into her doublet and drew out a small, satin-wrapped packet that contained a large square-cut emerald Nathan had found on the *Santo Domingo*.

"For the new baby," she said, kissing her aunt on both cheeks. "Have you named him yet?"

Christiana laughed and shook her head. "Alas, no. We have run out of fathers, grandfathers, uncles, and cousins to honor, so now we must just wait and see which name suits him."

Juliet smiled, but she was distracted by the fact that they were the only two speaking. Everyone's eyes were on her, some more expectantly than others, all of them tense with curiosity.

A further glance noted that the sack Crisp had deposited inside the doorway had not been opened yet.

"You show amazing restraint, brothers dear," she murmured, then added casually, "Silver. There are more than fifty crates of bullion in her hold, along with an equal number packed with gold, pearls, spices, even a few hundredweight of copper plating. I've barely scanned the manifests myself, but by all means, help yourself."

Jonas and Gabriel reached the sack in two strides. They had the neck open and the contents spilled on the desk before their father's laughter had stopped echoing around the room.

The next hour was spent poring over the cargo manifest, toasting each new and incredible discovery—some Juliet was not even aware of—and making crude calculations as to the value of the prize. An accurate tally would be impossible until each crate was unloaded, the contents weighed and assayed, but as an extremely conservative estimate, Geoffrey Pitt put the worth at well over two hundred thousand English pounds, a staggering sum when held against the normal cargo of a treasure galleon, which averaged between thirty and fifty thousand.

There was silence again, as Pitt redid his sums, but even if he was generous by half, which was not likely, it was easily the richest single prize taken since Drake had raided the treasure train at Nombre de Dios.

It was also the practical side of Pitt that prompted him to refuse another refill of wine and exchange a frown with Simon Dante. "Why would a warship be carrying so much?"

"And of such variety," Juliet added, thankful she was not the only one who could see past the dazzle of gold to question the nature of the treasure itself. "The gold bars were minted at Barranquilla, the silver at Vera Cruz, the emeralds from Margarita, and some of the spices are clearly off the Manila galleons. It's almost as if she made a circuit of the Main and took on all the extra cargo the other ships could not hold."

"What do we know about the captain . . . Aquayo, was it?" Simon asked.

Pitt searched a memory filled with countless volumes of facts and figures. "Diego Flores Aquayo. He comes from Seville. His uncle was the Duke of

Medina-Sidonia, *capitán-general* of *la Invencible* Armada. A galleon of the *Domingo*'s size and worth would have been a plum appointment from the king, but I agree he wouldn't have taken on so much cargo unless he was planning to return to Spain. I am somewhat surprised, however, that he would have risked it by attacking an English merchant ship, especially one that was not looking for a confrontation."

"I suspect the attack was more the initiative of his first officer, the *capitán del navío*," Juliet said. "He is definitely well seasoned. His name is Recalde," she added, looking at Pitt. "Don Cristóbal Recalde."

"The garrison commander at Nombre de Dios?"

Juliet nodded. "I didn't realize it at the time, unfortunately, for we were a little busy trying to manage three hundred prisoners, but he seemed to know me—or at least *of* me. He called me *la Rosa de Hierro* and said I was a bitch, just like my mother. I took it as a compliment," she said, smiling at Isabeau.

Isabeau frowned. "You said the *Argus* had already surrendered, yet this Capitán Recalde was continuing to hull her?"

Juliet nodded again. "We didn't see the opening salvos—there was a thick haze that morning and a squall had just passed by, but the English lieutenant said that the galleon had turned deliberately off her course to give chase. By the time we closed, the *Argus* was in shambles, her crew was screaming to surrender, and the Spaniard had arquebusiers in the tops firing down on them like ducks in a pond. They were not intending to take any prisoners, and we found incendiary loads in some of the cannon, suggesting they were going to burn anything left afloat. It was almost as if . . ."

"Yes? As if what?"

Juliet shrugged and took a sip of wine. "As if they wanted no witnesses left behind to report seeing them in the vicinity. There was something else. Later that night, the men in the tops reported seeing lights riding very low on the horizon. They thought they counted at least seven ships, headed north by northeast. I went up to take a look, but either they dipped below the sea line or spied us first and doused their lights, because I saw nothing. I didn't dare risk closing for a better look, not with the *Santo Domingo* in tow."

"It could give substance to the rumors we have been hearing for the past couple of weeks that the plate fleet is planning an early return to Spain," said Geoffrey Pitt. "Some of our normal sources of information have been showing an unusual reluctance to accept our gold, but we have sent out a scout to have a closer look."

"And what of this other treasure you have brought us?" Jonas planted his hands on his waist. "This . . . envoy from the king. What is it this time? A demand for Father to return to court and kiss his ring? Or does he want a larger share of the purse, perhaps?"

Juliet shook her head. "From what I have managed to pry from between the duke's teeth, it would seem the king is seeking to uphold the terms of the peace treaty between Spain and England. He has sent our lord peacock with his fine plumage and threats to warn all the brethren against further hostilities while the king of England and the king of Spain negotiate the terms of a peaceful coexistence. He says if we refuse, we risk being branded as pirates and traitors."

Jonas snorted. "In truth, I have never understood the differences between a pirate and a privateer save for a poxy piece of paper giving royal permission to 'trade by force if permission is denied.' I'm surprised you did not toss him overboard long before now."

"He is annoying enough that I probably would have . . . had he not saved my life on board the *Santo Domingo*."

Like bloodhounds scenting fresh meat, all ears perked in her direction and she felt an uncomfortable warmth spread up her throat to her cheeks.

"It was a trifling thing, of no account, and I repaid him tenfold by saving his mangy neck from the *Argus*."

"Then why is he here?" Gabriel asked.

"Mainly because we needed the English crew to help bring the galleon home and it would have looked peculiar to go out of our way just to disembark a duke and his manservant."

"I would have solved the problem in a more practical way," Jonas muttered.

Simon Dante held up his hand to end the discussion. "There is no harm in hearing what he has to say. But not tonight. Tonight we celebrate the victory of our *Rosa de Hierro*. Come. A feast awaits us on the dining table and I want nothing to spoil our mood."

It was hours before Juliet could excuse herself and climb her weary way up to her bedchamber. She had eaten far too much and drank far too much, and after Jonas had shaken off his displeasure at the presence of the king's man under their roof, they had sung too much. All the people she loved dearest in the world were in that room, and looking at Jonas with his flame red beard and raucous laugh, she could even feel the spirit of her grandfather beside her.

As tired as she was, she ordered a hot bath and soaked away the salty rime that made her hair feel like wire and her skin like parchment. When the last vapors of steam had expired, she toweled herself dry and donned a shapeless shirt for sleeping. She had learned from experience that while her brothers may have appeared to collapse into drunken stupors, they were not averse to creeping into her room an hour later and playing a prank that would prove costly if they found her. The last time she had outfoxed them, they had thrown her naked into a vat of indigo dye, and the stains had taken weeks to fade away.

As a precaution, she bundled a roll of pillows under the blankets of her bed and arranged it to look like a sleeping body. She doused the lamp and crept to the opposite wing of the house, careful to light no candles or leave any clues behind. With luck the Hell Twins would search her room and assume she had gone back to the *Iron Rose*.

The furniture in the room she had chosen was covered in white sheets, the windows latched shut. Needing air, she raised the sashes and opened the french doors, then went out onto the wide balcony to wait for the room to cool. Most of the lanterns on the lower tier had been doused and apart from the glow that came from several windows closer to the front of the house, the rest were dark. There was nothing as extravagant as the sixty-five bedrooms Harrowgate Hall had to boast, but there were half a dozen chambers on the upper floor that were furnished for phantom guests who never came.

The shrill humming from the cicadas was constant, a sound that took a day or two for Juliet to adapt to after several weeks at sea. The breeze rustling through the palms was similar to the rush of waves beneath the keel, and helped ease the transition. Far below was the lighted circle of the harbor with its cluster of ships riding at anchor. They looked almost insignificant from such a height, like toys in a pond.

She was not exactly sure when she realized she was not alone on the balcony, or how she knew the identity of the dark silhouette leaning back against the wall. The tingle in her breasts, perhaps, or the feathery shiver that ran down her spine.

"This is not a good night for you to be creeping about in the dark, your grace."

"I merely came out of my room, which is there," he said, turning slightly to indicate a set of open doors, "for a breath of fresh air. Furthermore, with all the shouting and singing going on below, sleep was proving to be somewhat elusive."

Juliet smoothed back a lock of hair that had blown across her face. "We are not accustomed to catering to the needs of houseguests."

"Or prisoners?"

"As it happens, we do have a sturdy hut on the

beach with bars in the windows and a bolt on the door. If you would prefer those accommodations—?"

"Mea culpa." He held his hand over his breast. "It was a poor riposte. All things considered, you have been more than generous."

"Benedicamus Domino." She issued the blessing with a mock bow.

"Ex hoc nunc et usque in seculum," he murmured. "You know the Catholic liturgy?"

"I make it a point to know my enemy's weaknesses and strengths," she replied in Castilian. "I know their faults," she added in French, "I know their foibles"—in Dutch—"and I know how to play one against the other," she concluded in Latin.

"All that," he mused, "and you can sail a ship through riptides, shoot a pea off the masthead—which Johnny Boy was only too proud to inform me—and wield a sword like the devil's own angel."

An eyebrow took a brief quirk upward. "I suppose you think a woman should be nothing more than an adornment for a man's arm?"

"Good God in heaven, no. I am in consummate awe of any female who can discuss more than fashion and the state of the weather."

She humphed and muttered disdainfully in Portuguese, "As long as they are soft and plump and lay beneath you like submissive starfish."

"A soft body can be a comfort at times," he agreed quietly.

His Portuguese was not quite as effortless as Juliet's, but the fact that he understood what she said succeeded in unnerving her again.

"Do you enter into every conversation with the intent to annoy?"

"Not every one," he admitted.

"Just those with me."

He smiled crookedly. "You cannot deny that you throw down your own share of gauntlets, Juliet."

"Which you pick up and fling back at every opportunity . . . *Varian.*"

His smile turned into a soft laugh. "I take my points where I may, for you do not allow too many openings. Your tongue is as sharp as your sword and I confess your proficiency with both weapons intrigues me. I believe I can say with complete and absolute honesty that I have never met a woman quite like you before. One who provokes the most violent urges to throttle one minute, and the next . . ."

She arched her eyebrow again. "Yes? And the next . . . ?"

Varian clamped his teeth and cursed inwardly. He had seen the trap and fallen into it anyway. Even worse, his eyes had lost the battle to remain fixed above her chin and were making a recklessly slow and dangerous journey down the length of her throat to where the collar of her oversized shirt hung loosely open.

He had not been able to sleep. Delivered to his room by the two stout bulwarks, he had been given stern orders he was to remain inside. Beacom was nowhere in sight, locked away in another room, he supposed. With not much else to occupy his time, Varian had taken advantage of the hot bath and hearty meal provided, but the instant he had stretched out on the feather mattress, the queasy feeling he had experienced on the jetty had returned. The room was on solid foundations but he was still moving, rolling with imaginary waves, and to avoid spewing his fine meal into his lap, he'd paced a while. He'd sat with his head in his hands and pondered his situation. He'd listened to the muted sounds of singing and revelry from somewhere below, and in the end, he had flung the french doors open and stepped out onto the veranda, fully anticipating another brace of guards posted there to turn him back.

What he found was a wide, deserted sweep of balcony. There were no barriers between the rooms, no guards to bar his way as he walked the full length of the one wing, then rounded the corner and strolled across the front of the house. He counted off more than a hundred paces before reaching the end. There he met an ivy-covered lattice wall that barred intrusion along the western wing of the house and he assumed that those were the family's private quarters, including the rooms that would be occupied by Juliet Dante.

He had remained a while to admire the truly spectacular view of the harbor but when the effects of the hot bath began to wear off and his various wounds began to ache, the thought of a little nausea became a small price to pay for a soft bed and clean sheets. He had retraced his steps, only to find he was no longer alone on the veranda. Someone else was standing in the shadows at the far end. Someone dressed in a thigh-length cambric shirt with her long dark hair left unbound in the night breezes.

"And the next . . . ?" she said again, jolting his attention back up to her face.

Varian's hands curled into fists by his sides. He had come perilously close last night to doing something that defied all logic; he could not afford to make the same mistake again.

"The next," he said offhandedly, "is of course an urge to turn you over my knee and paddle you until your face turns blue."

Juliet's eyebrow remained arched. She studied his face for a full minute in silence before the smile trembling at the corners of her mouth broke free of her efforts to restrain it. A tilt of her head released a deep, resonating laugh, which lasted so long and was so completely uninhibited, the joy of it caused Varian's rigid expression to falter and collapse.

"Well, it is true," he said. "And you must know you have that effect on people else you would not have perfected it over the years. Look at poor Beacom. You need only glance in his direction and he is reduced to a quivering puddle."

"Beacom *is* a quivering puddle. I am surprised you tolerate his company."

"He came with the title, unfortunately, and I have

not had the heart to send him out to pasture. He has no other family, no other interests; I have even caught him polishing boots at four in the morning when he is displeased with the job the bootboy has done."

"You have a *boot*boy?"

The question was asked with the same sarcasm she had slathered on the query of sixty-five bedrooms at Harrowgate Hall.

"It is a very old castle," he explained with a sigh. "It is also an extremely old title, and whether I like it or not, it comes with a great many responsibilities and obligations, not the least of which is to ensure the employment of the hundred or so villagers who have relied on the family for generations. It is not unlike the community you appear to have fostered here," he added, nodding in the direction of the bay. "If not for your family, where would they be? What would they be doing now?"

"Whoring and drinking somewhere else, I expect. It would be of little concern to us or to me."

The midnight eyes returned to scrutinize her face. "Now, that you do not do well, Captain," he said quietly. "You declare indifference, yet you care a great deal what happens to those close to you. Johnny Boy, for instance. If you worried so little about the people around you, you would not have noted a pinprick of blood on his leg in the heat of all that was going on today. Nor would you have asked Lieutenant Beck how he burned his face, or gone below each day to check on the men who were injured in the battle with the *Santo Domingo*."

" 'Twould be a foolish captain wh̶ ̶d̶ ̶not see to the welfare of her crew."

"And a foolish lord who allowe̶ starve over a harsh winter. Howe̶ taken great pains to remind me at̶ I have no friends here. My title b̶ position carries no influence, n̶ been in your company for less th̶ see how I might have made a c̶

my arrogance and pretensions, yet I ask only for the
chance to prove otherwise. Moreover, I would ask that
you be tolerant of similar errors I have made in judging you."

The offer and the way it was delivered with his
hands spread in supplication sent her head tipping to
one side, as curious now as she was wary.

He had a buttered tongue, that much was a certainty. She suspected there was a good deal more to
Varian St. Clare than met the eye, and not all of it
was the formidable physical strength he camouflaged
beneath the velvet and feathers.

To that end, she let her gaze rove down the pillar
of his neck and across the impressive breadth of his
shoulders. He wore only a shirt and breeches, no doublet, no starched collar. The shirt, in fact, was open
midway down his chest, revealing the wealth of
smooth hairs that formed a natural, dark breastplate.

"I think I have already been quite tolerant," she
murmured. "Especially after last night."

"Last night was a mistake. My behavior was . . .
totally inexcusable. I suppose I could blame it on the
rum, yet no . . . not even that in good conscience, for
I should have better control over my actions. I *do*
have better control, by God, and the fact that there
was moonlight, and starlight, and you were half
clad . . ."

His voice trailed away as he realized the same conditions existed before him now. The moonlight was in
her hair, sparkling off the dampened curls. She no
longer smelled like saltwater and canvas, and the collar of her shirt had slipped to one side, exposing the
smooth roundness of a shoulder to the starlight.

"At any rate," he continued, "it should not have
caused me to lose all sense of propriety."

"Are you saying you have better control over your
tonight? If so, I am glad to hear it, for I am in
to fight you."

was so soft it sent an unexpected spray
ippling up his arms. The infernal shirt

had slipped lower and likely would have come right off her breast if the nipple had not tightened and snagged the silky fabric.

"I have no wish to fight with you either," he said.

"Well then," she mused, "what shall we do instead?"

If there was still a moment when he might have reclaimed his senses enough to beg her pardon for the interruption and walk away . . . it was lost when she took a step from the rail, rose up on the tips of her toes, and pressed her mouth over his. Her lips were soft and the kiss was fleeting, but when it ended, he felt as though he had been struck by a bolt of lightning. The first bolt was followed by another as she slid a hand up and circled it round his neck, dragging his mouth down into another longer, bolder caress.

When it ended, he studied the hard sparkle in her eyes and felt more than just the tiny hairs across his nape begin to stand on end.

"May I ask why you did that?"

"Why did you kiss me last night? And if you say again it was a horrible mistake and you'll regret it to the end of your days . . . be warned that your days will end here and now, and in a most unpleasant fashion."

His jaw slackened a moment, then clamped tightly shut again. "I expect the answer you are looking for is that I kissed you because I wanted to."

"And why did you stop?"

"Really, Captain, I—"

Juliet laughed softly and stood back. "Does your hand still pain you?"

"I . . . I beg your pardon?"

"Your hand. Let me see it."

He drew a wary breath and slid both hands out of sight, clasping them behind his back. "The burns are much improved, thank you. The thumb is still bruised, but I can use it without screaming."

Juliet smiled and reached out, grasping his wrists and drawing them forward. She had remarked once before that his hands were big and capable, too strong

to have spent idle hours sitting at card tables or playing at dice. The fingers were long and tapered, blunt
at the tips with enough callouses to suggest he did not
always remember to shield them in kid gloves. They
were the hands of a swordsman, with wrists like iron.
Angling them into the light now, she could see the
redness from the rope burn was almost gone on the one
palm and if one had not been there to hear the thumb
pop from the socket, the faint swelling would hardly
tell the tale.

She brought the injured hand forward and placed it
over her breast. She heard him take another sharp
bite of air, heard it catch in his throat, but he did not
jerk away. Not a finger twitched, not a hair bristled,
and any other time she might have laughed out loud
to see the shocked rigor on his face.

Any other time she might not have been feeling so
damned unsettled and at odds. She was back in the
bosom of her family. Her ships were safe in the harbor
and she was being lauded as a hero. Her belly was
full of good food, her skin tingled from a hot soak
and a lusty scrub . . . and yet she had not been able
to eat, drink, or wash away this feeling of restlessness.
A bug had landed on her arm earlier and she had
nearly stabbed herself, for pity's sake. Now, just the
sensation of having his hand on her breast was setting
every square inch of her flesh on fire, warming her to
the demon that was already coursing through her
blood.

At the same time she became disturbingly aware of
the heady scent of his skin, the broad expanse of his
chest only inches away. The beating of his heart was
tangible against her fingertips, and lured by the open
shirt, she coaxed the linen slowly aside and rested her
hand on his warm skin. He was all muscle, hard and
sculpted, and when her fingertips started roving, she
felt a shiver race through his flesh.

"You managed to avoid answering my question,"
she murmured.

"I . . . scarcely remember what you asked." His voice was hoarse, forcing an indifference that broadened her smile and sent her hand searching farther afield. The hairs tickled her palm and she combed her fingertips through the springing curls until she found his nipple. A slow, speculative circle traced around the sensitive flesh had it stiffening into a hard little peak.

"I asked if you had better control over your urges tonight."

The question set the blood pounding through his temples, stinging through his veins even as her hands moved lower, sliding farther beneath his shirt to explore the bands of muscle that quickened across his ribs and belly. Appalled by his utter inability to deter her, he watched as she leaned forward and touched his chest with the tip of her tongue, then followed the same path her fingers had taken to his breast. When her mouth closed over his nipple, she sampled it like one might taste an offering of some exotic delicacy. Her teeth gently caught the skin, pulling the dark disk inside the heat of her mouth where she continued to torment it with her tongue.

His body turned to iron. His hands came up and gripped her arms, but still he did not push her away. There were tremors in his fingers, tremors in his throat as each breath came harsher than the one before.

Intrigued, Juliet took more of him into her mouth. At the same time, she started to gently ease the tails of his shirt free of his breeches. When the cambric hung over his hips in loose folds, she searched for the fastenings at his waist, releasing one button, then the next. She did not wait for the cloth to part completely before she slid her hands beneath and what she found there caused her own breath to falter in her throat, for he filled her two hands and still strained upward for more.

"Dear Christ." His voice rasped against her forehead. "Do your excesses know no limits, madam?"

"Not tonight," she replied, her lips nuzzling his

throat, the warm underside of his chin. "Not here, not now . . . unless you want there to be some boundaries such as do not do this . . . or do not do this . . ."

Varian groaned and his whole body shook as her hands stroked him. His grip tightened on her shoulders and she felt a massive shudder wrack his body as some of the pressure pulsed free, creaming her fingers with a threat and a warning.

His hands came up from her shoulders to cradle her neck. His tongue thrust fiercely between her lips to smother her mocking laughter and somewhere, somehow in the blink of an eye, the power shifted happily from her mouth to his. His lips, his tongue, ravaged her with none of the gentleness she had teased him with earlier. This was lust, heated and urgent, and she felt the effects curling between her thighs, shivering through her limbs.

Wanting more, she lifted the hem of her shirt and brought him forward so he could slide himself into the sleek warmth of her cleft. His flesh bucked and thickened beyond all conceivable thought, stretching until the veins beat against her fingers, and his mouth tore free of hers on a ragged gasp.

"Enough, damn you! Enough before I shame us both!"

For one wildly blind moment she thought he was going to push her away, but the hunger in his body was raw and pounding. It overwhelmed his every common good sense and he scooped her into his arms, carrying her across the veranda in brusque, powerful strides. He kicked aside the gauzy curtains that belled outward from his room and went straight to the bed, where he threw her on top, delaying only long enough to shed his clothes before joining her.

Juliet welcomed him eagerly into her arms. She was ready—sweet Christ she was more than ready—and she laughed for the sheer pleasure of it when he grasped two fistfuls of her shirt and tore it from neck to hem. He knelt above her a moment, his shoulders

gleaming in the candlelight, his eyes dark and full of
questions that had no answers.

Slowly, almost reverently, he placed his hands on
her breasts, then stroked them down to her waist, to
her hips, curving them around until they were between her
thighs and sliding into the soft, coppery curls. He
bowed his head and she writhed when she felt his
mouth and tongue painting her breasts and belly with
fire, but when he took his assault lower, she came
arching up off the bed.

"Wh-what are you doing?"

"You said there were no boundaries, Captain."

"No, but—"

"Or would you prefer to impose some now, such
as . . . do not do this . . ." He lowered his head and
touched her with the tip of his tongue, sliding lushly
down one sleek fold and up another. "Or this . . ."
The gentle lapping was replaced by a swirling invasion,
a series of wet, silky thrusts that sucked the breath
from her body and sent her melting helplessly back
onto the bed.

Varian probed and stroked until the resistance left
her thighs and he could feel the shock of discovery
fluttering through her limbs. He explored every tender
crease and crevice, layering pleasure upon pleasure
until she was no longer fighting the extraordinary intrusion but opening herself eagerly for more.

He obliged by bringing his hands, his fingers into
play and she was conscious of her own hands clutching
desperately at the bedsheets. She did not know where
to look, what to grasp to keep her from flying out of
her body and in the end, she flung her arms above
her head to catch hold of a bedpost but it was too late.

She rose off the bed in a taut arch, her body straining like a bowstring. Each ruthless thrust of his tongue
caused her to cry out into the shadows, to shudder
and writhe and eventually issue the frantic plea that
brought him sliding forward to replace the heat of his
mouth with the driving shock of his flesh.

Juliet crested before the first thrust was even complete; the second brought her hands down from the bedpost to claw frantically at his shoulders, then his hips. She could not have drawn a breath to save her life, for there was only pleasure, intense and unstoppable, great shuddering contractions of ecstasy that seemed to never end, never relent in heat or intensity.

Varian drew on every skill he possessed to resist the lure of those grasping muscles. He lifted her hips higher to change the angle of penetration and watched the silvery eyes glaze in disbelief as the shudders from yet another orgasm sent her head thrashing side to side, scattering the dark cloud of her hair across the bed. He kept her there, trembling and senseless, as long as he possibly could before his own pleasure broke in dark, rushing torrents.

The sheer force of his release brought him plunging forward into her body. He felt her legs twine around him like a vise and he flung his head back, pouring himself into each greedy roll of her hips until he had no more to give. A final, heaving shudder left him so utterly and immutably drained that he sank back into her arms and lay there panting, steaming in his own sweat.

Juliet fared no better. Her blood was thrumming through her veins, her heart was beating like a mad thing in her chest. Every shiver, every tremor, that raced through his big body found an echo in her own. She could feel his breath against her neck, the hairs on his chest where they lay crushed against her breasts. She felt exposed and vulnerable, lying there with a man sprawled between her open legs. Part of her wanted to push against his shoulders and shove him aside. Another part wanted to run her fingers up into his hair and turn his face so that she could taste the silky heat of his mouth again.

Varian lay there stunned. There had been nothing shy or tentative about her passion. It had been as fierce and primitive as her instinct for survival and it should not have come as any surprise that a young, vibrant creature like Juliet Dante would regard the act of engaging in intercourse any differently than she viewed her right to wield a sword or command a fighting ship.

Furthermore, as shockingly virginal as Varian himself felt at the moment, he was far from being a novice in the bedroom. At the same time, the act had never been more than a purely physical release for him. He had never, not once in all his years, felt such a resounding need to lose himself in a woman's body, to commit himself so completely to the giving as well as the taking of pleasure.

Whether he moved first, lifting his head out of the crook of her shoulder, or she moved, squirming slightly to encourage some of his weight to shift, it was not clear. But one minute they were searching their own thoughts, and the next they were searching each other's, their eyes locked, their breaths cooling the dampness on each other's faces. His hair had fallen forward, throwing most of his face into shadow. Juliet's, conversely, was spread beneath her like a tumbled cloud of dark silk, her features bathed in candlelight.

Why, he wondered, had not noticed until now the tiny raised mole at the corner of her mouth? It sat just above the curve of her lip and was the same dusky pink as her nipples. The rest of her complexion was flawless, smooth as silk, tanned a lush honey gold by the sun. Her whole body was tanned, making his seem even whiter by comparison.

Searching farther afield, he saw the swath of shiny skin on her arm where she had said she'd been burned, the countless nicks and tracings of fine white lines that could have been caused by knives or swords or a myriad other violent means.

His gaze returned to her face—a truly lovely face when it wasn't trying so damned hard to be fierce and unapproachable. The cheekbones were high, the brow wide, the eyes large and luminous. Her mouth, when it wasn't scowling, was lush and evocative and wreaked enough havoc on Varian's senses to make his toes curl into the bedsheets.

"Something amuses you?" she asked warily.

He made no attempt to curb his smile. "My own misguided perceptions, perhaps."

"Well, perhaps you could guide them elsewhere and give me ease to breathe."

"And forfeit the advantage I have so keenly won?"

She started to wriggle out from beneath him but found her wrists suddenly caught and pinned flat to the bed, her legs effectively trapped under his.

"What are you playing at now?"

"I am not playing at all, Captain. I will confess, however, that I am curious to know if this was just a simple diversion for you, or if you had some other reason for plying me with your charms."

"Do not flatter yourself by supposing it was anything *other* than a brief diversion." She released an extravagant sigh. "Faith, I did not think men needed a reason to bed a woman; I thought they simply needed the opportunity. Thus, having taken it, sir, you may now heave off me."

"In due course . . . if that is what you really want."

"What else *would* I want?"

The question had barely cleared her lips—in fact, the last word faltered and quivered away to nothingness as she felt his lower body press forward and pull slowly back.

He was growing hard again.

She, on the other hand, was all soft and buttery inside. She had thought that was the end of it, for none of her four lovers, not even her exquisite Frenchman, had done more than grunt and roll away when they were finished—and they had not had half the number of reasons to toss her aside as Varian St. Clare. She had been rude, mocking, and outright belligerent with him since the moment he had wakened on board the *Iron Rose*. She had further deceived him by letting him believe she was taking him to see her father when in truth, he was scarcely more than a hostage against whatever use her father might make of him. In truth, when she had kissed him out on the balcony, she had fully expected him to reject her artless attempt at seduction.

He had not only answered it, but with a single flick of his tongue he had turned the tables, and if it was possible to believe what she was seeing in the smoldering depths of his eyes, he was turning them again, offering her the choice of whether to stop or go forward.

It would be different in the morning, she had no doubt, for he would once again assume the mantle of king's envoy and she would again be the daughter of the Pirate Wolf. But morning was hours away and she had other things to ponder now . . . like how limbs that had been deadweights only moments ago were drawing themselves up and hooking around his waist, how a body that had seemed completely drained of initiative was now tingling everywhere, gathering strength from each slow, heated thrust of his flesh.

He released her wrists, pausing long enough to remove the torn halves of her shirt, and when he bowed a determined mouth to her breast again, it was with a boldly ominous "*En garde*, Captain."

She curled her lip between her teeth and had to bite down hard to smother the groan of utterly decadent pleasure as he rolled her onto her belly and pushed his arms between her thighs to spread them. She stretched up to grasp the bedpost and let her lips fall slack while the promised friction of all that heat stretched up and began to move inside her again.

Chapter Twelve

"*H*eave, damn you! Put your weight behind it!"

Exasperated, Juliet vaulted over the deck rail and joined the men who were in the process of winching a heavy thirty-two-pounder on board the *Iron Rose*. An inspection of the guns had revealed a hairline crack in one of the barrels, a flaw that could prove fatal if the cannon overheated and blew apart. The crew had disassembled the gun carriage and slung ropes around the barrel to hoist it out of the cradle and drop it over the side.

Juliet wrapped her gloved hands around the cable and added her weight to that of the men heaving and straining to lift the brass culverin into its wooden cradle. The effort left her winded after only a few moments and she found herself sweating and gritting her teeth to keep her feet from skidding out beneath her. Though she refused to think about it, she knew full well why her energy reserves were depleted. She knew it every time she walked or sat or ran her tongue across lips that felt so puffed and tender she imagined every man on board the *Rose* was snickering out of the corners of their mouths.

She still wasn't entirely sure herself what had happened last night, how she had ended up in Varian St. Clare's bed. She had been restless, too full of herself—and wine—after her triumphant return to the cay, and all that coltish energy had somehow been converted to lust. Now, in the harsh light of day, every scrap of wind that pushed her shirt against her skin had her nipples peaking like small beacons. Every time her hair swept her neck or cheek she imagined it was his lips searching, nuzzling, whispering against her ear.

The tenderness between her thighs was a constant reminder. She ached in places she had not known she could ache. When she glanced up—innocently or otherwise—toward the big stone house on the hill, all she could see was the bed they had shared, the splash of his dark hair on the pillow, the sprawl of his naked body on the bed. That would, in turn, make her remember how he had looked last night with the candlelight gilding his shoulders, his muscles bunching and flexing as he arched above her, his every sinew straining with intent.

She should never have touched him. It had been a foolish, reckless, careless impulse and she was no better off for having burned half the night away in his arms. This was no time to be distracted by a handsome face, an incredibly inventive mouth, or a dangerously seductive body. Dear God, he had only needed to trace a fingertip along her hip to bring her crawling over his thighs.

Worse, she had crept out of the bed like a thief before dawn. She had come on board the *Iron Rose* and worked alongside the men, hoping that pure physical exhaustion would erase any more foolish thoughts she might have.

The rope slipped through her gloves and she scrambled for a fresh purchase. The cannon weighed upward of two tons and the strain caused the metal cleats to scream in protest. The scream ended with a loud snap as the bolt broke and Juliet felt the cable spring back and go slack in her hands. The men on the line fell backward in a heap as the barrel came crashing down. It landed crosswise on the carriage and split the wooden truncheon into kindling before bouncing off and slamming to the deck. One of the mates who had been guiding the barrel toward the rail was standing in its path, and his foot was crushed to pulp on impact.

The gun pitched forward and pushed the bones in his lower leg up through the knee, breaking the skin and spraying blood across the deck. Two crewmen rushed to brace the barrel with staves to prevent it rolling farther onto their shipmate, while several more tried to pull the injured man free. The sickening shreds of flesh that hung off his ankle were quickly bound in canvas and he was carried, howling, below to the surgery.

Juliet sat gasping on the deck. It had happened so fast she'd had no time to react. She had fallen with the others, and while there was no reason to assign blame to anything other than a weakened bolt on the winch, she was angry at herself, angry at all the men who stood around scratching their heads and peering up at the pulley as if it was to blame for human carelessness.

"By the devil's caul, did no one think to inspect the bolts before we started hauling guns around?" She pushed to her feet and smacked the sawdust off the seat of her breeches.

"The winch was checked," Nathan said calmly. "It looked sound enough. The bolt just snapped, is all."

"Just snapped?" She whirled on him. "A good man has lost his foot, possibly his leg and that's all you can say? It just *snapped*."

Nathan shoved the brim of his cap back off his forehead, and ignoring the fact that she was captain, he snatched her around the arm and dragged her out of earshot of the rest of the crew. "What would ye rather hear? That someone climbed up there, sawed through the metal, an' stood to one side eatin' a plantain while they waited for the bolt to split an' slam down on one of his mates? Pin my eyelids to the mast if it would make ye feel better, but it were an accident, plain an' simple. Be thankful it weren't yer leg that were crushed, though it couldn't hardly put ye in any better of a mood if it were."

"My mood is just fine, thank you."

"Aye, for a harridan. Ye've been barkin' an' snarlin'

the whole blessed morning long an' the men are thinkin' they should just bare their backs an' take a dozen licks o' the cat now so ye can vent yer spleen all at the one time and be done with it. Ye're not doing anyone any good here, lass. Havin' ye bray an' stomp around won't get the work done any faster. Go ashore an' if ye're needed, I'll send one of the lads to fetch ye. An' *whup*!" He held a finger up to forestall whatever retort was about to burst from her lips. "If ye don't leave of yer own accord, I'll heave ye over the side myself an' let ye swim ashore."

They glared one another down for another full minute before Juliet dredged up a fearsome oath and stormed to the gangway. She swung a leg over the side and descended to one of the many boats bobbing in the water below. A harsh bark set eight oars in the water simultaneously and within a few strokes, they were flying across the bay.

Mounting the first horse she found tied beside the dock, she kicked a wet boot into its flank and galloped all the way up the slope to the house. Knowing she was in no fit mood to encounter any of her family, she followed the lower veranda around to the stairs at the rear. She took them two and three at a time and, without looking to the left or the right, walked straight to the double french doors of Varian St. Clare's room. She thrust them open and stood a moment on the threshold, her blood pounding fiercely in her temples.

Varian came awake with a start. He sat bolt upright, his dark hair spiked over his ears and spilling forward over his brow. The noise, the sound . . . whatever had wakened him was gone and could not be readily identified. He was alone—that much was confirmed when he glanced quickly around and searched the room. There was nothing, not even an indent in the bedding to show there had been another body beside him during the night.

He ran a hand through his hair and frowned. The

frown turned into a wince as he brushed the injury on his cheek—an injury that, oddly enough, had not troubled him overmuch during the night. None of his aches or bruises had intruded, though now, in daylight, he felt like he had been hauled beneath the keel of a ship encrusted with six months' worth of barnacles.

Frowning again, he made a second slow search around the room. Was it possible he had dreamed the entire incident? Was it possible he had spent the night alone and only dreamed that Juliet Dante had been there beside him?

No, he had not dreamed it. The lingering heaviness in his body belied any doubts he might have had, as did the redolent scent of sex on the bedsheets—the ones that were not scattered on the floor or tossed into a heap at the foot of the bed.

He groaned and sank back down onto the bolsters. He'd had wine, but only two small glasses, not nearly enough to make him dizzy with lust. The hot soapy bath—the first in over two months—had made him decidedly light-headed, but instead of putting him to sleep, it had sent him prowling out onto the balcony like a tomcat. Seeing Juliet there, clad only in a cambric shirt, had completed his fall from grace. Had she not stunned him by initiating the seduction herself, he likely would have thrown her over his shoulder and ravished her anyway.

Since he had already reached the conclusion that Juliet Dante was unlike any woman he had ever encountered before, the fact that she'd had him out of his clothes and damn near out of his skin quicker than he could blink an eye should not have surprised him, but it had. He had known too many women who were eager to make the conquest but then were paralyzed by propriety when it came to actually enjoying the deed. Juliet, on the other hand, made it quite clear she had no interest in making a conquest of any kind. She had simply wanted something and had taken it eagerly and aggressively.

His blood stirring at the memory, Varian rolled onto

his side. A single filament of auburn hair trailed across the pillow and he stared at it for several moments before plucking it up between his fingers. Long and shiny, he imagined it tangled in the rest of the silky mane, the curled ends teasing his flesh as she moved above him. It had been his enormous pleasure to let her straddle his hips and assume command of the ship, so to speak. A superb navigator, she had sailed them both into a maelstrom of bouncing bedsprings and juddering posts.

Only afterward, swallowing past the hoarseness in his throat and listening to the sound of his heart thundering in his chest, had he thought to give thanks for the fact that her family slept in the other wing of the house.

Yet as well as he had come to know her body, he was no closer to understanding what went on behind those pale gray blue eyes. She had wanted no part of him when they were not willfully engaged in acts of pleasure. She had wriggled to one side until they were not touching—difficult to do in a bed not much wider than the span of his arms—and only at the last, when neither of them could have raised a limb or exchanged a caress to save their lives, had she fit herself snugly into the warm curve of his body and drifted to sleep.

Varian stared at the dancing pinpoints of sunlight on the ceiling. He had no idea what time it was, no idea when she had left or how she had managed to extricate herself from his arms without so much as jostling the bed. He did not even want to hazard a guess as to what her reaction would be when she saw him today. Would she be embarrassed? Angry? Would she resent him for having exposed the softer, more vulnerable side that she strove so hard to keep hidden beneath all that thick-skinned armor?

Or worse . . . would she act as if nothing out of the ordinary had happened? As if it was her habit to take her hostages to bed and extract her pound of flesh before they were delivered to her family for their amusement.

Varian sighed, raked his hands more vigorously through his hair, and swung his legs over the side of the bed.

Never mind her, he thought sourly. What would his own reaction be when he saw her again? He had sold his soul to the devil and no doubt the devil would demand his due. He was the Duke of Harrow and he had all but forsworn his wild ways when he had agreed to the marriage with Lady Margery Wrothwell. The fact that he was not officially betrothed was small consolation, for it was understood by both parties that the engagement would be announced upon his return to England. Yet here he was, his body rife with lust for a woman he had known but three days. A woman who was more comfortable wielding a sword than a tapestry needle. A woman whose entire family held only scorn for the king, for England, for the strictures of a society that had dictated every facet of Varian St. Clare's life for the past twenty-eight years.

He had barely exchanged a dozen words with Simon Dante, yet he was more than halfway convinced he was here, as Juliet had so eloquently put it, on a fool's errand. Dante had a fortress here, so why should he concern himself with the dictates of a king who waved his scepter from three thousand miles away? If anything, James Stuart should be asking himself why the Pirate Wolf continued to go to the trouble of sending the royal treasury ten percent of his privateering profits. Surely after all these years he needed no letters of marque granting him permission to trade. From what Varian had seen of the firepower anchored in the harbor below, the Dante clan posed a formidable threat to any foreign port or authority and it would behoove the king to do whatever was necessary to ensure the Wolf continued to fly England's colors on his masthead.

Varian stood and gingerly stretched to unknot the muscles in his arms and legs. Dazzling blue sky showed through the open french doors, and the cool breezes that had played across their bodies through the night had been replaced by a moist heat. He cast around for his clothes, vaguely recalling he had torn them off with such haste he'd almost knocked over the bedside table. There was no immediate sign of his shirt or breeches, but his doublet was draped over the back of the chair and he stared at it grimly, not entirely eager to button himself into confining layers of padded velvet and leather. Moreover, the original owner of the garments had been neither as tall nor as broad across the shoulders as he, and in spite of the hasty adjustments Beacom had made, the sleeves were too short and the ruff of Spanish lace would not close. The wool stockings scratched and the pantaloons were stuffed so full of horsehair he felt like he had two gourds attached to his thighs.

Fostering this small streak of rebellion, he walked naked to the door. He stood with his hands braced on either side of the frame, his eyes closed tight against the glare of sunlight as he let the full blaze of tropical heat bathe his skin. He recalled Juliet's comment about all Englishmen being terrified of allowing sunlight to touch their flesh, and he had to admit, if only to himself, this was the first time he had greeted Mother Nature face to face. To that end, the sun's rays felt marvelous on his chest and arms; even his nether parts seemed to respond amiably to the new experience.

"I warrant it should take about ten minutes for your skin to turn red and start to blister."

Varian jerked his eyes open and brought his hands swooping down to cover his crotch.

Juliet was sitting out on the balcony, her booted feet propped on the rail. She was dressed in an airy white shirt and black breeches; her hair was gathered at the nape and tied with a leather thong. There was a second chair and a small wooden table beside her, the latter holding a huge tray laid with bread, cheese, an inordinately large mound of sliced meat, and bowls of exotic fruits Varian was not readily able to identify.

She followed his gaze. "I thought you might be hungry. And I wanted to thank you for last night."

Hairs that had not already risen at the sight of all this domestication riffled upright into spikes. "Thank me?"

"For providing sanctuary. My brothers searched high and low, thinking to haul me out in my bed-clothes and play one of their nefarious pranks—one, I am told, that involved paste and chicken feathers. They found the bundle of blankets I had left in my bed, but they did not find me, nor would they have thought to look in your room, so aye, I have you to thank for my reprieve." Her eyes narrowed and a smile lifted the corner of her mouth. "What did you think I was thanking you for?"

Varian had the grace to flush, and he did so in a magnificent flare of crimson that shaded everything, even the lobes of his ears.

"Rather an arrogant assumption, was it not?" she said softly.

Their eyes remained locked for one, two heartbeats before Juliet broke first and looked away. "You really shouldn't expose all that untouched skin to the sun too long. You wouldn't want to look like me, would you?"

She tipped her face up, letting the sun bathe a complexion that was already tanned to a golden hue.

"I would happily oblige, Captain, but my clothes seemed to have disappeared."

"No they haven't. I brought you new ones. You'll find them at the foot of the bed. I did not think you should walk around the island dressed like a Spanish don. You might present too pretty a target."

Varian turned, but halted again. "May I ask what you've done with Beacom?"

"You prefer his company over mine?"

"I didn't say that."

She opened her eyes and looked at him. "Get dressed, your grace. It is well past noon already and my father's patience has its limits."

"Noon?" He glanced up at the sun with a start and realized it must be on its descent, not ascent. "Good God, why did no one wake me earlier?"

"I did try, but the only part of you that seemed interested in rising was not the part of you my father would care to see so early on in your acquaintance."

Varian's jaw clamped shut and he retreated hastily into the bedroom. He found a plain shirt and buff breeches folded neatly at the foot of the bed. Both garments fit surprisingly well, as did the tall knee boots that were made of such soft leather, they molded to his feet like slippers. The shirt laced up the front and he was tying the last knot in place as he walked back out onto the balcony again.

Juliet was not in the chair.

He glanced down either side of the wide veranda, but she was nowhere in sight.

"I guessed you and my father would be about the same size. I see I was right."

He whirled around. She was leaning against the wall, her arms folded over her chest, one foot crossed over the other and balanced on the toe of her boot. Something flickered in her eyes a moment as they swept the length of his body again, but it was gone before he could put a finger to it.

"The cheese is excellent," she said, indicating the tray. "We appropriated it from a Dutch merchantman not long ago. The mutton we grew ourselves and the ale is passable."

"I am not overly hungry," he lied. "And if your father is waiting—?"

She gave her shoulders a little shrug. "Alas, you seem to have missed him. He has gone down to the harbor. You can just see him . . . there . . . through the trees."

Varian followed the thrust of her chin and saw Simon Dante, mounted on a huge bay stallion, cantering down the road away from the house.

"You have not gone with him? I would have thought you had a hundred things to do today."

"More like a thousand," she agreed grimly. "But I have already been to the ship and . . . and Mr. Crisp seemed to think I was only getting in the way. My mother reads Spanish far better than I, so she is locked away in the study with the manifests we took from the *Santo Domingo*. My brothers, having been thwarted of one pleasure, are amusing themselves by counting the barrels of pearls and coin being off-loaded from the galleon. Lieutenant Beck is being entertained by Geoffrey Pitt, while the rest of the English crew is being introduced to hot baths, good food, and sweet rum. As for your man Beacom, I sent him down to the warehouses with Johnny Boy to search through some of our vast inventory of velvets and lace to see if he could restore your wardrobe. That would appear to leave only you at odds, sirrah, and me to think of some way to amuse you for a few hours."

It was becoming all too commonplace of late to feel his skin tightening and his blood pulsing through his veins, and Varian did not know what to make of it. The rush was stronger now that he had experienced firsthand what his mind had only imagined until last night, but before he could dare question the sparkle in the crystalline eyes, she offered up a short laugh.

"Come. If you're not interested in eating, we can take a walk. I have something to show you."

She turned and headed for the stairs at the far end of the veranda, the blade of her sword reflecting flashes of sunlight. Varian cast a grudging, hungry glance at the tray and snatched up a wedge of cheese and a crust of bread before he followed.

There was a stone path at the bottom; one direction led around to the front of the house, and the other led through a garden and a small orchard of lime trees. They took the latter, with Juliet striding into the lead and Varian pressed to keep an even three steps behind. Her pace belied any notion they were out for a stroll and after five minutes, when the path turned to dirt and began taking a steep upward slant, he could feel the muscles in his thighs protesting.

The trail meandered and turned sharply to circumvent the occasional outcropping of rock, but for the most part it went straight up. Ferns grew over the path and brushed their arms and shoulders. The vegetation was lush and fragrant, heavy with moisture, and after a few hundred yards Varian began to stare at Juliet Dante's shapely backside, wondering if or when she ever tired. She seemed to possess boundless energy and did not look the least winded or dragging, not even when they broke clear of the treetops and had to follow some tangled, rock-strewn goat path to reach the top of the ridge.

"There is an easier way around the point," she said with vulgar cheerfulness. "But I thought you might appreciate the view from up here."

Throughout the climb, he had deliberately resisted the urge to look behind him. He was not particularly enamored of heights and knew that as steep as the path had been on the climb up, it would seem twice as precipitous looking straight down.

He stumbled over a crust of rock and used it as an excuse to catch his breath. Sweat crawled through his hair and down his neck, soaking his shirt to his back in great wet patches. Insects—who had blessedly remained behind under the shade of the trees—had stung his neck and arms in a dozen places. He spared a scowl upward at the boiling yellow glare of the sun, but when Juliet turned to glance over her shoulder, he smiled and waved her on.

"Just stubbed a toe."

"It is not much farther. I could carry you, if you like."

Her laughter drew another scowl, but when he looked up again, she had disappeared behind a gnarl of rock, leaving him alone and drowning in his own sweat on the goat path.

Biting off a soundless oath, he scrambled up the last few feet and saw her standing on the crest of the volcanic ridge. A quick and justifiably breathless glance around in all directions told him they had also reached the highest peak on the island. The endless shimmering blue of the ocean surrounded them in a vast blue circle, the surface gleaming pewter where the sun glanced off the waves. Varying shades of aqua, cobalt, and turquoise ringed the island, the shadings and striations created by the sandbars and reefs. The four outlying atolls looked like barren cones of rock, tossed there by some giant's hand to be beaten by the surf, while far below they could hear the thunder of the waves smashing against the cliffs of Pigeon Cay.

Turning a slow, full circle, Varian could also see down into the bowl of the volcanic crater, the green of the pastures, the swaying tops of the palm trees that looked like green-haired men listening raptly to some unheard chorus. He guessed the island was ten, twelve miles long at its widest point and rose perhaps a thousand feet above the sea. The roof of the big house was hidden from their vantage point, but the harbor looked like the inner surface of a seashell, deep blue in the center rising to a pearly gray along the beach.

This was Dante's kingdom. The secret lair of the Pirate Wolf, and although Varian had found many veiled references to such a mythical place in the ledgers and documents he had studied before embarking on his voyage, he never dreamed it actually existed.

"Tell me, your grace, when you are at home in your English castle, can you walk outside your door and see a sight such as this?"

She had her face turned into the sun, and tendrils of her hair were streaming back like rich dark sheaths of silk. She had her arms stretched wide to catch the wind, and her shirt was molded against her chest, outlining the perfect shape of her breasts, the tantalizing peaks of her nipples.

"I confess I cannot," he admitted softly. "But then, should one not fear that to see such beauty every day might render it less spectacular?"

"When I was young, I climbed up here every day and always found something new that I had not seen before. The color of the water, the pattern of a bird gliding on the air currents, the passage of a cloud . . . it was never the same as the day before."

"Have you no desire whatsoever to see what lies beyond the scope of the horizon?"

" 'Beyond this place, there be dragons,' " she quoted softly. "It was the warning written on all sea charts by the ancient mariners, who believed the world was flat. Father has sailed over that edge, and I will too some day. He says there are islands far on the other side of the world that are as different from these as the sun and moon, with volcanos that spew molten rock into the night like crimson fountains, and where spices are so plentiful you can smell them a week's sail away."

When he said nothing—and good God, what could he say when it was taking all his strength not to reach out and pull her into his arms—she turned and looked directly into his eyes.

"Tell me about your England. Is it always cold and wet, as I have heard?"

"We . . . endure more than our fair share of rain and fog, true enough. But when the sun does shine, the land is almost greener than you can bear."

"Not in the cities, surely."

"No," he smiled. "Not in the cities. Nor can I think of a one that smells of anything closely resembling a spice. But a great country cannot survive without thriving cities, and in order to thrive they must house the people who keep the factories and shops full."

"I do not think I could survive in a city. I detest walls and crowded places."

"You would like Harrowgate. It is well out in the country, surrounded by miles of green, rolling hills. There are sections of the house that are three centuries old, with rooms so large you have to shout to be heard from one end to the other. As children, my brothers and I were only allowed in certain areas lest we become lost and get dragged away in chains by the ghosts."

"You had ghosts?"

A sinfully roguish smile crept across his face. "Ask Beacom if you doubt me. He'll tell you there are noises and odd occurrences that cannot be explained, and he is convinced one of our more shadowy ancestors crept into his room some nights and rearranged his belongings while he slept. It was just brushes and shoes in the beginning, but then desks and chairs started moving. Once, his entire suite was reversed and when he rose to relieve himself, he did so in his wardrobe by mistake. It drove him quite mad for a while. He even threatened to leave Harrowgate Hall and seek employment elsewhere but Father said he was far too valuable a man to lose and sent me away to school instead."

Juliet's eyes sparkled. "*You* were the ghost?"

"He was easy prey, as you can imagine."

Juliet was imagining far more than he was inviting her to do. She was imagining him as she had seen him when she stormed back to the house, his arms still clutched around the bolster pillow she had given him as a substitute when she crept out of bed earlier that morning. Seeing him like that, realizing he would still be holding her so closely had she stayed, had taken the wind out of her sails, had stripped her of her anger, had left her standing there in the doorway feeling helpless and bereft.

Some of that helplessness flooded back now as she gazed into the midnight eyes. His face was unreadable, his thoughts untouchable, and she had no way of knowing if he was aware of how the blood pounded sluggishly through her veins each time he looked at her. Indeed, why should he? He'd made no attempt to touch her or broach the subject of what had happened between them last night. True, she hadn't mentioned it either, not directly, but that was only because she did not know quite what to say. It was also true that he did not need to touch her. The simple act of him standing there looking at her made her feel as if his hands were running up and down her body, stroking the tender places, making them hunger for more.

He smiled, and after a small hesitation, she smiled back.

"We can take the easier way down, if you like," she said casually.

"I am entirely in your hands, Captain." He bowed slightly and when he straightened, she caught her breath, for the guarded look in his eyes was gone. In its place was something else, an apology perhaps—to her, to himself—for his inability to pretend he did not want something that he wanted very much indeed.

Juliet felt a shiver deep down inside. It was a strangely isolated sensation, for the rest of her body had gone suddenly numb. She was vaguely aware of him moving closer, of his hand reaching out to catch at a lock of hair that had blown across her face. He tucked it behind her ear, then smoothed the backs of his fingers along her cheek and the resultant thrill of pleasure that rushed down her spine nearly took her down onto her knees.

Seconds ticked away on heartbeats and still he held her at arm's length. Then, just as he slipped his hand beneath her chin to tip her mouth up to his, she shook her head and warned him away.

"There are lookouts on every point of every ridge around the island. Easily six or seven are watching us right now."

He dragged his eyes away from her face with an effort and looked along the crest of rocks. She could see by the way his gaze flickered, then halted, flickered, then focused again that he located at least two of the sentries.

His thumb caressed her chin and without looking back at her, he murmured, "Then you might very well have to carry me back down the hill, Captain, for I am not altogether sure I can walk without grave difficulty."

Juliet glanced down. A second welter of prickles and shivers washed through her body and it was with some difficulty of her own that she took a subtle step back, then turned and started walking down the path.

Varian's hand remained hovering in empty air for a long moment and did not drop to his side until the crunch of her footsteps had faded away. He hung his head a moment and cursed his own stupidity, then forced himself to follow after her.

The path she had taken wound around the outer rim of the rocks where there were fewer trees and sharper breezes, but the descent was markedly less steep and gave the hardness in his body a chance to ease. Twice Varian caught sight of her ahead of him, but then he would round a bend or traverse a clutter of rock and she would be gone. He continued to curse himself ten ways to Sunday and almost missed the narrow fork in the trail that broke off from the main route. Something lying on the path caught his eye and he slowed.

It was Juliet's sword belt.

He hurried forward and picked it up, a flash of alarm sweeping through his body as he unsheathed the blade and looked around.

He searched the path, the surrounding bushes . . .

There! Just ahead, something else . . .

It was a boot. A tall black knee boot, and ten yards farther on, its mate.

Almost running now, Varian's first thought was that a wild animal had been stalking them, had leaped out of the bushes and attacked her. His second, more rational but equally paralyzing thought was that it might have been a two-legged animal lying in ambush. An animal who could remove a belt and boots and . . .

A splash of white turned him off the path and had him slashing through the tangle of ferns and vines to snatch Juliet's shirt off the branch. He saw an opening just ahead, hardly more than a deep fissure in the wall of rock, and looked around one more time, his fist gripping the hilt of the sword.

There was no one else in sight. There had been no sounds of a struggle, no torn branches to suggest she had been dragged here against her will. He looked at the shirt again and realized how precisely it had been placed, with an arm stretched out and pointing to the crack in the rocks. He glanced at the boots, at the belt, and realized they had all been left as markers as well, guiding him toward the fissure.

Bending low, he ducked through the split in the wall. Ten feet on the other side, he emerged into a cavern, the ceiling rising to a thirty-foot vault, the sides spanning fifty or more feet across. The earthy smell of damp stone and thick moss mingled with the warm steam that rose off the pool that took up much of the space inside. Although there were no torches, no visible cracks in the ceiling overhead, no other sources of light that he could see, the water shimmered an iridescent green. It was so clear he could see the pale, sandy bottom and the dark coiling shape that streaked below the surface.

Juliet rose to the top with one strong stroke, her hair and face streaming sheets of water. She saw him and swam easily to the side, where it was shallow enough to stand. There, she rose like some gleaming marble goddess, her skin shining, reflecting green lights from the pool, her hair clinging in a sleek curtain down her back and over her shoulders. She walked right up to him, naked as a sea nymph, and drew his mouth down to hers.

The kiss was brief, lush, and full of wicked promises as she smiled and backed slowly into the water again, the steam curling around her thighs like soft caressing fingers.

"You will forgive the brief delay, will you not? Everyone on the island would have known within the hour that you kissed me and I let you."

Varian waved the sword ineptly. "You had me worried that some wild beast had caught you and dragged you off into the bush."

"Like most who bear the Dante name, I am not that easy to catch." She laughed once, then dived beneath the surface and streaked away.

Wordlessly, Varian thrust the sword back in its sheath and set it aside. He stripped off his shirt, tugged off his boots, flinging them into the moss, then peeled his breeches down, hopping through a moment of acute discomfort as his enormous erection sprang free.

Juliet was on the far side of the pool, her body hanging in the water, her hair spread out in a wet fan around her shoulders. When she saw him walk into the soft sand, she jackknifed under again and vanished briefly in the shadows below.

Varian's long body cut cleanly through the water, reaching the spot where he had last seen her in a matter of a few powerful strokes. He trod water for a few moments, trying to see through the filtered layers of light and shadow to where she might be hiding, but did not see her until a splash told him she was back on the opposite bank.

Twice more they crossed paths, with Juliet spending more time under the surface than above. She brushed by his leg once and escaped, but the second time he was able to grasp her around the ankle and haul her back to where his feet could touch bottom. Slippery as an eel, she wriggled free again, and would have swum away if he had not planted his feet in the sand and pointed an ominous finger.

"Stay right where you are, dammit."

She watched him walk toward her, the sand kicking up in small clouds around his feet. It sparkled like a million shards of glass, lit by the same unknown source that fed light into the cavern.

When he reached her side, there was no preamble, no teasing foreplay. He cupped his hands beneath her bottom and lifted her against his body, bringing her down with gentle ferocity over the straining thickness of his flesh. His mouth was there to cover her gasp, and to turn her husky groan into soft, shallow sighs.

Juliet wrapped her legs around his thighs, tightly enough he needed only one hand to support her while the other rose and cradled the nape of her neck. His mouth was warm and ravenous. His hands were strong and very sure of themselves as they began to move her back and forth over his flesh.

A shamelessly feverish cry had Juliet flinging her

head back, gasping a plea into the steamy shadows above. The water began to churn around them with the movement of her hips, and a twisting, writhing effort to bring him even deeper inside ended with both of them clinging steadfastly to one another, not wanting a single shiver or spasm to go unspent.

Varian held her until the hot, pulsing contractions of her climax faded into warm shudders, then with her body still quivering around his, carried her to the bank of the pool and lowered her onto the cool bed of thick moss. He ignored her faint whispers of protest when he eased her legs from around his waist and draped them over his shoulders. He kissed his way down the trembling length of her body until his face was buried between her thighs, and when the cavernous walls echoed with her cries again, when he was hard and thick and strong enough to give her all the pleasure she could bear, he surrendered himself completely to the passion that was Juliet Dante. He thrust himself eagerly into the explosion of light that burst behind his eyelids and to the dark, exquisite peace that followed.

Chapter Thirteen

*J*uliet was wakened by the pungent smell from the large booted foot that was planted with a deliberate lack of care beside her nose.

She opened her eyes and followed the leather trail up to the amused face of her brother Gabriel. He, in turn, glanced wryly at the nude body of Varian St. Clare and murmured, "I suppose this helps to explain why Jonas and I could not find you last night."

She yawned and stretched, then pushed herself up on her elbows. "How did you manage now?"

"Nathan told me what happened on board the *Rose*, and when I couldn't find you at the house, I thought you might have come here . . . though I confess," he said after a pause, "I didn't expect you to have company."

She threw a scowl over her shoulder as she stood and waded into the pool. Gabriel looked away with brotherly disinterest as she rinsed the sand and moss off her body, and focused his attention on Varian St. Clare instead.

Varian had come awake when he heard their voices, and when he recognized the intruder as Gabriel Dante, he searched unsuccessfully in the shadows for his discarded clothing. His shirt lay like a pale blot against the darker green and it was Gabriel who spied it first and plucked it off the moss with the tip of his rapier.

"I don't believe we have had the pleasure of a formal introduction," he said, conveying the garment on the point of his sword. "But then my sister often neglects her manners."

Juliet emerged from the water. "Varian St. Clare, his grace the Duke of Harrow; my brother, Gabriel Dante, his grace completely lacking."

Gabriel executed a formal bow, something Varian could not do with a bundle of crushed linen clutched about his waist.

Juliet pulled her own shirt over her head, then found her breeches. "Your concern for my well-being warms me, brother dearest."

"You require further warming?" He glanced idly at Varian, who sat immobilized on the mossy bank. "Does he speak at all, or is that another of his appealing qualities?"

"I am quite able to speak," Varian said coldly. "It's just that you have appeared rather suddenly, and—"

"And now you fear you are in mortal peril of being driven to the chapel at the point of my sword?"

Varian's jaw muscles twitched while he groped to find an appropriate response, for that was, indeed, one of many disjointed images that had flashed before his eyes.

Gabriel did not wait for Varian's tongue to become unglued from the roof of his mouth before he cocked an eyebrow at his sister. "Good God, Jolly, if you were to marry the swiving fellow, that would make you a duchess, would it not?"

"The devil himself should geld you," she said on a sigh, "and slice off your tongue while he is at it, for I would sooner hang all day in a suit of tar and chicken feathers as deal with your misbegotten sense of humor. Furthermore, it isn't as if you have never been caught with your breeches down around your knees, brother dear."

"No, but all men are lusty beasts and it's expected, whereas you—" He touched a finger to the side of his nose. "You're a sly minx and lead all the louts to think the only blade you crave is the one that hangs in their baldrics."

She narrowed her eyes. "Unless you want to answer to *my* blade, you will keep your tongue firmly between your teeth and say nothing about this to anyone."

"Ah. And just what would my silence on this trifling matter be worth, dear sister?"

"Two unblackened eyes and two unbroken legs."

Gabriel's handsome mouth puckered thoughtfully a moment, then eased into a smile. "A fair trade, all things considered. Shall I assist you in finding your breeches, your grace?"

"I can manage," Varian said in a low growl.

Dante shrugged and resheathed his sword. "Fair enough. I'll wait outside, shall I? Give the two of you a moment for a final sweet kiss."

Juliet hurled a boot at his head, but he ducked in time and hastened toward the exit in the rocks. When she glanced back at Varian, he was stepping into his breeches and it was obvious from the frown on his brow that he was not amused. If the light had been better, she might have said his mouth was white around the edges. The fine patrician nostrils were definitely flared, the jaw was rigid, and when he raked an angry hand through his hair, the veins stood out on his temples like those on a leaf.

"Out of curiosity, what would happen back in London if a man and a woman were found naked together by a member of her family?"

"Assuming one was not the king and the other not a milkmaid, they would probably be wed before the week was out."

"Even if that man was a duke?"

Varian avoided meeting her eyes. "If he was a duke or an earl or even a baron, he would most likely try to buy his way out of any further commitment. Unless of course he had a scrap of honor about him."

"Are you an honorable man, your grace?"

He looked up. "I assure you I am prepared to accept full responsibility for my actions."

"By marrying me?"

He straightened slowly and his voice was as brittle as a dry stick. "I will happily discuss the details with your father as soon as I am given an audience."

"Without asking me first?"

The shadows prevented her from seeing more than a faint glint of light from his eyes but she did see that light flicker out for a moment, as if he had closed the lids in utter disgust—at himself for falling into such an obvious trap, and possibly at her for setting it.

"Of course. Mistress Dante, if you would kindly do me the honor—?"

Juliet laughed and interrupted before he went any further. "I would have to rise on a morning and see two suns in the sky before I would even *think* of marrying you, your grace-ship, and even then it would have to be for a far, *far* better reason than having spent a few hours naked together. Accept that we have enjoyed our little diversion and leave it at that. Unless, of course, you were hoping a physical dalliance would put me in thrall and win an ally to your cause?"

"My dealings with your father played no part in this, madam," he said with quiet resentment.

"Would you have refused and said, 'No, no, do not trouble him at a time like this,' had I taken you to him this morning, all a-blush like a blissful puppy, and insisted he listen to your pleas for peace?"

Varian shook his head, having gone from one ludicrous situation to another so fast he could barely keep up. "No. No . . . I . . . I doubt I would even have been able to face your father this morning, much less convince him to obey an edict from the king. Damn and blast, woman"—he twisted his hands into his hair in a gesture of frustration—"you were right! After what happened on board the *Argus*, I am not even certain I *want* to convince him. I am half inclined to encourage him and every other pirate and privateer who hunts in these waters to sally forth and smash the treaty to a million bits. Smash it hard, and smash it well enough that Spain will never recover!"

For several long seconds, the startling declaration was met with silence, the only intrusion a faint *blip blip* of water dripping down the stone wall.

"But of course, I cannot do that," he said, blowing out a harsh breath. "I am bound by my oath to present your father with the unpleasant alternatives he faces if he refuses to comply with the terms of the king's Act of Grace."

"Act of Grace?"

"An amnesty, if you will. A complete pardon for all past transgressions to every privateer who agrees to return to England until such time as a system of fair and lawful trade can be negotiated by the kings of England and Europe."

She wanted to clout him on the head, but she planted her hands on her waist instead.

"This is the important business you have been holding so close to your breast? This? This . . . Act of Grace?"

"I was under oath—"

"A pox on your oath, sir. Have you not been listening to a word I have said to you? The only way the Spanish will negotiate is if their cities are sacked and held to ransom. Drake did it. He sailed right into Maracaibo Bay, bold as brass, and demanded five hundred thousand ducats in exchange for keeping his guns from blasting the town to perdition—and he had half the firepower we do right now! Did you know Father sailed with Drake on those raids?"

"Are you telling me he's planning to raid Maracaibo again?" The question had come out heavily laced with sarcasm, but at the look on Juliet's face, Varian stopped and stared. "Juliet?"

"No. No!" she exclaimed with more conviction. "But he certainly could if he wanted to." She brushed past him to retrieve the boot she had thrown at Gabriel and started slightly to see her brother lounging in the shadows.

"I thought you were going to wait outside."

"And miss bearing witness to what might well be your only proposal of marriage? A sorry opportunist that would make me, would it not? And besides, I am seething with curiosity to hear the rest of the duke's arguments for peace. He is aware, is he not, that the king has made this generous offer before? Not two years ago," he said, coming forward to the edge of the pool, "another envoy came bearing documents titled an Act of Grace, and some of our brethren believed in the notion enough to sail into the port of Hispaniola, where they were guaranteed to earn a warm welcome from their Spanish counterparts. It was warm, all right. If you live long enough you could ask Captain David Smith how it felt standing on the deck of his ship, being the only one to have escaped from an ambush that saw four other ships trapped in the harbor, bombarded and set aflame, their crews thrown into shackles and led off to cut sugarcane for the rest of their days."

The tension stretched out for several long seconds. The eerie greenish light from the water touched the curves and angles of Gabriel's face and made his eyes glow out of the darkness like those of a big cat. Like his sister, he seemed capable of concealing his emotions until the wrong trigger was pulled and the spark hit the powder.

"I was not aware of any former Acts of Grace, no," Varian admitted.

"And now that you are? Do you still feel you can go to our father and present your offer without choking over the king's sincerity?"

"King James is no fool, though he plays the part well at times. He shares the former queen's disdain of the Spanish and while he sees no reason why they should hold a trading monopoly in these waters, he also knows that a declaration of war now would utterly deplete the resources of both countries. Spain lost their one and only chance to conquer England twenty-five years ago. We have heard rumors in the past that the dons kept trying to rally another armada to revenge their ancestors, but Philip III is not a zealot like his father, and their navy at home has never fully recovered from the devastating loss in men, ships, armaments. Conversely, our strength has grown by leaps and it is only a matter of time before we have a navy capable of challenging for supremacy at sea. A war now would set that back for many years."

"We have no intentions of declaring war," Gabriel said, the words so exactingly polite they were obviously meant to bait the recipient. "We'll settle for cutting out a few of the fat treasure ships when the plate fleet leaves Havana next month."

"You cannot do that," Varian said wearily. "You will never come out of it alive."

Gabriel tipped his head. "Zounds, Jolly. You could at least have picked a lover who had more faith in our abilities."

"I have an incredible amount of faith," Varian said. "But I also happen to know the fleet that is scheduled to leave Havana in four weeks' time is no ordinary fleet. There has been a drastic shift of power within the Spanish government and many high ranking officials have been recalled home. There are going to be an inordinate number of ships making the crossing—double, treble the number of usual vessels—and not all of them merchant ships."

"What are you talking about?" Juliet asked.

"As you undoubtedly already know, it was commonplace fifty years ago for Spain to send fleets of a hundred ships or more back and forth across the Atlantic. Over the past couple of decades, those numbers have been drastically reduced, in part because the fleets simply are not as profitable as they once were. The mines are playing out and they have to search farther inland for their gold and silver. Slaves die and have to be replaced, or they rebel and burn out the towns. Easily half the cargo comes overland from the Manila fleet, which has its own route between Panama and the Far East."

"You are not telling us anything we do not already

know," Juliet said, buckling her belt with an impatient slap of leather on leather.

"Then you also know that the single massive flota was reduced out of necessity to two much smaller treasure convoys—the Tierra Firme fleet, which arrives in Havana in late April, and the Nueva España fleet, which arrives in late summer. Both fleets are escorted from Cádiz to Havana by galleons which merely take on water and provisions before immediately turning around to escort the departing fleets back home. In an average year, it may be that thirty merchantmen arrive, fill their holds with treasure, and depart six months later, escorted by fifteen or so armed galleons."

"Closer to twenty," Juliet said dryly. "I could impress you with their names, if you like, their tonnage, weaponry . . . ?"

"I can appreciate that your information is very good, but are you aware that once every decade or so, there is a noticeable overlap, when ships of an arriving fleet remain in port longer than they should, or require repairs, or are impeded by weather? Some that are due to depart in April, for instance, are delayed until the September flota and vice versa."

Juliet arched her eyebrows. "And? What of it?"

"The last time it happened, there were seventy-five ships in the flota that sailed from Havana."

"Are you saying it is going to happen again?" Gabriel asked, all traces of indifference erased from his voice.

"I am saying it is indeed going to happen again," Varian agreed, "but in even greater numbers. Between our government's sources in Seville and dispatches intercepted for the Spanish ambassador in London, it would appear there will be closer to one hundred treasure ships—the sum of three overlapping fleets—gathering in Havana to make the crossing home."

"One hundred ships?" Gabriel whistled softly. "We knew there was more activity than normal on the shipping lanes, but . . ."

Juliet looked at Gabriel. "The reports we had from the Dutchman Van Neuk said there were an unusual number of ships anchored off Maracaibo. His exact words, I believe, were that he came close to pissing down both legs when he stumbled over a dozen galleons tucked behind a tiny leeward island that was normally used for trading with smugglers. He made away with all haste, but he said the patrols were thicker than he had ever seen them before."

"It doesn't prove anything," Gabriel said. "Van Neuk is a braggart. If he said he saw a dozen ships, it was likely closer to three or four." He looked hard at Varian. "And if we have reason to doubt him, why should we believe you?"

"Because I have nothing to gain—or lose—by lying to you."

"Except your life, of course," Gabriel pointed out.

Juliet waved a hand at her brother to hush him. "I am still at a loss as to why you think this would persuade us *not* to attack the plate fleet. If anything, your information would draw the brethren to the fleet like sharks in a feeding frenzy."

"I am telling you, because along with the extra merchantmen, they are also adding several squads of warships to the *guardia*. According to *our* sources, they are withdrawing more than half the ships in the Indies guard to supplement the normal escort fleet back across the Atlantic. That would add roughly another thirty warships to the *guardia,* none less than four hundred tons. They will be filled to the gunwalls with cannons and soldiers, and their only intent will be to kill."

"How do you know all of this?"

"You forget, I am not a duke by nature, only by the laws of primogeniture. I have been in the military for eight years, including three as Captain of the King's Royal Guard. What you may not know, and what could very easily get me killed if it were to become common knowledge, is that when I inherited the title and all the trappings that went with it, I did not resign my post in the army. I may have traded the uniform and gold braid for purple velvet and silver lace, but only because it made it that much easier to travel freely around Europe."

"You were a spy?"

"I prefer to say that I was in Seville to study the fencing techniques of Alejandro de Caranca, one of the most renowned masters in Seville. Among his other devotees were several high ranking officials in the government, including the admiralty. They are a boastful lot when they face an Englishman in the circle."

"And that is why the king thought you were so well suited to come here? Because you had a measure of success loosening the tongues of a few dueling Spaniards?"

"Actually . . . I volunteered for the task. In a further search for truth, were you to press the point of a blade to my throat, I might even admit that I wanted to embark on one last adventure before my life became cluttered with rents and politics, though if you repeat that in front of Beacom, I shall deny it to my last breath."

Juliet smiled crookedly. "It would seem you got more adventure than you bargained for."

"More indeed," Gabriel murmured dryly. "He can return home now and brag that he has fucked the daughter of the Pirate Wolf."

Varian's patience was already on the edge and Gabriel's crudeness gave it the final push. His fist came forward with the power and speed of an iron hammer, the punch catching Dante under the chin, cracking his head back, and lifting him off his feet with the force. He followed immediately with a second blow to the midsection, then a third that landed just below the breastbone and knocked Dante back toward the edge of the pool. The younger man staggered upright and his hand went immediately to his sword. The sound of steel sliding out of the sheath sent Varian stepping back, but only to lean over and snatch Juliet's blade off the moss.

"You don't want to do this," he warned.

"You don't know what I want to do," Gabriel replied, wiping a smear of blood off his lip.

The sound of the two blades slashing together shivered off the damp walls and sent Juliet leaping prudently to one side. She knew her brother's skill, suspected the duke's, and although she kept a hand close to the hilt of her dagger, she backed away and watched the two circle each other like cocks in a ring.

Gabriel moved cautiously away from the soft edge of the pool, his sword arm extended full and unwavering. Varian had a slight advantage in height and build, but Gabriel was solid muscle and sinew beneath the elegant clothing, and his skill far exceeded that of his burly brother. There was genuine pleasure in his smile as he brought the fight to Varian St. Clare in several blindingly swift parries, his blade cutting through the air in a series of silver flashes.

The stone walls rang with each echo as the swords crossed, touched, slid, and slivered together. The two men clashed without a break in stride or rhythm, each forward step brusque and efficient, each paced retreat calculated to draw the opponent here or there by intent. The ground was soft in places, the moss slippery underfoot, and once, when a lunge was overextended, the sword bit into rock and sprayed chipped fragments onto the ground.

They came together, swords high and crossed, both men grimacing with the exertion and the knowledge that they were more evenly matched than either had suspected. Steel slid in a shrill scraping protest, then parted when Varian caught Dante's blade and whirled it with a stirring motion, nearly wrenching it from his grasp. Startled, Gabriel recovered quickly and spun nimbly to the left, reversing into a counterattack that sent the duke splashing into knee-deep water. There was also a fresh cut on his cheek, barely more than a nick, but when his hand came away, it was slick with blood.

He stood there staring down at his fingers so long, Gabriel glanced at Juliet and grinned. He heard the hiss of steel beside his ear and realized his mistake, too late to prevent a thick lock of dark hair from being sliced away from his temple. Outraged, Gabriel vaulted into another attack to avenge the insult. It was answered by a blur of slashing metal, the thrusts coming so fast and furious, he was driven well back into the darkest shadows of the cave.

Juliet tracked their movements by the sound of grunts and oaths. At one point Gabriel made a gazelle-like leap from one stalagmite to another and balanced a moment on one booted foot while he parried and thrusted and engaged Varian in a breathless exchange of ripostes before vaulting onto level ground again.

"By God, you've a worthy arm, man!" he cried. "I would not have guessed it of a lace-necked nobleman."

Varian bared his teeth. "I'm glad you approve. And now will you listen to me when I say I am not here with your sister to earn the right to brag? It was never my intention to do so; it was never a thought in my mind."

"Never? Not once?" Gabriel scoffed openly. "Your intentions were noble, virtuous, and honorable? And you were not the smallest part relieved just then when she refused to marry you?"

Varian's guard dropped, just for an instant, but it was long enough for Gabriel to launch himself across the bank. It was his fist, not his sword, that smacked into Varian's jaw, spinning him around, sending him out over the ledge and into the iridescent water.

Gabriel watched him sink to the bottom, then turned to Juliet with a triumphant grin—a grin that ended in a yelp as his ankles were hooked and he found himself hauled off balance and dragged backward into the pool.

Juliet saw the horrendous splash and the huge cloud

of white silt that was churned up as they touched the bottom together.

In God's name, she thought as she moved closer to the edge, but they were still fighting. The pull and drag of the water was slowing their movements, but the blades were flashing and fists were striking at one another in a graceful underwater ballet before they both ran out of air and were forced to the surface.

The two dark heads rose in a font of bubbles and glittering droplets. Varian hung there for a few treads but Gabriel turned and swam for shallower water. He emerged, dripping and laughing, then stood doubled over at the waist while he fought to catch his breath.

Varian slogged into knee-deep water behind him, the sword still clenched warily in his fist.

"A draw," Gabriel gasped. "It must be declared a draw, sir, for I would hate to have to run you through after such a fine display."

"Only if you will concede my motives were not what you thought."

Gabriel prodded gingerly at his jawline, moving his chin to and fro to ensure it still functioned properly. "I will concede you have a sweet fist. I damn near bit off my tongue. As for the other, proof of your motives is not owed to me."

Both men glanced into the shadows where they had last seen Juliet, but she was gone.

Chapter Fourteen

$\mathcal{V}$arian slapped the side of his neck, killing one of the tiny buzzards that was gnawing at his flesh. As irksome as the insects had been on the climb up to the summit, the sun was well down in the western sky and they were like cannibals now, swarming around his head and shoulders in a dark cloud.

Juliet had not waited for them, and the path Gabriel took back led around the eastern slope, taking them past several batteries of black, long-snouted cannon. There were two men posted at each emplacement but that, Dante casually explained, could increase within minutes to half a hundred at the ringing of the alarm bell.

Once they were past the guns and making their way along the ledge that ran parallel to the channel, the vegetation thickened considerably. Through the palms and tangled vines of oleander, Varian caught glimpses of the water, noting that they were still fairly high up the side of the sheer wall. Here, the view and the perspective were much different from those from the deck of a ship passing through, for he could see where the path widened frequently into terraces, where men with muskets could stand in the camouflaged gallery and shoot down on any vessel that made it past the cannon emplacements. Looking down into water that was clear as gin, he could also see where thick cables had been woven into nets and rested flat on the bottom. On a signal, they could be drawn up and fixed tight to stanchions on either side of the passage, trapping any intruders in the middle.

Varian slapped again and spared a scowl at Gabriel's broad back. The younger Dante did not seem to be bothered by the fog of gnats; he kept to a fast pace and only slowed when he knew they were approaching a sentry post. His clothes were as wet as the dark curls of his hair, and his boots squeaked with moisture at every step. Despite the ready wit he displayed in the cave, he did not appear to have too much to say while they walked, and only spoke if asked a specific question.

"Your ship," Varian ventured at one point. "It is . . . the *Tribute*?"

"The *Valour*."

"A regal name."

Gabriel stopped so suddenly, Varian almost walked up his heels. "Near the end, just before we went for a soaking, you did something with your wrist. An imbrocade that followed through with a quarter twist. A pinch more pressure and you could easily have broken the tension in my wrist and sent the blade spinning out of my hand. You had the advantage, sir, but did not press it."

Varian would have answered but for the bug that flew into his mouth the moment he opened it.

"If you thought to win *me* as an ally to your cause, you were mistaken. Had you followed through, disarmed me honestly, then put the blade to my throat and held it there until I conceded the point, you would have scored higher."

"I will know better the next time," Varian said evenly. "I merely thought to—"

"Save me the embarrassment in front of my sister? Believe me, she probably saw what you did and it saved me nothing but endless entendres from her tongue. She is a clever girl, our Jolly. And if I might offer a word of caution, should you ever find yourself locking blades with her, you had best give it your all or she'll sliver you just for the insult." He paused and smiled faintly. "She's rather prickly in that respect."

"So I have noticed."

"Will you show it to me again? The imbrocade? It is a move I have not seen before."

Varian inclined his head. "Certainly. Though I could not find too many faults in your attack. You had me on my guard more than I would care to admit."

Dante grinned. "The devil you say. And were you speaking the truth? Did you honestly study under Alejandro de Caranca?"

"If you knew me better," Varian said evenly, "you would know that my word is my bond and men have died for doubting it."

Gabriel crossed his arms over his chest. "If you knew my sister better, you would know she is not easily swayed by a pretty face and a strong pair of arms. Whatever words you whispered in her ear while you had her beneath you will carry no weight if it ever came to a choice between you and the lowliest seaman on her crew. Speaking for myself, if I thought you intended to hurt the smallest hair on her head, I would slit you open stem to stern, tie you down in the sun, and watch the seabirds peck away your flesh until you screamed yourself into madness. Jonas would be even more creative, I'm sure, and Father . . . well . . . suffice it to say madness and death would be a blessing. Be wise and keep that in mind the next time you open your breeches."

Varian was accorded another flash of the handsome grin before Dante ducked back under the veil of greenery and began walking again. They went the rest of the way in silence, and by the time they arrived at the bottom of the slope, the air was purple with dusk and there were lights blazing in windows on both stories of the sprawling white house, more twinkling below in the harbor.

Juliet had not lingered outside the cave. When she was fairly certain the two fools would not kill each other, she had left and returned down the path, too furious to trust herself not to take her sword to both men.

Some of her anger had been vented with savage glee on the palm fronds that had got in her way on the trek down. Some continued to burn in her cheeks when she arrived at the house and started pacing to and fro, still wishing she had a pair of heads to break between her bare hands—Gabriel's for defending her when she needed no defending, and Varian St. Clare's because . . . because he was clever and deceitful and because she should have been able to leave his bed this morning with nothing more than a stretch and a yawn of satisfaction.

He admitted he was a spy. He admitted he had come to the Indies to experience one last adventure before retiring to his castle and the virtues of wedded bliss. Was Gabriel right? Was she just part of the adventure?

Even if she was, where was the harm in confessing it? She was more than happy to admit on her part that it was lust, pure and simple. Why complicate it further by seeking hidden motives? Why offer marriage like it was some kind of panacea? And why, by the devil's wrath, was it perfectly fine for men to act on their feelings of lust, but when a woman ventured into those waters, she had to be redeemed instantly from the depths of the perceived sin and cloaked in respectability, regardless if she wanted to be or not? He'd looked like he had a bone stuck in his gullet when he tried to spit the words out; had she said yes, would he have spun into a swoon like his wretched little manservant?

Juliet cursed and kicked an offensive pot of flowers out of the way. Her toes took the worst of the blow and she hopped over to the veranda to sit on the edge.

She heard footsteps and looked up. They were just emerging from the path at the far end of the garden, Gabriel in front, St. Clare lagging a few steps behind. They seemed to be walking easily enough in each other's company, with no evidence of the fight having continued after she left. Their clothes had dried for the most part, but the wind had played havoc with

Varian's hair, leaving it wild and shaggy around his shoulders.

"You may check his shirt for extra holes if you like," Gabriel said cheerfully, "but you will find him all of one piece. Is Father back yet, do you know?"

"I've not gone looking, but I heard horses arrive out front a few minutes ago."

"Ah. In that case, I will just go along and find myself a tall glass of rum to ease the pain in my jaw. By the way, his grace has generously offered to show me that pretty little twirling fillip he did at the end." He paused to swish an imaginary blade through the air. "And I have promised to let him feed the seabirds if he is so inclined."

He offered a polite bow and touched a dark curl before he continued on his way, leaving Juliet frowning up at Varian.

"Feed the birds?"

"With my own entrails," he explained succinctly, "if I unfasten my breeches again without giving it serious thought."

Juliet sighed and shook her head with visible frustration. "There are barely ten months between us in age. I expect that makes him feel the need to play champion."

"I thought he showed remarkable restraint. Were our positions reversed, and I found him *in flagrante* with my sister . . ." His voice trailed off a moment. "Juliet . . . I meant what I said back there. My offer was genuine."

She frowned. "And your mouth is just as stiff with terror saying it now as then. Save your chivalrous gestures, your grace, they are not needed or wanted here. I have enjoyed our trysts, truly I have, but if you keep plaguing me with offers of marriage, I will have at you myself with a blade. Speaking of which—?"

She held out her hand and Varian hesitated a moment before handing back her sword and baldric.

"You realize, of course, my dear mother—who has been trying to get me to propose to someone, anyone, for the past few years—would be crushed if she knew that the first time the words actually left my mouth, they were rejected out of hand. Twice."

"Your dear mother should have raised a more honest son."

He sighed and took a seat beside her. "I have been more honest with you, Juliet, than with anyone else in my life thus far."

"When were you thinking of telling me you were a spy?"

He pursed his lips. "Since the role was a small one, played many months ago, I did not think it was relevant. I am not here for any other nefarious purpose than the one I have already stated. I am not here to write down the names of your father's fellow privateers; we already know them. I am not here to assess your power or strength; that too is quite well documented. I grant you the exact location of this island comes as somewhat of a revelation, but since the best I can estimate is that we are somewhere within a day's sail of the Windward Passage, your lair is perfectly safe from exposure by me."

Juliet found the dark eyes waiting for her when she turned. "So much for Johnny Boy thinking you could not read a chart," she murmured.

"I am just as likely to be a hundred leagues out one way or the other but I do know the constellations that lie over the equator and we are considerably north."

"Is this supposed to win my trust?"

"Would it help to nudge you closer if I told you I am also aware of the upcoming rendezvous on New Providence Island? If my dates are not as muddled as my thinking, I would estimate the annual meeting of all the privateers should happen some time within the next fortnight."

"Did Gabriel tell you that?"

He shook his head. "I knew before I left London. That was where the *Argus* was bound."

"You were just going to sail into a harbor full of

privateers? Demand they haul in their guns and follow you back to England like docile lambs?"

"I was empowered to offer some excellent incentives aside from the amnesty and the pardons."

"Titles? Lands? Estates? Tossing a knighthood at someone who already rules the sea is rather like tossing someone a coin to fetch their trunks, when that someone already has so many chests filled with coins, there is a lack of warehouses to store them."

He held her gaze a moment, then spread his hands with a helpless shrug. "In that case, I have nothing else to offer but the truth. I am not here to spy on your family. I have no intentions of studying stars and charts and landmarks with the intent to reveal the location of this island to anyone, nor do I have any tawdry ulterior motive for"—he leaned forward, kissing her hard enough to suck the breath from her mouth—"doing that. And if my proposal appeared stiff with terror, it is because you are a very terrifying young woman, and because it has confused the bloody hell out of me to see how easily you have managed to twist my entire world . . . everything I knew up until a few days ago to be solid and real and unchangeable . . . into something I hardly recognize at all."

He raked a hand into her hair, but while it remained there and while his eyes continued to search her face, he did not try to kiss her a second time.

Juliet did not know whether to be disappointed or relieved. Nor did she know if she would have kissed him back or pushed him away if he had pulled her into his arms again. It was not even faintly comforting to know that she was not alone in her confusion, for if nothing else, she had assumed . . . she had *known*, dammit, that she could rely on his ingrained sense of ducal propriety to keep this thing between them on the lowest possible level of complication.

Next, he would be spewing declarations of love, and she would be expected to know how to respond.

She surged to her feet. "We should go inside. I am famished and my mouth tastes like seawater."

Varian was slower to rise, slower to clear his face and rearrange it in a less compromising expression. "If I am to meet your father, I would beg the chance to make myself a little more presentable."

"The clothes you wore yesterday make you look arrogant and self-serving. In truth, you will make a better impression in calfskin and cambric."

"I bow to your better judgment, madam."

"Do you indeed? Then brace yourself, sir, for the real judge and jury awaits you inside."

Varian had not yet made the acquaintance of either Lucifer or Geoffrey Pitt, though their reputations had certainly preceded them. The Cimaroon was possibly the tallest and broadest man he had ever seen in his life: a huge black mountain of muscle glowering in one corner of the room. His eyes were like two bottomless holes burned into his head, and when he peeled his lips back in a grin, the filed points of his teeth glinted like white daggers.

Pitt was only slightly less intimidating. He was not as tall nor as solidly built as the other men who crowded the great room, but the bulk of his muscle, Juliet had warned, was between his ears. He was of a similar age as Simon Dante—mid-fifties—but wore fewer weather lines on his face and showed no gray in the sun-bleached waves of his hair. His eyes were the color of jade, pale green and intently focused. A man who thought to tell him a lie was a fool indeed, for although his smile was deceptively friendly, his instincts appeared to be as sharp as a blade. Proof of this was in the way his mouth drifted upward into a speculative little smile as he looked from Varian to Juliet, then back to Varian as she finished the introductions.

"You will join us in a glass of brandy?" Simon Dante asked. "Or would you prefer to try our island rum?"

"Brandy, thank you. I'm afraid my stomach has not acquired a keen enough tolerance for your rum."

Dante was also studying the rumpled hair, the damp clothes, the fresh nick on his temple, as he filled a glass and handed it to him. "You look as if you've had a rough time of it, lad. What new torment has my daughter been putting you through?"

Happily, Juliet had not yet taken a mouthful of her own wine and when she coughed, it was just air.

"She offered to show me a breathtaking view of your island, and was kind enough to take me up to the summit," Varian said without missing much of a beat. "I must say, I am in awe, Captain, for you command the horizon as far as one can see in any direction. A pity you do not hold sway over the insects that attacked us on the way up and again on the way down."

"Vicious little beggars, were they not?" Gabriel agreed, raising his glass. "I was forced to use my sword to clear a path for us."

"You went up the mountain?" Simon looked at his younger son as if such a strenuous activity was not a common-day occurrence.

"It was a mood." He shrugged. "It came upon me unawares. Besides, someone had to chaperone these two. Jolly might have tossed him off the cliffs before we had a chance to hear his pretty speeches from the king."

Dante glanced pointedly at the bruise beginning to darken on his son's cheek, then turned to Varian and smiled as he raised his glass. "Your continued good health, sir."

"And yours, Captain."

They drank, their gazes locked over the rims of the goblets.

"And so you have come to offer the brethren an Act of Grace. All sins and past transgressions pardoned if they will but abide by the terms of the treaty with Spain—have I the fair gist of it?"

"There are a few additional incentives, but yes. That

would reduce the three pages of whys and wherefores in the king's intent to a single sentence."

"Was this act signed by the king's own hand? Or did he have one of his ministers do his dirty work?"

"It was the king himself. I witnessed the signing with mine own eyes. It was signed in the presence of the Spanish ambassador as well, who then sent a copy to Spain."

"You have this decree on your person?"

"Unfortunately, no. It was lost with the *Argus*."

Jonas snorted from across the room. "Convenient."

Varian turned and looked into the amber eyes.

"Well, it is true. I could say I was traveling with papers to prove I was the emperor of China, but if they went down with the ship, how would I prove it? For that matter," Jonas added, "we only have your word that you even are who you say you are."

"I have no good earthly reason to lie, sir," Varian said quietly. "And my word is good enough for most men of my acquaintance."

"Look around you. Do we appear to be like most men of your acquaintance?"

"Oh for heaven's sake." Juliet, who had been sitting with a leg draped over the arm of a chair, rose and went to the sideboard to refill her wine. "Why not just fetch a pot of boiling oil and have him pick a stone off the bottom. If his flesh melts off the bone, you will know he is lying; if it remains unblemished, you will know he speaks the truth."

The only one who responded to her sarcasm was Lucifer, who grinned and nodded as if he approved of the idea.

Simon gently swirled the contents of his goblet. "I am inclined to give our guest the benefit of the doubt—for the moment anyway—unless you have a damned good reason why we should not?"

Jonas snorted. "I don't trust him. That's reason enough for me."

Isabeau came walking through the open door. "If he had brown eyes instead of blue, that would be reason enough for you, Jonas dear, when your belly is full of rum."

She went directly to the enormous cherrywood desk in the corner of the room and slapped down a sheaf of papers. The topmost ones were curled at the edges; some still had bits of wax stuck to the parchment where the seals had been broken.

She joined Juliet by the sideboard and poured a full measure of wine, draining it before she turned to address her family.

"I have been reading for most of the day," she announced. "Aside from the manifests of crew and cargo, there were the logs—which I will get to in a moment—and an inordinately thick sheaf of personal letters entrusted to the capitán to carry home to Spain. The Spaniards are effusive, to say the least, and whine at endless length about the food, the bugs, the swamps, the conditions in port, the noise from the garrison barracks, how much they long to be going home, how they miss the warm plains of Seville, the breezes off the Pyrenees, the snow, the olive trees . . . pages and pages of tear-blotted script bemoaning their plight to lovers and mistresses and wives and families. I am ready to pull my teeth out to save them grinding together every time I read the salutation *mí amor*!" She paused and held out her cup for Juliet to refill. "Then there are the official reports from the commandants, from the *gobernador*, from the damned lackey in charge of seeing there are enough linens on the tables in the officers' mess. And the cook! Dear Christ weeping on the cross, the poor bastard is beside himself for the short supplies of vessie. Three pages he goes on about it. Three damned pages about vessie, written in a hand that looked like it used a chicken foot as a quill! For the blood of God, what is vessie? Is it the name of a girl or something to eat?"

When no one was able to answer, Varian ventured to raise a finger. "If I may, I believe it is the bladder of a pig, used for steaming meats and stews."

"Can it steam away a pounding head and bleary

eyes? If so, I shall demand a crate myself. As it is, I was driven to stab the letter a dozen times to gain relief. You'll find the shreds there, right beside a second letter from the same poor bastard, bemoaning the fact that although there were over twenty ships in Barranquilla preparing to embark for Havana to join the most glorious armada to set sail in his lifetime, alas he was not destined to be on board one of them."

"God bless cooks who aspire to greater things," Gabriel mused aloud.

"Happily for us, he was not always a cook," Isabeau said. "Apparently his family had wanted him to become a priest, but he preferred to worship at the altar of greed instead and I gather he was banished to Nueva España by way of punishment. Believe me, I know all of his miseries and complaints, even to the state of his bowels. You must be the Duke of Harrow," she said brightly, coming forward.

"Comtesse," he said, offering a formal bow. "Your servant."

"Comtesse? Beware of another stabbing, sir, if you address me thus again. You may call me Beau, and I shall call you . . . ?"

"Varian." He seemed startled by the instant informality, almost as startled as he was by his own dreadful faux pas in instinctively reaching for her nonexistent hand to kiss. "The honor and the pleasure is, of course, mine."

She studied his face through narrowed eyes. "I see my daughter has been practicing her stitchery again. You have improved, my dear," she added, smiling over her shoulder. "And thankfully so, for it would have been a shame to mar such a handsome fellow."

Varian touched his fingertips to the wound on his cheek. Apart from one brief glimpse when Beacom had shaved him yesterday, he had deliberately avoided examining the wound that ran along his hairline. Handsome was not a word he would have applied to what he had seen in that reflected mess of knotted threads and mottled bruises.

"As for the log," she said, turning to her husband, "it reads like a travel journal. The captain sailed her from Havana to New León, in Mexico, then south to Vera Cruz, where he took on his cargo of silver coins. From there he continued on down the isthmus to Nombre de Dios, where he agreed to carry crates of spices from the Manila galleons that were in excess of what the merchant ships could hold. He also acquired Capitán Recalde and a hundred troops from the garrison. A week after they left Nombre de Dios, it appears the *capitán del navío* of the *Santo Domingo* had an accident—he fell off the forecastle deck in a rainstorm and broke his back—at which time Recalde assumed the post. They touched in at Porto Bello, Barranquilla, Cartagena, and Margarita Island. At each stop, they took on cargo and more soldiers who were bound for Havana. At their last stop, after heading due north to Hispaniola, the captain was relieved to find a large number of ships waiting in port—eighteen of them, to be precise. Some of the troops he had taken on earlier were transferred to these vessels to ease the overcrowding on his decks, which had at one point reached nearly seven hundred men."

"Seven hundred?" Juliet asked.

"Not including the seamen. So you were even luckier than you realized, m'dear. If you had come across the *Santo Domingo* a week earlier, you would have been outnumbered six to one instead of just three to one."

Geoffrey Pitt was frowning. "Eighteen ships at Hispaniola? A normal count would be six or seven."

"And don't forget the Dutchman's report of seeing more ships than usual off Maracaibo," Gabriel added. "You might want to ask our guest about that, however. He has an intriguing explanation about three fleets overlapping, putting as many as one hundred treasure galleons in Havana waiting to leave for Spain."

"One hundred galleons? There hasn't been a fleet that size in—"

"Over twenty years," Varian said, saving Pitt the trouble.

"I should think closer to thirty," Isabeau said quietly. "That was the last time they ordered all of their naval ships, and most especially all of their warships, home, and no, it was not because of three fleets overlapping. It was in anticipation of launching *la Felicissima Invencible*—the biggest invasion fleet the world had seen—against England the following spring. Do you read Spanish, Varian?"

"Why . . . yes, yes I do."

"Good. Then this should be of special interest to you." She returned to the sheaf of papers she had left on the desk and raised the topmost sheet. It was a single page of heavy parchment bearing the remains of two wax seals and the florid signature of the governor of New Spain.

"It seems the king has recalled all of his top ranking officials and ordered most of the troops and warships home to Castile. He also indulges in some bragging, stating that they have had great success in lulling the English king into believing they are committed to upholding a lasting peace, and that with the return of the Indies fleet to Spain, they will at last have sufficient men and ships, as well as the financial means, to launch another invasion armada in the new year, whereupon they will finally avenge the honor of their noble ancestors as well as eradicate the heretics from England once and for all, restoring the power and glory of the One True God." Isabeau came forward and presented the document to Varian. "As I understand it, you have been sent here to convince my husband and the other privateers to keep their ships in port. Are you quite certain that is what you want to do?"

Chapter Fifteen

$\mathcal{V}$arian was invited to accompany the Pirate Wolf and Geoffrey Pitt to the chart room. It proved to occupy one of the largest areas on the main floor and was aptly named for the breathtakingly huge reproductions of continents and coastlines painted directly onto two of the sixteen-foot-high walls. The territories that comprised the Spanish mainland in the New World—the Spanish Main—occupied one full quadrant and included minute details of the coastline that flowed from the tip of Florida around the gulf coast to the New Kingdom of León, down to the Yucatán, Panama, and across the northern coast of Tierra Firme from Cartagena to Paria. Painted inside the great gulf were the islands of the Greater Antilles, the Baja Más Islands, and the Caribbee Isles. Each known city, port, cay, and islet was neatly identified, the sea-lanes and passages marked as well as the thin blue latitude line denoting the Tropic of Cancer.

England, the western coast of Europe, and the Mediterranean filled another wall, while the third was filled with shelves of books, racks upon racks of maps, charts, astrological tables. The fourth wall was interrupted by doors leading out to the terrace, but between the two tall banks of doors was an enormous table the size of a dining board, on which had been built a three-dimensional map of the Spanish Main. It showed islands with any recognizable landmarks, channels, reefs, coastlines, and rivers. Forts were represented by small stone blocks over which flew tiny flags identifying the nation that controlled the island or port. Most were Spanish, but a surprising number of French and Dutch flags showed that inroads were being made, especially in the easterly Caribbee Isles.

At either end of the room were desks, a drawing table, assorted chairs, and small reading tables, and—as Varian raised disbelieving eyes to the ceiling—suspended over all was a map of the star constellations identical to what one could see if one stood on the roof and gazed heavenward.

"My wife's handiwork," said Simon Dante, waiting an appropriate amount of time for Varian to absorb the stunning details and close his mouth again. "She was as restless as a pirhana through all three of her confinements and I either had to find something for her to do or maroon her on an island somewhere for several months each time."

"I confess, I am speechless. I have never seen such extraordinarily fine work, not even in churches or cathedrals. The king's admirals would ransom their souls to have a room like this."

Dante smiled to acknowledge the compliment and poured three glasses of rum. The evening meal had been accompanied by an extravagance of wines: a full-bodied Rhenish plonk with the soup course, a lusty Madeira with the plates of shrimp and lobster, and a dry, velvety Burgundy with the mutton and beef. French cognac had been served with platters of fruit and cheeses for dessert, after which sweet cane rum had been enjoyed on the terrace with fat Dutch cigars. Varian's head should have been reeling, yet it was oddly clear and focused. Anger undoubtedly played a major role in his sobriety, for he had not only read the document Isabeau Dante had presented with such a cool flourish, but he had studied a dozen others that taken individually might have added to nothing but rumor and gossip. Taken as a whole they spelled treachery and cunning, deceit and betrayal. His shock, his confusion, had barely permitted him to enter into any of the conversations that had swirled around the dining table. He had noticed that Pitt and Simon Dante had exchanged more than a few quiet words between themselves, studying him while they did as if they were trying to gauge his true character. Thus it was with some interest—and wariness—that he accepted their invitation to join them in the chart room.

"I understand you have seen military duty."

"I served in the army for nine years."

"You must have purchased your commission young."

"I was sixteen. I had two older brothers who were more interested in business and family affairs. The army offered a handy escape."

"Your brothers?"

"The eldest, Richard, died almost five years ago. Lawrence was killed in a duel."

"Which elevated you to your current status as duke? Yet it would appear you have remained in the king's service."

Varian shrugged. "There were power struggles within the court. It seemed a poor time to show a lack of loyalty when the wolves were circling."

"Loyalty is an admirable quality in any man, regardless of the reasons," Pitt said. "You must have excelled at your post to have found yourself promoted to Captain of the Royal Guard so young."

"I excelled in stupidity, if anything. I was handed a note one day warning of a plot to blow up the king when he opened Parliament the next day. I charged blindly ahead, searched the cellars, found the culprit, and tore the lit fuse out of the cask with only inches to spare."

Dante laughed. "No wonder the king has an aversion to Parliament now. Yet I doubt your post was given solely as a reward for plucking a fuse out of a cask of gunpowder. Old Gloriana had a keen eye for young gladiators as well. She could have ten bull-necked wrestlers stand before her and unerringly pick out the one with enough fire in his eye to win the match. Furthermore, anyone who can impress my son with his swordsmanship—you must show me this move he goes on about—does not wear a captain's uniform only because he is pretty. Nor is he entrusted to sail several thousand leagues to persuade a few dozen pirates to lay down their arms if he has not earned the trust and respect of his peers. Trust, I might add, that seems well placed, for you hold your own counsel well. I have a thought that you would be a formidable adversary in a game of chess. But enough flattery. Tell me about this king. What is the climate of the country with a Scottish monarch on the throne?"

"I warrant the people would prefer him over a Spaniard," Varian said quietly.

Dante smiled. "And you, sir. What would you prefer?"

"I would prefer not to be put in the position of having to choose."

The piercing silver eyes narrowed. "Neither would I. So we'll leave England to its fate, shall we? You can return to London boasting that you met the Pirate Wolf and with diligent and daunting conviction persuaded him to keep the peace. I, meanwhile, having been warned of the overwhelming odds against us, and threatened with the consequences of disobeying the king's edict, will keep my ships in port and let the richest treasure fleet in a decade leave Havana unmolested."

Varian felt the knot in his chest grow tighter. Looking into Simon Dante's eyes was like looking into a world of salt and sea spray, of endless horizons and booming canvas, of smoking cannon and bloodcurdling violence. He could only guess what kind of fortitude, cunning, and intelligence a man needed to survive for thirty years in the middle of the most dangerous waters on earth, but he could say with absolute certainty that neither cowardice nor caution had played any part in shaping his destiny.

"If there was another choice to be made," he asked quietly, "what would it be?"

Dante's eyes gleamed. "The way I see it, we have

but two options. We do nothing, or we attempt to do something. The nothing part is easy. It is the 'something' that cannot be entered into lightly and might require more than some of us are prepared to give."

"If you are trying to alarm me," Varian said, "you are succeeding."

"Good. Only a stupid man jumps off a cliff without looking first to see what lies at the bottom."

Pitt had crossed the room and was gazing up at the map of England. "The logical and practical thing to do is to send you home with all due haste, your grace, armed with as much proof as we can give you against Spain's duplicity. It would then fall to you to convince the admiralty that Spain has no intentions of keeping the peace. Quite the opposite: Philip has every intention of mounting another invasion fleet and declaring open war." He paused and glanced briefly over his shoulder. "Forgive me if I repeat myself, but it helps when I am thinking aloud." He turned back to the map. "At best, a fast ship in perfect weather with strong northeasterly winds would take five weeks to cross the Atlantic. Once it arrived in London, any letters or documentation would have to be studied and interpreted by twenty wise, bewigged councillors, who would then have to argue and debate the wisdom of trusting the word of a handful of filibusters, who, it would be further argued, might well have written the documents themselves in order to justify their own *guerre de course*. Depending on your powers of persuasion, your grace, there might be some canny admiral who might—and I say *might*—dispatch a ship to spy along the coast of Spain, but that is highly doubtful . . . no insult against your integrity intended. I am sure you would argue long and hard and be quite passionate in your convictions. Nonetheless, the royal council chambers are filled with old men. We have a king who has been more engrossed with commissioning a new version of the Bible than he has the state of his navy and army. He will hesitate and cavil and unless he has more evidence than a few letters from a disgruntled cook in Nombre de Dios, he will pat you on the head and thank you for your observations, then send you out to your country estate to shoot pheasant.

"Meanwhile, the Havana fleet will sail. It will arrive in Cádiz unmolested, adding roughly forty warships the size of the *Santo Domingo* and few dozen refitted galleons to their armada. They will then have the winter to prepare, to send flowery messages of harmony and goodwill to London, and in the spring they will launch a fleet full of the sons and nephews of the noble officers and valiant soldiers who died in the first failed attempt at invasion. They will sail with vengeance in their hearts, bolstered by the knowledge that England will not have a formidable force of privateers to come to her defense this time because we have all been commanded to keep the peace."

"You paint a rather bleak picture," Varian said.

"Can you find fault with it?"

In truth, he could not. The king had been flattered and puffed up with self-importance when the Spanish ambassador had begun discussing the possibility of opening the Indies to legal trade with England, and with his being a Scot, it would require more than thirty barrels of gunpowder positioned under his arse before he would acknowledge the possibility he had been duped.

"There is another option," Dante said quietly, dragging Varian's thoughts away from the royal council chambers. "It would demand a tremendous leap of faith on your part, and would likely result in charges of treason, sedition, and piracy. It would also require ballocks the size of thirty-two-pound iron shot."

Varian stared into the unwavering silver eyes. The silence in the room was so thick he could hear the muted hiss of the candles burning on the desk and the distant ringing of a ship's bell somewhere out in the harbor.

"You certainly know how to gain a man's attention, Captain."

Dante acknowledged the compliment with a slow grin. "I haven't even fired my heavy guns yet."

He crossed the room and pointed to the map of the West Indies, specifically to a cluster of dots just south of the Baja Más chain of islands and spine-chillingly close to Hispaniola. "We're here, on Pigeon Cay. Scattered to the south and the east are more than a score of islands and harbors that serve as home ports for"— he hesitated over the wording a moment—"similar-minded gentlemen of misadventure. As you can imagine, the departure of the plate fleets in the spring and fall draw a certain amount of interest from these gentlemen and on average, we could expect ten, maybe fifteen captains to rendezvous at New Providence. The flota is due to leave Havana within the next four to six weeks. If we act swiftly, we can dispatch our own small fleet of pinnaces to the neighboring islands and ports, and if we offer the proper incentive, we could easily rouse the interest of thirty, perhaps even forty captains curious enough to hear what you have to say to them at New Providence."

"What *I* have to say?"

Pitt walked past, clapping Varian on the shoulder. "You are the king's emissary, are you not? You brought documents stamped with the royal seal offering all privateers amnesty in exchange for keeping the peace, did you not? Well . . . we shall simply reword those documents to offer them full pardon as well as claim to full shares of the profits for every ship they capture or sink or otherwise deter from reaching Spain."

Varian's jaw went slack.

"Half of them cannot read anyway," Dante said, "so all you will have to do is brandish a scroll over their heads that looks official. The other half are noblemen who may have taken a turn down the wrong path at some time, but who are still staunchly loyal to king and country. We'll have to fetch you some fine ducal clothes and put a curl in your hair, but my daughter assures me you are the very image of a royal envoy when there is silvered lace at your throat and a brace of purple plumes in your hat."

"But . . . I have no such decree, nothing that even bears the royal seal."

Pitt smiled and tipped an eye at the painted murals. "You will. And it will look authentic enough the king would think he wrote it in his own hand."

"More importantly," Dante added, "you will have us standing behind you. Knowing the Dantes are committed, the captains will believe it and will join the enterprise if only to ensure they get their fair share of the prize. To that end, I can say with all honesty that unleashing thirty privateers on a fleet of treasure ships—especially if they are not burdened with the guilt of altering manifests to match the ten percent share they apportion to the crown—would produce the same results as throwing a handful of gold coins before a crowd of beggars."

"Can we not just tell them the truth? That Spain is planning another invasion and England needs their help?"

"The same England that has threatened to declare them pirates and placed bounties on their heads? The same England that turns a blind eye when one of their ships is captured and the crew is forced to work as slaves in their mines? The same England," he added quietly, "that let the last fleet of privateers who came to their rescue starve and die by the hundreds from typhus and fever on stinking ships anchored in the Thames? Have you ever been tarred and feathered, your grace?"

Varian flushed. He had been barely three years of age when Sir Francis Drake rallied England's sea hawks to defend her coast against the last "invincible" armada, but he remembered that many of the stories of tremendous victory had been clouded by the treatment of the crews afterward. They were forced to remain in port for months, unpaid, poorly provisioned, forbidden to go ashore. Hundreds of brave men

starved and died of disease and when the crown eventually did pay them for their services, it was not one-
fifth of what they had been promised. To add insult
to injury, the queen blamed Drake for failing to pur-
sue the fleeing Spaniards, and in the end, he fell badly
out of favor and was forced to retire in disgrace and
near poverty.

"The name and legend of el Draque still causes
grown men to tremble here in the Indies," Simon remarked dryly. "I thought him a bit of a puffer, myself,
but there is no arguing his successes against the Spanish. Sprinkle his name wisely amongst the rhetoric and
you give rise to the specter of glory and victory again."

"Thirty ships against a hundred are still improbable
odds, Captain."

"Indeed they are. That is why we will have to work
swiftly to improve them somewhat."

"I don't understand."

"The Spaniards are arrogant and because of their
arrogance, they resist change. Not only do they continue to send their treasure fleets back and forth twice
a year on a regular schedule, but their point of disem-
barkation, their route, the method of protecting them,
has not changed in over a century. Their fighting tac-
tics are predictable as well, for there is only one sure
way for vessels that are top-heavy and square-rigged
to gain the advantage, and that is to stand off and
pound an enemy with their guns, then close and de-
pend on their soldiers to carry the battle. That is why
more than half a galleon's complement is made up of
troops who wouldn't know a knot of speed from a
knot in a rope. For the same reason, their command
is split. There is a *capitán de mar* who oversees the
mariners, and a *capitán del navío* who commands the
soldiers and, in battle, commands the entire ship. Most
of the time, neither one knows anything about the
other's job; thus there is always a certain amount of
confusion on board—more so if the two commanders
dislike one another and turn the whole thing into a
power pissing match. More rum?"

Varian looked down at his glass, surprised to see it was empty. "Please."

After the men replenished their drinks, Dante tipped his head by way of inviting Varian over to the topographical table. He took a taper from the mantel and lit it off one of the candles on the desk, then touched the flame to the multitined candelabra mounted on each corner of the table. The candles there were framed by curved sheets of polished metal, which focused all of the light down onto the tabletop. The effect threw shadows behind the mountain ranges and gave an even more realistic sense of depth to the islands and channels.

Pitt, meanwhile, had reached under the table and produced a handful of small, carved replicas of galleons. He started placing ships in ports located all around the table, naming them off as he went, setting particularly heavy clusters at the two main ports of Vera Cruz and Nombre de Dios.

"Some time over the next four weeks, all of these ships will be leaving port"—he pointed across the table—"and making for Havana."

Varian watched with interest as Pitt and Dante began moving the carved ships out into the open water of the gulf, aiming them by squadrons in the direction of Havana. At one point he saw another movement out of the corner of his eye and glanced over at the door in time to see Juliet slip inside the room. She did not approach the brightly lit table, but remained back in the shadows and stood with her shoulders leaning against the wall.

"The Dutch like to hunt here," Pitt said, placing a ship that had been painted green off the islands marked Little Antilles. A blue ship denoting French privateers was positioned west of the Caribbee Isles, and a third ship, painted red, was tucked into the Baja Más Islands. "The French are determined to take possession of the southern Caribbee, so they concentrate their efforts there, whereas the English favor the Straits of Florida, where the galleons catch the gulf currents and begin their run out to the Atlantic. As long as we all have one common, rich enemy—the Spanish—there is a certain degree of polite civility between the various nationalities. This is not to say that a Dutchman would not blast a Frenchman out of the water if the opportunity presented itself, but as a general rule, we exchange information when it is to our mutual advantage to do so."

"For instance, if our brethren to the south and west were to be told about the increased numbers of treasure ships bound for Havana," Dante said, "they would happily embark on a feeding frenzy of their own. If they are even modestly successful, word of the attacks will spread through the rest of the fleet and rattle the *almirante*'s composure before his ships even leave port."

"The Spanish are predictable in another way." Pitt was still maneuvering his vessels toward the port of Havana, lining them up in an orderly procession facing north. "They like to place their most formidable warships out in front, scattering galleons of a lesser size and firepower down each flank, then bringing up the rear with more heavy ships. The treasure ships are here"—he pointed—"in the middle. A fleet this size will take at least two days to clear the port. Because of prevailing winds and currents at this time of year, it will become strung out over twenty leagues or more until the rear guard, acting like dogs herding sheep, can bring all the stragglers up into formation. Once the fleet achieves that final formation, they are nearly impregnable, which is why, once they are out in the open water of the Atlantic, only a fool would attempt an attack. But here"—he touched a long, tapered finger on the port of Havana and traced it along the passage that ran between the eastern coast of Florida and the Baja Más Islands—"here is where they are the most vulnerable, for there are hundreds of low, sandy cays to hide behind. The strongest currents run through this area and few ships of any size are able to put about once they are committed. All an enterprising captain need do is lie in wait until a comely bitch passes by, then come up fast and attack from behind."

"You make it sound easy."

"Do I? If I have given you that impression, pray strike it instantly from your mind. The conditions in the Straits are the same for the predator as for the prey, and while I grant you our ships are lighter and faster and have the distinct advantage in maneuverability, they do not turn on a nod. If we miss on the first pass, it could take an hour or more to regain the weather gauge and by then, the element of surprise is gone and the galleon's guns are primed and waiting."

"If we were to succeed, however," Dante said, "we would stand a damned good chance of breaking up the convoy, of driving some of the ships into taking cover behind the islands, where they would sail right into the waiting hands and guns of our fellow brethren."

Once again Varian was struck by the penetrating intensity of the silver eyes. It was the same look he had seen in Juliet's eyes on the deck of the *Santo Domingo* when she had been fighting the Spaniards, and it was the same intoxicating power he had seen in her eyes when they had climbed the summit and she had spread her arms wide to catch the wind.

Beyond this place there be dragons.

The whispered echo of Juliet's words came to him with a shiver of understanding. The ancient mapmakers had known more than they suspected, for he had indeed arrived at the edge of the world he knew and understood. Beyond this room, beyond the boundaries of this island paradise, there were dragons waiting, too numerous to even begin to count. The next step he took would decide his course. To go forward was to step over the edge of the horizon and risk whatever perils lay waiting there. To step back was to retreat to where things were rational, orderly, and safe and where risks were only taken by others more suited to the task. It was his decision to make and he knew that once he was caught up in the current, there would be no turning back.

Varian looked from Simon Dante to Geoffrey Pitt to the silent, watchful figure standing in the shadows. The tightness in his chest grew until he was almost light-headed from the pressure and without even glancing down to see how steep a drop it was, he felt himself starting to pitch forward over the edge of the cliff.

Chapter Sixteen

"Run out the guns, Mr. Crisp. We'll fire three rounds with an extra ration of rum for the quickest crew."

"Aye, Captain." A grin put Nathan at the rail looking down over the waist of the ship. The men had anticipated the order and had their faces tilted expectantly up toward the quarterdeck. They had cleared the jagged teeth of the coral reef and would have to pile on sail to catch up to the five regal pyramids of canvas ahead of them, but there could be nothing left to chance on this voyage. After sitting in port for eight days, Juliet wanted all the guns to be fired, swabbed, and packed with fresh loads. There was nothing more damning than a cannon that had sat unused in the tropical heat and dampness. Despite wax plugs, moisture from rain and dew could have seeped into the touch holes and degraded the powder, making it merely pop and fizzle when a match was applied. Her father and brothers had taken similar precautions, as had Geoffrey Pitt, who had brought his sleek *Christiana* out for her maiden voyage.

Lucifer had been placed in command of the *Santo Domingo*, the crew once again supplemented by Lieutenant Beck and his Englishmen. In truth, if not for Beck presenting himself before her with a smart salute and an offer to help sail the galleon, she was not sure the *Domingo* would have left Pigeon Cay. Beck had admitted that the idea was not his. It was Varian St.

Clare who had approached him, advised him of the situation they were in regarding Spain's intentions to amass another invasion fleet, and left it to Beck's conscience as to whether he wanted to take a fast ship home with the news or stay and fight.

Beacom, having been presented with a similar choice, stood pale and withering beside Varian, his hands clapped over his ears as the orders were relayed to roll out the heavy guns.

On Nathan's command, the gunners opened the ports, knocked out the wedges that blocked the wheels of the gun carriages, and heaved on the breeching tackle. The eight twenty-four-pounder demi-culverins on the main deck were run out as were the twelve thirty-two-pounder culverins on the lower deck. The chief gunner for the starboard battery walked quickly down the line checking the lay of the guns and the readiness of the men, passing out glowing linstocks to each crew as he passed. The chief gunner for the larboard side did the same, pausing once to kick the backside of a man who had allowed one of the cables to go slack.

"Larboard ready!"

"Starboard ready!"

"Three rounds hot, gentlemen. Fire at will."

The words were not out of Nathan's mouth when the roar from twenty exploding guns swept along both decks. The sound traveled through the planking and trembled up the masts. It was followed by clouds of dense white smoke that boiled from the snouts of the guns and brought the harsh stink of sulfur and cordite creaming back over the decks.

Taking advantage of the recoil, the crews heaved on the tackling lines again, hauling the beasts inboard. While one man swabbed the barrel with a sponge and water, another stood waiting with a charge of powder and a ladle. A third was ready with the rammer and cloth wadding, a fourth with a ball of cast iron shot. Another pricked the powder charge through the touch hole and added a measure of fine ignition powder

from a horn. When the crew was clear, the gun was
run out again and the glowing end of the linstock applied to the primer.

Juliet was justifiably proud of her crew. They could
fire two rounds in under three minutes. Each man
knew how to lay a charge so that if any one man fell
in action, another could step up and sight the gun,
adjust the elevation wedges and the training tackle,
load, and fire. That was something her father insisted
upon after witnessing the confusion caused in battle
when the lack of knowledge and training resulted in
guns falling silent.

The three rounds were fired and ended in a draw
between four crews. Juliet happily allowed full measures of rum for all, then ordered fresh charges loaded
and the guns secured from the ports. Men were sent
into the tops to add more canvas and within the hour,
they had closed the gap between the *Iron Rose* and
her brothers' ships, the *Valour* and the *Tribute*, to a
few hundred yards. It looked strange to see the Spanish galleon sailing in their midst but Juliet was pleased
to see that the changes Nog had made on board had
increased her speed considerably. She could keep
apace at a steady eight knots and as long as the wind
did not take a drastic shift in direction, the new sails
and rigging would allow for better maneuverability.
More than twenty carpenters had swarmed over her
from stem to stern, sawing away unnecessary bulkheads, stripping the fancy paneling from her cabins,
banging away the cabins themselves. They had canni-
balized the two castles fore and aft so that from a
distance she gave the silhouette of a top-heavy galleon, but up close she was a mere shell with catwalks
built around the upper bulwarks to give the impression of a full deck. The renovations were continuing
while she was under sail, for hardly a league passed
where there were not discarded sheets of planking
floating in her wake.

A sharp clash of metal brought Juliet's attention
back to the main deck. She moved slowly to the rail,

knowing what she would see before she got there. Simon Dante may have used his powers of persuasion to coax the Duke of Harrow into accompanying them to New Providence, but he had also informed her that Varian St. Clare was still her responsibility.

It had been Nathan's suggestion that they assign him something to do on board and overseeing the daily practice with swords and pistols seemed a likely choice. He hadn't balked at the notion, and by the way he slashed through the first five men who ventured into the fighting circle, he looked as though he had been craving the exercise.

After leaving the chart room that evening, Juliet had returned to the *Iron Rose*. She had spent nearly every day and night since then on board, supervising the repairs here and on the *Santo Domingo*. She had kept herself too busy to think about Varian St. Clare, had barely said more than two words to him in passing, and had made a point never to be alone with him at any time.

It was not that she feared what would happen. She had no doubt they would come together like two oiled snakes given half the opportunity. It was more a matter of proving to herself that she had the force of will to stay away, that she could remain detached and observe him from the rail of the quarterdeck just as she observed every other member of her crew—with an impartial, critical eye.

Each of the first two opponents who faced him managed a half dozen strokes before a twist of St. Clare's wrist sent their blades spinning out of their hands. The third made but one clumsy lunge before he was sprawling, red-faced, on the deck, a ducal foot planted solidly on his backside. The fourth and fifth lasted slightly longer but they were clearly no match for St. Clare's expertise and again, their blades fell victim to the slight twist and spiral that saw their weapons somersaulting over their heads.

One by one he went through the ranks. The circle was thickening, the combatants attracting more and more onlookers, some of whom began to grow resentful as each of their mates fell victim to one trick or another that saw them disarmed and chased away at the point of the duke's elegant rapier.

"It could get ugly down there, lass," Nathan murmured, standing by her shoulder.

"It could," she agreed.

The crowd parted to a rousing cheer and Juliet smiled. Big Alf had been fetched from the lower deck, undoubtedly dragged away from his regular duties in order to have him teach a lesson to the pretty duke. Big Alf was deserving of his name, for he was a tower of bulging muscle, with hair sprouting from every conceivable pore on his arms, back, and shoulders. His favored weapon was the short, broad-bladed cutlass, and every man on board had seen him take the head off an opponent with one effortless swing.

As solidly built as Varian was, he still could have fit three of himself inside Big Alf's galligaskins and canvas pinafore with room to spare. And no sooner had Big Alf appeared at the edge of the circle than the glowerings and grumblings turned to excited laughter. Here, then, was someone who would show this lubber the color of his flag!

Varian merely took the measure of his opponent for a moment, then walked to where Beacom was sweating himself into a puddle. He exchanged his elegant rapier for a thicker, flat-bladed cutlass and returned to his quadrant, working his wrist back and forth as if to accustom himself to the heavier weight.

To the encouraging whistles and hoots from his mates, Big Alf lunged forward. He had a grin on his wide, hairy face as his first few hacking slashes forced St. Clare into a defensive stance, but the grin quickly turned into a grimace as the duke held off every blow, deflected every strike that would have sent any other normal man scrambling for cover. Alf's face turned red and his swings became broader. It was only practice and the intent was not to kill or maim, but it was a fine line that marked the difference.

Not that it mattered in the end, for within four more strikes, Big Alf's blade was slicing through the thin air where Varian's head should have been, and was buried instead into two inches of solid oak. It bit deep and stuck fast but before he could pull it free, the edge of Varian's blade was lying along Alf's jugular.

The men fell instantly silent, their champion defeated.

Up on the quarterdeck, Nathan read the expressions on their faces and his warning came out like a low growl. "Lass . . ."

"Wait," she whispered. She was watching Varian; his mouth was an inch from Big Alf's ear, and his lips were moving, so slightly she almost missed it herself.

"Ye say what?" Alf perked his head up, then to everyone's surprise, began to roar with laughter. He dropped his hands from the blade he was trying to extricate from the mast and doubled over, slapping the tops of his thighs as if the joke was the best he had ever heard. Varian was grinning as well. He stepped back and ran a thumb along the edge of the cutlass. He turned to hand it to Beacom, who had fainted, and tossed it instead to Johnny Boy, who was as owl-eyed and dumbstruck as the others.

When Alf stopped laughing, he straightened and wiped his hands across his eyes to catch the streaming wetness. He clapped the duke soundly on the shoulder, which very nearly accomplished what the bout of swordplay could not, then glared a challenge around the circle.

"Aye, then. Who's next? A doubloon from me own pocket to the man who can at least make the bastard break into a sweat!"

"I'll take your doubloon. And two more from the duke for my trouble."

Varian turned to track the source of the voice. Juliet stood at the edge of the circle, her hands on her hips, her legs braced firmly apart.

"Well, sir? Will you make it worth my while?"

"Only if you make it worth mine," he countered smoothly.

Juliet's slow smile caused some of the men to chuckle in anticipation. "If you get the best of me, your grace, your pockets will be heavier by a hundred gold doubloons . . . nay, two hundred. But for that much, I'll want to see the weight of your wager beforehand."

Varian smiled. "As you well know, Captain, my pockets are empty. You will have to trust me for the amount, which I will be happy to deduct from the two hundred you will owe when we are done."

A murmur rippled through the men, some of them laughing, some of the more enterprising among them beginning a hot exchange of private wagers.

"I'll take it out in trade instead," she said with narrowed eyes. "You lose and you'll fetch and carry like a cabin boy for the rest of the voyage. You will go barefoot and scrub the decks alongside the rest of the crew, and you'll learn how to set a sail, how to tie off a reef, even how to boil up a pot of burgoo to the crew's liking."

Varian took his rapier back from Johnny Boy and raised the blade in a salute to accept the terms.

The men raised a cheer and some spread their arms to usher the others back and widen the circle. Juliet drew her sword and flexed the thin, tempered steel once before slashing it down in a glittering arc and touching the point to the deck.

Varian assumed a similar stance; then after exchanging a nod with Juliet, both blades came up and tapped lightly together to start the flirtation.

They started to move, taking deliberate, prowling steps clockwise around the circle. Their eyes were locked, their smiles fixed. The sun was almost directly overhead, eliminating any advantage to one opponent or the other. Similarly the wind was warm and steady, lacking any gusts that might cause a man to squint or a lock of hair to blow across the eyes.

Juliet gave her wrist a small flick, scraping metal against metal. She saw his eyes narrow but his arm remained rocklike and steady, fully extended. A split second later, his blade was in motion, clipping hers through a volley of short thrusts that were so fast, the two lengths of steel moved in a blur. With his forward foot pacing out his attack, he came halfway across the deck before she was able to reverse the momentum of the thrusts and drive him back to where he had begun. She did not let up but continued to parry and thrust, lunging forward and back, to and fro, even leaping to the top of the capstan to deliver a flurry of ripostes from a superior angle.

When she jumped down, she landed on soft knees and went into an immediate crouch, slicing her blade parallel to the deck and forcing him to leap like a scalded cat in order to avoid the cut.

When the exchange ended, she strode back to take up her position in the first quadrant, her blade extended, the tip etching small circles in the air.

Varian came away from the wall of grinning men and moved back into position. A glance down confirmed the source of the laughter, for the front of his shirt had been sliced open in half a dozen places. It was loose, but not overly so, yet she had cut the cloth without so much as scraping a pink line in his flesh.

"My compliments, Captain," he murmured. "You show a deft hand."

"Do I? Shall I show you another?"

To his genuine and immense surprise, she tossed the blade from her right hand to her left and without waiting for him to recover from his shock, came in on the attack again. Their blades clashed, thrusting and slashing, seeking openings to the left, then to the right. Both adversaries were leaping and weaving their way through the sea of parting men now. The fight carried unceasingly across the deck to the bottom step of the ladderway, then with a graceful, spinning leap, to the top of the quarterdeck and all the way to the crutch of the bowsprit before the tide turned and the aggres-

sor was driven back to the opposite ladderway. Varian
had his back to the stairs and knew they were close,
but he dared not glance away for the smallest breadth
of a second. It was time, he thought. Time to end it
while he still had the wits and wrist to do so.

Juliet saw the small spark in the midnight eyes and
knew it was coming. She had watched all of his previous matches, studied his wrist, his shoulder, his footwork, the muscles in his jaw—all points where a
minute signal might betray what was coming next.
And there it was. The slight downward twist of his
wrist as he braced for the next lunge. With each and
every challenger who had gone before, this slight bend
had allowed him to cut the edge of his blade beneath
theirs, then to run it the length of the steel while moving his own sword in a tight spiraling motion. The
resulting pressure caused his opponent's fingers to flex
open and the hilt to fly out of the hand.

Juliet saw his thumb slip back on the guard, a pre-
lude to executing the "fillip," as Gabriel had called it.
There was not even a tenth of a heartbeat between
the shift of the thumb and the bend of the wrist, but
she used it to bring her sword up and snap it down
hard when his balance was momentarily suspended.
Instead of coming up beneath her blade, Varian's was
forced down with a sharp biting cut that brought the
hilt springing forward out of his startled fingers and
turning a silvery somersault before landing neatly and
solidly in Juliet's outstretched hand.

There was a moment of deafening, awed silence before the crew broke out in a clamorous roar. She
raised both swords in triumph to acknowledge their
cheers, then drove Varian's point down in a flare of
sunlight, embedding the tip in the deck before releasing it so that the shaft quivered upright between them.

The look of absolute astonishment on his face could
not be feigned. His hand was poised in the air as if it
still held the hilt. The only thing that moved was the
fat bead of sweat that rolled down his cheek.

Juliet resheathed her sword. "I believe that gives me the win, sir."

Varian recovered enough to offer a deep bow. "Your servant, Captain."

"Indeed you shall be, sir. As for you," she said and moved to the rail to address Big Alf, "Mr. Crisp will make a note to deduct the sum of one gold doubloon from your share of the profits before you drink and wench them away."

"Well spent it was, too, Cap'n! Well spent!"

She waved her hands to bring an end to the hurrahs, and beside her, Nathan's voice boomed out, ordering them back about their tasks. All save Johnny Boy, who was called to the quarterdeck with a tilt of Juliet's head.

"Take his grace the duke down to the galley and show him where he might find the victuals to prepare me a tray for supping. Oh, and fetch him a pot of lampblack. I seem to have won a few scuffs on my boots that need polishing out."

She smiled at Varian, then handed the helm off to a snickering Nathan Crisp before going below.

Once inside her cabin, she closed the door and leaned heavily against it. She had got the better of him, but only by a hair's breadth, for he was lightning quick and more resourceful than she had anticipated. There was dampness between her shoulder blades, more curling the fine hairs across the nape of her neck—the humid price of pride.

Shaking her hands to ease the ache in her wrists, she went over to her desk. On a normal day, at noon, she would carry the backstaff up on deck and take a reading to determine their position, but since they were only a few hours north of Pigeon Cay, the need was not pressing. She looked at the new journal she had brought on board. She had entered their time of departure and the date, September 3, but otherwise the pages were blank. Chewing thoughtfully on her lower lip, she pulled out the chair and sat down. She

stood a moment later and removed her sword belt,
then sat down again, wondering how busy she should
look on the first day of a voyage.

Opening a drawer, she took out a quill and a small
knife, and trimmed the tip to a fresh point. She un-
screwed the pot of ink and set it in the well, then
ran her tongue across her teeth a few times between
thoughtful glances at the door.

Leaning back in the chair, she propped her boot on
the edge of the desk.

A distraction, that was what he was. Just a distraction that would be gone from her life soon enough.

Varian only bumped into two bulkheads on his way
from the galley to the captain's cabin. He balanced a
wooden tray in one hand and carried a jug of ale in
the other. The captain liked ale with her noon meal,
Johnny Boy had informed him, then proceeded to
show him where the wooden ladle was hung and which
barrel had been marked for the captain's personal
consumption. Not watered down, he had confided in
a whisper, not like the weaker brew allotted for the
crew's ration of two quarts a day. They'd all be
drunken sots otherwise.

Varian was still prickling over the laughter that had
followed him below deck. How a mere slip of a
woman had bested him with a sword was completely
beyond his ken. Johnny Boy had winked and told him
it was a good thing he had let the captain beat him,
and he had wanted to box the boy's ears. *Let* her beat
him? The thought had not even occurred after the first
exchange of ripostes; in truth, he had been hard-
pressed to keep her from slicing more than just his
shirt into ribbons.

He arrived at the captain's cabin and, having no
spare hands, knocked with the rounded shoulder of
the jug.

"Come."

He worked the latch with his elbow and pushed the
door open, stumbling through with just enough bal-

ance left to keep the tray from tipping onto the floor. She was sitting behind the desk, a leg propped on the corner. A quill was in her hand, the feathers brushing her lips as she twirled the shaft between her thumb and forefinger. The bank of gallery windows was behind her, glaring brightly with the reflection of the sun off the water. She had taken the thong out of her hair, and the dark auburn curls spilled loosely over her shoulders, the finest strands glowing fiery red against the light.

He moved forward slowly, setting the tray and jug down on the desk. She said nothing, she just watched him and twirled the end of the quill against the soft pout of her lip.

It was such a small thing. A feather dusting her lip. But then he saw where a dark curl of hair rested over her breast. From there, it was a graceless slip down to stare at the crease in her breeches at the top of her thighs. He felt another bead of sweat trickle down his temple and before he could even reason with himself, he was standing beside her, reaching down and pulling her up into his arms.

She could have stopped him with a word, but she didn't. She could have resisted, could have pushed him back and flailed him for the audacity, but she was too busy opening her mouth and taking the heat of him inside. She flung her arms around his neck and uttered a soft, throaty moan as his tongue lashed her mouth. Her fingers clawed into his hair so that even if he wanted to, he could not pull away until she had her fill.

Varian's hands went to her waist and tugged at the fastenings of her breeches. When they were unlaced, he pushed them down over her hips, then ran his hands everywhere the moleskin had been—around the swell of her buttocks, over the flat plane of her belly, down into the warm nest of soft curls. He ran his fingers between her thighs and groaned into her mouth when he felt how sleek and slippery-wet she was. He stroked again and this time found the source of all that heat and moisture, curving his finger up and thrusting it deep enough that she gasped and shuddered in his arms.

Without unmolding his mouth from hers, he lifted her and sat her on the edge of the desk. He managed to pull off one boot and one leg of her breeches before he reached a shaking hand down to the fastenings at his own waist. The laces were not fully loosened before he was sweeping the top of the desk clear behind her and easing her back onto the wood. He breached her hard and fast, each thrust winning a cry of pleasure from her lips. Her legs went around his waist and she kept him locked tightly in her embrace until they were both straining and clutching each other through a mutual and stunningly prolonged climax.

He did not stop after the first flush of ecstasy, nor even the second. At some point he tore off her other boot and cast her breeches to the floor, and they moved from the desk to the chair. She sat astride his lap while his hands roved beneath her shirt and started the incessant throbbing between her thighs again. A small shift of weight forward and he was there, thick and hard, stretching up until she gasped and clawed his shoulders and could not breathe.

"You are acquiring some bad habits, your grace," she whispered. "You have learned to take without asking."

His mouth nuzzled deeper into the curve of her throat and his answer was muffled. She didn't care anyway. She only laughed and arched her neck and felt him move inside her again, her body silky and lush with the overflow of their passion.

He lifted his mouth from her shoulder and watched the pleasure streak across her face, wondering why . . . when he had ever thought her anything less than beautiful. Her eyes, her nose, her mouth—especially her mouth when it was trembling around a disbelieving cry—they were what had conspired to keep him restless and unable to sleep for eight days and nights alone on Pigeon Cay.

"There?"

"Yes."

"Now?"

"Dear Christ, yes."

The shaky whisper of breath on his cheek made him smile, made his flesh pulse within her. She melted forward against his chest, but there was nothing she could do. He was in control. Her feet hung several inches off the floor and with nothing to give her leverage, she was at his mercy . . . for once. He tightened his hands around her waist and held her until she stopped squirming, then skimmed his fingers down to cradle her bottom again.

When she was able, she opened her eyes and glared into his.

"You will pay for that," she promised.

"The coin will be well spent," he murmured, his fingertips starting to roam in places that had her curling her lower lip between her teeth. A whimper brought her head forward so that her brow touched his chin and this time when he surged inside her, she groaned.

"Is it because I bested you with the sword? Are you determined to prove yourself superior with a blade of another kind?"

He laughed, low and soft. "If you had this kind of blade, madam, I would gladly concede without ever testing it."

"You will concede anyway," she hissed quietly. "I will have you on your knees begging, damn you. I'll—"

The knock on the door cut off whatever she was about to say and she froze.

"Cap'n, you in there?"

It was Johnny Boy.

"Cap'n?"

"What is it? I'm . . . I'm busy."

Varian's eyes narrowed. He slid his hands up to her waist and exerted just enough downward pressure to win a shivered curse from between her lips.

"Mr. Crisp sent me down to fetch the chart."

"Wh-what chart, dammit?"

"He says we'll be passin' Crooked Isle before the glass runs out an' he had a thought that he might like to know where the shoals lie."

Juliet released her breath in a frustrated hiss against Varian's throat. "I have to get it for him. He won't go away unless I do."

Varian relented. He lifted her enough that she could climb off his lap, but he kept his hands around her waist until her legs steadied beneath her.

"Just a minute," she said loudly. "I'm fetching the damned chart."

She walked quickly around the desk and crouched down to search among the rolls of parchment that had been scraped to the floor earlier. She found the chart and padded barefoot to the door, glancing back once before she opened it just enough to push the roll through.

"Here it is. Tell Mr. Crisp I'll be up on deck directly."

"Aye, Cap'n." The boy tipped his head and tried to see behind her, but she closed the door with a firm slap and threw the bolt. She waited, her head and hands pressed to the wood, but it was several moments before she heard the telltale sound of Johnny Boy's peg thumping away.

Even so, she couldn't move. Her legs were trembling, her thighs were running with pearly wetness, and the breath rasped hotly in her throat.

A glance told her he had not moved, not any part of him. He was still taut and full, his flesh quivering like his sword when she had driven it into the deck. Nothing moved except his eyes and they were inviting her back, promising she could take what she wanted with or without asking. She was not even aware of her feet touching the floor as she returned. She took the hand he held out to her and let him bring her back where she belonged, settling over him without a moment to spare.

The orgasm was shattering and intense, no more no less so than any other had been in his arms, and yet it was different. It had no beginning, and when it rushed through her, it had no end. The flood of sensations just seemed to recede for a time, knowing that another look, another touch, would bring the tide flowing through her again.

Chapter Seventeen

From a strategic point of view, New Providence was ideal for privateers and pirates alike. The entrance to the harbor was protected by an island that allowed two ways in and out, making it impossible to blockade with anything less than a fleet of warships. The hills behind the beach provided an expansive view of the horizon, giving lookouts plenty of time to issue a warning if hostile sails came into view, plus an ideal vantage point to spot merchant ships that were weaving their way through the island chain. Less than a hundred yards from shore there was a tangled jungle of tropical vegetation where an entire crew could vanish within minutes and never be found by pursuers. While there were no permanent structures erected, the beach could be transformed overnight into a city of tents, with canvas sails strung over spars stuck into the sand.

The island was also the ideal base for launching attacks against merchant ships traveling from the New World to the Old, in particular the Spanish galleons that had been using the Straits of Florida as a main route to the Atlantic since Columbus had first discovered land. Even those who chose a different avenue were fair game, for the island lay within a few hours sail from the Providence channels and the Mona Passage. Between one route and the next, there were thousands of low, sandy cays where a stalking ship could hide and pounce on its victim without warning, which was why vessels often banded together for protection, and why the rich treasure fleets were escorted by a small armada of warships.

Varian was on deck as the *Iron Rose* sailed toward the mouth of New Providence harbor. As stimulating as the approach to Pigeon Cay had been, this was less blood-pounding by comparison but equally as intriguing, for there were easily more than twenty ships anchored in the bay. Lookouts posted on the outer island had obviously recognized Simon Dante's silhouette and pennons. They waved and shouted hails across the water, curious to know about the Spanish galleon in their midst, a sight which filled the decks of every ship and brought men down onto the beach by the droves.

Ever a cautious man, Dante had elected to leave the *Tribute*, the *Valour*, and the *Santo Domingo* cruising offshore with the *Christiana*, but there was no mistaking the enormity of the warship, even at a distance. Jonas and Geoffrey Pitt were on board the *Avenger*, and Gabriel was sailing in with Juliet, though he was politic enough not to crowd his sister's quarterdeck while the ship was maneuvering into port.

He was, in fact, standing beside Johnny Boy in the waist of the ship, laughing and whooping along with the rest of the crew as the lad tied small molded cartridges packed with charcoal, lampblack, and copper filings to the tip of an arrow, lit the fuse, and launched the missile up into the sky. When the arrow reached the top of the arc, the packet exploded, sending a fountain of burning blue sparks showering over the water. The rockets were sent up in response each time one of the other privateers fired their bowchasers by way of greeting the new arrivals.

When several dozen arrows had been spent, Johnny Boy slung the longbow over his shoulder and happily caught the coins some of the men flipped at him for the show. Gabriel's contribution was gold, accompanied by a pat on the tousled head before he sauntered over to join Varian by the rail.

"I was not aware the longbow was a favored weapon so far south of English forests."

Gabriel hooked a thumb over his shoulder to indicate the quarterdeck. "Jolly thought it was something the lad could handle. Muskets and arquebuses are too heavy, too cumbersome to load and fire with just one leg. He is adept with a dagger and is able to throw one with the skill of a gypsy. But when he fit the bow to his hand, it was like fitting a woman's breast to the palm. In a matter of weeks he could shoot an arrow from one end of the ship to the other without taking out anyone's eye. Nog assisted in the endeavour by making him a special bow, sized down for his height and weight. After that, well, he was unstoppable. And there is, of course, a more practical side to the skill— aside from displays of flying sparks. Arrows can carry a pitch-soaked fireball to an enemy's sails from three hundred yards out and, with Johnny Boy sighting the target, can strike to within a finger's width of where it is aimed."

Varian glanced at the boy, who looked hardly old enough to have acquired such skills, much less that he should have been faced with the need to learn them.

"Are you well rehearsed for your role, your grace?" Gabriel asked, his eyes scanning the beaches, the surrounding hills.

"As ready as I can be with forged documents and a lie on my tongue."

Gabriel smiled. "Ah, but they are excellent forgeries, you must admit, and your tongue seems smooth enough to have already taken you places that few men have dared to go before. Mind, you do not seem to heed warnings very well, do you?"

Varian kept his gaze trained on the forest of swaying masts that filled the harbor, and refused to acknowledge the barb. Juliet had insisted on some degree of discretion throughout the past two days, although it seemed from the moment they had emerged from her cabin that first morning, the entire ship's crew was aware of their transgressions. Gabriel Dante had been on board less than half an hour and it was apparent that he had already been informed that their afternoon in the cavern had not been the end of it.

The golden eyes were not going to relent and Varian braced himself to meet them, but won a moment's grace as Juliet came up behind them.

"What are you two plotting?"

She was dressed in her black doublet and breeches. The black cape with the scarlet lining was as striking as the whiteness of the ruff on her collar.

"We were just discussing how truly handsome you look, Captain," Gabriel said, bowing over her gloved hand. "And . . . dare I say it? . . . happy. There seems to be a bloom in your cheeks these days and a wicked liveliness in your step. Indeed, I fear for the safety of Van Neuk's manhood if he attempts to pinch your rump tonight."

"Faith, he has been trying to pinch it since I was eleven."

"Ten years, without success," he mused aloud. "Perhaps, if he had condensed his efforts into ten days, he would have had more success."

Juliet smiled. "Behave. Or I will stab you."

Gabriel raised his hands. "I am only saying aloud what most of your crew is whispering behind their hands."

"Let them whisper. And when you go ashore tonight and bury your face between the breasts of the first whore who lowers her blouse, I pray you suffocate on your piety. Now, and again when you return to Pigeon Cay and explain to Melissa why your prick is red and itchy. Did you by chance meet my brother's paramour in your wanderings on the cay?" she asked, turning to Varian. "You could not possibly have confused her with anyone else if you had, for she stands over six feet tall, has breasts the size of ripe melons, and a temper hot enough to fry an egg."

The sudden infusion of dark blood to Gabriel's cheeks caused him to waver slightly with the light-headedness.

"Yes." Gabriel cleared his throat. "Well." He squinted up at the sky. "We should get ashore just in time for a sunset." He lowered his head again and after a few more moments of silence, his eyes slanted toward Juliet. "Yes, well, all right. Just be careful, that is all I'm saying. You would not want to give a room full of freebooters any reason to think you have gone soft, or worse, that you have been swayed by more than just the rhetoric of the king's envoy. I doubt Father would be too keen on knowing it either."

He tugged a lock of hair by way of a salute before he wandered away to talk to Nathan Crisp.

Juliet only sighed and placed her hands on the rail, turning to face the harbor. The scarlet plume in her hat was barely ruffled by the passage of air, indicating the *Iron Rose* had slowed considerably as she glided toward an anchorage. The *Avenger* was just ahead, a half-pistol-shot off their starboard side, and they could hear the running of the cables through the hawser, the splash of the huge iron anchor as it hit the surface of the water.

"He is right, you know," Varian murmured. "Perhaps we should—"

"Keep a modest distance from each other? Are you afraid of shocking the sensibilities of a tent full of privateers? Or are you afraid of what my father might do if he found out where you have been spending your nights?"

"I am not afraid of your father. Not entirely, that is." He flushed. "I just think—"

"You think we should behave with proper decorum outside locked cabin doors?"

Varian's breath caught, for her hand had slid between him and the bulwark and cupped around his groin. "It might be prudent to show a little restraint, yes."

She laughed and withdrew her hand. "Prudence *and* restraint? My, how you do test me, sirrah. Shall I test you, then? Do you have your speech prepared? Father will not want any time wasted on niceties. This late in the afternoon, most of the captains are likely drunk or well on their way, but first thing in the morning, he will be tossing you to the lions and you will have to be convincing. The fact that you have arrived under his protection will gain their initial attention, but the rest will be up to you. If you falter or show any hesitation . . ."

"What is there to hesitate about? If these men cannot disrupt the fleet, then England will be at war with Spain. There will not be peace on either side of the line. And exactly who is this Van Neuk?"

Juliet thought she saw the smallest flicker of green in the midnight eyes and almost smiled. "He is a Dutchman. Anders Van Neuk. He has been sailing these waters nearly as long as my father and fancies there should have been a stronger alliance made between our two families. A brutishly handsome devil he is, too. I was almost tempted, the last time we met, to accept his invitation to enjoy a private dinner on board his ship."

"What stopped you?"

She shrugged and answered honestly. "I'm not sure. Perhaps because every woman in every port brags about how big he is, how tireless, how magnificent a lover. And because if I ever did find myself carrying someone's bastard, I would not want it to look like every other yellow-haired, green-eyed bastard scattered throughout the islands."

Varian's reaction to her bluntness tightened the lines around his mouth. It was not the first time he had pondered the consequences that might result each time he spent himself in her arms. But to hear it stated so flatly, so matter-of-factly, that she would regard any child of his a bastard unnerved him more than if it had just remained an unspoken thought.

Nathan Crisp signaled from the quarterdeck and Juliet left to oversee the final moments of dropping anchor. Varian leaned his weight on the rail but could not stop his gaze from following her as she took the steps to the upper deck two at a time. The wing of

her cape was folded back over one shoulder, showing
a splash of crimson silk. The blade of her sword had
been polished until it shone, and so freshly honed
that it could slice a candle cleanly in half without
dislodging the top from the bottom. She was magnificent and his feelings for her grew more terrifying
every day, for what frightened him more than any
roomful of pirates, any indignant fathers or brothers,
or any war that might be looming ahead was the
thought that he might actually be falling in love
with her.

Anders Van Neuk was almost a caricature of what
every rascal in every ballroom in London described as
a pirate in order to titillate the females in the audience
and leave them swooning. He was tall, with incredibly
broad, square shoulders that tapered to a narrow waist
and long, powerful legs. His hair was bleached almost
white by the sun and hung in a mass of gleaming curls
past his shoulders, interlaced here and there with
braids strung with beads of pure gold. Long-lashed
green eyes blazed with fire. A thin, hooked nose and
full sensuous lips completed the picture and needed
no help from the studded black leather doublet and
crossbelts festooned with guns and knives of all size,
weight, and description.

He was by far the most impressive of the captains
and officers gathered in the makeshift tavern built out
of wooden spars and canvas sheets. Trestle tables had
been set up on the sandy floor, and busty women with
bare legs ran back and forth to the huge barrels
stacked out back to replenish mugs and pitchers with
ale. There were huge fire pits dug along the beach,
the coals glowing red under spitted pigs, goats, chickens, as well as a whole cow that had been butchered
into manageable quarters. Platters of bones and bread
crumbs littered the tables, evidence that some of the
captains had been in port a few days. Dogs fought and
snapped over scraps of meat while cabin boys set up

games along the beach, being too old to be left on board, too young to amuse themselves with the whores.

Varian took in all the sights and smells as they walked up from the longboats.

Beacom had taken extra care fussing with brushes to remove the smallest specks of dust and lint from the sapphire blue doublet and cape he wore. His stockings were without snags; his breeches were close fitting and absent any padding or pleats. The starched ruff around his throat was made of the finest linen crimped to quarter-inch folds, the front pinned in a descending vee over his chest by a ruby the size of a child's fist. Flanking him were the Dantes, and a more impressive display of wealth and power could not be imagined. Also in their company was Lieutenant Jonathan Beck wearing brand new garb that was augmented by a gold-link torque and medallion stamped with the official naval insignia. Isabeau Dante had thought the torque was a nice touch, though Varian had not dared to ask where she came by the medallion. He had not asked about the wax seal that appeared on the forged papers either, or the signature that was identical, even to the slant and scrolled flourishes, with James Stuart's.

Most of the captains knew Simon Dante on sight and shouted hails over the heads of their comrades. Some knew him only by reputation and they turned to stare, studying each member of the Pirate Wolf's party as if they had not believed all of the stories they'd heard to date. Many stalled when they came to Isabeau, confirming her identity with a quick glance down at the empty sleeve, after which their interest turned to Juliet, who simply returned their speculative stares until their eyes were sent back to their ale.

Van Neuk parted the crowd with long strides, presenting a wide grin that gleamed like shark's teeth through the neatly trimmed moustache and rusty orange beard.

"Simon Dante, you hoary old bastard! Still standing before the mast, I see."

Dante grasped a hand studded with rings on every finger and returned the greeting. "You've not kissed the gallows yet, Anders? I heard they caught you smuggling off Porto Bello last spring."

"A tasteless rumor—the catching, not the smuggling. They fired a few shots. I fired more, and wound up adding a new ship to my arsenal. A fine young brigantine that flies like the wind. God curse my soul, nothing that compares to a bloody great fortress like the *Santo Domingo*!" The glittering eyes sought Juliet. "Is it true, lass? Is it true you were the one to take her?"

She cocked an eyebrow. "The *Iron Rose* and her crew took her."

One green eye narrowed. "Single-handedly? Your brothers were not riding off your stern?"

Juliet crossed her arms over her chest. "If you doubt me, I can show you how it was done. I'll hole your *Dove* and send you to the bottom with her."

Van Neuk studied her a moment, almost raping her with his eyes. "Damn me if I'd not willingly let you hole me from the bottom or the top, lady love."

Juliet did not respond to his crude humor, but he must have caught another movement out of the corner of his eye, for the piercing gaze darted over her shoulder and narrowed again when he saw Varian St. Clare. "Who's this then? Looks like you've brought along one of the king's lightskirts."

Varian stiffened and his hand dropped instinctively to the hilt of his sword, but it was Gabriel who stepped forward, cutting between St. Clare and the Dutchman. "Business can keep until tomorrow, dammit. My mouth is as dry as camel dung in the desert and if it isn't wetted soon, my tongue will be stuck fast to my teeth and I will have no way of inquiring who—God keep me sane—those two lovely wenches were who were bouncing on your knee when we arrived."

Van Neuk chuckled. " 'Twasn't my knee they were

bouncing on, lad, and you're welcome to them if you've a mind, for I've done with my licentious ways. I've seen where my true heart lies," he added, grinning drunkenly at Juliet, "and I'm swearing an oath of chastity here and now until she gives me ease."

"Then I regret to tell you that you will be chaste for a very long time," Juliet said, patting him on the chest as she brushed past. She followed her father to a table that had been hastily cleared for their use and tipped her head at Varian to suggest he join them while Gabriel had the Dutchman distracted.

He sat beside her, releasing a long breath and a disbelieving murmur. "These are the men with whom your father purports to stop a Spanish fleet?"

"That's good," she said. "You look indignant and skeptical. That should win them over to our cause."

"If I look indignant and skeptical, it's because I *am* indignant and skeptical. They're coarse, they're filthy. They are blackguards and drunkards and . . . and good gracious sweet God, what is that woman doing on her knees over there?"

Juliet followed his shocked glance to where a woman was locked between the thighs of a red-faced brute, her head bobbing rapidly up and down in his lap.

"Definitely not behaving with prudence or restraint, I vow," she murmured. "Are you jealous?"

"I *beg* your pardon?"

"Beg me later," she whispered through a sly smile. "And I will decide if you are pardoned or not."

Juliet was still laughing softly when she turned and realized her mother had been watching them. The golden eyes were flitting between her daughter's face and that of the duke's, accompanied by a small frown that suggested she had heard the whispers, too, but had not quite believed them.

The beginnings of a defensive flush started to creep up Juliet's throat but it was forestalled when several pewter mugs spilling foam down the sides were slammed on the table, followed magically by platters of meat, loaves of bread, plates, and two large silver candelabras. Toasts were made welcoming the Pirate Wolf to the fold, and by the time Juliet remembered the soft query in her mother's eyes, her own were blurring from the laughter and the spirits.

Chapter Eighteen

The strong shaft of sunlight struck Juliet directly in the eye, prompting her to move her head to one side. It didn't help. The sun was nearly level with the western horizon, and the glare was causing the contents of her stomach to churn, her head to throb.

It had been a necessary evil to drink to each toast made in their honor last night, but as the evening wore on, the ale was bolstered by wine, the wine by rum, and it had taken all of her powers of concentration to make it back to the ship without falling out of the longboat. She did not remember climbing up the hull to the deck, nor did she remember getting from the deck to her cabin. When Johnny Boy had wakened her at four in the afternoon, she was still fully clothed, lying facedown in her berth with a thin string of spittle trailing out of her mouth.

She had not bothered to do much more than splash her face with cold water and drink half a pitcher of water straight out of the jug before descending to the longboat again and rowing across to the *Avenger*. Varian St. Clare looked just as bleary-eyed as he sat in throbbing silence beside her, too miserable to do more than grunt when she remarked that more ships appeared to have arrived through the day, for the harbor was a forest of masts from one end to the other. It was either that, or her eyes were not uncrossed yet.

Neither Jonas nor Gabriel had returned to the ship after their night of drinking, but Simon Dante met

his daughter at the gangway with a cheerful, totally
unaffected smile, despite the fact that he had swilled
half his fellow captains under the boards before they
swaggered out of the tent at dawn.

Now she was standing in that same airless tent,
swamped by the stench of sweaty bodies, old ale, and
women who had been on their backs most of the night.
She wore the clothes she had slept in and the velvet
was stifling, the cape kept slipping off her shoulder,
strangling her, and one of the scarlet plumes in her
hat drooped annoyingly over her left eye.

She adjusted the brim for the tenth time, and instead of thinking about how much her head hurt, she
tried to concentrate on the discussions that were buzz-
ing around her. Simon Dante had addressed the captains first, wasting no time on oratory. He gave details
of the letters captured with the *Santo Domingo*, mentioned the various rumors from different sources concerning the strange numbers of ships in port. At this
point, several captains volunteered their own eyewit-
ness accounts of increased activity along the Main, and
when they started to speculate over the reason, Dante
introduced Varian St. Clare, his grace the Duke of
Harrow, come all the way from London with the explanation and a lucrative offer from the king.

Varian, taking his cue from the Pirate Wolf, kept
his words to a minimum. His eyes had more red in
them than white, and his mouth compressed into a
tight line whenever there was an outburst of noise
from the company, but he won everyone's attention
when he produced the royal decree that guaranteed
complete amnesty to any privateer who was willing to
aid in diverting the Spanish ships. When he added that
the king was further prepared to waive the ten percent
tithe due the crown on each cargo taken as prize, the
tables rocked and jumped with the force of the pewter
mugs thumping on the boards.

Asked why the king was being so generous, he did
not lie more than was absolutely necessary. Peace negotiations with Spain had broken down, he said, and

the king of England wanted to strike a blow where Philip would bleed the most—in the Spanish treasury.

Privateers were a suspicious, wary lot, and even though some of them could not read, they all demanded to inspect the royal Act of Grace, to frown over the embossed wax seal, to tap a thoughtful finger over the king's signature. Some put their marks on the parchment without hesitation after being assured that the Dantes were committed. Some, who had signed private articles of privateering with two or three of the other captains, were bound by those articles to discuss all ventures among themselves before voting yay or nay, but it only took a word, whispered in the right ear, for the estimated value of the *Santo Domingo*'s cargo to sweep through the crowd.

To a man, they signed and at the end of the meeting, there were thirty-seven signatures or marks, including the five that represented the Dante ships. There was still a long night of drinking and more debate ahead, but by the time the sun finally dipped below the dunes, Juliet's head was on the verge of splitting. It was necessary for Varian to remain and weather the questions thrown out by the captains, but she moved discreetly to a seam in the canvas walls and ducked out into the clean night air.

The first thing she shed was the cape, flinging it away in the sand like a twirling fan. The hat was next, after which she tore at the fastenings of her doublet, stripping it off and flinging it over her arm. The laces on her shirt were next. She parted the cambric almost to her waist to let her skin breathe, then took a knife to the annoying ruffles around the collar, casting the lace away in the soft sand behind her.

She climbed the dune and followed it to the far end of the beach, where the noise was reduced to a distant hum. Tucked behind a low tumble of rocks she found a shallow tidal pool, and although the stronger currents and tall waves were just the other side of a narrow breakwater, the pool itself was calm, the long, smooth water rippling over the fine granules of sand.

Dropping her doublet and hat on the beach, she sat on a rock and removed her boots, her sword belt, her pistols. With bare toes curling into the cool sand, she waded knee-deep into the water and just stood there, her head tilting side to side to work the tension out of her neck, her hands scooping water to splash on her throat and chest. Out in the harbor, each ship blazed with lamps hung from the rails and rigging. The moon would be late, but there were half a hundred torches flickering along the distant shoreline, and as the sky grew darker, stars began to appear, singly at first, then in clusters, glittering like pinpricks through some vast black cloth.

Juliet raised a hand, tracing a fingertip through the bright stars of a familiar constellation.

"That would be Sagittarius, the Archer. A fitting symbol, all things considered."

Juliet whirled around. Anders Van Neuk was stretched out on the sand, his hands laced behind his neck to support his head, his feet crossed at the ankles.

A quick glance told her he was alone. A longer glance, augmented by a silent curse at her own stupidity, showed that he had placed himself within arm's reach of her clothes, her sword, her guns.

"I caught your signals, lass, and about time, too."

"What signals?"

"Toffing your hat every time I looked at you. You could have just walked up and grabbed me by the arm—or aught else for that matter—and I'd've followed you just the same. Mind, I'll admit this is a mite more romantic, for you look like a nymph freshly risen from the sea."

"Anders, it's late and I'm very tired. If you thought I was signaling you to join in some romantic intrigue, you were mistaken. I was merely itching to get out of that tent."

"Itching? Aye, I know the feeling well," he said quietly. "I've had an itch for you, lass, longer than I can remember. And if you put your teasing ways aside, you'll admit you've had the same damned itch, one you almost let me scratch the last time we met."

Juliet bit the inside of her lip. She did remember a moment, scant though it had been, when her curiosity had almost got the better of her. She had been with Gabriel, and they had recognized the *Dove* at anchor when they passed French Key. The two ships had put in to barter a portion of their cargo to the Dutchman in exchange for sheets of copper plating, and a combination of foolish circumstances had placed the two of them on deck under the stars with his hands up her shirt and his tongue halfway down her throat.

"That was a mistake. We had both been drinking, and—"

" 'Twas no mistake, lass. You were as hot for me as I was for you. 'Twas your brother who interrupted us, plague take him, but it'll not happen again. I've taken precautions this time to ensure we'll not be disturbed."

He raised a hand and snapped his finger. Almost immediately, the silhouettes of four burly men stepped out from behind the rocks and stood with their arms crossed over their chests, their grins showing through their beards. Four more appeared on the left and another two came over the crest of the dune. In all, they formed a protective semicircle around the little inlet, leaving no escape other than the sea.

Stupid, stupid, stupid to have wandered so far down the beach.

Stupider still to have unbuckled her sword and guns, leaving her with only her wits, which were in damned poor shape, yet sobering fast. She was a strong swimmer. It would be a hellish long pull through the currents that ripped across the mouth of the harbor, but with luck she would not be dragged out into the ocean before she had a chance to pour a few broadsides down the Dutchman's throat.

No sooner had the thought passed through her mind than she heard a faint splash behind her. Before she could react, a thick arm had snaked around her waist, another around her neck. Juliet twisted around and thrust two fingers in the direction she thought her attacker's eyes should be. She hit one, feeling it squish against her fingernail, but was too far off center and missed the other. Even so, he howled and loosened his grip enough that she was able to turn and drive a knee into his groin.

She broke free but heard more footsteps splashing through the water. There were five of them this time, converging on her like mongrels, laughing, reaching out to grab her arms, her legs, her waist. The first one to touch her had his nose smashed and the bones driven into his face by the heel of her hand. The second roared and spun away, his cheek cut open by the wedge of coral she swung up from the sandy bottom. She started to run for deeper water, but someone snatched her hair from behind and jerked her head back. Someone else clubbed her temple with a fist, causing an explosion of pain in her head that made her limbs turn momentarily to jelly.

A moment was all they needed to lift her out of the water and carry her to shore. She was squirming and swearing by the time they dragged her free of the surf, but they only tightened their grip and lowered her onto the sand like a sacrificial offering. They stretched her arms out and pinned them flat, they spread her legs impossibly wide, and someone planted a boot firmly on her hair to keep her head anchored to the ground.

Anders Van Neuk stood and brushed the sand off his breeches. He looked down at her, shaking his head as if he was terribly disappointed in her behavior.

"We can do this one of two ways, lass. You can show a little proper enthusiasm, or you can lie there with all these fine lads watching. Either way, I'll be between your thighs and I'll be enjoying myself."

"My father, my brothers, will kill you," she hissed.

"Aye, that is a consideration," he agreed, beginning to unfasten buckles and belts. "But I figure by the time they start to wonder what's happened to you,

you'll be tucked up safe and sound on board the *Dove* and we'll be underway."

"They'll come after you. They'll hunt you down like a dog and flay the skin from your body strip by strip."

"It's your own skin you should be worrying about now, lass, and how much of it will be left when the Spaniard finishes with you."

"Spaniard? What Spaniard?"

"Ah, now, there's the beauty, you see, in flying the Dutch flag. Happens I was in Porto de Manatí not four days ago when a shipload of Spaniards came in, rescued off some small hillock of sand in the middle of nowhere. One of them was a real handsome fellow, no ears, no manners to speak of, but then show me a papist who does. At any rate, it seems he lost his ears on the *Santo Domingo* and was most anxious to make the acquaintance of *la Rosa de Hierro* again. So anxious, he's offered to give the man who brings you back to him ten times his weight in gold—which in my case, is considerable, you will admit."

"You would sell me to a bloody Spaniard for gold!"

"If it was just the gold, lass, I'd sell you back to your father for the same amount. But the thing of it is, the Spaniard is also offering a Let Pass, good for as long as we sail these waters, giving us the right to trade in any port, purchase any cargo, take away as much profit as we can carry in our holds. I grant you, it takes away the fun of blasting the bloody papists out of the water, but it saves my guns and my ships, and it will make me a rich, rich man. In truth," he added, "it was my intention just to tap you on the head and take you back to Porto de Manatí trussed up like a guinea fowl, but . . ." He paused again and the hard green eyes roved down her body. "You look such a tempting morsel all wet and shiny, I'm of a mind I should sample the wares first . . . just to make sure it's worth all the trouble."

His hands went to his waist and began to unfasten the leather thongs that bound his codpiece. Juliet twisted and writhed, she swore and spat, but on a

word from Van Neuk, the hands clamped around her
wrists and ankles tightened like iron shackles. A grunt
warned her he was free of his breeches, and Juliet
cursed again when she saw him drop onto his knees.
His flesh was thick, jutting out at the base of his
belly like a wooden club, and as he worked the fore-
skin back with one hand, he tore open her shirt and
reached for her breasts with the other. His nails were
long and ragged, the palms tough as leather, and she
had to clench her jaws to keep from screaming as he
scratched and kneaded and nearly clawed her nipples
off her body.

His men started to make lewd suggestions. One offered to hold her mouth open if he wanted to give
her a taste of what was to come. Another offered to
shut it with his fists to spare them all the steady stream
of oaths and curses she spat at them. The Dutchman
merely slapped her hard across the cheek to silence
her, then took a sharp dagger to the inseam of her
breeches. The point sliced her twice where her squirm-
ings forced the knife to cut more than the cloth, but
he was not deterred. His fingers probed her crotch
and the knife was starting down the other leg when
the sound of steel striking steel broke his concentration and he turned to search out the cause.

Two men with swords were fighting up on the dune,
and as Van Neuk watched, one of them—his own
crewman set there to warn of any unexpected company—screamed and fell, clutching his belly with his
hands. The swordsman whirled and came running
down the beach, sending up clods of sand behind him.
Two more Dutch crewmen drew cutlasses and charged
to meet him, but a stab and a slash sent them screaming onto the sand.

Anders growled and barked an order. The boot
shifted off Juliet's hair and she was able to raise her
head in time to see Varian St. Clare meet his new
attacker with a fierce display of cuts and strokes that
sent the man's weapon flying up in the air. Varian

caught it and brought both blades slicing down across his opponent's neck, nearly severing the head from the shoulders.

Three more of the men holding Juliet leaped to their feet and ran into the fray. Juliet was able to make a grab for the knife Anders still held poised over her crotch. She caught his wrist and twisted it back, thrusting it upward toward his chin. He reacted, but too slowly to deflect the aim, and willing every ounce of strength into her fists, she jammed the knife up and in, feeling it cut through cartilage and bone, splitting the windpipe and scraping all the way to the back of his skull.

Van Neuk's eyes bulged. He clawed at her hand, trying to drag the knife out of his throat, but it was lodged too deep in his brain and he was already dying. Juliet rolled out from beneath him as he pitched forward onto the ground. She sprang to her feet and ran for her sword belt, drawing her blade, twirling in a spray of sand to meet the two men who were hurdling around the rocks and coming after her. Her rage was at such a peak that she pierced the first man straight through the chest, punching the blade clean through his spine and out the back of his doublet.

The second brute managed a swipe with his cutlass before she dropped him, and when she whirled to find a new threat, the two shadows that had hung back against the rocks scrambled up the dunes and were swallowed into the night shadows.

"Are you all right?" Varian ran over, wiping spatters of blood off his face.

For a moment she was too furious to answer. Furious at herself, furious at Anders Van Neuk, furious at all mankind.

"Juliet—?"

"Leave me alone! Just . . . *leave me alone!*" She started to walk back down the beach, but stopped after only a few steps and stood there panting, staring at the lights in the distance. After all the talk, all the

bravado, all the displays of skill and strength to prove
she was the equal to any man, a bastard with a penis
could still have taken it all away from her.

When she could trust herself to speak again, she
turned and looked at Varian.

"Where did you come from? How did you know
where to find me?"

"I saw you slip out of the tent. Then I saw the
Dutchman leave right after. I thought, by the look on
his face, he was up to no good, so I made some excuse
and followed. Are you all right? Did he . . . *hurt* you?"

She followed his gaze down. The one leg of her
breeches was split and hanging from her thigh like a
skirt, and where her thigh showed through, it was
smeared with blood.

"The bastard cut me. Other than that . . . no, I'm
not *hurt*. I would not have let him *hurt* me either, so
if you're standing there waiting for me to thank you
for saving me from being *raped*, you will have a
long wait."

She brushed past him and leaned over the body of
the Dutchman. There was no question he was dead.
His eyes were wide, glazed, staring at the huge dark
stain that had spilled beneath him in the sand, and his
hands were still frozen around the hilt of the knife
protruding from his throat.

"He's lucky he died so easily," she muttered. She
glanced around at the other bodies sprawled in the
sand and pointed at one of the smaller ones. "That
one will do. Help me get his breeches off."

A few minutes later, Juliet was lacing herself into
the dead man's garment. She was cold, suddenly, and
thankful for the warmth of her doublet. Gathering up
her belts and hat, she started back down the beach,
but once again she stopped and retraced her steps.
With Varian watching, she dragged the half naked
body over beside that of Anders Van Neuk. She arranged it facedown with the buttocks in the air, then
took her knife and sliced the other leg of her dis-

carded breeches, leaving them clutched in the
Dutchman's bejeweled hand.

"Let whoever finds them think he died buggering
one of his own men," she spat.

After scuffing any telltale tracks she had made in
the sand, she led the way back toward the lighted end
of the harbor, saying very little until they drew near
the long row of beached longboats.

"I would appreciate it if you did not mention this
to my father. I think he was counting on the bastard's support."

"What about the men who escaped? Will they not
tell a different tale from the one down on the beach?"

Juliet offered up a crooked smile. "I will be surprised if the *Dove* is still in the harbor come morning.
If it is, then a new bastard will have already assumed
command, one who will not care how he came by his
captaincy, only that he was saved the trouble of taking
it himself. Murder is a natural means of attrition in
this line of business." She tossed her hat into the first
jolly-boat they came to and shoved the keel into the
water.

"Where are you going?"

"Back to the *Rose*."

"I'll come with you," he said, following her into
the surf.

"*No*! I mean . . . no, I would rather you didn't.
Besides, you might be needed here."

He tucked a finger under her chin, tipping her face
up to his. She tried to flinch back but he caught her
by the shoulders and made her look at him.

"Will you not allow me even one small illusion,
madam? That you might need me just a little more
tonight?"

She looked into his eyes without answering, without
moving. His thumb caressed her chin for a moment,
sensing another rejection in the tremor he felt there,
but when his hand started to drop, she caught it, stopping him before he could turn away.

"Actually . . . I might need your help. Just a little."

She swayed and started to slump forward. Varian caught her under the arms and when he lifted her, he felt where her breeches were soaked along her thigh.

"The bastard cut me," she whispered again. The words, muffled against his throat, trailed away as her body went limp and her head fell back over his arm.

Chapter Nineteen

"*I* don't faint. I have never fainted in my life."

"All right. We will say that you lost so much blood it was a wonder you lived to draw another breath."

Juliet's eyes narrowed. "We will say nothing at all, sirrah. And look you here"—she pointed to the cut on her thigh, which although far from being a scratch, had certainly not been life-threatening—"half an inch deeper and it would have pierced the main vein."

Varian obeyed and looked. The cut was as long as his hand and had bled profusely, but the edges were sealing without the need of stiches. There was a smaller slash farther down her leg and two deeper ones near her ankle, where the Dutchman's knife had taken several stabs at catching the bottom of her breeches. He suspected the latter would cause the most discomfort when she tried to put her boots on.

Varian had spent the night simply holding her, for once they were back on board and he helped strip away the bloody breeches, her bravura finally failed her and she began shaking like a leaf.

The sight had struck him like a physical blow. She was always so sure of herself, so much in control, in command of her emotions, that the sight of something so utterly female, so impossibly human, made him want to slay dragons for her for the rest of his life.

He had bathed the blood from her thigh, tucked her into a clean new shirt, and sat on the chair cradling her in his arms all night.

She sighed and nestled her head against his shoulder. "I just heard the watch bell and the sky is growing lighter. Johnny Boy will be knocking on the door soon to bring me my biscuits and cheese, while your man Beacom will be wringing his hands, convinced we have slit your throat and buried you in a sand dune."

"Beacom is learning to adapt quite well to my long absences."

She sat forward and stared into his eyes a moment before she kissed him. There was nothing provocative or seductive about it. It was just a kiss, a coming together of lips and breaths, the touching of flesh to flesh; nevertheless the contact produced a ripple of pleasure through both of them.

"Thank you," she whispered.

"For what?"

"For last night. For being on the beach, for bringing me back to the ship and tending my wounds."

"Believe me," he murmured, "it was my very great pleasure to rescue you. And of no lesser consequence to discover you are human after all."

"You had reason to doubt it?"

"Reason? Do you have any idea what wealthy young noblewomen your age are doing at the moment in England?"

"I can only guess," she said, venting an elaborate sigh. "Embroidering monograms on linens? Anguishing over which frock to wear for dinner? Which of the Bard's plays to attend?"

"For a certainty they are not planning how to attack a Spanish fleet. And had they been assaulted by a brute like Van Neuk, chances are they would have remained in shock the rest of their lives. Good God, Juliet. You are the captain of a fighting ship. You wear breeches and boots and sing sea chanteys with pirates until the sun comes up. You sleep an hour a night, if that. You wield a sword like a demon fairy and you have a shipful of sailors hanging off your every word and command. Look, for pity's sake, what you have made of me in less than a fortnight. You have me carrying false papers, bearing false witness, committing acts of treason and sedition, not to mention corrupting poor Lieutenant Beck into following suit. You have me sleeping on wooden floors and enjoying it as if it were a feather bed! In truth, if there were any more women like you in these Caribbean Isles, I would worry for the safety of all mortal men who trespass here."

Her face tightened a moment before she wriggled off his lap. She searched around the clutter of papers on the desk a moment to locate tinder and flint, then lit a candle.

Varian stood to stretch his legs, wincing as he straightened the knuckles down his spine. He flexed his arms and raked his fingers through his hair, then wandered out onto the gallery.

Night was receding as if some giant hand were drawing back the blankets. A thin band along the eastern horizon was pink and gold and pewter gray, the colors changing almost moment to moment as the sun rose higher. There were still torches and bonfires visible on the crescent of the shoreline. The breeze was cool, but laden with the threat of tropical heat, and it brought the smell of woodsmoke, of cookfires, of sand and salt and fish over the harbor. Most of the ships riding at anchor had huge lamps burning on their upper decks and Varian could see the silhouettes of tiny figures in the various stages of changing watches.

There were so many men, yet they entrusted their fates to so few. Did they ever question the decisions of their captains? Were they ever apprised of the incredible odds standing against them before they embarked on a venture such as the one they were about to undertake?

In theory the main thrust of the plan Simon Dante had fomented with the various captains sounded straightforward enough. Each privateer should try to capture at least one enemy ship. Thirty-seven privateers would reduce the size of the fleet by almost half—an impressive postulation until one remembered there would be Spanish warships in the convoy that had anywhere from forty to sixty guns in their batteries. Some of the smaller privateers mounted but ten or twelve and would have to band together if they were to present any kind of a threat.

The *Argus* had mounted ten guns, most of which had been silenced after the first Spanish broadside.

Varian's thoughts were dragged unwittingly back to the heat of battle, to the noise, the fires, the cannon blasting, the men fighting like demons with no apparent order or purpose other than to kill the enemy. It had all seemed like so much lethal chaos, yet he must admit—if only to himself—that it had been thrilling. Exhilarating, even. As if he had bared his breast to the devil and come away unscathed.

But that was not quite true either, for he had become very scathed indeed. He had allowed himself to be seduced by a sea witch, one who encouraged him to relish the sensation of hot sun on his skin, the sweat of hard labor on his brow. He had killed those men last night without hesitation, the lust for blood almost as potent as the lust he was feeling now to spread his hands wide and catch the wind.

"How long before the fleet sails, do you suppose?"

Juliet joined him on the gallery. She had pulled a pair of breeches on, careful of the fresh wound on her upper thigh, and was in the process of tucking the back of her shirt into the gaping waist. "It could be a week, it could be three weeks. We will know more when Jonas and Gabriel return from Havana."

Varian sensed the unease in her voice and knew it was there with good reason. The Hell Twins had volunteered to take their ships as close as they dared to the great Spanish port in order to scout the harbor, the war galleons, the state of readiness of the fleet.

"Fortuna favet fatuis," he murmured.

"Fortune favors fools," she translated. "You think it a foolish enterprise?"

"I honestly do not know what I think, other than it

is probably quite mad to assume we can do more than annoy the Spaniards."

"True enough, but then it is also true that we can be very annoying."

Her eyes shone in the pearly dawn light. Her skin looked satiny and luxurious and his hand could not resist the temptation to reach out and brush a lock of hair back from her cheek. His fingers trailed down her throat and onto the swell of her breast, where he found the nipple through the cambric and rolled it beneath his thumb until it was firm and taut. He saw the dark centers of her eyes dilate and sent his hand roving lower, sliding between the unbuttoned edges of her breeches to curve into the soft cluster of hairs. A single finger, then two explored the folds and contours. She grew tense as his fingers probed deeper, undoubtedly remembering the Dutchman's brutish manhandling, but Varian was so gentle, his intentions so sincere, she eventually had to lean against his arm and take her pleasure, moving into the sleek rhythm with a soft sigh.

When her body finished melting over his hand, he smiled and brought her into his arms, kissing away the wetness that shimmered along her lashes.

"And you think *me* a madwoman?" she whispered against his chest. "Do you suppose we could attract any more attention by standing on deck naked?"

Varian glanced over his shoulder. The *Avenger* was anchored a hundred yards off their starboard bow, thankfully not visible from where they stood. There were ships off their stern, but the light was not strong enough to have won any curious stares.

"If you are concerned about your reputation, Captain, we could move back inside," he murmured.

"A pox on my reputation," she said, laughing haltingly. "Sweet Christ, but I am going to miss you."

"I am not going anywhere just yet, madam. You'll not be rid of me so easily."

When she recouped her senses enough to look up, he saw the same tightness he had seen on her face not five minutes ago. He was not so misguided to assume he was beginning to know a tenth of her expressions or what secrets they kept hidden, yet this one bore an unmistakable shadow of foreboding, one that was clear enough to trigger an alarm at the back of his neck.

The feeling grew when she averted her eyes and pushed out of his arms, backing up almost to the gallery door.

"Do you recall meeting Captain Robert Brockman yesterday? A tall, gray-haired Englishman with a patch over one eye?"

Varian nodded and she needed to take a deep breath before she continued. "His ship, the *Gale*, is one of the fastest in the harbor; she has made the crossing to England in under forty days. One of the reasons his ship is so fast is because it carries only eight heavy guns and . . . and because of that same reason, he has agreed that his services might be put to better use in making a run for England. Father believes the king should at least be made aware of what is happening here. If we do manage by some miracle to delay or scatter the fleet, it might give the admiralty back in London enough time to put ships to sea and intercept the rest of the flota before it reaches Spain. Since you have made such a big to-do about how much the king and his council trust you, he thought, naturally, that you should be the one to carry the warning home."

When Varian did not say anything, when he simply continued to stare at her, Juliet appealed to his sense of logic. "It isn't as if anyone actually expected you to fight alongside the rest of us." She held up a hand, warning him to silence. "And before you splutter protests, reminding me of your years in the infantry will win you no favors either. Little toy soldiers dressed in red, who march in fine straight lines and oblige their enemy by presenting bright, steady targets, are no match for cannon fired from three hundred yards away. You said yourself you were well out of your depths here. You admitted that on a battlefield with artillery and cavalry, you would gladly fight battles and win wars, but at sea, all the rules change. And you were right. You have tasted battle on board a ship, sir; you should know, therefore, that there are no rules but those of survival. Your own personal survival," she added with emphasis. "For in most instances, there is very little time to worry about the man next to you. There is no room for error. No room for distraction either."

"Is that why you are sending me away? Because I have become a distraction?"

Juliet sighed. "There is no point in arguing with me. The decision was made before we left Pigeon Cay."

"Really. And when were you going to tell me?"

"I just did."

A muscle shivered in his cheek. "And is that to be the end of it? I have no say in the matter?"

"In all honesty," she said evenly, "you never did. You're a duke, for heaven's sake, a member of the British nobility and the king's official representative in the Indies. It behooves us all to keep you alive, to keep you breathing long enough to return in your *official* capacity and explain why we have disobeyed the crown's orders and attacked the flota."

"I am not that easy to kill; I would have thought I proved that much at least last night."

She colored slightly. "Last night was a display by a master of the sword against louts who hide in corners and slit throats in the shadows."

His gaze strayed to the faintly purplish bruise on her temple. "You were not so dismissive when it was your throat being threatened."

"Nor am I so easily swayed by a warm body and a smooth tongue. Are you under the impression, *your grace*, that because we have bedded, it gives you leave to challenge me at every turn?"

"If I have learned nothing else these past two

weeks, *Captain*, I have learned that you maintain two very different personalities, one that I am free to challenge, and one that I am not."

"Precisely so. And in this instance, you are not."

"You excel at dueling with words as well as steel, Juliet, but is it because you are afraid of making friends, of growing too close to anyone, or of letting anyone get too close to you?"

"I am not afraid of making friends, sir. I am afraid of losing them. As for growing close . . . I am not too addled by the wetness on my thighs to see that it was a huge, unfathomable mistake to have ever touched you. I should have sent you running back to your room that first night on Pigeon Cay. At least then you would not be suffering any illusions of who and what I am. You would still be anxious to return to your England and your unsuspecting betrothed, who has undoubtedly embroidered your monogram on a thousand pillowslips in your absence. Go home to her, Varian. Go home to your sixty-five bedrooms, your bootboys, and your rolling green fields. That is where you belong."

"What if I disagree?"

She looked startled for a moment, but in the next, her jaw was firm, her shoulders squared. "Frankly, at this point, it doesn't matter if you agree or not. You are going home, sir. The *Gale* sails tonight, on the evening tide, and you will be on it."

Before they had departed from Pigeon Cay, Nathan Crisp had grudgingly given up his quarters for the duke's use. It was a ten foot by ten foot cabin located forward on the lower deck containing a narrow berth and a stool that had three mismatched legs. Beacom had been installed in the tiny locker adjacent to the cabin, furnished with little more than a hammock strung between two beams. The bulkheads were thin, built out of half-inch planking, and so it was that the valet yelped and was spilled out of his hammock when the door was slammed and he could hear angry pacing inside the quartermaster's cabin.

He dressed quickly, smoothed his hands over his hair to flatten the spikes, then hastened out of his cubbyhole to knock lightly on his master's door.

It was jerked open so violently, the small wooden box Beacom carried was nearly startled out of his hands. A glimpse at the midnight eyes was more than enough to warn the manservant that his master was in a black mood; he did not need to hear the curse that sent Varian back to pacing the breadth of the cabin.

Beacom cleared his throat.

"Good morning, your grace. I trust you slept well. Will you be requiring a shave?"

Varian turned away from staring out the eight-inch porthole and glared at him a moment, as if trying to remember who he was and why he was there. "A tempting thought, Beacom, but do I look like I want to sit down and have someone press a razor against my throat?"

"Ah . . . no. No, in truth you do not, your grace. Perhaps some victuals? Or ale?"

"Perhaps you should just stand out of the way and let me think."

Beacom stepped prudently to one side and was about to set the shaving box down when he noticed the lid of the sea chest was open, the contents tumbled out of their orderly folds.

"Were you looking for something in particular, your grace?"

"What?" He followed Beacom's gaze to the chest. "A clean shirt. Breeches. Stockings. I am the king's envoy, dammit. I should at least look the part."

Beacom's eyebrows inched upward. He noticed, for the first time, that Varian's current shirt and breeches bore what looked suspiciously like spatters of blood amid the saltwater stains, the creases, the scuffs of dirt. "Indeed, your grace. So you should."

While Varian stripped, Beacom hastened to find clean stockings, breeches, and a white camlet shirt. Varian snatched each garment that was held out to

him and made no attempt to do so much as button a
cuff of the peasecod doublet on his own. He stood
rigid while Beacom attended him. He sat and allowed
his hair to be brushed smooth, and even tipped his
chin up without complaint when Beacom approached
somewhat hesitantly with the starched neck ruff. But
when the valet searched for the ruby brooch to pin it
down in front, it was nowhere to be found.

"Looking for this?"

Beacom gasped and whirled around, slamming himself against the bulkhead, but Varian merely turned
to acknowledge the sound of the door swinging open
and Simon Dante's presence at the threshold. The tall,
jet-haired privateer had to bend to duck below the
lintel, as did his oldest son, Jonas, who did not come
all the way into the room, but remained in the doorway, filling it with his big body.

Varian's reflexes were quick enough to catch the
object Dante tossed to him. Without looking down,
he knew it was the egg-sized brooch that had been
pinned to his collar the day before.

"It was found on the beach, not ten yards from the
bodies of the captain and eight crewmen from the
Dove."

Varian manipulated the brooch inside his hand,
grudgingly aware of the promise he had made Juliet
last night.

"You wouldn't happen to know how it came to be
there, would you?" Dante's voice was level, but his
gaze was hard. Hard and cold, just like Juliet's had
been when she looked him in the eye and told him to
go home.

Dante frowned, obviously unaccustomed to waiting
for explanations once they were demanded. "If your
memory needs refreshing, allow me to tell you what I
know. Eight bodies were found on the beach late last
night, including that of Anders Van Neuk. At first it
appeared as though he had been stopped in the act of
sodomizing one of his own men, and if that had been
the case, it would have ended there, the devil take

him and good riddance. Unfortunately it did not end there. Two of Anders's men, bleeding from various wounds, were found hiding in the trees and, when questioned, told a somewhat different story."

"They said they happened across you trying to climb on top of Juliet," Jonas growled. "When they ran to help, you and your manservant fought them off with swords."

The accusation was followed by a muted squawk and a dull thump as Beacom banged his head on a beam.

"Beacom was nowhere near the beach last night," Varian said calmly. "He never left the ship."

The Pirate Wolf glanced at Beacom and pursed his lips. "Frankly, I didn't even give it consideration. Apparently Gabriel didn't either, and by the time he had finished bloodying his knuckles, he had managed to wring an entirely different story from the men's throats."

Varian pushed to his feet. "In that case, you are free to believe the version that makes the most sense."

"They said," Jonas screwed his golden eyes down to disbelieving slits, "you came out of nowhere and put five of them on the sand without breaking stride. Said you looked like a great bloody bat with your cape flying out like wings."

Varian stared a moment, then turned to finish dressing. He plucked his cloak off the wall peg and tossed it to Beacom, who, in turn, had to pry himself away from the bulkhead to carry it forward and drape it over his master's left shoulder. He ran the ties under the arms to fasten it in place, then fetched Varian's sword belt and buckled it around his waist.

"Going somewhere?" Dante asked casually.

"Your daughter has told me I am. To England, with all haste."

"And . . . you are not happy with our decision to send you home?"

"I am neither happy nor unhappy at that particular decision. What does not please me, Captain Dante, is being set forth like a pawn and deemed dispensable once the opening gambit has been played."

"If you have been given that impression, sir, it was not my intention."

"Was it not?"

Simon shook his head. "No. It was not. In fact, it was not even my idea to send you home. Certainly not to insist we send you in one of our fastest ships with one of our best and most indispensable captains."

"Then why . . . ?" The question escaped Varian's lips before he could bite it back. The answer was there before him: it was Juliet, of course. It was her idea, much as she had attempted to shift some of the blame. He was, after all, her chattel, her prize, her responsibility, and he, like the *Santo Domingo*, could be disposed of any way she saw fit.

"The captain of the *Gale* is taking on extra provisions and fresh water," Dante was saying. "He should be ready to leave on the evening tide. All the papers and documents you will need to take with you are back on board the *Avenger*, so whenever you are ready—"

"I am ready now," Varian said abruptly. "If you have no objections, I will accompany you to your ship, then leave from there for the *Gale*. I would be remiss," he added, forcing a tense smile, "if I returned to England having never set foot on the infamous *Avenger*."

"As you wish. Can your man manage the chest or shall I send someone—?"

"Oh, I can manage it sir!" Beacom was so ecstatic at the thought of actually going home that he could have flown up to the deck with the sea chest balanced on his head. "Yes indeed, I shall be right on your heels!"

Simon nodded once at Varian before he turned to leave. At the door, he paused and looked back. "If it is any consolation, the decision to send you back was made before we left Pigeon Cay. In light of everything that has happened since then, she might not be quite so adamant about it."

"Nothing has happened to change her mind, Captain," Varian said quietly. "That much I do know."

Juliet was determined that a cut on her thigh would not keep her from going about her daily routine. As much as the fabric chafed, as much as her boots rubbed against the fresh wounds, she spent the better part of the day with Gabriel, having accompanied him out to the *Valour*. She did not ask about his bruised knuckles and he did not ask about the purple splotches on her jaw and cheek. They knew, just by glancing into each other's eyes, what had happened, and it was more to Gabriel's credit that he held his tongue, for he had clearly been surprised to see how close she had come to tears several times throughout the morning.

The *Valour* and the *Tribute* weighed anchor just past noon, leaving Juliet no choice but to return to the *Iron Rose*, and it was there, six hours later as dusk was settling again, that she stood on the quarterdeck and watched as the crew of the *Gale* began maneuvering the nimble ship through the congestion of ships in the harbor. Dozens of lamps and lanterns were hung from her rigging, casting a glittering reflection across the surface of the water as she moved toward the open sea-lanes. One by one those lamps were being extinguished, for once she was clear of the outer island, it would be safer to run dark toward the horizon.

Juliet lowered the spyglass. She had recognized Captain Brockman standing tall on the quarterdeck, his shock of gray hair making him easy to identify. She had not seen any other familiar figures invited to join him on deck to mark the departure. No one with broad shoulders, dark hair, or a dashing cavalier's hat on his head.

It was just as well.

So far throughout this endless, insufferable day she

had managed to keep her captain's face intact. She had done that by keeping busy, by not thinking about him, by not once going below to her cabin where everything she looked at would undoubtedly remind her of him. The bed, the desk, the gallery, even the chair for pity's sake, had all been used for other than what they had been intended and she was not sure she could look at them just yet without feeling the taint of his presence.

How she could have allowed herself to become so besotted, she had no idea. Not the how of it or the why or the when. She just knew that when she had seen him standing at the gangway this morning, prepared to disembark with her father, she had felt her heart crack open and the pieces slide down into her toes. She had wanted to shout that it was a mistake, that she really didn't want him to go, that what had seemed so logical and necessary a week ago left her feeling helpless and confused now.

From the outset, she had never been dishonest with herself or him as to what she had wanted. She had taken him to her bed because she had wanted his body, had craved the numbing release of a few well-wrought orgasms to help ease the restlessness and the tension that had been clouding her thinking. With that foolishness burned out of her system she had fully expected to be herself again, tough, strong, resilient.

But instead, she found herself distracted, unable to concentrate on the simplest of tasks. Something as second nature as calculating distances, speeds, and plotting the course they would take in the morning had turned into monumentally impossible equations that had Nathan Crisp frowning and chiding her for making basic errors. She had cut herself on the binnacle. She had nearly stumbled headfirst down a ladderway. She had stared blankly when Nathan had asked her questions for the second and third time.

It had also occurred to her more than once that this was the way her mother behaved when her father was overdue returning to Pigeon Cay, but if this was what

love felt like, then perhaps it was for the best that
Varian St. Clare was leaving.

If it was love, it was a foolish, witless thing, for she
was under no illusions as to how ludicrous a thought
it was that there could be any future between them.
Their worlds were so different, there was no end to
the reasons why neither could adapt to fit in the other.
She lived by instinct and passion, he lived by rules
and social dictums.

In a month, he would be back in England taking
strolls along the Thames, recounting his adventures
with a dangerous band of pirates to a rapt crowd of
tittering females. He would be back in his own world,
surrounded by beautiful women in gauzy dresses who
displayed soft white flesh and perfumed cleavage. He
would be reminded of his responsibilities as the Duke
of Harrow and grudgingly or not, he would do his
duty. He would take the bride his mother had selected
for him, he would gaze into her eyes and pledge his
troth, and then afterward, he would take her into his
bed, into his arms . . .

She made a strangled sound in her throat and
turned away from the rail. Nathan Crisp was directly
behind her and raised an eyebrow in askance.

"If ye give the order, there is still time to hail Cap'n
Brockman an' have him heave to."

"Why in heaven's name would I want him to
heave to?"

Nathan grimaced. "To save us all a deal of grief.
Ye've been like a she-cat with turpentine up her arse
all day, and I don't see your mood improving any the
farther away he goes. Give me the word and I'll run
up a signal. We'll fetch him back on board so's we
can get on about the business ahead without needing
to worry that you'll have us firing on our own ships."

"Sometimes," she said slowly, "you overstep yourself, Mr. Crisp."

"An' sometimes," he paused, moving so close she
could smell the sincerity on his breath, "ye try so hard
to prove ye don't care about something, ye only end

up twistin' yerself in tighter knots. If ye want him
back, we'll fetch him. Simple as that an' no one would
fault ye for it. Not after what he did last night."

"Last night?" she whispered.

His grimace deepened at the look of shock on her
face. "Ye didn't think it would stay a secret, did ye?
Not with yer brother lickin' the tar out of every man
on board the *Dove*. Whole crew knows. Whole fleet,
probably, and there isn't a man on board wouldn't
shake the duke's hand for savin' them the trouble of
blastin' the Dutchman to hell where he belongs." He
stopped and glanced at the mouth of the harbor,
where the *Gale* was putting on more sail, picking up
more speed as she neared open water. "Ye don't have
but a minute to decide, lass."

Juliet turned her head to follow the privateer's
progress. Most of her lights were doused now and as
she sailed toward the darkness of the eastern sky, her
huge mainsails were unfurled, shaking out full and
pale against the fading light.

Juliet watched until the ship rounded the island and
sped out of sight.

"We will be weighing anchor at first light," she said
quietly. "Have all made ready by then."

Nathan stepped back. "Aye, Cap'n."

She tipped her head and looked up. "Skies are
clear, we should have fair weather ahead. If the wind
holds we should be able to make the Devil's Teeth in
two days. By then, Mr. Crisp"—she met his eyes—
"we will be far too busy to remember that we even
had this conversation."

"Aye, Captain," he agreed after a moment. "No
doubt we will."

Chapter Twenty

*T*he serpentine chain of islands known as the Devil's Teeth were perfectly configured for an ambush. Dozens of small, uninhabited atolls and islets were strung out in an elongated crescent some fifty miles long flanking the eastern boundary of the Straits of Florida. Simon Dante had provided the other captains with detailed maps and charts of the cays, letting each decide where to position his ship where it might be put to best effect. Some preferred the hit-and-run method, lying in wait, concealed behind one of the islands until the galleons straggled into view. Then, like dogs culling sheep out of a herd, they would pounce on the slowest ship and engage it in battle.

The Spanish captains were notoriously without mercy, even to their own. If a ship floundered or managed to get separated from the pack, and if the *capitán-general* did not think it worth his while to jeopardize the safety of the other ships in the flota, the galleons would be sacrificed to the scavengers, tossed like a scrap of raw meat to a hungry pack of wolves.

They would not know exactly how hungry those wolves would be this time out, or that it would take more than a few paltry ships to appease their appetites. The privateers would be spread out the entire fifty-mile length of the cays, luring ships singly or by twos and threes into traps from which there would be little chance of escape.

The *Iron Rose* was bound for a pair of atolls midway down the chain marked on the Dante charts as Spaniard's Cay and Frenchman's Cay, names that denoted ships of those particular nationalities that had been waylaid on previous hunts. Looking innocent enough from the deeper water of the Straits, the islands sat where the sea bottom rose sharply in ridges and terraces, and where the currents that fed off the Gulf Stream drove many an unwary ship onto shallower banks that were often no more than two fathoms below the surface. Once there, a canny vessel waiting on the other side of the bank could pound away at the trapped ship until the white flag of surrender was run up the mast.

With that goal in mind, it was Simon's intention to use the *Dove* as bait—a more practical solution than blowing it out of the water as Juliet had originally craved to do. He proposed setting the Dutchman and the *Avenger* in plain view when the flota came in sight, both seeming to appear damaged and floundering in the water. There were few Spanish captains who did not know the *Avenger*'s silhouette on sight, fewer still whose arrogance would not provoke them to throw caution to the wind if there was a chance they could be the one to bring the infamous *Pirata Lobo* to ground.

Meanwhile the *Santo Domingo* would be stripped of her guns and mortars. They would be deployed along the beaches of the two small islands that flanked the narrow passage through the atolls. It was only wide enough for one ship at a time and once the galleons were committed to chasing the *Avenger* through, they would be caught in a deadly cross fire from the two batteries on shore. The *Iron Rose* and the *Christiana* would both be waiting out of sight behind the islands, while the *Santo Domingo* could be used to block the retreat. They would also be taking an additional hundred men on board, the volunteers coming in lots of five from any ship who could spare them. The extras would be needed to man the batteries on shore once the guns were in place.

The *Avenger* had led the fleet of privateers out of New Providence, setting a brisk pace north, skirting any islands that might have Spanish ships patrolling their waters. Following close on Dante's stern, flanked by the *Iron Rose* and the *Christiana*, was the newly appropriated *Dove*, whose crew had been given the choice of either submitting to their new captain—Isabeau Dante—or being sold to the Portuguese to work the cane fields. It made for an impressive sight to see nearly forty ships sailing out of port, all flying the Union Jack on their mastheads. Only once before had Simon Dante seen such a sight, and that had been on the eve he had sailed out of Portsmouth with Francis Drake to defend England against the threat of another Spanish fleet.

True to her prediction, Juliet was kept so busy during the daylight hours that she rarely gave a thought to Varian St. Clare. It was more difficult after dark, when she ran out of excuses to retire to her cabin, but there, too, after the third night, she could almost fall asleep without having to fight the urge to run her own hand down between her thighs.

Before they reached Frenchman's Cay, two of the captains broke away to set up their own ambush near the tip of the chain of islands. Captain David Smith had his own score to settle with the Spaniards and, together with Captain Peter Wilbury, had bid to take up the first position. The combined guns from the five ships in their group would announce the arrival of the plate fleet as it entered the Straits. Dante's guns would in turn give warning to the next ambuscade and so on all the way up the fifty-mile span of the Devil's Teeth.

Juliet dropped anchor midafternoon in the shallow water less than a half mile off the tiny island. The *Santo Domingo* lay alongside the *Rose* while the *Avenger*, the *Christiana*, and the *Dove* took up a posi-

tion behind Spaniard's Cay. Simon Dante, Pitt, and
Juliet rowed ashore with their quartermasters and
chief gunners to walk the length of the beach. They
surveyed the slope of the dunes with an eye to digging
the gun emplacements, checking to see if the channel
between the two cays was as they remembered. They
were pleased to see a thick line of trees less than fifty
feet from both beaches.

Out of the fifty-two cannon the galleon had originally mounted, four had already been removed to replace guns on board the *Iron Rose*. Thirty culverins,
twelve demi-culverins, and six eighty-pound mortars
would be broken down and transferred ashore, divided
equally between the two islands. There was a good
deal of backbreaking work ahead, but there, too, they
had the crew of the *Dove* to supplement the labor
force as well as the extra hundred men who would
eventually man the batteries.

"It should take two weeks," her father said grimly,
"with all of us skinning our knuckles and blistering
our backs. At first light, we'll send some hunting parties out to scout for rocks, cut down trees, fill sacks
with sand for constructing defenses. I also want search
parties to walk the entire perimeter of both islands to
make sure there have been no unpleasant changes
since our last visit."

Pitt concurred. "It wouldn't hurt to put a couple of
pinnaces in the water, too, maybe check the outlying
islands on either side."

"If memory serves, only one of these two islands
has a source of freshwater, the other"—Juliet pointed
to the beach on the opposite side of the passage—"is
barely three miles long."

"We'll need lookouts," Simon said, noting the arrival of the next boatloads of men on the beach. Isabeau had come across on one and when he saw her,
a sly smile stole across his face. "I will volunteer Beau
and myself to check out Spaniard's Cay, while you,
Juliet"—he waved at one of the men coming up the

beach—"take one of the lads with you and find a good vantage point above these trees."

"Aye, Father." She turned, expecting to see Lucifer loping up behind them, or at the very least, one of her own crewmen armed to the teeth with pistols and powder horns.

Instead, she saw Varian St. Clare striding up the beach, his dark hair blown about his face, his long legs forcing Isabeau Dante to almost run to keep apace. He wore a plain white shirt and dark breeches. His sword was strapped to his hip and he wore crossbelts that held a brace of pistols snug across his chest.

His steps slowed as he approached the small group at the water's edge. After nodding to Simon and touching a finger to his brow to acknowledge the smile on Geoffrey Pitt's face, he walked right up to Juliet, took her hand, and started walking toward the trees without so much as a by-your-leave.

She was so startled she actually followed him half a dozen steps before she dug her heels into the sand and stopped.

"Where the devil have you come from? You're supposed to be on a ship bound for England!"

"Unlike his daughter, who is too proud and pigheaded to listen to reason, I was able to convince your father I would be of better use here. In fact, we got along rather famously after we started sharing some of our anecdotes about the stubborn, willful women in our lives. After hearing about the very first meeting between your mother and father, I can see you came by your threat to geld me honestly. And is it true you were such a nuisance when you were small that your brothers trussed you up like a chicken and hung you by your ankles off the end of a bowsprit?"

Juliet, open-mouthed, glanced back at her parents, neither of whom looked the least abashed.

"We saw the *Gale* leave," she said, turning back.

"So you did. Lieutenant Beck was not entirely pleased to take my place, but he could see the need

and recognized his duty. Beacom was only too thrilled
to accompany him and offer his services on the voyage
home. Not only that, but he has taken some private
letters back to England explaining my delay. Now
then, shall we go along? We have a fair climb ahead
of us and only a couple of hours of daylight left."

He gave her a brief smile, then started walking, the
sand sounding like crushed eggshells as he strode
toward the trees.

Juliet stared. After another full minute, she glanced
back at her parents a second time, but they had already headed off, hand in hand, toward one of the
boats. Geoffrey and Nathan were talking together, the
latter grinning and scratching his chin as if he should
have known something had been in the wind.

By the time she looked back at the trees, Varian
had put several hundred feet distance between them
and she had to walk smartly to keep him in sight. She
made no overt effort to catch up to him. Her thoughts
were spinning too fast to even believe that he was
there, let alone that her father had spent more than an
hour discussing gun deployments and defenses without
giving her so much as a hint there was anything afoot.

Anger put a new snap in her stride as she began
closing the gap. The island boasted one tall peak and
several smaller ones that stretched out several miles
in length, descending like the knuckles on the spine
of some ancient creature. The path, if it could be
called such, was jagged and steep in places, with terraces of long grasses and tangles of bush in between
that had not seen a human foot for centuries. The
vantage, as they climbed nearer the top, was as domi-
nant as the one from Pigeon Cay, giving a sweeping
view of the surrounding area. The water shone like a
rippled sheet of pewter beneath the sun, stretching out
across the Straits for twenty leagues before it met the
coast of Florida. To the north, the next island in the
chain was visible as a vaporous blue haze linked underwater by a high shelf of reef. To the south, Spaniard's Cay rose like the hump of a dolphin's back, the

summit mostly rock surrounded by a ring of trees and pale pink sand.

Juliet had lost sight of Varian, but knew he could not be too much farther ahead. She passed through a narrow belt of long, lush grass and was about to climb the last ten feet or so to the uppermost ledge of rock when she saw him. He was leaning against a boulder off to one side, his long legs crossed at the angles, his arms folded over his chest.

"Why have you stopped? We haven't reached the top yet."

"I think this is high enough, don't you?"

"High enough for what?"

"To clear up any misunderstandings that might be between us."

She glanced around, not so much to assure herself they were alone but to save her eyes from being trapped by his. "I'm sure I don't know what you're talking about."

"Don't you? When I came up the beach back there, do you have any idea how close you came to being thrown down in the sand and ravished there and then, before your mother, your father . . . before God Himself?"

"They would have killed you if you'd tried."

He smiled. "I doubt that. In fact, it was your mother who suggested I just drag you off into the bushes and keep you there until you came to your senses. She said that was the only way your father managed to convince her she could be stronger with him than without him."

Juliet narrowed her eyes warily. He had removed his crossbelts and pistols, she noticed. They were on the rocks beside him alongside his sword and baldric. "She said that, did she?"

"She also said you were very much like her—sometimes to her sorry regret. That you are always so damned determined to prove you don't need anyone's help getting through life, that you sometimes forget that other people do."

"Are you saying you need my help?"

"Call it a character flaw. The need to comprehend the incomprehensible. Although I think *need* is perhaps too strong a word. *Desire* might be better suited. The desire to understand you and the need to understand myself."

"What are you having trouble grasping? You came here to do your duty to the crown. You have done it. Two weeks ago you were eager to see the last of us, to get back to your England and your rolling green hills and well-ordered life." She waved an arm, vaguely indicating the stretch of blue water. "You had your chance three days ago to leave. You didn't take it. And now you need my help to understand why you did not?"

"Oh, I know damned well why I did not. You see, I have spent the past twenty-eight years of my life wandering around without any real purpose, without any real ability to stray off the path that was chosen for me, the one that was set out in a straight line from the day I was born. I said I became duke by default and that part is true, but ten years ago, had you stood me beside my two brothers you would have been hard-pressed to tell the three of us apart. We dressed the same, talked the same, were educated by the same tutors. I expect we even made love the same, for we were all taken to the same brothel for our initiation into the earthy delights of a woman's flesh.

"My older brother studied politics because that was what he was expected to do. My middle brother learned finance and the law so that the family business would stay in the family. I joined the army because that's what third sons do. We even—all of us—agreed to marry women that were chosen for us because, while you had at least seen love up close and knew it existed, we were never exposed to anything so . . . earthy and uncivilized. Our parents were polite the two or three times a year they attended the same balls and court functions. They never touched, never—God forbid—smiled. When Father died, Mother's first priority was assuring we all had the proper wardrobes. I had absolutely no idea love could produce actual physical pain. Not until I watched you stand on top of Pigeon Cay with your arms outstretched, vowing you would one day sail over the horizon to see if such things as dragons truly existed. Do you have any idea how truly pitiful a moment that was for me? There I was wondering if there had ever been an instant in my life that I actually believed such a thing as love existed, while you were convinced there were mythical creatures lurking just beyond the horizon, waiting for you to discover them.

"I think that was the very first time I knew what the pounding in my chest was all about. It was the moment I fell in love with you, though there were occasions afterward that made me think, ah, that was the one. Or, no, perhaps that was it. I have had three days and three very long nights to think about it, you see, and . . . I guess I was hoping you had been just a tiny bit miserable about sending me away."

She stared at him, watching his lips move, hearing the words he was saying. And she had followed them right up to the point where he said he loved her. That was where her mind had frozen, where every single thought had slammed to a halt.

"I realize you made it quite shockingly clear from the outset that all you wanted was a pleasant diversion," he added, somewhat uncomfortable under her stare. "I just thought . . . I assumed . . ."

When she continued to stand there, saying nothing, he sighed and pushed a hand through his hair. "Of course, that would be assuming a great deal, would it not? It would assume you gave a damn one way or another. That you didn't just send me away because you'd had your fill of me, but because you were afraid it wasn't just a diversion anymore."

Something hot and stinging welled along Juliet's lashes, blurring him into a blot of white shirt and blowing dark hair. A blink sent a splash down on her cheek and a soft gasp parted her lips, for it was all there. All of it was in his eyes. How much he loved her, how much he wanted her, how desperately he needed her to want and love him in return. It was terrifying and thrilling at the same time to realize she had that kind of power over another human being, and to know that someone had that same kind of power over her. Not the kind of power won with a sword or a knife or a blustery command, but the kind that would come in quiet moments, with a look or a touch, or in the promise of a smile.

"I sent you away," she whispered, "because I didn't think . . ."

He pushed away from the boulder and moved closer. "You didn't think . . . what?"

"I didn't think . . . you could love someone like me."

He raised his hand, touching a fingertip to the fat tear that rolled slowly down her cheek. "Someone like you?" he murmured. "Someone who takes my every breath away? Someone who makes me want to be more of a man because she is so much more than any other woman I have ever had the privilege, the honor, the pleasure of knowing? Someone for whom I would gladly slay dragons the rest of my life?"

Juliet felt a flush rising up into her cheeks. Her eyes met his briefly, the tears brimming with damnable persistence as if once started, they would never stop. All four of his fingertips were wet now and he tried using his thumb to stanch the flow, but they just kept coming.

"You never thought it would happen to you either?"

She shook her head. "No. I never really thought it would."

"And? Has it?"

It was a foolish question, for of course he knew. He had known it before she had even acknowledged the possibility to herself that this wild beating in her chest, this molten heat in her limbs, the pleasure of simply have him sit with her through the night and hold her, was more than anything she had ever expected. She did not know how or when it had happened, but he had not just won his way into her body; he was inside her blood, a part of her now, flowing through her veins like life itself.

Juliet was looking studiously at the hollow at the base of his neck, unable to lift her gaze above the level of his collarbone. Even when he tipped his head, trying to make contact, she bowed hers lower, leaving him no choice but to thread his long fingers into her hair and gently turn her face up to his. He must have seen the answer to his question shimmering in her eyes, for he smiled and closed his own. She thought she heard him breathe a faint "Thank God," but she could not be sure, for in the next heartbeat, he was kissing her cheeks, her eyes, her temples, her brow. He brushed her lips lightly two or three times before his mouth came down hard and firm over hers but by then her arms were already around his neck, and she was partly laughing, partly sobbing as he swept her up off her feet and spun her in a dizzying circle.

She heard him say her name over and over, and she shuddered violently, knowing she wanted to hear it said that way, hoarse and ragged with passion, forever. Her own lips moved, and whether the words she uttered had substance or not, she could not tell, but at least she knew without any further doubts or hesitation that she wanted to say them, and that, for the time being, was enough.

Chapter Twenty-one

The *Contadora* was among the thirty-two warships anchored in a protective semicircle around the harbor, and one of the larger warships that comprised the *armada de la guardia*. There were fifty-nine merchant ships inside the ring of galleons, their captains increasingly anxious about the coming voyage to Spain. As early as last summer, the captains, the island governors, the officers in every garrison along the Spanish Main, had been on edge, knowing that it was important for the vast armada to reach Spain safely. The king needed the ships and the treasure the flota carried. Almost more than the gold and silver, Spain needed her best soldiers and officers if the plans for the new invasion of England were to succeed.

Common sailors and officers below the rank of captain were not told in advance that the treasure fleet would be larger than usual. Seamen were notoriously loose-tongued and privateers from every nation would have descended on them like locusts. Nor were they told the Indies would be stripped of her biggest warships. Those same loose tongues would have been bragging about how they planned to exact revenge for the fleet of 1588, and Spain would not only lose any advantage of surprise back home, but there would be open war with the English privateers in the Caribbean.

Of those who did know something was in the air, there were very few entrusted with all the details, fewer still who had realized the full scope of the enterprise until their ships were approaching the rendezvous in Havana and they saw the crowded conditions of the harbor. At the same time, most reported that there had been increased attacks on the ships attempting to reach Havana. Each cluster of ships that arrived brought stories of French and Dutch marauders thick as flies on a rotting corpse. Seven ships had been sunk or captured, and another twelve had turned back to their home ports not wanting to risk their valuable cargoes.

The *Contadora* had sailed from Vera Cruz. She mounted forty-eight big guns, which was enough of a deterrent against the privateering vessels that plagued the smaller, unescorted merchantmen. Her captain, Luis Ortolo, had been recalled from his normal duties patrolling the coastline off Cartagena, and this would be his first trip home in five years. On board for the voyage to Spain were twenty-three important passengers, including the former governor of Nueva España and his family. Also on board was Captain Diego Flores de Aquayo and several of his officers who had themselves been victims of the marauding privateers. News of the stunning capture of the *Santo Domingo* had spread like wildfire through the fleet, adding to the tension that was building incrementally in the harbor with each tale of attacks and sinkings received. For a ship so large, so heavily armed to have come under such a brazen attack, how could smaller vessels expect to defend themselves?

Earlier that evening, the obese, red-faced Aquayo had retold the story again for the benefit of the new passengers on board the *Contadora*. His version of the attack also built incrementally with each telling, and on this particular night, there were seven heavily armed ships involved in the *Santo Domingo*'s demise. Although her crew had put on a valiant defense, had nearly emptied her armory of shot and inflicted savage damage on her enemies (sinking at least one ship in the conflict!), the capitán had felt it a merciful necessity to surrender before the pirates slaughtered them to the last man.

Credit was lavishly bestowed on Don Cristóbal Nufio Espinosa y Recalde for his bravery and courage. The capitán had offered resistance to the final possible instant and bore the bloody scars to prove it! The lower halves of his ears had been shot away, leaving gnarled black scabs, the remnants of which were still visible beneath the precisely curled waves of his hair.

Recalde himself had remained rigidly silent through most of Aquayo's recitation of the events, though there was the occasional flicker of exasperation in the ebony eyes when the embellishments grew almost too outlandish to believe. But there had been no refuting the identity of the attacking ship, and for that, the governor, Don Felipe Mendoza, could heartily agree that Capitán Aquayo had indeed been lucky to escape with his life.

"*La Rosa de Hierro*. The *Iron Rose*." The governor had shaken his head in disbelief. "We were under the mistaken impression this was but the name of a ship. We knew, of course, there were sons who sailed under the crimson flag of the *Pirata Lobo*, but to think of a daughter having such boldness! She must be so mannish and ugly it is beyond the ability of a godly man to conceive of her as a woman."

The statement had been met with a general rumble of agreement around the dinner table. Also partaking of the exquisite wine and artfully prepared platters of food were three dark-haired, doe-eyed beauties—one of whom was the governor's wife, the other two his daughters. The latter were seventeen and fifteen respectively and because neither was permitted to set foot outside her cabin without the protective shadow of her duenna, these dinners in the company of so many handsome officers rendered them both flushed and breathless by the end of the evening.

"Is it true, señor capitán?" the elder daughter had

asked, her intrigued whisper inviting Recalde to look up from his soup. "Is she so ugly she could be mistaken for a man?"

"We were but briefly in her company, señorita Lucia."

"Oh come now, Don Cristóbal," Aquayo boomed. "Surely you cannot forget a chest like an iron barrel, a face brutish enough to frighten the devil himself. Had I a daughter like that, I would lock her away in a cellar from shame."

Recalde's gaze hardened. "I did not say I have forgotten her face, señor *capitán-general*. In truth, it is burned permanently on my mind and shall remain there until I see her standing before me again. In chains, of course. With a rope around her neck."

"With the reward you offered the Dutchman for her capture, I am certain your vision will be realized soon."

"I harbor the same vision of her father," said the captain of the *Contadora*. "You speak of the devil, Don Diego; then surely this man is his spawn. He appears out of nowhere and rains hell down upon our ships. He prays upon the weak and strong alike, as if he fears nothing, not our guns, not our numbers, not our might."

"He is a man," Recalde said coldly. "Cut him and he bleeds. Shoot him and he dies."

"The problem, Don Cristóbal," said another officer, "is getting close enough to either cut him or shoot him. There is not a man in this room who can even boast of having seen this Simon Dante face to face."

Recalde held his silence. It had been his fondest hope, before they departed from Havana, to have one last chance to avenge himself upon the Dantes. Father, daughter, it made little difference. It would have been a fine way to begin the new enterprise against England, with a victory against her most prolific sea hawk.

The loss of the *Santo Domingo* while under his command was an insult that would not go unanswered, regardless of how long it took. To that end, he almost considered it an inconvenience rather than a pleasure to be returning to Spain. A thousand things could happen between now and when the war with England was successfully resolved. *La Rosa* could be caught by another captain. She could be killed attacking another ship. She could fall overboard and drown and Recalde might never have the pleasure of seeing her pay for her crimes.

The conversation at that point had drifted, naturally, into debates over the upcoming enterprise against England and no one seemed to notice he was not participating. No one except Lucia, who had been looking at him all evening as if he were a succulent morsel of some rare, exotic sweetmeat.

Knowing she was watching, he let his gaze slip boldly down her neck and into the valley of her cleavage. At seventeen her breasts were small and shapeless but through the wiles of modern fashion, they had been pushed up and squeezed together to crown impressively over the bodice. She had a fine olive complexion with large fawning eyes and while she chattered incessantly about her upcoming wedding to the son of one of the richest families in all of Spain, Recalde thought of other ways to put that mouth to good use.

His gaze shifted deliberately to the younger sister, who was seated farther along the table. She kept her eyes downcast most of the time but Recalde had caught the plumping effects of an impatient sigh heaved whenever her sister would steer the conversation back to herself.

Thankfully, the ladies retired early and at the first opportunity Recalde begged his leave of the governor and the captain, using his wounds as an excuse to retire early from the table.

It was not entirely a lie. When the shots had torn off the lobes of his ears, the pain had been excruciating. The bitch had been standing close enough when she fired that he still bore scorch marks from the powder burns furrowed into his cheeks. A fraction of an inch higher on either side and he would have lost his hearing. As it was, he suffered headaches and still had a constant ringing in the left side, an annoyance that affected his ability to distinguish between the sound of the breeze rushing through the trees onshore and the soft whisper of a silk skirt approaching across the deck.

"You find our company boring, señor capitán? The conversation dull, perhaps?"

He was at the rail, listening to the water slap against a hundred hulls, when the dainty figure stepped up beside him. It was the governor's youngest daughter, Marisol, the gauzy ends of her lace shawl fluttering gently in the night breezes.

He looked past her shoulder but the stanchly bulked figure of her ever present duenna was nowhere to be seen.

"I can promise you, señorita, it was not the fault of the company," he said, bowing gallantly. "If anything, I feel it is my own presence that must insult the beauty of such tender eyes as yours."

"You refer to your wounds, capitán? But I do not find them offensive in the least. Indeed, with your hair arranged so carefully, they are hardly visible at all. I have some knowledge of healing herbs, taught at the Convent of the Holy Sisters in Madrid, and if your wounds pain you, I might be of some small assistance."

Recalde stepped back as she stepped forward, a hand rising instinctively to protect his damaged ears from her curiosity. He did not need this now. He did not need a coddling, mewling novitiate keening over his wounded vanity.

"There is a chill in the air, señorita. You might be wise to return below."

"Nonsense. It is so warm the dampness wets my skin like dew." She slipped her shawl off her shoulders and, ignoring his suggestion, placed her hands on the rail and gazed out across the harbor. "How beautiful," she whispered. "How entirely, wondrously beautiful. I think I have never seen so many ships gathered in one place. They glitter and twinkle just like the stars, of which I have never seen so many as there are here in the New World." She looked up and her face fell, for it had rained all day and the sky was still thick with clouds.

The entire ocean beyond the harbor was black, not a point of light to be seen anywhere. It was like staring into a great black void, and the awe was reflected in Marisol's voice.

"It is so beautiful, yet so terrifying at the same time. I find myself looking at the many endless, boundless leagues of water and thinking we are so small, so insignificant. A few lengths of wood held together by nails and pitch, afloat by God's grace, at the complete mercy of the wind and weather. Does it not frighten you, capitán, to know your life may be spent on such a whim? That a storm could strike or a leak could erupt and we would sink to the bottom without a trace?"

"You worry yourself needlessly, señorita. This ship is as sound as a fortress. And we will not be alone on the ocean-sea. We will be in the company of a hundred other galleons, an armada that will stretch from one edge of the horizon to the other until we arrive safely home."

"Home." She sighed wistfully. "Alas, I was so happy, so thrilled when Papá told us we were coming to the New World. I was so thankful just to be free of the convent, I thought I would die of excitement before we ever reached Vera Cruz." She paused and glanced at him sidelong. "Do you think that a shameful thing to say? That I was glad to be away from the prayer stools and the smell of incense?"

"I see little shame in telling the truth."

She smiled and moved her hand an inch closer to his on the rail. "Then I shall shock you by saying it was nothing at all what I expected. The villa was magnificent and we wanted for nothing, but Papá would not let either Lucia or myself outside the gates.

In two years, I was permitted to drive into the city of Vera Cruz only once, and then with so many guards in our escort, it was impossible to see through the wall of horses. Lucia was terrified the whole time of being waylaid and raped, and so Mamá punished me for her fears."

"Then that is a true shame, for Vera Cruz is an elegant, beautiful city."

"Yes, I know." She sent another smile, another sly glance in his direction. "I said Papá only permitted us to leave the villa once. I did not say I only left it the one time. The gardener's son was very much in love with me and took me often through the rear gates. He showed me things that would keep Mamá in a swoon for a month if she knew."

Recalde returned the smile. "If she knew you were up here on deck with me now, without your duenna, she would do much more than swoon."

"Would she indeed? Are you a dangerous man, capitán? Have you a reputation for taking advantage of unchaperoned virgins?"

The girl was flirting with him. She was pretty enough to make the game interesting, but she was also spoiled and rebellious and obviously thought herself an exotically daring vixen to have snuck outside the villa walls with the gardener's son.

"I can assure you, señorita, your reputation is perfectly safe with me."

She pursed her lips and feigned a moue of disappointment. "And here I was hoping you were different from the others."

"Different? How so?"

"The other officers, they look at me like I am the governor's daughter. They prance and simper and speak of nothing but the weather. Whereas you, capitán, look at me as if you could see beneath my bodice and, if provoked, would rip it open and take what you wanted without troubling to ask."

"And if I did? What would you do?"

"I might scream." She moved closer and traced a

fingertip along one of the prominent veins on the back of his hand. "Or I might tell you that I have not been a virgin for a very long time and that I would give you what you want more than willingly." She looked up into his face, her own arranged in an expression the gardener's boy must have found seductive. "Do you know where my cabin is, capitán?"

"I know."

"My duenna snores like trumpet blasts and I have never been able to tolerate her in the same room with me at night. If you were to scratch on my door later, you would find me quite alone."

Recalde's gaze flicked briefly into the shadows and he smiled. "If I were to scratch on your father's door right now and tell him of our conversation, I'm sure you would not be alone much longer."

The girl stiffened. She withdrew her hand from his, curling the fingers into a fist that trembled with the childish urge to reach up and scratch the arrogant face to ribbons. With a swirl of wide skirts, she was gone, her anger and humiliation making her run back along the deck.

Almost before the sound of her footsteps had faded, another figure detached itself from a niche in the bulkhead behind them, her dark eyes blazing with anger.

"So. You would have my little sister kneeling at your feet as well, señor?"

"I did not ask for her company. She followed me out here on her own initiative."

"Really." Lucia's eyes narrowed. "Had I not been standing here, would you still have sent her away?"

Recalde smiled and took several measured steps toward her, crowding her back into the darkness of the niche. He resumed where they had left off before the interruption, scooping her breasts free of her bodice and hiking her skirts above her waist. As she had the three previous nights when they had "accidentally" met on deck, she welcomed him with a grasping eagerness, whimpering when he impaled her on his flesh and rammed her repeatedly into the hard planking. In a trice her flirtatious whimpers turned into voracious snuffles of pleasure and he was forced to clamp a hand over her mouth, wary of the watchmen posted on the deck overhead.

His own release was swift, accomplished with a piquant savagery by imagining it was Juliet Dante clutching at him in fear, oozing his revenge from every orifice of her body. When he finished, he simply pushed himself away, leaving the girl quivering where she stood against the bulkhead.

"*Por Dios*," she whispered, her skirts sliding slowly down to cover her bare legs. "My little sister would be dead if you did such a thing to her. I myself wonder if I can survive six weeks at sea. *Por Dios Misericordiso*," she laughed softly. "I wonder if I can even walk back to my cabin."

Recalde started to tuck himself back into his breeches. "If you are displeased, I'm sure there are others on board who would be happy to show you more deference, señorita."

"You jest, capitán." She smiled and gingerly reseated breasts that had been suckled and bitten red back into her bodice. "The oaf I go home to marry is fat and balding—much like your Capitán Aquayo—and the thought of even letting him touch me is sickening. He is rich and has the king's ear, and so I must marry him but you, my handsome capitán, you will give me the memories I need to see me through the horror."

"I am flattered to have won your consideration," he murmured dryly.

"Oh yes, you have won it," she agreed, reaching out to stop him before he had fastened his breeches all the way. "As you shall win it every day and night for however long it takes to cross this vast ocean-sea. Not only that, but I shall see that you crave me just as much as I crave you so that when we return to Seville you will not easily forget me."

Recalde had more than half forgotten her already. He was staring out over the rail, his gaze fixed on a point far out where the sea met the sky. He narrowed his eyes and backtracked to search the blackness more carefully. There was nothing visible to the naked eye, yet for a moment he thought he had seen something. Even then, it was not so much that he had *seen* something; it was more like he had *sensed* something, had felt a presence lurking out there, crouched low on the eastern horizon.

His hand fell instinctively to his waist, but he was dressed for formal dining, and the belt he normally wore that housed his brass eye scope was back in his cabin. It was probably nothing. There were a dozen patches patrolling the approaches to the harbor, not to mention lookouts on every high point of the coastline. Only a madman would sail this close to Havana the eve before the armada was due to sail.

He gasped and looked down, jerked back to the present by the feel of an angry hand insinuating itself beneath his clothes and clutching around his flesh. He was about to swat it away, swat her away, when a startled grunt marked the realization that it was not her hand at all that was demanding his full attention.

Gabriel Dante lowered his spyglass. The wide stretch of coastline a league away showed few lights on either side of the dazzling expanse of bright glitter that identified the port of Havana. He and Jonas had not been able to bring their ships too close during daylight hours, but with the rain and heavy ceiling of cloud shielding them, they had thought to take advantage of the opportunity before breaking north.

Both ships ran dark. No fires, no lights, not even a pipe was allowed. The smallest pinprick of red could carry for miles on such a humid, heavy night. They had even gone so far as to change their regular canvas sheets to those stained with indigo dye, a practice that had successfully allowed them to get within five hundred yards of an enemy in the past. Tonight even Jonas was exercising caution, for there were patches and pinnaces patrolling back and forth along the straits and approaches, some of them running just as dark as they were and equally difficult to see.

They had both been astounded to see the crowded conditions in port, and they had not needed to see the larger warships maneuvering toward the mouth of the harbor to know that the flota would begin making the massive exodus any day now. Having noted this significant repositioning of the warships, Jonas was taking the *Tribute* in as close as he dared to see if he could get a count of exactly how many of the heavily armed galleons would leave with the first flush. After that, it would be time to lay on canvas and beetle back to the cays with all haste.

Gabriel rubbed a hand across the back of his neck. He raised the glass and took another sweep of the shoreline, but the four pataches he had already identified were presenting obvious silhouettes against the lights of the harbor, and were not giving the hairs on his neck a reason to stand on end. As a precaution, he walked to the larboard side and swept the horizon behind them. He did not see anything on the first sweep, not even on the second. But on the third he picked up a pale silhouette cutting swiftly in from the west and heading straight for the *Tribute*. It was another ship, larger than a patache, with at least three masts and high towers fore and aft.

A galleon. Running dark.

Gabriel aimed the glass at the *Tribute*. Knowing his brother was watching his back, Jonas would likely have most of the sharpest eyes on board searching forward. As if that fear needed confirmation, Gabriel saw no visible change in speed or direction from his brother's ship. He was moving necessarily slow, with only his indigo topgallant and topsail mounted on the foremast, steerage tops on the main and mizzen. He would have to shake out the sails on all three masts soon if he wanted to build up enough speed to maneuver away from the galleon before the Spaniard drew within effective range of his guns.

"Fuck me," Gabriel muttered aloud.

"Might not have to," his helmsman said dryly. "Pleasure might be all theirs," he added, pointing to two more ghostly specters closing fast on their own flank.

Gabriel swung his glass around and sure enough, the *Tribute* was not the only vessel in trouble. A pair of bloodhounds, coming from seeming thin air, had taken the scent of the *Valour*. They must have found him the same way he had found the pataches, by pinpointing his silhouette against the bright lights of the harbor. It was a stupid, careless, and potentially dangerous error in judgment to have come in so close, and they would be lucky to find the speed to outrun them before all hell broke loose.

"All hands up top," he ordered calmly. "Open the ports and clear the decks for action. On my signal . . ." He stopped and glanced swiftly at the *Tribute*, still apparently oblivious to the danger looming in the darkness. Jonas wouldn't be able to see any signal shy of a gunshot or a flare, and if they were going to do that . . .

"As soon as they're primed I want the gunners to fire a full broadside."

"A broadside, sir? But we're still well out of range and won't accomplish more than letting them know we're not wogs."

"I suspect they know that already. But if you can think of a better way to get my brother's attention, I am all ears."

The helmsman grinned. "Aye sir. Full broadside it is."

"Oh, and Riley . . . since we're not doing more than spitting in the pond, load the guns with double charges of powder. Might as well give the bastards an impressive show of fireworks while we're at it."

Recalde groaned. Lucia was abusing him with the same degree of determined savagery he had displayed earlier, and he was not only seeing stars, he was seeing lights explode across his vision. Moments later, he saw

more lights, but by now the muffled volley of thunder
from the first explosions had rolled over the harbor
and Recalde knew it had nothing to do with Lucia's
skills with her mouth.

"Jesús Cristo!" He twisted his fingers in her hair
and jerked her head away from his groin, all but kicking her aside in his haste to run to the rail. Far out
in the soupy darkness of the night, a ship was firing
its cannon, the concussions reflecting orange and gold
across the water and in the hovering thickness of the
air.

There were running footsteps above and below him
as other members of the *Contadora*'s crew were drawn
by the exchange, likely the same reaction as on board
every galleon in Havana harbor. Fingers pointed and
stabbed the air excitedly as a second ship opened fire,
then a third . . . then a fourth! There were two smaller
silhouettes in front—one of them shockingly close to
the harbor—and three much larger ones behind. The
two smaller vessels were being driven toward land, but
as they piled on sail, their speed increased and they
were able to peel away, one to the east, one to the
west.

The one to the west found open water, but the one
heading east was met by the patrolling pataches, bristling with ten guns apiece. As the pataches drew
within range and opened fire, the vessel had to veer
yet again to avoid sailing into range, but by then the
galleons had used their forward speed to good advantage and were emptying their batteries as fast as the
crews could load and fire.

Recalde was transfixed by the scene unfolding less
than a league away, as was every other man on board.
His hands gripped the rail as if to crush it, for he
could tell by the silhouette that the trapped vessel was
an English privateer.

"Use your chain shot," he urged, willing his command to carry across the distance. "Take down her
sails. Close in tight, by God, and you'll have her!"

Like a fascinating dance executed in excruciatingly

slow measures, the privateer backed his sails, hoping to elude the converging pataches and outrun them to the open sea, but instead, he ran straight into the guns of the two closing galleons. All five ships were spitting orange flames, some of the shots striking their targets, some throwing up tall spouts of white water on the sea. The echoes of the shots did not take quite so long to reach the harbor now, but the ships were engulfed in clouds of white smoke that hung in the air like a blanket and drifted toward shore, cloaking the action from view.

In the last clear glimpse Recalde had, the privateer was struggling. Her sails had been holed by shot and some hung in tatters. There was a fire on the upper deck, almost indistinguishable from the constant blasts of the guns on both decks, and when she moved out of sight behind a low promontory of land, she left a wide streamer of smoke boiling out behind.

Chapter Twenty-two

*I*t had taken twelve backbreaking days to remove the guns from the *Santo Domingo* and mount them in batteries onshore. Frenchman's Cay had a natural embankment that sat like a shelf along the length of the beach, but the earthworks on Spaniard's Cay had to be laboriously trenched and built. There were few complaints aside from aching muscles, however. Food was plentiful and the days, stretching into September, were neither as hot nor as humid as they might have been a month earlier. Morning came with the ringing of a ship's bell and the men would work until well after dark before crawling into the hammocks they'd strung among the trees. Canvas tents were erected along both beaches but most of the men preferred to sleep under the stars.

Juliet worked alongside her crew. The culverins each weighed between four and five thousand pounds, fired shots that weighed thirty-two pounds apiece, and required a powder charge of eighteen pounds each time they were primed, all of which had to be transferred from the galleon to the tents erected on shore. What Juliet lacked in brute strength she made up for by supervising the reassembly of each gun carriage on shore. The brass barrels had to be bolted to the trunnions, then the sights adjusted by driving in a quoin for the proper elevation. When the last monster was winched overboard, rowed to one of the beaches, and hauled to its final resting place, she ordered Crisp to

sail the *Iron Rose* through the channel so that each
gun could be aimed to achieve maximum damage
when fired.

Four types of shot were stacked in makeshift maga-
zines built behind the tree line. Ball shot was effective
for holing the decks and hulls. Chain shot, consisting
of two cast iron balls attached by a length of chain,
would wrap around spars or yards and reduce them
to splinters. Grapeshot was used mainly for keeping
an enemy under cover. Dozens of small round balls
were packed into the throat of the cannon and, when
fired, would spray across a deck in a wide fan, killing
or maiming anyone exposed. The fourth and last type
of shot was sangrenel, a cloth bag filled with jagged
scraps of metal. The bag disintegrated when the powder ignited, and the razor-sharp bits of iron sheared
through flesh and bone like hot knives through lard.

Varian St. Clare worked, stripped to the waist,
alongside the other members of the crew. Spending
long days in the sun, his skin started to turn a deep
bronze, making his smile appear wider and whiter than
before. Muscles that had not been soft to begin with
hardened to oak, and laughter that had not seemed to
come easily before had the men around him grinning,
especially when he was laughing at his own inability
to do things that came second nature to seamen. As
good as he was with a sword, he was all thumbs when
it came to wielding a glaive or a black bill, both weapons that were used for fighting in close quarters when
there was no room for fancy footwork or orderly
quadrants. When instructed on the use of a boarding
pike, he managed to somehow hook his own breeches
and fling himself through the open gangway. And
when he climbed the rigging one day, he shouted at
Juliet to show her how well he had done, only to twist
his foot around a ratline and dangle upside down in
a shroud until someone stopped laughing long enough
to go up and rescue him.

Regardless of how menial the task, he showed a
willingness to learn. He spent an afternoon with Na-

than being shown the finer points of how to set a sail, and when Nog Kelly demonstrated the proper way to nail together one of the gun carriages, it was Nog who took out a front tooth with a hammer, leaving Varian, his grin intact, to finish the job. He even went hunting one afternoon with Johnny Boy and while he skinned the inside of his forearm learning to shoot the long-bow, he proudly presented Juliet with the coconut he had skewered through the heart.

Juliet was smiling more, too. It seemed to start at first light when she opened her eyes and found herself curled against Varian's big body, and it was the last thing she did at night when they lay naked and sated in each other's arms. It was unfortunate that reality kept intruding or she would have been quite content to while away her days swimming in the tidal pools and making long, languorous love.

"They should have been back by now," she said, scanning the clear and disturbingly empty horizon with her spyglass. "It has been nearly three weeks. We've moved cannon, laid traps, built fortifications. Faith, we've even taught you how to climb a tree and bake crabs in the sand."

At least once a day Juliet made the climb to the highest vantage point on the island. Most times Varian accompanied her, which meant they would not quite make it directly there or back without taking some manner of detour. On this particular day they had arrived at the top well before sunset and relieved the two lookouts an hour before the regular watch was due to be changed.

Standing behind her, he swept her hair to one side and placed a kiss on the sensitive curve of her neck. "Your brothers strike me as being more than capable of looking after themselves. Indeed, I would allow they are the type who would show their backsides to the Spanish and run before them like hares taunting a hound."

She lowered the glass and sighed. "But three weeks. The pinnaces we've sent out have seen nothing either.

No ships. No fleet. No movement whatsoever in the Straits and frankly, Father is concerned some of the other captains may grow impatient and leave."

"Maybe the French and Dutch privateers did their jobs too well and the viceroy of Nueva España has ordered the fleet to remain in port."

"Maybe the next time you crack open a coconut you will find it filled with gold doubloons."

His hands slid down from her shoulders and circled around to cradle her breasts. "You dare to mock me, madam? I, who this very day risked life and limb to catch a turtle so that you might dine on *potage de tortue* tonight?"

She leaned against his chest, her nipples rising instantly beneath his palms. After three weeks she would have thought the fires within would have burned down to more tolerant levels, but no. A touch, a look, the crooked little smile he seemed to have reserved for her alone, could start an entire welter of sensations flaring to life inside her.

They flared now and within a few laughing breaths she had him on his back in the grass. Straddling his hips, she tugged his shirt free of his breeches, shoving the loosened folds up under his arms to expose the bulge of muscles across his chest. She laid her hands flat on the hard surface, letting the dark wealth of hair tickle her palms and fingers before dragging them down over the smoothness of his belly. When they encountered the wide black belt he wore, she watched his face while she unfastened it and reached for the buttons below.

The first few days they had been on Frenchman's Cay he had attempted to maintain the neatly trimmed imperial and thin moustache, but for the past fortnight, he had forsaken the blade and the chestnut stubble on his face had filled in thick and smooth. He had also taken to wearing his hair in a tail with a bandana tied around his brow to keep the sweat out of his eyes. When combined with the loose cambric shirt, the chamois breeches, the tanned skin and gleaming white smile, he looked increasingly more like a pirate, less like a duke, than she would ever have envisioned the first time she saw him on the deck of the *Argus*.

"Do you not miss your purple plumes at all?" she asked in a low murmur, her hands inside his breeches now, his body tensing beneath her.

"I, ah, beg your pardon? I'm afraid I wasn't listening."

She laughed and shook her head to negate the question and was about to bend over and distract him further when her gaze strayed to the rocky knob of land that marked the peak of Spaniard's Cay. The vantage points of the two islands were perhaps three-fourths of a mile apart, too far to hear the sound of an alarm bell, but close enough to see the small puff of white smoke that rose from the signal fire. She sat straight a moment, then reached for her spyglass and pushed to her feet.

"What is it?" he asked. "What's wrong?"

"I don't know. I can't quite . . ."

Juliet cursed the angle of the sun and the glare that was causing spheres of colored light to refract around the inside of her spyglass. It was just a speck well to the south, lost between every other trough of the waves, but she soon recognized the sleek lines of the *Christiana*. Geoffrey Pitt had taken her out three mornings ago to do a little reconnaissance of his own along the cays.

"It is Mr. Pitt, coming in hard and fast."

She trained the glass west and scanned the distant horizon but it was still clear. The *Christiana*, however, was skimming over the waves like she had a fire under her keel, and Juliet thrust the glass in Varian's hands.

"I have to get back down to the beach. Will you stay and wait for the watch change? It's probably nothing, but if you see anything unusual . . . anything at all, light the signal fire and ring the bell."

Varian nodded, fastening his breeches and tucking his shirt back inside. "Light the fire, ring the bell. Aye, Captain."

She did not acknowledge either his salute or his grin; she was already gone.

The *Christiana* barely cut her speed until she was through the channel. There, she backed her sails to make a graceful, sweeping turn behind the islands, but instead of ordering an anchor into the water, Pitt dived over the side, swimming ashore with long, easy strokes even as the *Christiana* ran up sail and caught the wind again.

By then there was quite a crowd gathered on the beach, including Simon, Isabeau, and Juliet.

"I was anchored off Running Rock when one of Captain Smith's scouts came in," Pitt said, emerging from the water, shaking droplets from his hair. "The fleet has left Havana. The vanguard should pass the southern end of the cays some time tomorrow. I've sent Spit north to spread the alert and give the other captains time to sober their crews."

Simon Dante nodded. The wait was over. There was still a question in his eyes, however, one that Geoffrey Pitt could not answer.

"There's no word. No one has seen or heard from either the *Tribute* or the *Valour*. Smith did say that his men ran down a French merchantman for sport and heard there had been a battle fought off Havana. They didn't know who was involved, just that a couple of privateers were in a skirmish, and at the end of the day, two ships were sunk."

"Were they ours?" Isabeau asked softly, standing by her husband's side.

Geoffrey shook his head. "He didn't know."

No one slept that night. The last of the powder barrels were taken ashore and final preparations were made along both embankments. At first light, the *Avenger* weighed anchor and towed the almost useless hulk of the *Santo Domingo* to the western side of the cays. At Geoffrey Pitt's suggestion, they had decided to revise their original plan slightly, using the galleon and the Pirate Wolf's ship as bait. Without the *Tribute* or the *Valour* contributing their firepower, they needed the Dutchman's guns on the other side of the channel. The Spaniards were not entirely stupid. If they saw a pair of privateers drifting in shallow water close to two islands, they might well see the trap for what it was, especially if they had just come under attack farther south.

While her father towed the galleon into position, Juliet walked the beach for the tenth time, turning a critical eye to anything that might betray the presence of men or guns on the shoreline. The tents had all been struck, the barrels of powder were well back behind the trees and covered with scrub. The cannon had sheets of canvas draped over their snouts, which had been painted with pitch and covered with sand to look like part of the landscape. No fires of any kind were permitted apart from the two covered pots of hot coals that were kept smoldering behind each gun line to light the fuses.

When there was nothing more to be done, she climbed to the peak accompanied by Varian and Geoffrey Pitt, for once they went on board their respective ships, they would be blind until they received a signal from the lookouts.

Juliet's first thought when they reached the top was that the *Avenger* had towed the *Santo Domingo* surprisingly far out, well beyond the strip of turquoise that marked the edge of the coral bank. Her second thought was that if she hadn't seen for her own eyes that the tatters and ruins were a ruse, she would have believed the *Avenger* was a wreck. Torn sheets of canvas hung from skewed yards. Rigging lines had been loosened; cables and spars hung over the rails dragging sails in the water to make it look as if the *Avenger* were dead in the water. They had even rubbed charcoal dust on the masts and rails to make it appear as though a fire had raged out of control on the decks. On a signal from the lookouts, buckets of oakum would be set alight on the decks of both ships to send up clouds of thick black smoke.

Beside her, Varian looked up at the stunningly clear sky. There had been a haze earlier in the morning, hanging like a pale shroud around the islands, but the sun had burned it away and the sky was clear in all directions, which was why he frowned.

"What is that? Thunder?"

Juliet tipped her head, listening to the low, throbbing rumble that was barely audible above the sway of the trees.

"Not thunder," she murmured. "Those are Captain Smith's guns. It has begun."

The vanguard of the Spanish treasure fleet came into view less than an hour later. Pitt, Juliet, and the two lookouts crouched down instinctively when the first sails appeared on the horizon, and while Varian knew it was quite impossible for anyone to detect their silhouettes from such a distance, he ducked as well. Two, three, five, eight majestic towers of sail and timber came into view, their sheets white against the blue sky, easily identifiable by the large red crosses painted on the canvas. The galleons in front were massive, equally as big if not bigger than the *Santo Domingo*, and normally would have been sailing in an open vee formation behind the *almirante*, like migrating geese, with the smaller treasure-bearing ships inside the protective shield of warships. But as the convoy drew closer, they could see something had staggered them.

"They look to be shy a few guards on their right flank," Geoffrey muttered. "God bless Captains Smith and Wilbury. And look there, well in the rear . . ."

He stabbed the air excitedly with a finger, training his glass on the far southern limit of their view. Juliet followed suit and smiled, though Varian could only squint and wonder what had caught their attention.

"Here." Pitt laughed as he passed over his spyglass. "Look just past the point of Spaniard's Cay."

Varian put the leather-bound glass to his eye and brought the horizon into sharper focus. The ships were still small and he doubted if he could have distinguished a galleon from a longboat at this distance, but there was no mistaking the thin plume of smoke he could see tailing out in the wake of one of the ships that was separated from the pack and obviously struggling to rejoin the convoy.

"We'd best get down to the ships," Pitt advised, standing and brushing the sand off his knees. But Juliet was already running ahead, her long legs scything through the long grasses, her hair streaming out in dark ribbons behind.

Chapter Twenty-three

It was almost too easy. The lead ship in the convoy—the *almirante*—ran up a series of flags signaling for the fleet to slow, then for two of the warships to pull within hailing distance. After receiving their orders, the pair peeled away and, undoubtedly stinging from the first surprise attack on the fleet, came to investigate the two smoldering ships adrift along the banks. The Spaniards knew these deceptively tranquil ribbons of azure and cerulean well, marking the area Baja Más—shallow waters—on their charts. They had lost enough vessels to know it was not outside the realm of possibility that a privateer could have become trapped by his own arrogance and not been able to escape the superior firepower of the galleon. Both ships looked badly crippled, and when they drew closer, they could see Spanish officers, their helmets winking in the sunlight, waving them on from the deck of the tall aftercastle.

On board the *Avenger*, Dante could almost pinpoint the moment when the capitán of the first galleon realized the wounded vessel belonged to the *Pirata Lobo*. The gun ports swung open prematurely on all decks. Sailors and soldiers alike crowded the rails, and clambered into the yards, some even leaping in the air and cheering at the thought of the ten thousand doubloons in reward that would now be theirs to share.

Dante ordered sails unfurled in the tops, only as

many as were needed to swing the *Avenger* gently away and make it appear as though they were attempting to limp to sanctuary behind the two islands. When he was through the channel—impressed that he could not see a single gun beneath its camouflage— and clear on the other side, he ordered the rigging lashed tight and the tattered sails replaced with taut new sheets. He tacked hard and swift to starboard, taking the *Avenger* in a tight circle that would bring her back around in position to meet the warships when they emerged from the channel. Isabeau had relinquished command of the *Dove* to Pitt and he already had the ship in position on the leeward side of Frenchman's Cay; together with Simon Dante, they would sandwich the galleons in a deadly cross fire.

Juliet, meanwhile, was set to bring the *Iron Rose* out from behind the island, sealing off any possible retreat by aiming her guns down the throat of the channel. Since ships did not move at the flip of a penny, the entire process took the better part of two hours, but by the time the galleons noticed the *Rose* bearing down on them, the first warship was already in the channel and the second one, encouraged by the waving, shouting crew on board the *Santo Domingo*— most of whom removed their helmets and lowered the backsides of their breeches as the galleon passed—was committed to follow.

The men on the shore batteries waited until both warships were caught between the islands. The pitch- and sand-coated tarps were removed, the fuses lit, and the first rounds of chain shot were blasting through the air before the Spaniards even realized they were trapped. Grape and sangrenel cut the men out of the tops, while the chain shot tore the rigging and ripped holes through the sails and decking. Not one in five guns on the galleons responded. Crews on the lower decks, shielded behind the bulkheads, managed to fire sporadically, but because the ships were built so high out of the water, every single shot flew well over the heads of the men onshore, kicking up explosive founts of sand, stone, and palm fronds hundreds of yards behind.

Conversely, once the galleons' sails and rigging were obliterated, the guns onshore were adjusted and trained point-blank on the hulls. The resulting damage from the thirty-two-pound culverins and eighty-pound mortars was terrible. With nowhere to turn and no effective means of fighting back, the Spaniards were forced to run the length of the deadly gauntlet only to emerge at the other end and find themselves facing the guns of the majestically resurrected *Avenger* and the *Dove*.

Dante's gunners fired but one broadside before the first galleon ran up half a dozen white flags. One desperate officer who crawled up out of the smoking shambles of the high quarterdeck stripped off his shirt and waved it frantically over his head to gain the privateer's attention before another round tore them to shreds. The second galleon ran into Pitt's guns and suffered the same fate, surrendering to the cheers and hoots of the men leaping out from behind the shore batteries.

The *Iron Rose*, gliding past the western end of the channel, saw that her guns were not needed but fired a single round into the trees by way of a salute. Juliet ordered the ship to come about, keeping one wary eye on the rest of the flota, another on the lookouts who had a better vantage from their height and would signal if any other ships broke away from the pack. From a purely avaricious standpoint, she hoped they did. Her men were eager and willing, her cannon were fully primed and hungry for action.

For a time she blockaded the mouth of the channel, assuming there were likely scores of steel-helmeted Spaniards making imprints of spyglasses around their eye sockets. They had seen the entire ambush unfold. They would know by the pillars of smoke rising behind the islands that their sister ships were lost. They would also have identified the *Avenger* and probably the *Iron Rose*; what they had no way of knowing was how many other privateers lurked out of sight behind the islands hoping to lure them into a trap.

"What do you suppose they're going to do?" Varian asked quietly.

Juliet shook her head. "They may be predictable, but they are not cowards. They won't be quick to run. See there, the *almirante* is already slowing, signaling the other guards to form a strong line."

"Lovely sight, ain't it?" Crisp remarked, standing on her other side. "How many do ye count?"

"Eight guards, twenty-three merchantmen," Juliet said absently. "They'll be trying to decide now if it is better to pile on speed and get the treasure ships to safer water above the banks, or delay and wait until the rest of the fleet closes the gap."

She trained the glass farther south, but there were only four or five stragglers on the horizon hastening to catch up to the first group. There was no doubt more would be coming. It just depended on how many ships had departed Havana in the first wave, how far they had become strung out, how quickly the slowest ship moved within the convoy.

"If they choose to run, it will be fine odds for our friends farther north."

"Aye, they'll've heard our thunder an' they'll know the storm is on the way." Nathan winked at Varian as he said this, then chuckled. "Mayhap, if the galleons are all swallowed into the shoals an' vanish without a trace, the Spaniards will start thinkin' there be mysterious powers at work in these waters."

It was a good jest and won a smile from Varian, who truth be told, would not be struck to his soul with disappointment if the fleet decided to cut their losses and move on. Eight warships and twenty-three merchantmen—Juliet had said it so calmly, as if facing their combined firepower would be like strolling down Mayfair on a sunny afternoon.

The thought left him wondering, not for the first time over the past weeks, what his mother's reaction

would be if he were to stroll anywhere in London,
indeed in all of England, with Juliet Dante on his
arm. For a certainty the stanch-lipped matriarch would
drop into a swoon that would require an entire nest
of scorched feathers to restore her senses. He could
also envision the expressions on the faces of his
friends and acquaintances when he recounted how he
met his ravishing pirate wench, how he had stood by
her side on the deck of a tall ship and watched those
silvery eyes dare the entire Spanish treasure fleet to
come feel the heat of her guns.

Unfortunately he could only see one of those silvery
eyes himself, for the other was still fastened to the
spyglass. Something in her expression had changed.
Her jaw was rigid, her lips were pressed into a thin
white line, and despite the warmth of her tan, the
blood was draining from her face, leaving her skin a
sickly yellow. She was no longer looking at the *almirante*, challenging it to sally forth. Her unblinking stare
was fixed on a pair of ships near the rear of the pack.

She reached out, grabbing empty air before she was
able to snatch hold of Crisp's arm.

"What is it, lass? What do ye see? Is it more company coming, then?"

She couldn't answer. She could not even lower her
glass to look at him, and Nathan snapped his own
brass and leather glass open, holding it to his eye
again.

Varian scanned the distant line of ships but saw
nothing with the naked eye that would explain Juliet's
frozen expression. The galleons had definitely huddled
closer together, though there were still a few stragglers
riding well off the starboard flank.

Crisp swore and lowered the glass, squinting out at
the water a moment before he raised the glass and
leaned forward over the rail as if it would bring him
that much closer.

He gasped, sucked the air into his lungs a moment,
then released it on an explosive curse.

"Jesus wept," he hissed. "It's Cap'n Gabriel's ship. It's the *Valour*. And she's sailing under a Spanish flag"

Gabriel stuck the end of his tongue into the socket at the back of his mouth and toyed with the empty space. It was the only part of him that was able to move. The ropes around his wrists and ankles pretty well assured he could not get up and walk around, nor even wipe at the blood that had crusted over his eye. And if he raised his head, the bastards would know he was conscious again and the beating would resume.

It had taken the efforts of two warships and four pataches to finally drive him ashore off Havana, and while he would gladly have fought to the death, as would all of his men, it would have been an arrogant waste of good lives. Jonas and the *Tribute* were away and clear—he surely would have heard the Spaniards' boasting if they were not—and if Gabriel knew anything at all about his brother, it was that he was as persistent as a mongrel. He would not allow his little brother to be shackled in chains and bound to oars in a slave galley. Moreover, when Jonas told their father what had happened . . . damnation, but he could almost feel sorry for these Spanish bastards.

All but one.

Gabriel had recognized him at once from Juliet's description. The narrow, hawklike face, the dead black eyes, the missing earlobes. He surmised the bastard must have been important, or had a great deal of influence, or had simply shown he was vicious enough to deserve the privilege of "questioning" the prisoners, for he had not only been among the first to come on board the captured *Valour*, he had subsequently assumed command.

Capitán Cristóbal Nufio Espinosa y Recalde.

The name, like the pain from the myriad of bruises his henchman had battered onto Gabriel's body, throbbed through his head like a religious chant. That and kill the bastard, crush the bastard, choke the bastard.

Just give me one chance at the bastard. One small opening.

It was apparent they had decided the *Valour* was not too badly damaged to be of some use to them back in Spain. Gabriel could hear sawing and hammering, and part of him was pleased his ship was being repaired. Another part hoped they were good carpenters, for it quickly became obvious their sailors did not know how to handle so much power and response from the helm. They were accustomed to sails that were square-rigged, set in configurations that were fixed. The Spaniards had little or no knowledge of how to adjust the sheets fore and aft to catch the best draft of wind and that was why, after one near collision with another galleon, the *Valour* had been relegated to a position outside the orderly vee.

Gabriel was being held belowdecks in what had been his quartermaster's small cabin. The door had been smashed off its hinges and there was only a chair nailed to the centre of the floor. There was always at least one guard posted in the outer passageway, but more often two, as if they still considered him, trussed and battered, a dangerous threat.

You bastards have no idea.

When Recalde came to visit he brought a lamp, but otherwise it was gray and murky, the only source of light an eight-by-eight-inch porthole with the hatch partly closed. The air was thick with particles of floating dust, and because they had kept him bound hand and foot to the chair for two days without relief, the smell of his own blood and urine was a constant incentive to stay alive, to wait for that one unguarded moment.

He could only imagine what he must look like. The first day they had stripped him down to his linens, searching for any weapons he might have hidden in his clothes, and never bothered to dress him again. Two days and several interrogations later, skin that was not splattered with blood was bruised a dark blue. He had a cut over his eye they took particular pleasure in reopening on the first punch of each session. There was another on his cheek, and he knew his lips were a swollen mass of splits and scabs. He hadn't been able to feel his feet or hands or even wiggle his fingers since the day before; the ropes were bound tight to ensure there was no possibility of him working them loose, and for all he knew, his fingers had turned black and fallen off. He had very little hearing in his left ear but couldn't tell if it was a result of the beatings or because it was just full of congealed blood. The right side was still functioning. Enough for him to hear the cannonading early that morning. Enough to hear the more recent volleys that had brought Recalde striding into the cabin and soiling his own gloves by dealing Gabriel a blow to the jaw that genuinely knocked him out for a few minutes.

He opened his good eye a crack, wondering if the Spaniard was still there. Recalde was quiet as a python and had fooled Gabriel before.

The thought was barely finished when his hair was grabbed and his head jerked upright. The grunt that escaped his lips was not feigned, for each time the bastard pulled him up by the hair, it felt as though his entire scalp was about to rip off.

"I see you have come back to us, Señor Dante," Recalde said in clear English. "Ah ah." He held up a warning finger. "If you spit at me again, I shall instruct Jorge to cut out your tongue."

Gabriel rolled his eyeball in Jorge's direction. A massive, ugly brute, he would have made Lucifer look like a delicate princeling. His fists were the size of sledgehammers, his shoulders resembled a series of powder barrels strapped together, the muscles bulging in hard, round shapes. Most of the damage on Gabriel's body had been accomplished by bored slaps and lightweight punches and Dante had no burning desire to see what the leviathan could do with a blade.

Recalde released the clutch of hair, pleased to see the comprehension in the wolf cub's eyes. "A wise decision."

Gabriel started to let his head sink forward again, but stopped when he saw Recalde's gloved fist move as if to snatch back the fistful of hair.

"I am not a man who believes in coincidences." Recalde leaned down so that his breath bathed Gabriel's face with the smell of garlic. "It was no coincidence we caught you and your brother scouting Havana. It was no coincidence our ships have been under recent attack off the coast of Hispaniola. Nor was it a coincidence—albeit both ambushes were brilliantly executed—that our fleet has come under attack twice today."

He straightened and clasped his hands behind his back. "It is no wonder your family has a reputation for audacity. Had this infernal ship sailed faster, however, I would have been able to stop this latest travesty before two more of our fine vessels were lured to their doom."

"You should have put me at the helm," Gabriel croaked. "I would gladly have sped you directly into the heart of the fray."

Jorge took an ominous step forward, but Recalde held up a hand. "No. No, the offer is a generous one, and I accept. You may indeed go topside, Señor Dante. In fact, your crew is there already, waiting for you to join them, to lead them as we go forth to meet the infamous *Pirata Lobo*. Jorge, untie the gentleman. Careful of his hands, they are so swollen the skin might burst if the blade slips the smallest degree."

Gabriel did not feel the knife parting the ropes. Moreover, his hands and feet fell like leaden weights the moment they were free, and he was fairly certain he would not be able to stand on his own.

Recalde signaled to a pair of guards who were waiting out in the passageway. All bustle and efficiency, they hastened into the cabin, taking Gabriel up under each arm and dragging him out between them. They hauled him up the ladderway, his feet slapping the steps like wooden blocks, and when they reached the deck, they paused a moment to allow Capitán Recalde to climb ahead of them to the quarterdeck.

By then, Gabriel's horror was such that his battered eye cracked open of its own accord. His gasp of outraged disbelief came out sounding more like a cry and drew equally helpless cries of rage from his crewmen when they saw the broken condition of their gallant captain.

Each member of the *Valour*'s crew was stripped to the waist, bound hand and foot to the shrouds, to the rails, forming a shield of human flesh around the upper deck.

Gabriel was taken up to the quarterdeck, where his arms and legs were similarly bound, spread-eagled, to the ratlines in plain view of anyone with a spyglass. He started shouting profanities before the ropes were applied, as did his men, and when the din became more annoying than amusing, Recalde nodded to several of his soldiers, who started savagely lashing the naked backs, shoulders, bellies of the bound men. They whipped and lashed until they were drenched with sweat, spattered with blood, and the din had been reduced to whimpered curses.

"Now then." Recalde stood on the quarterdeck behind Gabriel. "I am sure your family would like to see that you are alive and . . . *reasonably* unharmed for the moment. Shall we go and pay them that visit now? I am particularly anxious to renew my acquaintance with your sister," he murmured, reaching up to touch a mutilated ear. "As I recall, I made a promise to her at our last meeting and I know my entire crew is looking forward to honoring it. Jorge first, I think. The poor fellow's prick is so big, even the whores are terrified of him, but I think *la Rosa de Hierro* would be eager to accommodate him if she thought it might save your life. What do you think, Señor Dante? Does she value your life enough to sacrifice her own?"

"Go to hell," Gabriel snarled. "Go straight to bloody hell."

Recalde sighed and nodded to Jorge, who lifted a bucket full of the salted brine used to preserve meat and threw it over Gabriel's head and body. Some splashed the man hanging next to him, whose back had been slashed by a whip, and he let loose such a scream it set all one hundred and twenty of the *Valour*'s bound crewmen quivering in the lines.

Gabriel made no sound. Every muscle, every sinew in his body remained clenched through the inconceivable agony of brine seeping into his open wounds. Just when he thought he might be able to open his eyes and breathe again, he heard the order to put on all sail and felt the *Valour* leap forward with a response. They were breaking away from the fleet and heading straight for the cays. Moreover, they were not going forth alone. Following in their wake were three of the biggest warships in the fleet, their gunports open, their decks cleared for action.

"Gabriel," Juliet whispered. "Dear God, it's Gabriel . . . there, in the shrouds."

Crisp's lips moved but the oaths were either too foul to vent or the air in his lungs suddenly too sparse to give them sound.

They had fired another shot to alert her father and Geoffrey Pitt that more company was imminent, but there had been no quick way to warn them of the fact that one of the four ships was the *Valour*. Juliet had sent a messenger back in a jolly-boat, but that was before they bristled out to meet the oncoming threat and saw the human shield. Neither the *Avenger* nor the *Dove* had come through the channel yet and Juliet had to assume they were still dealing with the first two galleons. There would be prisoners to disarm, perhaps even set ashore under guard, to ensure they would not retake the ships and strike from behind.

Juliet knew she could not strike out alone against four ships, she simply did not have the firepower. And if the *Valour* had been taken over by the Spaniards, she would not even have speed as an advantage, for the two ships were well matched and any attempt she made to come in fast would be met with an equally nimble counterattack from her brother's ship.

Not that any of that mattered now. As soon as she saw the crew tied to the shrouds, it changed everything. Every scrap of nerve, courage, and bravado sank to her toes and she knew the mind-numbing shock of real fear.

"What are yer orders, lass?" Crisp asked softly. "The men are lookin' to ye."

"Dear Christ," she muttered. "If we fight, we'll be killing Gabriel and every other man in his crew."

"They'll be killed anyway. An' if we run, the bastards will make straight for the channel. They'll know the men onshore won't fire an' neither will yer father. Then we'll all be in a fine mess."

"Wait," Varian said. "Look . . . they're slowing down, they're splitting up."

The trio watched as the warships took down sail and carved wide swaths through the water to line up in a blockade formation a league offshore. The only ship that continued to move forward was the *Valour*, and inside half a mile, it too presented a broadside, gliding parallel to the shoreline.

It was not the most gracefully executed insult, for there were yards aligned wrong and the ship turned far too slowly, something Juliet noted but was helpless for the moment to know how to use to their advantage. All she could think of at the moment was her brother tied helplessly to the shrouds. She wasn't quite ready to dismiss his life as easily as Crisp, though she understood emotion had no place on the deck of a fighting ship. They had all understood the risks before they left New Providence. They understood the risks each and every time they sailed out of Pigeon Cay.

She glanced quickly over her shoulder, but there was still no sign of the *Avenger*. Turning back, she caught Varian's eye and held it a moment, wondering if he, with his annoying ability to read her thoughts, could read them now.

"The Spaniards are soldiers," he said quietly. "They think like soldiers, not like seamen."

"What of it?"

"A parley," he advised.

"What?"

"Ask for a parley. Find out what they want, what they are prepared to do to get it."

"I already know what they want," she snapped. "And I know damned well what they are prepared to do to get it."

"Then use it to buy some time. Send me over under a white flag and let me talk to them."

"*You?* Why the devil would I send you?"

"Because I am the Duke of Harrow. I am the king's emissary and still have the power to negotiate a truce."

"A truce?" She nearly spat the word. "They don't want a truce, they want blood. Mine and my father's."

"Just so, but they also don't know if it is just you and your father they have to deal with. Thus far, they have only seen the *Iron Rose* and the *Avenger*. For all they know, there could be a dozen more ships lying in wait behind the cays."

"You want to try to *bluff* them?" She looked at him even more aghast, if that was possible. "If they don't believe you—which they won't—they will kill you. At the very least, there is no guarantee they won't tie you up in the shrouds alongside my brother."

"I am not that easy to kill. You should know that by now. And if they tie me in the shrouds beside your brother, I will be in excellent company. Lower a boat and show a flag," he urged gently. "Let them know you want to negotiate. It is what any good general would do, and what any well-trained soldier would expect."

Her eyes remained locked to his in an unrelenting grip while a hundred different reasons for denying his request flashed through her mind. One above all set the blood pounding in her temples, not loudly enough, however, to drown out the grim command she gave to Nathan Crisp to ready a jolly-boat and find a white flag.

"Give me five minutes," Varian said, glancing over her shoulder at the glowering quartermaster. "And four of your strongest oarsmen so I don't have time to change my mind."

He looked at Juliet one last time, then dashed below to find clothes more suitable for a king's emissary. The royal blue velvet doublet and breeches he had worn to impress the privateer captains were crushed but wearable, and he was struggling to fasten the starched ruff around his neck when he heard the cabin door open behind him.

When Juliet saw how badly his fingers were fumbling the task, she took the ruff and the ruby brooch gently out of his hands. "Let me do that before you stab yourself. I would have thought you had acquired some skill in dressing yourself since Beacom's departure."

"Pressed to speed, I am much more adept at *un*-dressing, as you well know."

She looked up and caught the intense look in the midnight eyes.

"Just between you and me," she admitted softly, "I do my shaking afterward. Especially when I have done something truly stupid and realize how lucky I am to have survived." She smiled softly and touched his cheek with a fingertip. "You won't do anything truly stupid, will you?"

He would have answered, but he was distracted by her hands moving around to the nape of his neck, tying a narrow leather strap beneath the starched white ruff. Sheathed in the strap was a knife that slid beneath his doublet and hung against the clammy skin between his shoulder blades. She then knelt down in front of him and unfastened the garter below his knee, shoving his breeches up high enough to allow her to strap a second, needle-thin filleting knife to the inside of his thigh. Another went around his left calf before she adjusted the cuff of his boot. The last, a short double-edged serrated blade, she slid inside the front of his breeches.

"I doubt there are too many men—even Spaniards—who would search there for a weapon," she said. "But I would have a care how you sit."

After passing a critical eye over his form to see if she could detect any of the knives, she helped him strap on his baldric, giving the polished hilt of his rapier an extra touch for luck.

"If you can get close to Gabriel—" Her voice faltered and he tucked a forefinger under her chin, tilting her face upward.

"I'll tell him." He studied her face a long moment, as if committing every pore and eyelash to memory, then kissed her lightly on the mouth and straightened to indicate he was as ready as he was ever going to be.

Chapter Twenty-four

Isabeau Dante stared at the messenger and asked him to repeat what he had just said.

"It's Captain Gabriel's ship, Cap'n Beau. It's the *Valour*. Spaniards are at the helm, coming in fast with three more galleons on her flank."

"And Captain Juliet?"

"She's standin' fast, Cap'n, waitin' on orders."

"Oh, dear God." Beau glanced at the closest of the two smoldering galleons they had herded into the elbow of Spaniard's Cay. Simon had gone on board the first to dictate the terms of surrender; Pitt was on board the second, several hundred feet away. Neither ship was close enough for a hail to be understood and she called over one of the fastest swimmers, dispatching him over the side with the urgent news. Before he had cut ten clean strokes through the water, Beau had ordered men into the tops and by the time the swimmer reached the hull of the first galleon, the *Avenger* had shaken out every scrap of canvas she could carry and was underway, heading down toward the southern point of the cay.

When the Pirate Wolf heard the gasped message from the lips of the soaked crewman, he was livid enough to fire a shot from a handy swivel gun across his wife's bow. She did not stop and he hailed Geoffrey Pitt with a savage bellow. Within minutes, they were both on board the *Dove* piling on sail, but were out of position and were forced to make a wide, slow turn, hampered by the lack of wind coming over the crest of Frenchman's Cay.

The Spanish captains, their ships reduced to smoking ruins, saw that they were being abandoned and screamed at their officers to find enough sail to hoist into the broken spars and effect an escape. Both ships beat a retreat due east into open water, hoping to put as much distance as they could between them and the ferocious teeth of the Pirate Wolf.

They would not get very far.

Isabeau, meanwhile, had rounded the point of Spaniard's Cay. She took in the scene at a glance, the three warships formed in a threatening line and the *Iron Rose* drifting almost at a standstill, looking small and vulnerable and as valiant as David must have looked facing Goliath. There was a jolly-boat making its way across the choppy water to the *Valour*, and even at that distance, the white flag on the stern was clearly visible.

"An English duke?" Recalde paced a slow circle around Varian St. Clare, the sunlight glinting off the cone-shaped peak of his helmet. "I confess I am intrigued to know why you would be keeping company with such a notorious band of pirates."

"It was not by choice, I can assure you," Varian said. "My own ship was recently waylaid by Dutch privateers, who planned to hold me to ransom. The Dantes apparently paid what they demanded, thinking to rescue a fellow Englishman from the clutches of the cheese-eaters, but I have yet to find a reason to thank them. Especially now," he added, tugging on a cuff to straighten it, then brushing an annoying fleck of lint off the velvet. "I dislike being forced to do anything at gunpoint, whether the hand holding the gun is English or Spanish."

Recalde pursed his lips. "You are saying they forced you to come and parley?"

"They thought a proposal delivered by me would

carry more weight than if it came by way of a filth-encrusted sailor."

"Ah. From one gentleman to another?"

"My dear captain, while you might wear the veneer ably enough"—Varian paused and glanced pointedly at the naked, bleeding men that were bound to the rigging lines—"I see nothing that would lead me to believe you were anything quite so elevated as a gentleman."

Recalde, whose head had been tilted to the right while he listened, now tilted it slowly to the left as he studied Varian's face. "Unfortunately, señor, gentlemen do not retain their manners long in the jungles of Nombre de Dios," he murmured. "Particularly when one deals with criminals and misfits, one quickly learns that they do not respond to manners, only to a show of strength and a willingness to be completely ruthless. As for this . . . *proposal* you bring, while I am amused and flattered by the Dante audacity, I can assure you that nothing less than a complete surrender will suffice."

"If that is the case, then it may be perceived that we do indeed have a problem, for the captain of the *Iron Rose*—"

"The captain of the *Iron Rose* will present herself to me within the hour, señor, or she will not only be condemning her brother to death, she will be responsible for the deaths of every man who served on board this ship."

"Whereas I have been empowered to tell you that unless you stand down at once, the rest of the Dante fleet"—Varian almost stumbled when he turned and saw sails to the north, coming around the point of Frenchman's Cay, and sails to the south where the *Avenger* was now standing off Spaniard's Cay—"will show no mercy when they raze your ships to the sea."

"I believe a situation such as this would be called a draw, would it not?"

"You may be sure Captain Dante is sincere in her threats."

"As am I, señor." He raised a hand and one of the
scarlet-clad soldiers touched a glowing fuse to the
touch hole of a swivel gun mounted on the deckrail.
"Shall we see who blinks first?"

Juliet reacted without thinking.

She had watched the jolly-boat take Varian across
to the *Valour*, had followed the flash of blue velvet as
he climbed up the hull and went through the gangway.
After that, she had only been able to catch glimpses of
royal blue amidst the sea of scarlet tunics and molded
leather breastplates.

Then the round of grapeshot had torn through the
wall of crewmen with horrifying results and she knew
the negotiations had met a violent end. She did not
have time to think. She did not have time to absorb
the shock of seeing helpless men blown to pieces. She
only had time to react and trust her instincts.

At less than three hundred yards, it was not possible
to build enough speed to cut in swiftly under the *Valour*'s guns, deliver a broadside, and peel away again
without coming under heavy fire herself, but no one,
not even Nathan Crisp, balked at the order to do just
that. With every scrap of furled canvas suddenly dropping from the yards, the *Iron Rose* surged forward to
close the distance between the two sister ships and,
at the last impossible moment, heeled sharply about,
presenting her broadside.

Delivered at point-blank range, every shot smashed
into the hull of the *Valour* with devastating results,
the iron balls tearing through the timbers of her outer
skin and plowing through open ports, unseating cannon and obliterating the Spanish gunners who manned
them. Shots that did not rip an exit through the opposite hull ricocheted around the lower deck, turning it
into bloody chaos. The Spanish crews, unused to English gun carriages, fired wild, and while many of the
shots tore into the *Iron Rose*'s sails and rigging, a
lucky number went wide.

Counting off every precious second it was taking

the gunners on board the *Iron Rose* to reload, Juliet could see the Spanish arquebusiers on board the *Valour* taking to the rails and rigging. Gabriel's upper battery, she knew, held five swivel guns, but to her ever-increasing outrage, she could see that they were not being mounted on the gunwalls to fire at the crew of the swiftly approaching privateer. They were being fired, one after another, at the men screaming in the shrouds. Before the fifth gun discharged, a streak of blue velvet ran across the deck, his sword flashing, his white neck ruff stark against the tanned face and flying chestnut hair. He was able to clear a path to one of the swivel guns, to cut down the man holding the fuse before it could be lowered to the touch hole, then to slash his way through three more men before he was finally brought down under a crush of red-and-black-clad soldiers.

Juliet had no time to ponder Varian's fate as the *Iron Rose*, moving too fast now to avoid a collision, backed her topsails and slid beam on through the water so that when she rammed the *Valour*, it was broadside to broadside, the impact causing a huge gout of foaming water to spew up between them. The gunners had reloaded by then and fired another round of sangrenel and incendiary shot, which blasted straight into the damaged hull, taking out most of the cannon that were left on the lower deck and starting fires wherever the pitch-soaked scraps of flaming canvas settled. Up in the tops, crewmen with muskets started to answer the deadly fire from the Spanish sharpshooters, but they were hampered by the human shield and many died where they stood, unable to make a clear shot.

Juliet screamed for grappling hooks to lash the two grinding ships together.

Their first desperate attempt to board was turned back by volleys of gunfire. Juliet had mounted all her falconets on the starboard rails, but the men who were firing them into the opposing tops were being picked off with terrible precision. Until they could clear the yards, the men on the deck of the *Iron Rose* were exposed and helpless.

Juliet was pinned against the bulwark on the quarterdeck, already bleeding where a musket ball had nicked her arm. Nathan was crouched beside her trying to reach the helmsman, who was draped over the whipstaff, a red bloom spreading across his back.

A lone figure appeared in the hatchway below the quarterdeck and, after taking a deep breath to steady himself, ran through the hail of musket balls to seek shelter behind the bulkhead.

Johnny Boy set his quiver of arrows beside him. Using the lip of the deck as cover, he began firing at the Spanish arquebusiers, shooting them out of the yards with swift and deadly accuracy. He was able to launch his arrows between, over, and under the writhing shield of human flesh, where the uncertain aim of muskets had made it impossible to return the Spaniards' fire. He loosed one arrow after another until the first quiver was empty, then reached for the second and began making a noticeable gap in the Spaniard's defenses.

"Away!" Juliet shouted. "All hands up and over!"

The men of the *Iron Rose* needed no prompting. As soon as the muskets were silenced, they were swarming over the rails, their knives in their teeth, their cutlasses and pikes raised to meet the sea of soldiers flowing across the *Valour's* deck toward them. They clawed their way over the bloody remains of shattered crewmen, cutting down others who were still alive and screaming to be freed. Those who had their bonds slashed joined the fray with rage in their hearts and eyes, joining the charge against the Spaniards with anything they could grasp to use as a weapon, even with bare fists if nothing else was at hand.

Juliet emptied the four pistols she wore in her belts, then flung them aside and fought through the crush of helmeted soldiers with her sword in her right hand, a dagger in her left. Arrows continued to fly overhead and bodies fell screaming from the yards into the

mêlèe below. The gunners on board the *Iron Rose*
fired another raking broadside into the *Valour*'s belly,
sending chunks of planking and hot cinders rising on
explosive forks of orange flame. Rigging lines were
cut along with the freed crewmen, and yards swung
loose, hurling more Spaniards off balance. As soon as
the *Valour*'s crewmen were freed from the rigging, the
Rose's bowchasers began firing up into the tops, earn-
ing the alternate name they bore with bloody justification: murderers.

Water began to pour through the holes in the *Valour*'s belly. Smoke and steam choked the passages and
ladderways. Seamen who had thought to remain below
were forced up on deck, where they were cut down
by privateers or shot by their own soldiers in the
confusion.

Juliet fought her way to the quarterdeck, where she
had seen the greatest concentration of scarlet doublets
and steel breastplates. It was also where she had last
seen her brother, his body jerking and twisting in outrage against his bonds. He had been shouting encouragement, cheering on the men of the *Iron Rose* as
they attacked his ship, at the same time screaming for
someone to cut him loose so he could join the fight.
Juliet was almost there when she found herself cornered against the bulkhead below the quarterdeck,
fending off attacks from a clutch of Spaniards armed
with heavy cutlasses.

Nathan was on her left. He lunged at one of the
soldiers to block a thrust, deflecting it with a powerful
strike from his own blade. The steel snapped at the
hilt but the Spaniard had a dagger in his other hand,
which he drove forward and plunged hilt-deep in Nathan's shoulder. He jerked it back and would have
stabbed again but the intent was foiled as a thin slash
of steel came out of seemingly nowhere and sent the
Spaniard's dagger spinning across the deck, the fist
still clenched around the hilt.

"We're going to have to stop meeting like this, my
love," Varian said, pausing to flash a grin before he

moved to stand beside her, shoulder to shoulder, facing their attackers. His face was bloody, his ruff was gone, and a sleeve of his doublet was parted at the shoulder, revealing a deep gash in his upper arm. He was bleeding from another cut on his thigh, but it did not seem to hamper his strides as he helped her clear a path to the ladderway.

With her back amply defended, Juliet vaulted up the steps to the quarterdeck. Crewmen from the *Rose* had swung across on cables and were engaging an enormous giant of a man in one corner, while on the opposite side of the deck, a Spaniard wearing the steel breastplate of an officer fumbled with something at the rail. At first she could not see what he was doing, but then he turned, his hand gripping the long brass monkey-tail of a loaded falconet, swiveling the iron barrel around to aim the muzzle into the shrouds where Gabriel was tied.

Juliet saw the spitting linstock. She saw the officer's mouth draw back in a grin, heard something that sounded like a deep, slow distortion of a curse. She saw the flat black eyes staring out at her from beneath the curved sweep of his helmet and recognized Cristóbal Recalde at once. The shock halted her a moment, long enough for him to show her the glowing fuse he was lowering toward the touch hole of the bowchaser.

Juliet heard herself scream. She was aware of her feet carrying her forward, but her steps seemed to drag and her legs were so heavy it felt as if she were slogging through waist-deep quicksand. Gabriel turned, again so slowly the beads of sweat on his brow looked like droplets of syrup glistening where they fanned through the air. Their gazes met, for just an instant, but it was an instant that lasted an eternity, filled with broken images of every smile, every laugh, every childhood prank they had happily suffered at each other's hands. His battered lips were moving, he was saying something she could not hear, but by then she was reaching out, she was leaping into the air, she was smashing into Recalde's chest and shoulder just as he touched the hissing fuse to the powder hole.

Juliet seemed to hang there in midair as the powder sparked and flared. The delay was just long enough for her to know she had knocked Recalde's hands away from the barrel, but then she heard the louder boom as the main charge exploded. She saw the gleaming iron beads of grapeshot bursting out from the flared maw of the gun, but instead of spraying the shrouds where Gabriel was tied, they were now aimed straight at her chest. . . .

Immediately after the *Iron Rose* opened fire, all three Spanish galleons put on sail and started forward to join the attack. The first to reach the battling ships was swinging into position to unleash a full broadside when Isabeau brought the *Avenger* cutting across her path. Gunners on both vessels were ready, but the privateer was lighter, faster, bolder than the Spaniard, and the *Avenger*'s cannon made short work of the rails and ports on the larboard side, blasting great holes in the decking and unseating whole gun carriages, sending them rearing back on cracked timbers. The Spaniard retaliated by tearing holes in the *Avenger*'s tops, but she was already trimmed to fighting sail and merely shook off the affront, coming hard about and firing a hot round straight down the bows, blasting the tall forecastle with a series of broadsides that enveloped both ships in clouds of smoke.

Breaking free of the sulfurous yellow fog, Isabeau ordered more sail and brought the helm about again, closing the circle tighter this time, knowing the greater threat was not from the galleon's fixed batteries, which were ineffective at less than three hundred yards, but from the scores of marksmen that lined her yards and rails like fire ants. If allowed to get close enough, they would slaughter the valiant fighters on board the *Iron Rose* and the *Valour*. With Lucifer at the helm, she brought the *Avenger* in again on a swath of curling blue water, this time sweeping the Spaniard's upper decks and tops with a barrage of chain and sangrenel.

The remnants of the tall forecastle were obliterated. Bits of planking and somersaulting bodies flew through the air, blown there by a series of domino-like explosions that erupted in bursts of orange flame along the deck. It was a spectacular amount of damage from one cannonade and while Isabeau knew her husband's crew was efficient, she did not think they were capable of striking the galleon on both sides at once.

It took nearly half a minute for the second ship to come streaming out of the smoke and reveal herself, and when she did, Isabeau's eyes widened in surprise again, for it was not the *Dove* as she had expected. It was the bristling and battle-damaged *Tribute*, with its red-haired captain standing before the mast, his raised fist coming down hard as he called for another round of incendiary shot.

"It's Master Jonas," Lucifer said, grinning ear to ear. "And lookee what he brought wid him!"

The big black Cimaroon grinned and stabbed a finger north, pointing through the haze of smoke. Geoffrey Pitt's ship, the *Christiana*, with Spit McCutcheon at the helm, was bearing down from the north leading a squad of three privateers, while a second brace of ships, obviously in Jonas's company, broke away from the *Tribute* and raced after the remaining two Spanish galleons, both of whom were attempting to turn and retreat back to the fleet.

Isabeau heard the swish of another keel and saw the *Dove* coming up fast on their stern. She could see Simon standing on the quarterdeck, his hands on his hips, his long black hair streaming out in the wind. He signaled Lucifer his intentions, then started to peel away in the direction of the *Iron Rose*, but not before he gave Isabeau a very different kind of signal, one that put a flush in her cheeks and a revitalized edge of defiance in her voice as she turned to relay new orders to the helm.

*   *   *

Varian was a step behind Juliet up the ladderway. He absorbed the scene on the quarterdeck in one glance but was too late to stop her from taking the wild leap across the path of the falconet. Everything happened so damned fast it was reduced to a blur of motion! She was there one moment, in the air the next, slamming into Recalde, knocking him hard into the rail. The gun exploded, but without Recalde's hand to steady it, the recoil swung the barrel sideways, so that it discharged its load of grapeshot in a wide spray. Some went wild, whistling through the air so close to Varian's head that he felt his hair move. Most of it spattered like a hail of pebbles into the back of the huge giant who was fending off the efforts of half a dozen seamen with swords and cutlasses. He staggered with the impact, driving himself forward onto the outthrust blades of the *Rose*'s crewmen. Even so, they had to skewer him several times until he finally gave one last bellow of rage and crashed facedown on the deck.

Varian ran to Juliet's side. She wasn't moving and when he grasped her shoulders to lift her off Recalde, he could see the side of her face was covered in blood. The Spaniard, meanwhile, struggled to his feet and drew his sword from its sheath.

Varian's rapier blocked a slash intended to cut across Juliet's throat. The blades met and slid together, locking for as long as it took Varian to leap to his feet and break Recalde's hold. Their swords parted and slashed together again, touching, clashing, striking in a series of quick, lethal ripostes that drove the two men forward and back across the width of quarterdeck.

If Juliet's prowess with a blade had startled him, Recalde's skill was at least expected, for the Spanish were without equal as swordsmen. It took all of Varian's considerable dexterity just to parry each stroke, to keep from being driven into the binnacle or over the rail. Like a shark scenting fresh blood, Recalde aimed for the torn shoulder, the wounded thigh; he kept his strokes coming fast and clean, never taking two steps where one was sufficient, rarely executing a feint, preferring to wear his opponent down with cool, slashing precision.

Gabriel, meanwhile, had been cut down from the shrouds and helped to the deck. His feet were still too swollen to support him but he crawled on his knees to where Juliet lay slumped against the bulkhead. His hands were stinging like the fires of Hades and although he had regained some movement, they were clumsy and it was all he could do to cradle her against his chest and probe beneath the blue bandana for the source of all the blood flowing down her face.

Varian made the classic mistake of taking his eyes off Recalde for a split second. He had seen Gabriel moving over by his sister, gathering her into his arms, but she had seemed so limp, the need to know if half her head had been blown away overcame Varian's instincts to keep all of his attention fixed on Recalde's blade.

The glance cost him dearly. He felt the steel punch into his rib cage and start to plunge inward. He jerked back before the thrust could be completed, but the blood began to pour from his side, soaking through his doublet and leaking down onto his breeches. When he backed away, Recalde pursued. When he stumbled over the body of the giant Spaniard and nearly lost his balance, Recalde did not give him a chance to regain his balance, but battered him into the corner with a deadly offensive that sent him crashing down hard on one knee and left his head and shoulders exposed.

Standing over him, Recalde raised his rapier, the point angled down on a slant that would carry it down through Varian's spine for the coup de grâce.

"It would seem, after all, that you were the one who blinked first, señor."

"Not this time, he bloody well didn't," Juliet hissed.

Recalde whirled around. Juliet was behind him, swaying on her feet. He saw her sword slash out like a dart of silver blue light, the tip seeking the gap beneath his arm where the armor met his sleeve. At the same time, Varian retrieved the knife that was sheathed between his shoulder blades, while Gabriel found he had recovered enough dexterity in his finger to wrap it around the trigger of a pistol he grabbed off one of his crewmen.

Recalde's body shuddered with the three strikes as the dagger pierced his belly, the shot tore through his neck, and Juliet's blade pushed clear through his chest. He staggered back and came up sharp against a broken section of the rail. The wood gave with a loud *cra-a-a-ck* and he fell backward over the deck, dead before he splashed into the churning water below.

For several moments, no one moved. There was still fighting going on in the waist of the ship, but the Spaniards were beginning to throw down their arms. The men from the crew of the *Iron Rose* and the *Valour* were cheering, watching the *Tribute*, the *Avenger*, and the *Dove* lead their small fleet against the three warships, cutting off their retreat, crowding in with all guns blazing.

Juliet's knees wavered and Varian was by her side in a stride to support her. There was a deep gash on her temple where she had sliced it on the edge of Recalde's helmet, but as bad as it looked, she was smiling. She threw one arm around Varian, another around Gabriel, who tolerated her sisterly affection despite the squeezing pressure on his wounds.

Varian was hardly better off. There was a hole in his side, a slash in his arm, a stab in his thigh, and someone would have to stitch his head again. For a man who had arrived in the Caribbean with one small scar from a childhood mishap, he was charting quite a few new lines and welts.

Gabriel eased himself out of Juliet's arms and hobbled to the rail to look down over the ruins of the gun deck.

"My ship!" he cried softly. "Look what you've done to my ship!"

But Juliet did not respond to his battered grin when he turned around. Her arms were around Varian's neck and their mouths were firmly locked together. Clutched in her right hand was her sword, in her left the crushed folds of the Spanish flag that had, until a moment ago, flown on the *Valour*'s masthead.

Chapter Twenty-five

On board the *Iron Rose*, Simon Dante walked from one side of the great cabin to the other. His steps were slow and measured, and when he reached the far side, he turned and paced back. His hands were clasped behind his back, and his head was bowed. Now and then he looked over at the berth where Nog Kelly was in the process of knotting the last stitch in his daughter's temple.

"Skull might be cracked," Nog declared solemnly. "At the least, she'll be hearing bells and walkin' into walls for the next few days—longer if she tries to get up to do more than piss in the pot. Her shoulder will hurt like a bastard, too—she's lucky it's only black an' blue an' swole up an' it isn't broke—but if she's not plannin' on throwing herself at any more Spaniards wearin' steel breastplates, it'll heal up fast enough. Other than that . . . few cuts, few scrapes."

"She will have plenty of time to heal back at Pigeon Cay," Simon Dante said evenly. He saw Juliet's eyes swim open and narrowed his own in a warning. "There will be no arguments either. Nathan has a hole in his shoulder, half your crew is licking wounds, Gabriel's ship is at the bottom of the ocean, and between the pair of you, we couldn't manage one captain with enough common sense to know when to run and when to fight. Which brings me to the other addle-witted female in this family."

He turned the full power of his glare on Isabeau, who

was sitting on the corner of Juliet's desk winding a clean strip of bandaging around a wound on her stump.

"That I, of all people, should have been cursed with two women who—"

"Love you dearly," Beau said sweetly, "and tolerate your bouts of ill temper with enduring patience."

"*My* ill temper? *Your* patience! Madam! You took my ship into battle! You risked your life, the lives of my crew, the well-being of my vessel—"

"To go to the rescue of your daughter and son . . ."

"To go to the . . . ?" He stopped and clamped his lips shut. "I should send you back to Pigeon Cay as well."

She smiled. "You could try."

He muttered a curse and aimed his stare at the next victim. The cabin on board the *Iron Rose* was crowded. Gabriel and Jonas stood in one corner slouched against the wall, the former almost unrecognizable beneath a swollen, closed eye, multiple bruises, and lips that looked like two slabs of raw meat. Jonas, who had shadowed the convoy all the way from Havana hoping for some opportunity to cut in and regain his brother's ship, had a gash down his cheek, another on his arm, and a grin a mile wide splitting the red fuzz of his beard. He had his good arm draped around Gabriel's shoulder and every now and then ruffled his brother's hair as if he still could not believe the Hell Twins were together again and both alive.

"You find something amusing?" Simon asked.

"Aye, Father, I do," Jonas boomed. "A brother who smells like a vat of pickled herring, for one thing. For another, a sister who has ballocks the size of Gibraltar, inherited from a mother who can outsail, outshoot any bloody papist on the water. Add to that three fat galleons loaded to the gunwalls with treasure, and I'd say we have a fair bit to put a smile on our faces. Oh, and did I mention a father smart enough to find the wife to give him the sons and daughters of whom I speak?"

Dante glared at him a moment, then looked at Geoffrey Pitt. "Am I mad, or are they?"

Pitt shrugged. "A little of both."

The silvery eyes narrowed. "I knew I could count on you, my oldest and wisest friend, for a definitive answer."

"Come and sit here," Isabeau said, patting an empty corner of the desk. "Let Nog have at you with his needle and thread."

"See to the duke first. By the look of it he has more leaks."

Varian had been standing quietly by the berth, his wounded arm cradled across his midsection. He had shed his doublet when Juliet had insisted she would not allow anyone to touch her until Nog checked his ribs. But the bleeding had stopped and the pain was manageable, and one look from the midnight eyes had sent the carpenter back to Juliet's bedside. She was stitched now and so was Gabriel. Nathan's shoulder had been cauterized and, together with Spit McCutcheon, he was organizing the prisoners and assigning crews to sail the prize ships back to Pigeon Cay.

The *Valour*'s wounds had been too grave to repair, and after removing everything of value, her ports had been opened to let in the sea. Jonas, who had met and joined forces with three privateers who were late reaching the rendezvous at New Providence, had sent them chasing after the pair of galleons that had initially been caught in the ambush, with the result that there were now five Spanish ships—six, including the hulk of the *Santo Domingo*—surrendered to the Dantes and anchored in the lee of the two islets. One was given to the privateers who had arrived with Jonas, the spoils to be divided among their crews; another was given to the two ships who had accompanied the *Christiana* back to port, drawn by the thunder of the guns. Both ships would remain at the ambuscade, as would any crewman from the *Valour* or *Iron Rose* still hungry to fight, while the injured would be sent back to Pigeon Cay on the *Rose*.

Of the three remaining prize ships, one would be
taken over by Gabriel until a more suitable replace-
ment for the *Valour* could be acquired. The *Santo
Domingo* was useless except as a decoy, and to that
end, Simon Dante planned to fill her with barrels of
powder and send her forth to meet the next wave of
Spanish warships. The vanguard had been in such a
hurry to flee north, they had dispatched but one pin-
nace to carry a warning back to the rest of the fleet
to be on the alert for ambushes. The *Christiana*, skimming the waves like a low-flying bird, had intercepted
the courier and sunk her before the alarm could be
delivered; thus there was an excellent chance of more
galleons sailing blithely to their doom on the morrow.

In truth, the day's work had been more successful
than even Simon would have imagined. The damage
to the *Avenger* was not severe enough to send her
home yet and the carpenters would work through the
night to effect repairs. To have gained five and lost
only one ship—the *Valour*—was remarkable, and if
the rest of the adventurers were half as lucky, the flota
would be reduced by half before it neared the northern exit of the Straits. There, it was Dante's further
intention to form a blockade line of privateers, whose
very presence, after harassing the flota every league
of the way, would surely send any remaining ships
scrambling back to Havana.

For the time being, however, it was taking all of his
strength and concentration just to keep a stern eye
trained on the recalcitrant members of his household,
for if a tenth of the pride he was feeling ever burst
free, he doubted he would ever gain control again.

To aid in that effort, he focused on Varian St. Clare,
the only occupant of the cabin who had not already
begun to chatter like a clutch of boastful gulls and the
only one who might still be intimidated by the silvery
glare. The duke was finally allowing Nog to attend his
wounds, though he had not moved from the side of
the berth, and he had not let his hand stray farther
from Juliet's than a breath would take it. With the

smallest flicker of pain that had crossed her face, his fingers had been there, curling around hers. Even more remarkable, her fingers curled back.

Catching a fleeting glimpse of himself standing in much the same position twenty-five years ago, the legendary Pirate Wolf smiled and shook his head. "You should have fled when you had the chance, your grace."

Varian looked over at him. After a moment, he smiled back. "Have you ever regretted that you did not?"

Simon glanced at Beau, who was laughing at something Jonas and Gabriel had said. "No. Not for one single blessed moment."

"Then that is good enough for me."

Two hours later the *Iron Rose* weighed anchor and slipped away just as the dawn was rising in pink streaks across the horizon. Nathan plotted a course that would take them well to the east before turning south and heading for home. They were accompanied by three pinnaces that would run far enough ahead to give fair warning of any other traffic on the sea-lanes.

Varian left Juliet asleep on the berth and went to stand at the gallery door, watching as the two islands grew smaller and smaller off their stern. His side was aching and his arm was throbbing. If he closed his eyes he could isolate and identify every cut and scrape he had earned over the past twenty-four hours. For a certainty, he was not entirely unhappy to be returning to Pigeon Cay. On the other hand, it had been an exhilarating twenty-four hours and he had to wonder again if it eventually became blasé to men like Simon Dante, who lived every day as an adventure.

The smell of gunpowder and burned canvas still permeated the air inside the cabin, and after a glance back at Juliet, he stepped out onto the narrow balcony. The wind blew his hair and the foam leaped high off the curl of the ship's wake, sparkling like handfuls of diamonds where it fell back into the sea.

A pair of dolphins swam alongside, their bodies sleek and gleaming beneath the blue water; now and then they crossed behind the wake, leaping over the waves and diving below again in gray streaks.

Varian heard a bump behind him and turned just as Juliet slipped out onto the gallery. She was holding her head and swaying slightly with the motion of the ship and he was by her side in half a step, his arms around her waist, a frown creasing his brow.

"You were given specific orders to remain abed, Captain."

"You weren't there," she whispered. "I opened my eyes and you weren't there."

He gathered her gently into his arms and felt her press her face into the curve of his shoulder. "I'm here now. And will be for as long as you want me to stay."

She tipped her face up, slowly, as if it weighed twice as much as usual. Her eyes were glazed, the centers dilated from the steeped decoction Nog Kelly had forced her to drink. But she was smiling. "I think I would like both of you to stay."

"Both?"

"Indeed. There are two of you. There is two of everything, in fact, and I was hoping I found the right door to walk through on the second try."

She tried to raise her hand and touch his cheek, but the pain from the bruises across her shoulder and chest made her reconsider. And then something else caught her attention and she looked past the canted hull of the ship toward the eastern sky where the sun was hot and bright and promising a clear day ahead.

"I see two of them," she whispered softly.

Varian glanced down and saw the dolphins gliding side by side through the water. He was about to remark that her vision was improving, when he realized she was not staring down into the water at all. He followed her gaze and felt his blood surge in his veins as he remembered.

"As I recall, that was one of your stipulations, was

it not? That you would have to rise on a morning and see two suns in the sky before you would consider marrying me?"

She tipped her head and looked up at him with a slightly accusing frown as if he had somehow managed to arrange the phenomenon. Then her eyes settled on his mouth, on the smile that was widening as she watched.

"You will see no tightness there at all this time, madam. Just the sheer, unadulterated pleasure of seeing you have to honor your word. And thank God for that, since I have already spoken to your father."

"You have?"

"I have," he said and lifted her hand, pressing it to his lips. "He thinks I would show more sense marrying into a nest of hornets, but I told him I have already been well stung. And before you ask, no. I would never expect you to live in England. Moreover, it has taken me these past few weeks to realize I would be happier here, sailing with you to the edge of the world."

"You want to slay dragons with me?"

"Every last one, my love. Every last one."

A split second before the arrow struck, the girl's instinct sent her ducking back into the shadow of the cottage door.

The shot had come from one of the half dozen longbowmen who stood at the edge of the clearing. With lethal calm, their eyes stalked fresh victims, and as soon as one was found, they nocked their arrows, drew the strings taut, and fired. Behind them, laughing and shouting encouragement, were four mounted knights, their gray wool gambesons devoid of any distinguishing crest or blazon. The sleepy English village, innocent and unaware only moments before, was under attack by men who did not want their identity known—and for good reason. An ambush on unarmed villagers broke every law, defiled every precept of the knighthood's code of honor.

The first flight of arrowheads had been wrapped in pitch-soaked rags and set alight before being dispatched. The mists at dawn had been thick enough to conceal the raiders' approach, but the wind now passed through the clearing like an errant hand, sweeping the fog away. That same wind fanned the sparks, sending flames leaping across the roofs, and within seconds, columns of coiling black smoke rose from the cluster of mud-and-wattle cottages.

The three swaybacked asses in the village were too old, too workworn to even bleat an alarm as the flames licked across the thatch and ran down the walls. They were also dead after the second flight of arrows, as was the solitary milk cow and the brace of fat hogs.

As the roofs burst into flame above them, the men ran out of the cottages in a panic, snatching up pitchforks and scythes as if the handmade tools could afford any protection against the bowmens' three-foot-long shafts of barbed ash. They were followed by their women, who pushed and dragged children, urging them to run for the perceived safety of the woods. Goats and chickens added to the confusion, for most were too insignificant a target for the archers—seasoned marksmen who drew their bows with unrelenting accuracy and felled the husbands, fathers, sons first. The killers were also patient. They tracked a man as he ran behind the wall of a burning hovel, then waited for the heat and smoke to drive him out into the open again. The women fared no better. Several were sprawled on the ground, arrows jutting from their backs.

Amie remained crouched in the doorway of the smithy's cottage, her eyes watering from the smoke, her nose burning from the waves of heat that were sucking the air out of her lungs, her back and shoulders being scorched through the threadbare cloth. Her choices were to break for the forest or be enveloped by the roaring flames overhead. The trees were fifty paces away, but there was nothing between them and the cottage save for a miserly vegetable patch scratched into the earth.

Clenching her teeth around a half-sobbed prayer, she darted through the door and ran as fast as she could to the feeble protection afforded by a low

mound of hay. Over the sound of her heart pounding
in her chest, she heard the telltale *whoosht* and *thunk*
of an arrow furrowing into the earth a few inches from
her foot, but she was already running again, weaving
this way and that in an attempt to elude the archer's
aim. She was slight of build and wiry. The only soft-
ness on her body was in the vicinity of her breasts,
which were pressed almost flat inside a frock that was
two sizes too small. Her hair was braided and hung in
a long brown tail down her back; the hem of her skirt
was pulled up between her legs and tucked into her
belt so that from a distance, it was possible to mistake
her for a lad in an ill-fitted jerkin.

She heard a shout, followed by two more sharp
thunks as arrows kicked up clods of dirt close on her
heels. She felt the spray of pebbles against her bared
calves but did not once look away from the bed of
ferns that grew in the shadow of the trees. The ferns
were thick and green, high as her waist, covering the
ground like a canopy, and she knew if she could just
make it that far, she might have a chance. . . .

She heard another *whoosht* and dove for the under-
growth. Something punched her in the back of the
shoulder and helped propel her forward, but she
barely skidded to her knees on the spongy loam before she was on her feet again, scrambling deeper into
the sea of ferns. She ran one way for a dozen paces,
then veered sharply to the left for a dozen more. She
kept running, changing direction every few wild moments, trying to ignore the shouts and screams that
filled the clearing behind her. The wind was a blessing
now, keeping the tops of the ferns swaying and dip-
ping in constant motion, helping to conceal the direction of her flight.

Another sound brought her briefly to a halt. She
risked a glance behind her and confirmed the dreaded
thud of horses' hooves scything through the saplings
and underbrush. One of the knights had left the scene
of slaughter and was pursuing her—with almost lazy
confidence—into the greenwood. Even at a hundred

paces, he was huge, his destrier enormous as it trampled a wide swath through the ferns. The knight had his visor lowered, and there was not much to see between the iron grating that covered his eyes, but while she doubted his face would be familiar to her, she knew why he had come. He and others like him had been hunting her for over a month, and now the villagers were paying the price for sheltering her.

Smothering a sob, she ducked again and lunged deeper into the woods. The main vein of the creek that ran past the village was somewhere close by, but she had spent most of the past seven days in a fever and was not familiar with all the paths and turns. She was running blind, disoriented by all the green, the shadows, the new and excruciating pain in her shoulder that was forcing her to hold her arm in a hard curl against her chest.

Without warning, the saplings thinned and the ground took a sheer plunge downward. She had found the creek, but it was at the bottom of a steep embankment. Driven by another brief glance behind her, she grabbed an exposed root and started to ease herself over the edge. The lip of earth crumbled under her weight and she slipped, only managing to break her fall by clutching at a second root. The action jerked her injured arm, and she felt the iron arrowhead grind against bone. Barely able to bite back a scream, she let go and dropped straight down, landing on a bed of decades-old decayed leaves. The momentum of her fall sent her rolling onto the shaft of the arrow and she heard the ashwood snap, but not before the iron tip was pushed all the way through the flesh of her shoulder, tearing through the coarsely woven wool in front.

Nearly blinded by the pain, she dragged herself under the tangle of roots that overhung the bank. She made a last, feeble attempt to rake some of the decayed leaves over her legs to conceal them, but a chill unlike anything she had ever felt before slithered across the base of her neck and began to spiral down through her belly, numbing her all the way to the tips of her toes.

He was there. He was above her on the embankment, and his laughter came to her softly over the creak of saddle leather as he guided his horse down to the lower bank. A moment later, the jangle of his spurs told her he was dismounting, and through her own sobs and pleas, she heard the sinister whisper of a sword being drawn from its sheath.